THE ULTIMATE SACRIFICE

Maisie Hill

ARTHUR H. STOCKWELL LTD.
Torrs Park   Ilfracombe   Devon
Established 1898
www.ahstockwell.co.uk

© Maisie Hill, 2006
First published in Great Britain, 2006
All rights reserved.
No part of this publication may be reproduced
or transmitted in any form or by any means,
electronic or mechanical, including photocopy,
recording, or any information storage and
retrieval system, without permission
in writing from the copyright holder.

British Library Cataloguing-in-Publication Data.
A catalogue record for this book is available
from the British Library.

This is an entirely fictional story,
and no conscious attempt has been made
to accurately record or recreate
any real-life events.

ISBN 978-0-7223-3726-4
ISBN 0-7223-3726-4
*Printed in Great Britain by
Arthur H. Stockwell Ltd.
Torrs Park   Ilfracombe
Devon*

Chapter One

The sun beat down on the assembled troops on the quayside at Alexandria, North Africa, 1942.

There was immediate interest as the senior medical officer stepped forward to speak. "I know you have been warned about the perils of being in this part of the world. Be careful about what and where you eat and drink. There is one thing left for me to warn you about — sexual intercourse."

At once the listening men focused.

The Scottish brogue of the medical officer belied the hostile way he eyed the men before him. "I thought I would leave my warning until now so it will be fresh in your minds when you reach Cairo or wherever. If you can't go without sex, then make use of what you have been provided with. I've found that some men put their penis where I would not put my walking stick. There will be little sympathy from me for VD patients."

Abruptly he finished and marched away, leaving his listeners still and thoughtful, especially the newly enlisted ones.

Captain Purcell approached his colonel. "Permission to dismiss, sir."

"Granted, Captain. Get the disembarkation into action immediately. We are sitting targets for enemy planes."

"Yes, Colonel. Sergeant Major, let's go."

The quayside was now heaving with frenzied activity as the ship rid itself of its cargo of troops, machines, and weapons.

The young captain, papers in hand, called out four names: "Sergeant White, Privates Jones, Harvey, and Woods, come with me at once."

The four chosen, briskly left what they were doing and followed

the officer to the far end of the quay where three vehicles were standing. These were brand new and were of a design and size different from the rest.

The sergeant studied them with interest. "These are new, sir. I haven't seen anything like them before."

"They are especially for reconnaissance, Sergeant."

"I see, sir."

At that moment the colonel came up. "We must get away at once, Phillip. This place is unhealthy. I'll lead the way, you second, and Andrew in the rear."

"Yes, sir. Ready whenever you are."

The colonel moved quickly away. The captain turned to his men. "You heard the colonel. Let's get going. Jones, you take the wheel for now. We'll take it in turns to drive. Sergeant, you'll sit in the front with us, and Harvey and Woods behind. Now get our kit in the back."

In a short time the three reconnaissance trucks were edging their way out of the docks, leaving behind mayhem as the main cargo of men and machines were being prepared to depart.

They drove past the usual shanty town, belonging to the local dock workers, until they reached a decent highway where the trucks were able to instantly increase speed. This provided a breeze for the grateful occupants of the vehicles.

"Are you all right sitting there?" the officer questioned the other two, who were perched high on some boxes behind, but who were able to peer through the small aperture into the cabin of the truck.

"We're fine, sir. This is better than sitting further back in the truck. From here we can see out of the windscreen."

"They're frightened of missing something," the sergeant quipped.

Captain Purcell stared with interest at the passing scene. "I haven't been to this part of the world. The local people seem very poor."

"Very much like India, sir. I could never understand how some of our men took to India. A few even married some of the local women. God knows how they'll survive if they ever come to Britain!"

The officer listened, taking in the sergeant's views. "And how about you, Jones? Is this new to you?"

"Oh yes, sir. This is my first time away from Wales. There is nowhere like your own country." The lilting voice emphasised his point.

"Come on, Taffy, there are more sheep than people in your country," the sergeant broke in.

There was a good-natured grin from the Welshman, who was obviously getting used to this banter.

"This is our first time abroad too, sir," said Harvey from the back.

"Join the army and see the world," the sergeant announced with a wry laugh.

"Well, you should know, White, because you're the one full-time soldier here," the officer pointed out.

White was quick to seize his opportunity: "When I put my kit in the back, I noticed that it was stacked with tents and gear. Are we going to be under canvas, sir?"

"Yes, Sergeant, for most of the time."

White fell silent, digesting this.

"So we won't be seeing Cairo, sir?"

Woods sounded disappointed. The others laughed.

"You're thinking of what the colonel from the medical corps said. We're not going anywhere near Cairo, so there won't be that temptation," the officer assured him.

"We lived a lot under canvas in India, and got used to it," said the sergeant. "This heat does not make much difference. Have we got far to travel, sir?"

"A fair distance. We'll be briefed by the colonel when we arrive. At this moment I only know the barest details."

For the next twenty-four hours they travelled along the highway, filled mostly with military traffic, the occasional civilian car, many oxen carts and dilapidated lorries.

Early on the second day they left the highway, turning off onto a potholed road.

"This isn't a road, it's more like a country track," Jones complained as he avoided the holes and cracks.

As they jolted onwards, the captain succumbed to the intolerable heat, thirst and cramped conditions. He shifted around, trying to ease himself into a more comfortable position. He glanced at his

men and saw that they were also silently suffering. "The countryside is changing. Now we're not even passing through villages. This place is deserted," the officer pointed out.

"Well, sir, this road must lead somewhere." Jones was being logical. "It's well used, even though it is in such a terrible state. Probably caused by those heavy ox carts they use here."

"Or tanks, Jones," the officer suggested.

It was late afternoon before they finally reached their destination. The small cluster of buildings lay within a wall which almost encircled the village. It looked picturesque under the blazing sun.

Everywhere appeared deserted, but as the three vehicles ground to a halt people began to emerge from doorways. The women and children stayed back, surveying the newcomers, whilst several men approached the soldiers.

One, who was obviously the leader, bowed low as he spoke in passable English: "Greetings, sir," he said to the colonel. "We have been waiting for you. Come, we will show you."

The village men led them to a largish building nearby. When the door was unlocked, they entered and found the place full of equipment and stores. It was extremely clean, but, most of all, felt cool in the torrid heat of the day.

The officer in charge looked well pleased. "This is good. Much better than I expected. We'll use this as our office and communication centre," he told his two fellow officers. He then turned to the leading villager: "Is there some land where we can put our lorries and tents? What shall I call you? What is your name?"

The man bowed again as he replied, "Aberdoo Groomer, sir. My name is Aberdoo Groomer. I am headman here. There is some land where you and your lorries can live."

They were led outside to the rear of the building where there was a medium-sized plot of land. It was screened off from the rest of the village so gave some privacy.

"We will be a little cramped, Colonel," the captain observed.

"Yes, we will for now, but there will be men coming and going all the time once we are organised. We'll manage." He turned again to the headman: "This is good, Aberdoo Groomer. Thank you, and where is the water?"

"At the other end of the village, sir. My people will work for you

and bring you plenty water. We have worked at the latrines for you." He pointed to where two very small wooden huts stood on the far side. Then a crafty smile accompanied his next words, "We'll talk money tomorrow."

The colonel smiled as he agreed, "I can see why you are headman. We will talk." The colonel instructed his two junior officers: "Right. Let's get going. Tents to be erected, lorries emptied of our personal belongings, then parked. Come, Sergeant Major," he ordered.

The tents had to be packed in tightly but nobody was complaining. They were just thankful to have arrived.

"I'm looking forward to a decent wash and shave. Is there any water?"

"Yes, Captain. The villagers have brought enough to keep us going till tomorrow. The sergeant major is fixing up a shower. It's a bit rough and ready, but it will do. He is also writing out a rota, sir."

"Sounds fine, Sergeant. I'll be glad when it's my turn."

When the darkness had descended the village took on a new identity. Kerosene lamps cast a mellow glow over the harsh primitive scene. In the cooler air the villagers had come to life. Noisy laughing children scampered around, pausing only for the briefest secretive glance in the direction of the strangers. The adults looked striking in their long white Hausa robes as they intermingled with one another, each one seemingly at ease and content.

The three officers sat at the large open window of the office, looking out at the village nightlife before them. They gratefully sipped their drinks, then the colonel sighed, "I feel almost human again now that I've washed and changed. This is adequate for us, for we are only three. That large tent will make a good communal mess for the men."

"Andrew and I will shortly go along and see how they are," the captain promised the colonel.

He was amused when they put in an appearance, for the men had certainly made themselves at home. Several small tables had been pushed together and around this they sat — some playing cards, the rest watching. Sergeant White was dealing the cards when they entered, and there was a pile of money in the middle of the table.

Cigarette smoke filled the air, and filled beer glasses completed the picture.

"I can see you have all settled in," was the dry comment from the officer, directed mainly to the sergeant.

An impudent grin greeted his words as the sergeant told him, "You're right, sir. I'm trying to retake some of my money, especially from the sergeant major. He has more of my money than I have."

This brought sarcastic laughter from the men as the sergeant major protested: "That's not true, sir. We all know what a crafty player he is."

Serious for the moment, White asked, "Do you think the colonel would permit me to try to get our dhobi, I mean our dirty washing, done by some of the village women, sir?"

"I should think so, for we would all benefit. We'll mention it to him. Do you have the sentry organised?"

"Yes, sir, although I am sure there won't be much thieving here, nor noise when they pray. They will just use their prayer mats. The sergeant major can tell you that living near their mosques can be bloody noisy."

As the two young officers walked away, Andrew remarked, "One can clearly see who the two old soldiers are."

"It stands out a mile. They have served together in India and elsewhere. We are just wartime soldiers. At times I feel quite inadequate."

Their first morning in the village started with a briefing by the colonel. He commenced, "We have been given the task of tracking down and monitoring the German forces known to be in the vicinity. We will have to be on our guard at all times for they could just suddenly appear from anywhere. It is calculated that they are intending to swiftly move on to meet the bulk of their army at some prearranged place. Do not underestimate Rommel's men. They are first class and have become accustomed to this territory and conditions here. They have already been in this area for some while. Our main priority is to find their stores depots, especially the fuel dumps. In fact, fuel is the real priority. There will be three search parties. I shall lead one, with the captain and the lieutenant leading the other two. The remaining few men will man the base here, overseeing the weekly deliveries of petrol, oil, stores and, very

important, incoming mail. In the field we will keep in daily contact with the base here at specified times. We should be ready to commence in two days' time. I think I have covered the important issues. No — there is one thing I have not mentioned. It is a good idea for Sergeant White to organise our laundry."

"Yes, sir. I will see to it right away."

It caused some amusement when the sergeant arrived back from the village a little later with two of the women and a handcart, pulled along by several small boys.

"It didn't take him long to get organised," Purcell remarked to the others as they watched out of the window.

There was a knowing chuckle from the sergeant major, "White is the best at this type of thing."

The captain continued to watch as the cart was piled high with bundles of soiled clothes. The sergeant disappeared for a moment, only to re-emerge from the large tent, carrying large bars of soap which he handed to the women.

"Army rations. Trust him!" the captain observed.

When all the dirty clothing was collected, the sergeant surprised his watchers by taking charge of the now heavy cart. He trundled it away with the small boys trying to help, whilst the women walked serenely alongside carrying the precious bars of soap.

This caused much surprise to the village headman, who was at that moment approaching the office. He stared hard after them.

"Here comes more trouble," sighed the colonel.

After civil greetings, the headman was keen to get down to negotiating, but the colonel was prepared.

"Well, Aberdoo Groomer, I have made a list of the money we will pay your people. Take it away, read it, and talk about it."

The man gingerly took the list and, after quickly running his canny eye over the figures, bowed low as he accepted the proposed payments. "It is good, sir. I will go and show and talk with my people," he grinned.

After the headman had gone the colonel shifted uneasily in his chair as he told the others, "I've done it wrong. He did not argue or haggle, so I have obviously overpaid."

Sergeant White returned to the office some little time later and

boasted, "After a lot of haggling I have reached a fair agreement with the women over the laundry." He suddenly stopped, whilst a shrewd wary look blotted out his pleased grin. "But there is something that worries me, Colonel. I gave the kids some chocolate. As the older one took it he said, '*schokolade*'. It was quite plain, sir — *schokolade*. That is German for chocolate, isn't it? I think the enemy has been here." He turned to the captain: "Do you remember saying to Jones that tanks could have spoilt the road that leads to here? Well, I think you are correct, sir."

Absolute silence was the immediate reaction to the soldier's words as each man thoughtfully considered them.

"Of course, I could be wrong. There could be some other reason for this kid using a German word," White hastily added. Then quick to change the topic he asked the colonel, "Did you do well in your dealings with the headman, sir?"

"Not as well as you've done, Sergeant."

"Permission to leave, sir," White requested, now eager to be gone.

"Granted, Sergeant, and keep your eyes and ears open to anything that seems suspicious."

"Yes, sir."

Captain Purcell was the first to speak after he had left. "I think he is correct. The enemy have been here."

"And I am inclined to agree," said the lieutenant, whilst the sergeant major nodded his agreement.

The colonel was already planning. "Now we have a problem. When we are away, the men left here will be extra vulnerable. I think the answer is for you, Sergeant Major, to remain here and take charge."

"Right, Colonel. Let's hope we are never outnumbered."

"I know that is a possibility, but I have a gut feeling that it was only a few that came here and, hopefully, they were just passing by. That is why the villagers are keeping quiet — they don't expect them to return. I hope to God we can trust them, for this village is so remote and off the beaten track the people here have become a law unto themselves."

"You can't blame them for that, Colonel," replied the sergeant major. "It is only survival. I have been in this situation before, in India. If we treat them fairly, then I am sure we will find them loyal."

"To us, you mean?"

"Yes, sir. After all, we will be bringing in a regular supply of money to the village. They are not stupid."

"Well, there is no other alternative I can think of. I was warned that we would be strictly on our own and would have to fend for ourselves once we were in the field."

"I will start to organise safety precautions at once, sir. We may be only a few, but, with the help of the villagers, we should be able to put up some defence if it were ever needed."

"Excellent, Sergeant Major. I will leave it in your hands."

"We are never allowed to settle anywhere for long," Sergeant White complained two days later as they headed away from the village.

The truck sped along as best it could, leaving behind a trail of choking dust. Even though it was early morning the heat was already suffocating, sapping the energy of the soldiers as they sat unusually quiet and listless. There were no other signs of life as they made their way onwards.

After several hours they had a welcome break and gingerly climbed down from the truck.

Harvey quickly lit the Primus stove so as to make tea. With experienced hands he passed round the steaming mugs to the parched men.

"This is good. Tastes like tea my mother makes," complimented Jones.

"It's not as good as your mother's, Jonesy. The milk is powdered, and wait till you taste the eggs, for they're powdered too. Still, I'll make an effort to feed us."

"As long as we have some beer for our sundowner," White broke in. "That's what really matters. Of course it will have to be rationed. What do you think, sir?"

"I will leave that to you — and the water. Two pints per man a day."

"Yes, sir."

"We have only enough for ten days — that is, the essentials — water, food, and petrol and oil for the truck," the officer pointed out. He studied the map. "According to this we are entering a suspect area, so from now on we will go at a slower pace. Watch out for

any fresh tank tracks."

"Are we near the desert, then, sir?" asked Woods.

"We are on the outer edge — that is why it is so desolate and lonely."

He spoke the truth, for the remainder of the day they met no one, nor did they see any tracks.

It was late in the day when they finally called a halt.

"Pull over there, Jones," the captain instructed. "This is where we'll stay the night. We will be sheltered by those dunes."

Harvey and Woods made a rough sort of lean-to, with a tarpaulin attached to the truck and held up by several steel poles, under which the two men began to unload collapsible chairs and a small table. The other three brought out the tents and sleeping bags. They set to work and within a short time it bore some semblance to a small camp. As the darkness fell the comforting light of the lamp shone out.

Captain Purcell looked at his watch. "It's time to make contact with base. Are you ready, Woods?"

"Yes, sir."

The soldier sat at the table and commenced, whilst the others sat silently around, watching his every move. He followed the written message which the officer had placed on the table, then waited. After a short while he began to scribble furiously as he received the incoming call from the wireless.

As the sergeant remarked later, "It can be hell if contact with base is lost."

"Especially if you are in a place like this," Jones replied, looking out into the inky darkness.

"Is everything OK at the base, sir? I mean, no sign of the enemy?" asked Harvey.

The captain, who was reading the communication, looked up. "I should think so, for this seems a normal reply."

They ate their supper afterwards in the cool of the night.

"I'm sorry it's just hard tack," explained Harvey, "but this is what we'll be eating most of the time. I thought I would make dried-egg omelette for breakfast."

"Well, at least we can wash it down with our couple of beers in the evening," said Woods as he pushed his food around his plate.

"When shall we wash and shave — night or morning?" Purcell asked.

"I think morning is best, sir. We can shave and smarten up whilst Harvey cooks his dried eggs," the sergeant said.

"And we must be careful that we bury all of our rubbish. There must be no trace of us being here," the captain reminded his men.

For the next two days the soldiers followed this same procedure — looking for signs of the enemy during the day, and making solitary camp at night.

On the third day they came upon their first fresh sighting of the enemy's existence.

"Tanks," the officer confirmed as he knelt down to get a closer look at the tracks in the sand. "They were here this morning. There was a stiff wind in the night, so old tracks would have been covered. I am tempted to follow them, but have been given strict orders not to take such action. I have to report to base first," the officer complained.

He took out his map and compass and after roughly working out the direction and the number of miles they had travelled that day, he made a cross on the map. He then passed it over to Private Woods to check.

That night as they sat together, awaiting contact with base, there was an unusual happening.

"Quiet a moment," Jones broke into the conversation of the others. "I'm sure I can hear something."

There was instant silence as they all listened intently.

"I can't hear anything," whispered Harvey.

"I can," said the sergeant. "You're right, Jonesy. It's very faint, but I can hear something. Can you, sir?"

"Not at the moment, but I think we should douse that light."

They sat in the darkness until the drone of an approaching plane could be clearly heard by all.

"Then I wasn't hearing things, boys."

"No, you weren't, Jonesy. You heard before any of us," said the sergeant.

"It's a bit strange," mused Woods. "First, sign of the enemy, and now a plane."

"It could be one of ours, but we can't afford to take that risk," the captain pointed out.

They waited until the plane flew directly overhead, shattering the stillness of the desert. Then, in a matter of seconds, the roar receded as it flew away.

"That was a Jerry plane." The sergeant's voice was sombre. "We soon learned to recognise them at Dunkirk. They put the fear of Christ into us."

Just then the eyes of the five men were drawn to a ball of fire which was hovering in the sky.

"It's dropping flares — probably to confirm the exact position of their tanks. They are very confident. I reckon they could be nearer than we imagined," was the captain's thoughtful comment.

They gazed in fascination as that part of the sky was bathed in a glow which began to slowly fall earthwards, then disappeared from view.

"We'll have something to report tonight, sir."

The officer noted the sergeant's voice was taut with anticipation.

"It must be time to make contact with base, sir," Woods prompted.

"We dare not light the lamp yet. Can you manage with my torch?" Purcell asked.

"Yes, sir, if someone directs it onto what I'm doing."

"I will, sir," Harvey volunteered.

The young captain sat still and hushed as Woods began his evening ritual, for he felt this bound them securely to that small village and the others.

Woods despatched his message and then waited. There was a grunted signal from him as the answer came through. It was a lengthy one and he at once handed it over to the officer, saying, "They want you to confirm that you clearly understand these orders, sir."

"Right now?"

"Yes, sir. They are waiting. The colonel has unexpectedly turned up there."

Captain Purcell studied the words before him. "I understand the orders and will act upon them. You can confirm this, Woods."

Now there was a marked difference in these men. Gone was the lethargy as the officer brought out the map and spread it on the table.

"Bring that light nearer," he said.

He studied the map again. "I make it there."

"Is that where we're going, sir?" White asked.

The officer nodded and pointed to the map: "This is roughly where we are now, and there's where we are bound. We'll be much nearer some form of life there. It's probably a small watering hole. We should meet up with the colonel, if all goes according to plan. We leave early tomorrow morning."

"It'll be great to see other faces for a change," Jones said.

"What's the matter, Jones? We've been on our own for only a few days, so what are we going to be like after a few months?"

Sergeant White's shrewd observation silenced everyone as they realised the truth in his words.

"How are we measuring up as a team?" the officer questioned next morning as they bumped and rattled their way along.

There was a brief pause as the sergeant considered. "Not bad, sir. We haven't been tested yet, and are . . . "

"Rookies, except for you," Purcell butted in.

"Well, yes, sir. That is it, but we are coping so far."

"That is good to hear. I must admit I was worried."

"There is nothing to worry about, Captain. I'd like to see any other officer do better in these circumstances."

The bond between them was already growing.

It was noon before they reached their destination, and it turned out to be what the officer had half expected — a small watering hole amidst several derelict buildings. It was entirely deserted.

The soldiers looked down at the discoloured unhealthy water. Their expressions were grim.

"Well, we can use it for washing and shaving, but it isn't fit for anything else. I suppose the locals drink it — better than nothing," White said.

The officer looked around at the depressing place and ordered," We had better get ourselves established before the colonel arrives."

The men were silent and uneasy as they followed the usual routine.

Even White seemed affected. He cast jittery glances at the shacks nearby. "I think I should have a closer look around, sir," he quietly said as he reached for his rifle.

"Shall I go with him, sir?" asked Jones. "I've finished what I have to do here."

The officer consented, so the two soldiers, with their rifles at the ready, made for the buildings whilst the other three watched.

With surprising agility, the captain noted, they silently entered the first building, then in seconds they re-emerged and gave the thumbs-up signal to the others. This was repeated with the second. The third building was the furthest away, standing a little behind the other two and partially hidden from the watching soldiers.

The minutes ticked away, but there was no sign of the sergeant and driver. All was quiet and still.

"Let's go," the captain commanded in a low voice; "and have your weapons at the ready."

He signalled for the other two to approach in different directions, so as to encircle the buildings. They skirted along the outside walls, gaining as much cover as possible. In the intense heat there was a sickly stench of rotting wood and decay.

The officer stopped short at the entrance and strained his ears. With great relief he heard the unmistakable tones of his sergeant. Still with extreme caution, he slipped inside and quietly edged nearer. As his eyes grew accustomed to the interior gloom he made out the figures of the two men busily searching among debris at the far end.

The captain did not proceed any further for the moment, but peered into the deepening shadows around them to make sure they were alone. He noted that this building was not so dilapidated, and was much larger than the other two.

He turned towards the two soldiers and called, "What have you found?"

They spun round.

"Bloody hell, sir. We could have shot you. We didn't hear you come in. You did that quietly," White said.

"As good as those Red Indians I saw in the films when I was a boy," a shaken Jones added.

Purcell smiled as he told him, "Go and tell Harvey and Woods to go back to the truck, for the colonel may arrive. You go with them, but be careful as you step outside. Make sure they know it is you."

"Yes, sir."

The Welshman gingerly went to the open door and began to

whistle one of his native tunes. The familiar sound soon brought his two comrades out of hiding, and there was relieved talk amongst them as they walked away.

"Come and see what we've found, sir." White's tone was serious. He pulled out a wooden box into the middle of the floor and gently lifted the lid. "It was hidden over there in the darkest part, and was covered with this dirty old cloth." He pulled out some binoculars and handed them over for inspection.

"These are of excellent quality. There is the maker's name on the side. I can just about read it in this light." The officer peered closely. "They are German. Did you realise this, Sergeant?"

"I had my suspicions because their equipment is the best."

The captain knelt down and began to rummage amongst the contents. "Books — some sort of logs and diaries. They were keeping records."

"They do look official, sir. Quite important, I would think."

"Yes, they do. My German is hopeless. I can only make out the odd word. What else is in the box?"

"Look at these." The sergeant grimaced as he handed over some letters. "I'm sure it is mail from someone's home, sir."

Phillip Purcell felt a twinge of conscience as he opened the letters and scanned what was written. "It is mail from their families. You are correct, Sergeant. What the hell is it doing here?"

The sergeant was still searching among the piles of papers lying in the bottom. "Look at this, sir."

The officer reached for the articles offered. A look of realisation passed between the two men. "Two German identity tags. Let's have a thorough look around, but first, is there anything else in that box?"

The soldier went painstakingly through the rest of the contents. "There are only papers, sir."

"Come on, then."

They both quickly moved outside, just as the colonel's truck drew in and parked alongside theirs.

"It's the colonel, sir. He's made it."

They hastened over to the hot and weary newcomers.

"I'm sorry we are late, Phillip, but it has been a hell of a drive. Is everything going well?" asked the colonel.

"Yes, thank you, sir, although there is something I'd like you

to see, straight away."

The captain and sergeant led him to the opened box lying on the floor.

"This was hidden there, in that dark corner, and was covered with this cloth. We found these inside, as well as several other personal items." Purcell handed over the identity tags. "White and I are going to search around outside before it gets too dark, sir."

They left the colonel going through the contents of the box.

"You know what we're looking for, Sergeant?"

"Earth that has been recently disturbed — graves."

"So we are thinking along the same lines."

"Yes, sir."

The two soldiers widened their search. They were joined by Harvey, Woods, Jones and Smith (the colonel's driver).

"Can we help, sir?" asked Harvey.

The captain told him, "We are looking for freshly dug graves."

Jones swore softly. "Is it something to do with that box, sir?"

"Yes, it could be two German soldiers. Their identity tags were in that box."

Jones swore again.

For the next hour or so the men searched diligently, but the coming of the night finally beat them.

"The answer isn't here, I'm afraid," Purcell said. "We had better join the colonel."

"Any luck?"

"No, Colonel."

"I wonder what's happened to them."

There was no response to this from the rest, and a sense of unease hung over the little band of men.

"I shall forward everything to headquarters and they can take the necessary action. They will probably use the information contained in their letters from their families. It will be passed on to the Red Cross. Talking of letters, I have brought a stack of mail for you all from home."

This was the lift they all needed. The mail was distributed amongst them.

"Our first mail from home," the sergeant crowed as he elbowed his way nearer to the lamp.

A silence descended, broken only by the rustle of paper as the mail was read and reread. Then they carefully folded and pocketed away these precious links with home.

After the others had left for their beds, the two officers sat talking.

"Now to get down to the reason for this meeting," the colonel commenced. "You're doing well, Phillip, in such a short time. Andrew and I have not found a trace of the enemy so far, but I suppose that could be put down to many things. Anyway, it has been decided that you should push on further, especially after your sighting of that plane."

"Sergeant White recognised it as an enemy plane."

"He was almost certainly correct. There is something important around there, and it has to be located. Those are our orders. We have brought you another week's supply of stores, which we will transfer to you in the morning. You are to penetrate further into the desert, using the same tactics as before, but this time do not get in touch with base unless there is an emergency. From now on, Phillip, you're strictly on your own."

"Yes, sir. I understand."

The changeover of supplies was completed early next day. Then the colonel and his driver left.

The sergeant stared after the departing vehicle. "We are going on, sir?" he asked.

"Yes, Sergeant, for another seven days. We'll leave now and I can brief you on the way."

Suddenly, Jones stiffened and warned the others, "There's something coming from over there." He pointed.

There was no questioning as each man quickly armed himself.

"Find the nearest cover," the officer snapped.

They piled into the nearest building and took up positions. There were many cracks and holes making it ideal for observation. The noise grew louder as into view came a solitary motorbike.

The driver was extremely accomplished as he sped over the hardened track. Behind him, his pillion passenger hung on for dear life. They roared up to the truck and stopped dead. For a few seconds they stayed there, surveying the truck, then calmly looked around.

The soldiers stayed quiet, and kept well out of view.

With unhurried arrogance the bikers dismounted and walked up to the truck. They were Arab in appearance, dressed in the customary flowing robes. The only difference being the high-powered gun which was draped across each man's chest. They opened the door of the truck and peered inside.

At a given signal from the captain the soldiers emerged from their hiding place, keeping the strangers covered.

With instant reaction the two men twisted around to face the oncoming soldiers. As they approached, the bike driver put up a hand in a friendly gesture.

The officer immediately responded in the same manner. "Do you speak English?" he hopefully asked.

They looked at each other and shrugged. Their faces were almost hidden under long strips of cloth which were twined round and round, ending tucked up under their headdresses. Only their noses and the top parts of their faces were visible.

"Real desert men, these are, sir — real vultures," the sergeant remarked.

Their eyes switched to him as he spoke — eyes that were calculating, hard and cruel.

The sergeant stood his ground and stared back. "I could drop you in a second if you put a foot wrong, you bastards," he promised.

The hostility between the three men festered.

"Hold on, Sergeant," the officer urged quietly.

The driver of the bike then glanced at the captain and began to fumble amongst his robes. He slowly and carefully brought out a small water container which he uncorked, then turned upside down to show that it was empty. He then pointed to the watering hole.

"They have come for water. We will show some friendliness. Bring out one of the containers from the truck, Harvey."

The soldier did as he was bid and replenished the mens' drinking water. In all this time the two strangers did not utter a word, but followed every movement with their sharp wary stares.

The captain fidgeted, now doubly anxious to get away. "Are we ready to go, Sergeant?"

"Yes, sir, right away," White answered, never once taking his eyes off the strangers, although, like the others, he had lowered his gun. "Shall I ride in the back, sir? I want to keep these two in my sights as we drive away."

"Yes, certainly. Let's go."

With a brief salute to the two men, he signalled the soldiers to move. White was swiftly seated in the back. The strangers knew that, although it was out of sight, his gun was surely trained upon them. They stood stock still, just watching.

The engine roared into life as Jones pulled away. He glanced into the mirror. "They still haven't moved. They are just standing there looking at us," he reported to the others.

"Looking at our sarge in the back, you mean, Taffy. They knew that they were in his line of fire. Mind you, I wouldn't trust them an inch," said Woods.

It was a full hour before the sergeant was relaxed enough to join Harvey further back in the truck. "I can still get a clear view out of the back," he assured them.

The officer glanced back at him: "I felt a strong urge to get away, even before they turned up. There was an atmosphere about that place."

"I wonder what their real reason was for going there. I don't think it was only for water. Maybe they came back for the box, sir," suggested Jones.

Nobody answered as each soldier began to succumb to the heat and the monotony as they retraced the way back into the desert wilderness.

Only when the day was ended and they sat under their makeshift canopy in the comparative cool of the night did the morning's events crop up.

"I would like to make a suggestion, sir," the sergeant ventured as all eyes were turned on him. "It might be a good idea if I kept watch tonight. I could stay in the truck. It would be the best vantage position to see any intruders. There will be strong moonlight for the moon is almost full."

"Do you think there could be intruders around tonight, Sergeant?"

"Yes, sir. This is their territory. They probably know it like the backs of their hands. It would be easy for them to follow our tyre marks."

"But what about the noise, Sarge? Remember this morning?" Jones broke in.

"There is a difference. Now they will be looking for us. This morning they stumbled on us by chance. Now they know we exist."

"It is a sound idea, Sergeant, so we will keep it up for the next few nights," the officer agreed.

"I won't be getting much sleep tonight," Harvey admitted; "there was something evil about those men."

"Well, I certainly didn't miss the way they looked at you, Harvey." The sergeant grinned impishly as he spoke, "One quite fancied you."

There was a ripple of laughter from the rest, as the soldier in question coloured a bright red.

"Well, I don't fancy being a bumboy, Sarge," he protested.

Now there was no banter in the sergeant's voice as he asked the captain, "The Germans are blond, fair-skinned and blue-eyed like our Harvey here, aren't they, sir?"

"Yes, they are, many of them. Hitler is keen on keeping pure the Aryan blood."

"That's what I thought, sir."

The soldiers became thoughtful, although not one voiced his suspicions.

The night passed peacefully, as did the following ones. Nor was there any evidence of the enemy in close proximity.

"Last week we had plenty of action, but this week none," moaned Woods, who was missing the daily contact with base.

"The colonel was so sure that we were near the enemy, but he could be wrong. I suppose it must have appeared that way, for usually the first few days on any new mission are quiet and uneventful," the captain reasoned. "I think we were close to the enemy but they have now moved on."

"We could go on for weeks like this, sir," White pointed out, "and it can be bloody monotonous. I have always liked being in action."

"At least we will be heading back on the seventh day," said Harvey.

This day finally dawned, and the men were elated at the prospect of returning to base.

They travelled until midday, when they stopped for a break. Jones, forever the wanderer, strolled away from the others and

climbed a nearby dune.

"He must be mad in this heat," Sergeant White remarked as they lazily watched him.

Jones reached the top and stood surveying what lay before him. The others turned away, losing interest, but were immediately startled when the captain scrambled to his feet.

"Look at Jones, he has been shot," he called as he ran.

The soldier was tumbling down the dune like a limp rag doll, falling this way and that.

For a second the others stared in horror, until the sergeant ordered, "Stay here, but cover me as best you can."

He swiftly followed the captain over the red-hot sand. Just as he reached the two men, the officer was dragging Jones to his feet.

"Go easy, sir."

"Not to worry, White. He isn't shot."

Jones was struggling to find his breath; he coughed and retched. Then he pointed upwards. "Tanks," he managed to spit out, then collapsed.

"Come on, let's take a look," the captain said.

They toiled up the dune, and, when near the top, crawled forward on their stomachs. They cautiously peered over the top.

"Enemy tanks — ten of them," the officer whispered as he focused his glasses on them. "They have stopped and the crews are gathered around the leading one. Here, take a look."

The sergeant studied long and hard. "They are smoking and just walking around. It seems they are taking a break, like us. We would have run into them if we hadn't stopped here. Luck is with us, sir."

"We have a problem. Which way are they heading now? We won't know for sure until they move off. There is a chance they might come back this way, so we must be ready to duck out of sight."

"Again we are lucky, sir, for there are plenty of large dunes around to hide behind."

"Yes, I agree with that. We must tail them, Sergeant. This opportunity is too good to miss. Go and bring the truck and men nearer, but be careful of noise, for we can't be sure that we are out of earshot."

"Right, sir, and I will tell Jones what is happening. I will leave him where he is for the moment, for he still looks bushed."

The two soldiers looked down upon the slumped figure below

them. Captain Purcell resumed watching the enemy until the sergeant rejoined him.

"Anything happening yet, sir?"

"I'm sure it won't be long before they move. I can see that you've brought the truck nearer." He laughed as he looked down at the vehicle immediately below them. "I have to be careful that the sun doesn't catch my glasses. We don't want to alert them to the fact that we are here."

"The men are ready too, sir. They will pile into the truck the minute they see us rushing down."

The officer went back to his binoculars and after a few minutes he crowed, "The front tank is moving. Look, Sergeant, they are pulling away from us. Now we can safely tail them."

Knowing that the noise from the tanks blocked out any sound he might make, the sergeant shouted, "Just what we wanted, Captain, and they haven't spotted us."

The two men made their downward rush.

"I will take the wheel for now," Purcell said as he jumped in behind the wheel, shoving over a still-dazed Jones.

The sergeant scrambled in the other side just as the truck started. As they emerged from behind the dune the last tank was disappearing from view.

"We'll keep this distance between us whilst we are among these dunes, but we'll have to stay further back when we reach open ground."

"It'll be easy to follow them for they are stirring up clouds of dust, sir."

"Oh, you're back with us, Jones. Are you feeling better?"

"Yes, sir. It gave me a bit of a shock seeing the enemy tanks like that."

The captain laughed as he told him, "I feel a bloody fool now. I thought you were shot, Jones."

"Well, sir, I did come down like a rocket and knocked all the wind out of my body. I thought I was choking, sir," Jones admitted.

For the next two hours they continued to shadow the enemy, who were still unaware of their existence. Being afternoon it was unbearably hot and suffocating. The five soldiers were tense and alert, not once giving thought to the intolerable conditions, made

worse by the slow, steady pace they were forced to adopt.

"It must be murder in those tanks." Woods was sympathetic.

At that moment the truck jolted to a halt as the officer switched off the engine. "Look, there is no dust now," he quietly observed.

"And no noise either, sir," White pointed out.

They listened. All was deadly still.

"We will go on by foot. I hope to God they haven't finally realised that they were being followed. We'll climb this nearest dune to see what has happened. We must be absolutely quiet. Leave the truck doors open so that we can make a speedy getaway if needed. Out we go," the officer ordered.

The five men moved across to the dune and began to noiselessly climb upwards. When they reached the best vantage point they were astonished at what lay below them. Stretched out for a sizable distance was a cunningly concealed fuel dump. Rows and rows of large metal drums were stacked high, all covered with sand-coloured tarpaulins.

At one end several huts had been erected. Purcell trained his binoculars upon these. "They house the keepers of the dump, I should imagine," he told his men.

"I can't see any guards posted, sir," White commented.

The officer scanned everywhere. "I cannot see any. The only security seems to be that barbed-wire fence."

"There are some men coming out of the huts," Woods interrupted.

They watched with interest as these enemy soldiers approached the newly arrived tanks, which had parked near to them.

"They are going to fill them up, sir." Jones sounded envious.

"This place is really well camouflaged. No wonder it took some finding," Harvey admired. "There must be thousands of gallons stored here."

The young captain lowered his glasses and looked at his watch." It will soon be getting dark. There will be a full moon tonight, so if we are going to strike it should be sooner than later. We still have the advantage of surprise."

"There is one problem, sir," Jones intervened. "We are low on fuel ourselves. It worries me, sir."

"That is a chance I took when I decided to follow, I'm afraid."

Sergeant White was quick to respond with, "We'll find a way to get some, sir — we have to."

Just then the sound of the tanks starting up drew their attention.

"They are coming this way," exclaimed Woods.

"Keep down," was the officer's urgent order.

The hidden men could only listen as the tanks drew nearer. Suddenly the noise stopped.

"They are directly below us, sir," the sergeant whispered.

The officer nodded his agreement and then looked at each man in turn. "We haven't got much in the way of arms, but we'll put up a fight if it comes to it."

The minutes ticked agonisingly by as the soldiers lay there. A look of amazement passed between them when on the still air there wafted up boisterous laughter and talk from down below them.

"I am going to take a look," Purcell whispered some minutes later.

The others watched as he crouched, absolutely still, taking in the happenings at the foot of the dune.

Then, very slowly, he drew back and crawled to them. "They're refuelling and have no idea that we are here — well, not yet."

"Do you think they are preparing to leave, sir?"

"I couldn't tell, Sergeant. I know what you are thinking. They may see the truck, but there isn't much we can do about it. We can only hope for the best."

"Maybe they will leave in another direction," suggested Harvey hopefully.

The soldiers sat tight for the next half hour, listening to the enemy's movements below. Then all went quiet — not a sound to be heard.

"That was sudden," Woods breathed.

The officer silently signalled the others to follow him as he made for the top once more. The sight of the enemy walking away to the huts raised their spirits.

"It looks as though they are not going anywhere for a while, sir," said White.

"They might even stay here for the night," Jones added.

"Talking of night, it will soon be upon us. We have a lot to do before it gets dark and the moon rises. We must get down to the truck." The officer was already leading the way down as he spoke.

In the fading light they gathered some necessary items from the vehicle.

"The first priority is to get more fuel."

"I can get through that barbed-wire fence, sir," Jones volunteered.

"But there will be a certain amount of din as you negotiate those drums. We can't take that chance."

"The captain is right, Jonesy," the sergeant broke in. "The best bet is the tanks."

"Exactly, Sergeant. They are nearer to us, and will give some cover if any of the enemy should wander outside."

"Then I can do that, sir. I have often had to siphon off fuel from our tractors back home." The Welshman would not be put off.

"Can I go with him, sir?" asked Harvey.

"Yes, and the sergeant too, for he reckons he has the knowledge to unlock those fuel caps on the tanks."

"I have, sir. I have been able to manage most locks in the past."

The officer chose to ignore that. "You can take an empty fuel can each. That should be sufficient to cover the added distance back to base. Woods and I will keep you covered as best we can. Just give it another few minutes to make sure that the coast is clear."

In the gathering gloom the soldiers waited, holding the precious cans. Some lights appeared in the huts, shining out brightly, but at a comfortable distance away.

"Off you go. Best of luck."

The trio moved away in the failing light. Purcell and Woods watched anxiously as the shadowy forms of their comrades ran, almost bent double, towards their targets.

Within seconds they had reached the first tank. The sergeant began to investigate, whilst the other two stood alongside, shielding him from the enemy's view.

The captain and Woods could see the muffled beam of the torch as the sergeant struggled with the fuel cap.

"Their equipment is so advanced it might be too sophisticated for him. I should have gone with him, but then, I know far less about it than he does," the officer fretted out loud.

Now the sound of music wafted out on the still night air, as the unsuspecting enemy relaxed.

"The moonlight seems to be getting brighter by the minute, sir," Woods said.

"I'm not sure whether that is going to be a help or not. It would be better if we were able to finish before it gets too bright, for if it

should go wrong then we are clearly visible, as well as being heavily outnumbered."

"We won't think about that, sir."

The two men waited for what seemed ages, before the other three returned. The captain and Woods ran forward to help them.

"This is bloody heavy," Harvey panted as he slowly stumbled along.

"Put it down. I'll have a go," the officer instructed.

There was no halting until the small band of men were round the side of the dune and safely out of sight.

"Well done. You have been successful with those fuel caps then, Sergeant? I have been worried because everything they have is so advanced."

"Yes, sir. They gave me a bit of trouble. Permission to smoke, sir. I could really do with one."

"You stay here and smoke to your heart's content, Sergeant. We're going to fill up the truck."

He was still smoking when they returned some little time later.

"Now we have come to the second part," the captain told them. "Jones, you have the truck ready to move the instant you get the signal from Woods." He turned to Woods and handed him the torch. "You and Harvey stay here. It is out of sight of the enemy, but you can see the sergeant and myself. We intend to blow up the fuel dump and make our way back here. So, the truck should be ready and waiting for us to get the hell out of here. We aren't really equipped for this sort of thing, but we are going to try. Should it all go haywire, don't hang around, but get away at once. You are good at navigating, Woods, so I would expect you to make it back to base."

"Yes, sir."

The officer reached into a small container he was carrying, and gently handed over two hand grenades to the now tense sergeant. "Two for you, and two for me. I am good at throwing, Sergeant. How nifty are you?"

"I will make sure that I put a great distance between these things and us, sir."

"Bet I beat you, Sergeant."

"You're on, sir."

With the whispered well-wishes from the other three soldiers, the captain and sergeant started forward. Being brilliant moonlight,

the visibility was now excellent, so they had to make use of every available shadow.

After some way, the officer stopped and looked across to the huts, which were now considerably nearer. Although they were only wooden prefabricated buildings, there was a hospitable air about them as lights shone out and the sound of voices and laughter came through the open windows and doors.

"This will do," Purcell whispered.

They closed in against the barbed-wire fence, drew the pins from the hand grenades, then pitched them away as far as they could. For a split second there was nothing, then the most horrendous explosion rent the peace of the night, spilling sand and debris over the two prostrate men lying on the ground. Great sheets of flame leapt high into the sky.

"Are you able to get back, sir?" the sergeant shouted as he prodded the stunned figure beside him.

The young officer reacted immediately as he began, with his hands, to shovel away the sand which had half buried him. The sergeant helped him to his feet and, keeping close together, they lurched away from the blazing inferno. Several times they were thrown to the ground as more fuel cans exploded, making the flames leap even higher.

Woods and Harvey rushed headlong over the sand to help them, dragging them roughly along to safety. They reached the waiting truck and scrambled aboard.

As they drew away, Jones shouted, "Look at that," as two tanks were tossed high in the air like toys.

That was their last glimpse of the fiercely blazing hell, as they tore away into the desert. But the noise of the still-exploding fuel dump followed them for many more miles.

Jones drove slowly and carefully now, aided only by the moonlight. There was complete shocked silence amongst the soldiers as they rumbled onwards.

After a while, Woods fidgeted then spoke out, "I would like you to confirm my calculations, sir — just to make sure we are on the right track."

"Shall I stop, sir?" asked Jones.

"Yes, anywhere here will do. We need a drink."

Harvey handed round the nightly ration of beer. "Is anyone hungry?" he asked.

They were not in the mood for eating, but gradually their tongues loosened.

"Did you see what happened to the huts?" Purcell questioned.

"They collapsed right away, sir," Woods told him.

"Any immediate sign of survivors?"

"No, sir. None."

A silence followed, then White quietly spoke: "War is bloody. It's either you or them. It doesn't help to think or brood."

"Poor bastards!" Harvey commiserated.

The subject was closed.

"If I can have the torch, compass and map now, I can confirm your calculations, Woods. Then we must push on, for everything will be drawn to this area, especially planes."

"Yes, sir."

After more miles of travel, they halted at what the officer deemed to be a more safe distance away from the blazing inferno. Here they washed, changed and even ate a little.

"At base they will be wondering why we haven't turned up," the captain pointed out. "We must now get in touch. With all that has happened in the last few hours there is a risk that our contact could be intercepted. Are you ready?"

"Yes, sir," answered Woods. The soldier read out the words as he despatched them: "Enemy fuel dump located and destroyed. Mission accomplished. We have the necessary fuel to return to base. Is that correct, sir?"

"Yes, Woods. All correct."

The soldiers sat subdued, awaiting the reply.

Then the answer came through: 'Not bad for five men on a reconnaissance. It will take some beating. Return to base.'

A knowing smile accompanied the officer's remark to his men. "That was dictated by the colonel," he told them.

They drove on through the night, taking turns to drive, sleep, and navigate. This remainder of the journey was uneventful after the trauma of the previous day.

Daybreak found them at a small village, not so far from base.

"We will stop here and have a snack."

"Yes, sir. It'll only be tea and hard tack, sir."

"That will do for now, Harvey."

As they relaxed, Sergeant White surveyed the scene before them. "Permission to do a bit of business, sir."

"What here, White?"

"Yes, sir. I recognise some travelling traders. They go from village to village."

"Very well, but don't be long."

The sergeant went to the truck and after a few minutes brought out a wrapped bundle which he tucked under his arm. He jauntily walked over to where several men were gathered and deliberately turned his back on the watching soldiers as he began to parley with the traders.

After a while he returned, still clutching a wrapped bundle.

"I bought these for our village washing women and their kids," he told the others as he undid the bundle to display its contents. There were brightly coloured beads, bangles, sandals and some smooth shiny stones.

"What are these?" the captain asked, pointing to the stones.

"The kids play a game with these, sir. I used to watch them in India. These presents will make sure that we will get our washing done well, and we have got a lot of it. They will be washing non-stop for days."

"I do hope that you are not out of pocket, Sergeant, for these traders are very canny?" Purcell slyly probed.

The answer was quick in coming: "Don't worry about that, sir, because you saw me haggling and bartering."

"Something else you learnt in India, Sergeant?"

"Yes, sir. I just part-exchanged some of our rations. It always works, sir."

The captain raised his eyebrows but let it go at that.

The soldiers were relieved to reach base and find everything exactly the same.

At the earliest moment White was off, bearing his gifts. "I'll go and organise our laundry again, if that's all right with you, sir."

"Under that tough skin beats a large heart," Harvey observed.

"Well, White, what did they think of their gifts?" Purcell later asked.

For once the sergeant seemed embarrassed. "They went mad, sir. It's not often that they are given anything. You should have seen the kids' faces. I am working class, so I could appreciate their feelings. Your class couldn't understand, if you beg my pardon, sir."

"I suppose you're right, Sergeant. It is a matter of experience."

After the captain had walked away, the sergeant told the others, "I feel I can speak freely to the captain. Funny that, because he is everything I am not, and he is a lot younger."

"But you do come near to the edge sometimes, Sarge," Woods told him.

"I know I do, but that's how I am."

As that day drew to a close, the colonel and his two junior officers sat, once again, in that small village.

Great wafts of smoke billowed from the colonel's pipe as he contentedly relaxed.

"It seems ages since we last did this," the lieutenant observed. "Your exploits are on everyone's lips, Phillip."

The colonel chuckled: "The communication wires have been red-hot. I suspect we have been a bit of a joke with the rest, especially the heavy tank brigade. It was said, 'These extra reconnaissance units — who needs them? We have got our own.' Now who is laughing?"

The two younger officers delightedly agreed, although Purcell did point out, "It was luck really, sir. We were just in the right place at the right time."

"I don't want to hear anything like that, Captain. We'll keep that to ourselves." The older man then paused and puffed thoughtfully on his pipe. "We'll be leaving here in the next few days and will be joining the main force. There is going to be a showdown between us and Rommel's men. There has to be. The enemy is massing his tanks and heavy armour, flinging down the gauntlet. Montgomery is sure to pick it up. We'll be moving right into the intended battle zone. Should be interesting."

"What will happen to this place, sir?"

"It is intended to still keep it operational, with the minimal number of men. I have already told the headman, and he is

pleased with the arrangement."

"I'm glad to hear this, Colonel," Purcell continued, "for out in the desert we thought of this village as a secondary home. These people need to be rewarded."

The villagers were genuinely upset when the time came for the soldiers to leave. Sergeant White was the main centre of attraction for the washing women and their children, who had come in the morning's early hours to wish him goodbye. They openly wept as he embraced the children before entering the truck. The headman and the rest were also in sombre mood.

"You know you still have some of our men here, Aberdoo Groomer. Take good care of them. Our money will still come into your village to help you."

"Yes, Colonel. Thank you, sir. We will treat your soldiers like our own brothers, sir. We will be sad not to see your faces. Allah be with you, Colonel."

"Thank you," the colonel said as the trucks moved away.

The soldiers did not look back.

Their journey was depressingly boring until they reached the main highway.

"God Almighty! Look at this," Purcell muttered, as they watched the passing, never-ending stream of military vehicles, all heading in the same direction.

The three reconnaissance trucks joined the main flow, but not for long. A few miles further on they turned off onto a secondary road.

"Back into the wilderness," the captain bantered.

"Well, I feel more secure there, sir. Being part of a large force can have its drawbacks. The fewer the vehicles, the more chance of making a good getaway if the going gets rough," the sergeant said.

"Do you notice that our sergeant is always thinking of retreat, sir?" Jones noted.

"Better to live to fight another day, that is my motto, Jones. Will we be doing the same thing as before, sir?"

"Exactly the same, Sergeant. Only this time we'll be actually in the fighting zone. And don't ask me where that will be, for it could be anywhere at any time."

"So, from now on, we'll be in the thick of it, sir?"

"Yes, Sergeant. This is when it all starts in earnest, so I've been told."

By midday the three trucks had parted, each following their assigned route.

For a further three days Purcell and his men didn't encounter anyone as they roved the desert waste.

"Although we haven't had a sighting, I sense we're not so far away from contact. Of course it could be some of our own force," the officer told his men.

"Knowing our luck, sir, it will probably be the enemy," Harvey put in.

They travelled on further and, upon rounding one large sand dune, they lurched to a halt as a scene of destruction met their startled eyes. Scattered before them lay many tanks, destroyed, blackened and charred. Some were in grotesque positions due to the intense bombardment they had received. Sticking up from the sand were weird twisted shapes of heavy metal. There was an absolute quietness and stillness about the place — almost peaceful.

"It looks and feels like a graveyard," the captain sombrely observed. "Everyone out. We'll take a closer look."

"There are as many of our wrecks here as theirs, sir," White pointed out.

"Yes, you're right, Sergeant. There's been quite a heavy skirmish here — losses on both sides."

"Is there a chance that some have survived, sir?" asked Woods.

"I shouldn't think so, but we'll make sure before we leave."

They slowly and laboriously inspected each wreck, trying to prise open the many hatches which were jammed fast. The hot metal seared their hands as they toiled.

Other wrecks had gaping holes, into which the soldiers peered. "Nothing in there, sir," they reported.

"It looks as though this battle took place about three days ago. What do you think, Sergeant?"

"Two to three days, I should say, sir."

"So if anyone had survived, they would have been removed from here?"

"I would have thought so, sir. It's not likely that these were the only tanks fighting here. Some must have got away and taken the wounded with them."

"And this is the resting place for the others. That would account for the awful stench coming from those tanks we couldn't open. I said it felt like a graveyard," was Purcell's parting comment.

It was two days later that they experienced their next sighting of the enemy.

"There's something moving on the horizon, sir. I just caught a glint of something shining in the sun," Harvey said.

The captain was quick to use his binoculars. "Several enemy staff cars, and one is flying a flag," he told his men.

"Must be top brass, then, sir," White pointed out.

"I wonder where they're going, and what they're up to," the officer said.

"It could be Rommel, sir," Woods suggested.

"I shouldn't think so, Woods. Out here without an armed escort or back-up? I hear he is always very well protected."

"But they also say he likes to be in the middle of whatever is going on, sir," interrupted the sergeant, "a lot like our own general."

At that moment there were startled yells from Harvey and Woods in the back.

"Three enemy armoured trucks approaching from our rear, sir."

"Get going, Jones," the officer ordered as the sand around them began to erupt with exploding shells. "Drive like mad, man, before we take a hit."

"Yes, sir. Any special direction, sir?"

"Over to the right. There appear to be dunes on the horizon there. We'll try to shake the enemy off when we reach them."

"Yes, sir."

Jones drove like the excellent driver he was, zigzagging away, whilst the other soldiers grimly hung on.

Several shells came perilously close, spilling red-hot sand over the occupants.

"Are they gaining on us?" Purcell questioned the two in the back.

"No, sir. They're heavier than us, so are slower," Harvey told him.

"Pity their shells aren't," the sergeant put in quickly as two more

exploded on his side of the truck.

"You're doing well, Jones," the captain encouraged. "The more we outpace them the less danger there is from their ammo."

"Yes, sir."

The next few minutes were hair-raising for the five soldiers as the chase continued.

Then Woods gave a delighted yell, "Two have pulled away and are going off in the direction of the staff cars. Now we are being followed by only one."

"I had completely forgotten about the staff cars," Purcell said.

"So had we, sir," the others agreed.

"We're pulling away even further, sir," reported Harvey.

"The number of shells has lessened, making it quite bearable now, sir," said the sergeant.

"Don't tempt fate, Sarge," Jones warned. "It will only take one swerve in the wrong direction, and it will be curtains for us."

"Don't think of that, Jones. You're doing fine," praised the captain.

"You'll give him a big head, sir. He'll be wanting an extra beer tonight," Sergeant White laughed.

"The remaining truck is pulling away too. They have given up," the two men in the back shouted with relief.

"They're rejoining the others," Purcell speculated, "to escort and guard their staff cars against any further interference. We must have given them a shock."

"What if we had been a tank, sir?" asked Woods.

"We wouldn't have got so close. Our dust trail would have alerted them earlier, for one thing, and then there is the question of noise. I have a notion that they have tanks in the near vicinity, so we were lucky this time."

"I still maintain that there was very top brass in those cars, sir, but we'll never know for sure," the sergeant complained.

"I should think that is the case, Sergeant. Now, Jones, keep your foot down, for the sooner we reach those dunes the safer it will be for us."

"Yes, sir."

Later that afternoon, safely tucked away amongst the sand dunes, the five soldiers unwound.

"Have the tarpaulins over the truck and this lean-to been made really secure?" the captain questioned.

Woods answered, "Yes, sir. They are very secure."

"Good. In the daylight they are our only protection against being spotted by planes. Tonight we'll not light the lamp."

"I can drink my beer just as easily in the dark," boasted the sergeant, making them laugh. "I take it you're feeling uneasy, sir?"

"Yes, Sergeant, I am. We're too near for comfort."

"I felt uneasy when we were being chased this afternoon. I was petrified with fear. As Woods and I were sitting in the back, we could actually see those missiles heading towards us," Harvey told them.

"We were all scared to death, if the truth were told," the captain agreed.

So they sat completely in the dark that night. Even the talk was subdued, Purcell noted. This was with the exception of Sergeant White, who had already experienced being in the middle of the action.

The young officer voiced his thoughts: "We'll tread warily from now on. Before, it was reconnaissance; now it is a case of remaining alive." He glanced down at his notebook. "This information we have gathered will be vital to our side."

"When will we be reporting back, sir?" asked Jones.

"In three days' time."

"I still miss our nightly contact with base, even though I know it's impossible now," lamented Woods.

"Not only impossible, but deadly dangerous," Purcell confirmed.

It was in the early hours of the following morning that the officer awoke with a sudden start of alarm. He lay there, still and alert, listening to the even breathing of the others. Something had awakened him, but what? He lay there for some time and was beginning to drift off again when he heard it once more. It was heavy gunfire in the distance. Now it had disturbed the others.

"Captain, are you awake? Do you hear that, sir?"

"I've been awake for some time, Sergeant. At first it was sporadic, but now it's increasing in volume. It sounds as though a night tank battle is taking place."

"What shall we do, sir?" asked Woods.

A torchlight beamed as the officer looked at his watch. "It's never too early for tea, is it, Harvey? We'll just sit tight for the time being, but we must be ready to move should the occasion arise. I should say the fighting is some few miles away, but that could all change."

"Shall I make some tea, then, sir?" asked Harvey.

"You may as well, because sleep is out of the question."

With the aid of torches Harvey handed round the brew, whilst the captain scribbled furiously in his notebook.

The heavy gunfire pounded away in the distance with increasing intensity.

"We'll climb the dune when we've finished our tea," he told them. "There must be something to see and record. All information is valuable, especially at this stage in the campaign."

From the top of the dune they watched as part of the sky was lit up by the battle going on.

"One can imagine what the heat and noise must be like in the midst of that."

"All hell let loose, I should say, sir," said the sergeant.

"This engagement can't last for long. Such ferocity — not even the strongest and heaviest armour could withstand a barrage like that."

"It's as bad as when we blew up the fuel dump, sir." Woods recalled.

"True, Woods, but we're not gaining any advantage by being here, so we'll sit tight until dawn; then we'll depart," Purcell ordered.

There was still no sign of abatement in the fighting as they left next morning.

"We must be really on our guard, for we may run into reinforcements. This battle is far from over," said the officer.

It was later on that same day that they had their first sighting of the enemy going into action. Concealed behind some large sand drifts they watched as a long line of tanks and armoured vehicles snaked its way along.

"So, I was right about reinforcements," the officer remarked as he followed their progress through his binoculars. "I was hoping they would be ours. We must do something in this situation, Woods."

"Yes, sir."

"We'll take a chance and try to get this information through immediately. It's a risk worth taking."

"Yes, sir."

"Without backup ours are goners, sir," the sergeant agreed.

"Come on, then, Woods, let's put our heads together and work out our position as best we can."

"Yes, sir."

In a short time Woods was ready to despatch.

"I've almost forgotten how to do this, sir," he joked.

"I know, Woods. You've repeatedly mentioned your withdrawal symptoms. Get on with it, man."

"Yes, sir."

The others laughed.

For the next few minutes Woods worked and then sat hopefully waiting. Then to his and the others' amazement he made contact.

"That was lucky, sir. I never expected that," he said.

"Neither did I. Let's see what our orders are. They acknowledge our report and will act accordingly." Here the captain frowned: "We are to immediately return to our place of rendezvous. It sounds as though I might be in for a rollicking, Sergeant."

"I shouldn't think so, sir, not for one moment. We have put only ourselves at risk, and your main aim was to aid our side in battle. Under those circumstances, in my opinion, sir, you made the correct decision."

"Well, let's hope that others think the same as you, Sergeant. We had better obey orders and leave immediately."

The soldiers piled into the truck.

Jones carefully drove out from behind the sand drifts, then stopped dead. "Would you look at that," he breathed.

"It's those two bastards on their bike," White exploded.

The five stared with disbelief as the two bikers sped along, unaware that they were being watched.

"Where the hell did they come from, and, what's more to the point, where are they heading?" asked Purcell.

"They're going to hang around out of sight until the fighting is

over," Harvey put in; "then they'll be in there for the pickings."

"I said those bastards were like vultures," the sergeant hissed.

"More like the carrion crows that we get back home, Sarge," Jones pointed out.

White turned to his officer. "What are we going to do, sir? We could go after them and blow them off that bloody bike, but, if we're going to do that, we'd better make it quick. We only have a couple of hand grenades, but we've done well with them so far."

Purcell deliberated as he looked at the two bikers speeding away from them. But there was no time for an answer, for at that exact moment a sheet of belching, shooting flame engulfed the two bike riders.

"It's a flame-thrower," gasped the sergeant. "Where did that come from?"

"Pull back, Jones. Pull back to where we were," ordered the captain in a panic.

Jones did as he was ordered.

From where they were hidden they saw two enemy vehicles approach the smouldering remains. Filled with fear and apprehension, the soldiers watched as one of the enemy left the now halted vehicles. Walking over to the charred heap, he studied what lay before him on the ground. He straightened, then, using his field glasses, carefully scanned all around him.

Captain Purcell felt a sickening jab of nerves as the glasses swivelled in their direction. "Is this it?" he whispered, half to himself.

"No, we've got away with it, sir," replied a thankful sergeant as the enemy soldier returned to his vehicle.

Within seconds the Germans had left, heading in the direction of the recently passed convoy.

"That was close," breathed Woods.

"That could have been us."

"It certainly could have been, sir," the sergeant answered.

"What a way to die, but at least it was instantaneous. Seems like a rough sort of justice."

"Yes, we're all of the same mind on this one, sir," White said.

"They did something terrible to those two German soldiers," put in Harvey. "Their identity tags confirmed that."

"It doesn't bear thinking about," shuddered Jones.

"Well, we can't afford to lose any more time here, so let's make a move; and everyone keep a sharp lookout."

"Yes, sir," they replied as once again they left the sand drifts and headed for open ground and danger.

Nerves were taut as they proceeded the first few hundred yards.

"Anything to report? Any sighting of movement of any kind?" asked Purcell.

"Nothing, as far as I can see, sir," answered White. "It's as quiet as a grave on this side."

"Same here in the back, sir," Woods told him.

"So far, so good. With a bit of luck we'll soon be leaving this area of action. Without any further complications, our rendezvous should be reached by early evening."

As each minute passed, the morale of the five men rose as Jones swiftly accelerated away from this perilous zone.

Rendezvous turned out to be a large gathering of the military force centred around an oasis.

"We'll have a job to find the colonel amongst this lot, sir," the sergeant commented as they edged their way inwards.

"There aren't many of our type of truck around, so that will make it easier, Sergeant — although this fading light is a hindrance."

Some few minutes later, Harvey blurted out, "I've just spotted them. You'll have to reverse, Jones. They're over to our left, next to some tanks."

They found the two reconnaissance trucks neatly tucked in beside the towering bulk of the tanks. Jones adeptly drew in alongside them.

The soldiers were quick to alight. They looked in both vehicles, but they were empty.

"Are you looking for your colonel, sir?" The voice belonged to a crew member of the tank nearest to them.

Purcell turned and saluted. "Yes, I am. Any idea where he is?"

"Over there, sir. Inside that large tent. You'll find him there, sir."

"Thank you." The captain turned to his men. "I'll go and find the colonel. I shouldn't be long."

"Permission to brew some tea, sir?" the sergeant said.

"Granted, Sergeant. I'll have mine when I get back."

The inside of the tent was well lit, so Purcell was quickly able to

locate his colonel, who was engaged in conversation with several senior officers.

Awaiting the opportune moment to politely interrupt, the captain glanced around with interest. He looked in vain for Andrew, but he was nowhere to be seen.

"Captain Purcell." The colonel had suddenly spotted the lone figure.

"Yes, sir." The captain made his way through the crowd.

"Have you just arrived?"

"Yes, Colonel."

The colonel turned to the other officers. "This is Purcell."

The captain smartly saluted the officers.

"Excuse us, gentlemen, but my captain and I have to talk. Come, Phillip, we'll find somewhere more suitable."

Purcell quickly fell in behind his colonel.

They reached the quiet and darkness outside where the older officer immediately slowed down. "Let's walk for a while. This camp is dimly lit as you can see. I cannot think straight with all that noise and commotion back in there."

"It seems that I might be in for a reprimand, sir," ventured Purcell, "but I had to break cover and call for assistance. The enemy reinforcements were moving in before our eyes, and our men were in danger of being hopelessly outnumbered."

The colonel stopped and, in the gloom, peered at his junior officer.

"You're not in line for a reprimand, Captain. Is that what you thought? It was sheer coincidence that you made contact when you did, for, in fact, we were desperate to reach you."

"Were you, sir?"

"Yes, Phillip. You see, something has come up for which you are admirably suited."

"Has it, sir?" Purcell didn't sound at all convinced.

"Yes. We are all agreed you are just the type of man that is needed."

"To do what, sir?"

Here the colonel hesitated. "You know what headquarters are like, Captain — they keep everything close to their chest. The one detail disclosed was that this mission should only last for a few days and then you will return to your own unit. You are to leave for Cairo at daybreak tomorrow."

"So I leave for this mission tomorrow at daybreak?"

"Yes, Phillip. Report to the tent. Shall we now return there for a drink?"

"No, thank you, sir. I'll have an early night. What about my men, Colonel?"

"Tell them to report to me tomorrow morning."

"Yes, sir. May I tell them what is happening?"

"Yes, Captain."

"One other thing, sir — have our reinforcements got through yet?"

"Apparently they have, for there are reports of a major battle in progress there. Good night, Phillip, and good luck."

"Good night, Colonel, and thank you."

With reluctant steps the officer made his way back to his men. He pondered on this latest twist of events.

His sense of unease was immediately picked up by the sergeant.

"You weren't long with the colonel, sir. Do you still want that tea?"

"Yes please, Sergeant."

"Another brew-up for the captain," White instructed, then he drew up a chair. "Sit here, sir. You look a bit down. Has there been trouble over our breaking our silence?"

Purcell shook his head. "No, nothing like that. I have been ordered away on a mission. I leave at daybreak tomorrow."

The four other men went very quiet and attentive.

"Are you allowed to say what sort of mission, and where, sir?" the sergeant questioned.

"Only headquarters know that. The one fact the colonel could tell me was that it should only last for a few days, and then I will be returned to my unit."

Immediately the others brightened.

"That isn't too bad, is it, sir?" asked Jones.

"You'll be back before you know it, sir," Harvey told him as he handed the captain his tea.

"You are to report to the colonel in the morning," instructed the officer. "I shall finish this and then I will get my head down, for I must grab a few hours' sleep."

"We'll see that you are up and away on time, sir," White promised. "I was talking to some of the tanks' crews, and they were saying

that there was a buzz going round that our next stop was a place called El Alamein. They are expecting a really tough time from now on. The enemy is massed around that area and ready for action. This is going to be the big one, sir."

"I wish I were going with you, Sergeant."

"You might well be, sir, for you could be back by then. There's one thing we know for sure, you'll give a good account of yourself, sir, no matter where you are. But, of course, we'd sooner you were with us. We're a team, sir — a damned good one."

With that glowing endorsement the captain bade his men goodnight and retired to his tent.

Chapter Two

When he finally presented himself at headquarters, Purcell found the place throbbing with activity.

He was greeted at the desk. "Yes, Captain, we've been awaiting your arrival. Corporal, escort the captain to the appropriate room."

The officer was led away down numerous corridors until they reached the selected room.

Expectant, curious faces were turned towards him, and he immediately sensed that they had been discussing him.

He saluted the major, who had come forward.

"Hello, Purcell. I'm Grant, and this is Sayer and Moss."

The two sergeants saluted.

"I'm afraid I'm late, Major, but we were held up by the largest convoy I've ever seen."

"I'm not surprised. It's been murder here for days. Come and sit down. I will brief you right away."

The four men took their seats around the large desk which was covered with the inevitable map.

The major commenced: "There is some urgency about this business. As you can see, this map covers the Mediterranean and its islands. You will be landed here" — the major pointed — "from one of our submarines under the cover of darkness. There will be local people awaiting your arrival. All the necessary plans have been laid, so it was just a matter of our selecting the right men this end." He pointed again to the particular island. "The enemy have recently installed extra equipment and arms to this part, and these are presenting an added threat to our fleet. They have to be demolished as soon as possible. Sergeants Sayer and Moss are experts in this field, whilst you, Captain, have the other necessary

requirements. You've proved this only recently."

The young officer cringed with embarrassment.

"So that is your task," the major went on. "You will be given every assistance by your contacts there. They are tried and true, so you can trust them. Have you any questions?"

"Are we going to return by submarine, sir?" asked Sayer.

"Yes, Sergeant. You'll be given instructions on that when you disembark at the island. All eventualities are covered. It has been thoroughly thought out." The major then looked at each man in turn and asked, "Is everything clear?"

The three soldiers nodded their assent.

"We shall go and have lunch, and then you will proceed to port, for you will be leaving tonight."

The three soldiers didn't become really acquainted until they were at sea. They sat together within the cramped confines of the submarine. The unfamiliar surroundings and noises left them subdued and apprehensive.

"I can't stand boats, let alone subs," Moss whispered, not wanting any of the crew to overhear his remarks.

"I must admit I have never wanted to join the navy," Purcell mused.

"Nor me," Sayer agreed.

"How long will we be on this sub, sir?" asked Moss.

"When we boarded, the captain told me that we should be put ashore tomorrow night, provided there are no hitches."

"It can't come quick enough for me," Sayer said.

"Have you done anything like this before?" Purcell asked.

"Neither of us have. Have you, sir?"

"It's the first time for me, too. Well, there has to be a first time for everything, I suppose. At least you are both experts with explosives, so I will feel secure in that field."

"We hear that you have done well yourself with explosives, sir. We were impressed."

The captain laughed as he confided, "It was a chance sighting of a few enemy tanks which led us to a large fuel dump. My sergeant and I just lobbed a couple of hand grenades and got lucky."

The following night found the three soldiers in an inflatable

dinghy, being rowed ashore by two of the crew. They sat in total darkness.

After a while the pounding of the surf signalled that they were nearing the beach. As the water became more shallow, the sailors jumped out and began to expertly drag the dinghy up the beach. The soldiers had received their orders, so they too joined the sailors a few seconds later. With combined effort they beached the craft, then, very quickly, the soldiers unloaded their belongings.

"You shouldn't have to wait long, sir," one of the crew whispered; "as you know, we picked up the shore signal some time ago."

"Thank you, and give my thanks to your captain," the officer told him.

"Will do, sir. We hope to pick you up in twenty-four to forty-eight hours from now. Best of luck."

The soldiers watched as the sailors boarded the dinghy and disappeared into the darkness.

"Have your guns ready. We're in enemy territory," reminded the captain.

They huddled together near some rocks. There was only the crashing of the waves to be heard.

Moss gave a whispered warning: "I saw a glimmer of light, just for a second, further along the beach."

The three men strained their eyes.

"There it is again," Moss insisted.

"I saw it, so here goes." The officer switched on his shaded torch for a brief moment.

They anxiously waited, their nerves jangling.

Suddenly out of the inky blackness their contact joined them. "We weren't that far apart, were we?" he asked quietly. "We'll make the introductions later. Come on, let's get the hell out of here. Give me something to carry."

They sorted out the baggage between them, making sure that nothing was left behind.

"I'll lead the way. I have a rope tied around my waist. Each of you will hold on to it so that I can guide your steps. This is the only way in this darkness. I know this place like the back of my hand."

"I'll bring up the rear," the captain said as they fumbled around feeling for the lifeline.

"Are we ready?" the voice calmly asked.

The others gave their answer as they slowly began to stumble after him.

After a while he spoke again: "We're now going to climb. We've reached the path that takes us to the top. It is steep and rough but I'll go slowly. If you get into trouble, then tug on the rope. Do not speak."

They slipped, plodded and sweated their way upwards. At last the top was reached.

"It's easier going from now on," was the whispered encouragement.

They clung on to the rope as they progressed in the blackness. Now the sound of the sea was below them, made much clearer by the sharp breeze which whipped around their ears.

They soon arrived at their destination, for it was only a little way in from the path they had just climbed. They turned in through a small gate which led up a stone path to a building, outside of which they stopped.

Their contact let go of the rope as he fumbled around; then there was the sound of a key in a lock.

"Come on in," he ordered.

They trooped in after him. He edged past them again to shut the door and drew some bolts across.

"Now we are safe," he announced in a normal voice, "but keep still until I light up."

They blinked momentarily in the glare of the light, and then saw that they were inside a typical fisherman's cottage. Their eyes turned to their contact. He was a tall, swarthy, dark-haired young man with a pleasant good-natured face — not strictly handsome but attractive. He stared back at them with curiosity, his dark eyes twinkling.

"I thought you were . . . " the captain started.

"British," he interrupted.

"Well, yes."

"My English is good because I was brought up there. I left here as a very small boy. My uncles have restaurants in London, so I can fluently speak both languages. Of course, the enemy don't know this. I had returned here for a holiday when we were overrun and occupied. It is as simple as that. Now, make yourselves comfortable. We're safe at night for there are heavy shutters to the windows. My name is Theo. I will make us something to eat now."

"This is Tom, John, and I am Phillip," the captain introduced. "Is there anything we can do to help?"

"No. We will eat first, then we can talk and make plans."

"That was great, Theo," Tom complimented him after they had finished a surprisingly good meal.

"In London I learnt to cook too," he laughed.

They then got down to the serious task.

"I was told that we would be met by contacts," the officer queried.

"And you met only me," Theo put in quickly. "There are two of us. You'll meet him tomorrow. I met you because I am the one with the expert knowledge of this part of the seashore. I am puzzled. Everything here has been quiet and settled for some time, then suddenly we are told to expect you. Why this urgency? There's not a large installation of guns here. Now, if it were on the other side of the island, then that would be a different matter."

"Apparently our navy are finding them an added threat. It has only recently come into use, hasn't it?" asked Purcell.

"Yes, that's true, but I still think that the guns on the other part of the island should be the target. Still, I suppose they know best." Theo then placed a piece of paper on the table. "This is a rough sketch of the installation. I go there regularly to deliver fish and milk to the ten men stationed there. This is how I survive — by doing some inshore fishing and helping out on a nearby farm. My cousin, Dimitri, owns and runs it. He is the other contact I spoke about."

The soldiers studied the sketch.

"So you come and go to this place quite easily?" asked Moss.

"Yes, I'll be going every day this week. Sometimes it works out like that." He hesitated for a moment. "We were hoping that you could accomplish your task without throwing too much suspicion on us. We want to go on living here after you've gone. It's better to be a good live contact than a useless dead one."

"Don't worry, Theo. We'll keep that uppermost in our minds," Purcell assured him. "These daily visits to the enemy — is there an agreed time for you to call there?"

"3.30 in the afternoon."

The captain thought for a moment. "Well, Sergeants, we'll plan our course of action tomorrow, and carry it out the following afternoon."

"Yes, sir," they both agreed.

The three men talked and planned far into the night, until they grew tired and weary.

Theo showed them into another room. "It's cramped, but you should sleep well. It's safe here, for I never have visitors. I keep my own company."

After he had gone, the soldiers lay on their makeshift beds quietly chatting.

"I'm not happy about this one, sir," Sayer confessed.

"Neither am I, Sergeant. There are too many loose ends for my liking. We've been hastily pitched into this, and then are expected to be finished and ready to depart in a couple of days. Then we have Theo."

"Do you trust him, sir?"

"I do, because he seems to be as troubled as us. It all appears to be too hurried and slipshod. I'm wondering how our contacts would react if everything should go wrong. With the best will in the world, would they be able to withstand the pressure? Let's hope it never comes to that."

Purcell lay for ages, going over their situation in his mind until, like the other two, he drifted off into an uneasy sleep.

At daybreak the soldiers were awakened by noises from the other room.

"It's Theo," Sergeant Moss confirmed. "I've been awake for ages. He's lighting the stove."

They lay there listening to the background sound of the sea.

"Such noise after the stillness of the desert!" Purcell commented. "I wonder how my team are faring."

"It makes me homesick, because I'm from Cornwall," said Sayer.

The smell of brewing coffee greeted them when they joined Theo.

"I'd forgotten the smell of early morning coffee," Purcell told him.

"There is milk but no sugar, I'm afraid. Drink and eat at once, for I start work early. My routine today mustn't be altered in any way."

The storm of the night had given way to a calm warm day. They silently walked with Theo along a well-worn path, safely shrouded

and protected from view by high thick hedges on either side.

This continued until it ended at a narrow tarmac road. The three men remained, as Theo cautiously emerged onto the road and looked around. He then beckoned them forward.

"This is where we part company," Theo told them. He pointed to the wood on their left, bordering the road. "You take to the trees, but not too far in for you want to be able to see where I'm going. Just follow as best you can, but don't leave the cover of the woods. About half a mile along this road lies Dimitri's farm. I'll make sure that it's safe for you to join us there. Get as near to the farm as you can." With a cheery wave he briskly strode off.

"Let's get into those trees," the officer ordered.

They lost no time, for Theo was already well on his way.

"He's fit," panted Moss as they crashed through the undergrowth in an effort to catch him.

"I thought the same last night when we climbed that cliff path. He was like a mountain goat," Sayer observed.

"We're doing well. He is on a level surface and isn't hampered with this load." The captain was referring to the amount of gear they had strapped to their bodies.

From a distance they followed him, until he reached the entrance of the farm. He paused for a moment and then was lost from sight.

The soldiers reached the spot opposite, and squatted out of view. The small farm was clearly visible, together with some barns and outhouses. The only sign of life was a thin spiral of smoke wafting from the chimney.

The sun was already growing warmer as it filtered through the foliage. The soldiers carefully eased their heavy loads from their backs.

"We could be in for a long wait, sir," Moss said.

"Not too long. Remember, last night Theo worked out the timetable."

"Here comes someone now," Sayer interrupted.

An old woman came out of the door and slowly walked into one of the barns. As the soldiers watched, Theo also emerged, accompanied by another man.

They led out a sturdy farm horse from the stable. They then harnessed the horse into a large cart that was standing in the yard. The next ten minutes was taken up with the loading of bales of hay

and other farming implements.

"He's going to be busy," Sayer remarked as they watched.

When all was ready, Theo came to the edge of the road and, after making sure it was deserted, beckoned.

The other man stared as the soldiers warily moved out into the open. He was older than Theo, but of a similar appearance.

"Theo has told you about me," he said. "I'm Dimitri."

"You speak English too," the officer exclaimed.

The man laughed. "Not good, like Theo. I was in London at my cousin's restaurant. Then my father died, so this farm was mine. I live here with my old aunt. Don't worry about her. She is deaf and her eyesight is bad."

Theo was clearly impatient to be gone. He butted in, "We had better go. This is the best time to be in the fields near the enemy. They are used to my being here at this time, so will take no notice. We have piled the cart up high so you'll not be seen on that side, and if you walk on the inside next to the hedge you'll be even safer."

"Theo talks true and is clever. Go now and remember everything he's told you," Dimitri cautioned.

The soldiers positioned themselves alongside the cart as instructed and they moved off.

Nearly three quarters of the way along the length of the field Theo stopped the horse and cart. Immediately the soldiers froze. Suddenly the reassuring sound of pounding hooves was to be heard as animals rushed headlong towards the cart.

"Bloody hell, goats," Sergeant Moss muttered as he went down under the onslaught of several huge ones which had barged wildly round to where he was.

The other two men were of little help, as they had been roughly shoved headlong into the hedge.

Theo appeared, shouting and wielding a heavy stick, which caught both men and beasts alike. There was a general stampede as the goats made their escape to the field side of the cart.

The soldiers gingerly picked themselves up. Theo could be heard as he unloaded the fodder for the hungry animals. Peace reigned as they settled down to feed.

"Are you hurt?" Theo asked when he came round to them. Then not waiting for an answer he went on, "We graze the goats and the

few cows together. The goats are wild and crazy."

"We weren't expecting anything like that," Purcell admitted.

Theo laughed as he told him," You see farming can be dangerous." He grew more serious as he inspected the hedge. "The goats have done us a favour. They've made a hole big enough for a man to get through."

"That's where I landed," the officer told him.

"Well, you need to get into the next field, so here is as good a place as any. I'll fill up the gap once you're through. From now on, take care not to be seen."

The soldiers pushed their way through the hedge. Bending almost double they skirted further down the field.

When they reached the bottom, the captain carefully parted the hedgerow. He looked through and whispered, "Our target is now directly in front of us, with the actual gun installation nearest to the cliff edge." He dropped to his knees to study Theo's rough map, which Sayer had produced. He indicated. "We'll make for here," he said.

They left the security of the enclosed field and swiftly crawled along to the nearest clump of bushes, where the officer used his binoculars. The pounding of the sea was much louder now.

"There isn't much cover from here to the cliff edge, but if we use what little there is, and continue on our hands and knees, we have a fair chance of making it," Purcell reasoned.

Firstly making sure that their backpacks were firmly secure, the three soldiers started their arduous course over the rough terrain that led to the top of the cliff.

They proceeded, pulses racing, limbs aching, all the while expecting to be detected by the enemy. When they finally made it, they nimbly tumbled over the edge, falling down some way, landing in a niche close to some rocks. The men, by now winded and still cramped, lay exhausted.

"It could have been a sheer drop down to the sea, sir," Moss observed once he had regained his breath.

"Not according to Theo's sketch. He accurately pinpointed the dangers we would encounter if we took this course of action. I took a chance and gambled on his loyalty and integrity — so far, so good."

"I see, sir. I'm not much good with maps."

"But he's the best with explosives, sir," Sayer intervened.

"Well, that's what matters," Purcell told them.

The hot mid-morning sun bore down on them as they lay there. The officer's mind was working overtime. "I've been thinking," he interrupted the lethargic silence that engulfed them, "why do we have to wait until tomorrow? We're placed in the best possible position here, directly below our target. We should take advantage of what we've achieved so far today. Even though we were to spend today planning and preparing, there is no guarantee of success tomorrow."

"You mean destroy the target today, sir?" asked Sayer.

"Yes, Sergeant."

"I hate hanging around — it makes me nervous. I'd sooner get on with it," added Moss.

"Theo told us that he would be making deliveries to the enemy at 3.30 this afternoon. That gives us ample time to finalise our course of action," the captain reckoned, now eager to get cracking.

"Then we'd better make a start, sir," agreed Sayer, "for we'll take some time laying charges amongst these rocks."

"Down here, Sergeant?"

"Yes, sir. It's about the right distance below our target."

"The idea being to destabilise the installation in as many ways as possible, sir," Moss added. "You'll see, sir."

The two sergeants got to their feet and began to poke and probe amongst the rocks and boulders around them.

"We'll start here and work our way upwards," Moss suggested to Sayer.

"Couldn't be better," the other replied.

"Is there anything I can do?" asked Purcell.

"Yes, sir, but it'll be mostly fetching and carrying, I'm afraid," Sayer told him.

For the next few hours the soldiers laboured, laying the explosives, all the while working their way upwards. The officer watched, fascinated, as the sergeants deftly accomplished their task, oblivious to any distraction.

"That should do it, sir," Moss finally announced. "Now we have to find a suitable place of concealment."

"There is a rough track over to our right. Let's start from there," Purcell said. "At least our load will now be lighter to carry."

The soldiers scrambled through the jagged rocks, following the track upwards. Sometimes there were only inches to spare as they squeezed themselves and their kit through. Very soon they reached the top.

Crouched down behind the last barrier of rocks which separated them from their target, they gently eased themselves from their backpacks.

The officer looked at his watch. "We still have time to spare, so we'll rest and prepare for the next stage."

"We set the time of detonation of the bombs at 3.30, sir, so will keep to that time for the next lot. That should give us a little time to reach a safer range, but we'll have to move quickly," Sayer explained.

"Then we'll approach the target at 3.00. That should coincide with the arrival of Theo."

"Yes, sir, if it all goes according to plan," answered Moss.

"And those bloody goats keep their distance," added Sayer.

"I'd give anything to be able to survey the target from here, but that's out of the question, so we'll still have to depend on Theo's sketch," Purcell complained.

The three soldiers studied their next move.

"We'll make for this clump of bushes, but from then on it's open ground, so we'll crawl as before."

"It would be better, sir, if you remained in those bushes," Moss put in quickly.

The captain looked surprised, then irritated.

"He is right, sir." Sayer had noticed that look. "We'd feel more secure knowing that you were covering our backs."

"And we'd work quicker as a pair, sir. That's how we've been trained," Moss pointed out.

The officer relented. "Yes, you're correct. I'd be a hindrance. I'll join you as soon as you give the signal."

At precisely three o'clock the soldiers clambered over the last remaining rocks, and crawled to the nearest clump of bushes. The officer scanned the gun emplacement, looking for any sign of movement from the apertures that housed the firing crew and their weapons. Now, at close quarters, the long barrels of these looked deadly menacing.

His eyes dropped to the two sergeants crouched beside him, and

he knew that they were weighing up their options. Returning his gaze to the target, he was relieved to see that there was still no sign of the enemy.

"We're off, sir," Sayer whispered as they moved forward.

The remaining officer felt a spasm of fear as they crawled onto the open stretch of ground that led up to the target. Now, steadily watching for any trouble from the enemy, his nerves were taut and tense.

For the next agonising while he concentrated on the part he was playing and never once lowered his eyes to see how the sergeants were progressing, although he desperately wanted to.

Only after what seemed to be a reasonable amount of time did he drop his gaze to that open stretch of ground. His heart pounded wildly when he saw that the sergeants had gained comparative safety directly below the target.

They carefully and methodically worked, using the contents of their backpacks, which were lying open beside them.

The sergeants then paused, looked up and signalled for the officer to join them.

With one final check that they were still undetected by the enemy, Purcell started to crawl towards them. As he did so, he saw them feverishly dig into the earth right next to the foundations of the target and gently place the bombs into the holes they had just dug. They then became even more quick and decisive as they prepared to leave.

Sayer looked at his watch as the captain reached him. "Time is ticking away, sir. We'd better get clear."

The three soldiers wasted no time as they wormed along the ground, making for the next clump of bushes.

Here they stopped as the officer got his bearings. "We'll make for that small wood over there," he directed.

They continued like this until they reached the small copse where Purcell called a weary halt. They sank into the leafy shelter and lay there, worn and spent, until their hearts' beating became more normal and their breathing less laboured.

"We've covered a fair distance, sir," Moss muttered.

No sooner had the words left his mouth, than there was an almighty explosion. To the officer hiding there, it brought back the vivid memory of that blazing inferno in the desert. Added to this

din was the rumbling of falling rocks and earth.

Just as suddenly the noise ceased, and there was an uncanny eerie silence. Even the seabirds were quietened.

"It sounded as though everything we planted was detonated." Sayer was very matter-of-fact.

"And that was a hell of a lot," Moss whispered back.

"Everything is stunned and still. I can scarcely believe it — so unlike the last time," the officer recalled.

"But that was an ammunition dump, sir — much worse than this," Moss told him.

"I've just realised how hungry I am," Sayer butted in.

"Then we may as well eat now, for we'll have to stay here until nightfall. Of course this entirely depends on our not being detected by the enemy. We'd better keep a lookout, for the area could soon be swarming with Germans. I'll take first watch."

"Yes, sir," the sergeants answered.

But the calculations of Purcell were wrong, for the three soldiers remained securely hidden without any sighting or contact with the enemy.

Under the cover of the night they emerged from their hideout. This time they were able to walk erect.

"It's good going this time, sir," Sayer whispered as they stumbled along over the scattered debris. "Anything must beat belly crawling."

"I agree with you there, Sergeant."

"We must be getting near to where we planted the ammo, sir," warned Moss.

The moon was already half risen, making their progress easier. They now picked up pace as they headed in the direction of the target.

Now they could make out the outline of the barracks. The soldiers halted.

"It appears to be deserted. We'll go slowly and investigate," whispered the captain.

They crept around the building, reaching the back.

Then Purcell, who was leading, stopped. "Look at this," he gasped.

Even in the semi-darkness they could see that this part was demolished — ripped asunder by the blast. Some of the roof was missing, allowing the moon to shine down on the devastation below.

"Now we'll see what effect you've had on our real target. I need extra light. Here goes." The officer switched on his torch.

The bright powerful beam picked up even worse devastation. The gun installation had completely disappeared. That part of the ground where it had stood had slipped and fallen to the beach below, dragging rocks, boulders and a great deal of the cliff with it.

Purcell switched off his torch. "It looks like a . . ."

"Landslide, sir?" interrupted Moss. "That's why we planted the explosives in the way we did — to make it initially appear like some sort of a landfall."

"And halfway down the cliff too, to make it look more like the real thing. The enemy will probably inspect it closely, but they'll never be totally sure," added Sayer.

"And all done in a few hours. Well done! Now all we have to do is get back safely onto the sub tomorrow night."

"Yes, sir," the sergeants enthusiastically agreed.

"We'll strike out for that wood opposite Dimitri's farm."

There was no difficulty in reaching the farm, for the soldiers were becoming familiar with the surrounding countryside. Squatting in the woods, they looked across for any sign of activity at the farm, but there was none.

"We'll make a move to the farm. There is plenty of cover should we need it," Purcell decided.

With great caution they approached and eventually secreted themselves in the large hay barn on the further side of the farmyard, overlooking the fields beyond.

Sayer pointed over to where some rickety steps led up to the loft.

The officer nodded his agreement, so they mounted them quickly but quietly.

The sweet-smelling hay was everywhere. Bales were stacked far into the rafters of the roof. The men stood grouped together looking around them.

"If we move these bales around we could get a distant glimpse of the barracks," the officer whispered.

"What's left of it, sir," Moss observed.

With steady pushing and heaving there was soon a narrow passageway leading to the far part of the barn. The soldiers gingerly

crawled through until they came to the outer edge. There they carefully prised some openings, which allowed them to see the fields below them. Their eyes immediately fixed on the remains of the barracks, standing proudly defiant in the moonlight.

As they stared, an enemy truck with dipped headlights emerged from the far side of the barracks. It drove slowly up to the closed gate leading into the large field nearest to the watching soldiers.

At the gate the driver waited as a figure jumped out and opened it, allowing the vehicle to pass through, then closed it.

"Do you see what I see?" the startled captain asked the sergeants.

"It's Theo," they answered together.

"Replace that hay quickly. We must get nearer so that we can see and hear a little of what is going on." The officer was already crawling back through the bales as he spoke.

They clambered up and perched high on top of the hay, well out of sight, near the top of the steps. There was a view down to some of the farmyard outside.

They had just made it, for the truck was now near. There was a pause as the driver of the truck waited for the opening and closing of the farm gate, and then it slowly passed by. It stopped, now out of their sight. There was a slamming of doors, and the unmistakable guttural tone of the enemy's language. All noise then faded away as they obviously entered the farmhouse.

"They've gone inside, sir," said Moss.

"They seem to be on friendly terms, sir," observed Sayer.

"First appearances can be misleading, Sergeant. We'll have to wait and see."

The soldiers waited for over an hour before anything else happened. Then the engine of the truck started up. It whined in reverse gear until it reached the entrance of the hay barn, where it stopped.

The hidden men watched as Theo came in accompanied by the driver. The two were in deep animated conversation as Theo drew out a cask which had been hidden under some hay in the corner. After uncorking the cask he sampled the contents, then passed it on to the other, who did the same.

Still conversing in fluent German, they left, with the driver now in possession of the flask.

Seconds later the truck roared into life, this time leaving the

farm by the road.

Silence reigned once more.

"His English is excellent, but so is his German. He neglected to tell us that." The officer's whispered muttering was bitter.

"He certainly was on the best of terms with that driver. I did trust him, but not now," Moss whispered back.

"We're due to be picked up tomorrow night, as you both know. Until then we remain hidden. We'll make contact at the last possible moment so that neither Theo nor Dimitri are able to warn the enemy."

The soldiers dozed fitfully all night, which was not surprising after the traumatic events of the day.

Daybreak came, and the three listened to the awakening of the birds and the general early morning farm noises.

Later, Theo and Dimitri could be heard going about their work.

"It's going to be a long day just waiting," sighed Sayer.

"We should rest all we can, for we'll need our wits about us tonight," Purcell warned, "and there is a good chance that the enemy will be back today."

"To the barracks, sir?"

"Yes, Moss. To investigate and see what they can salvage."

Sure enough, there was much coming and going of the enemy during the day. The hidden soldiers listened as numerous heavy vehicles passed by out on the road as well as some actually calling at the farm.

"Theo and Dimitri are having plenty of callers today," said Moss.

"I wonder if they are under suspicion. I hope not," the captain worried, "but then how could I so quickly forget how at ease and friendly together they all seemed last night."

"Yes, sir, and we heard with our own ears how fluent Theo's German was. We have no proof that he's not with them," said Sayer.

Eventually, the day began to draw to a close, so the soldiers prepared to depart.

"Theo will be leaving for his home now. We'll follow across the fields, making sure that we're near the road so that we can use it when we are really sure it's safe to do so. If we hear anything

coming, we'll use the cover of the woods that run alongside the road. Now, let's get away from here," the captain told the sergeants as they carefully descended the rickety steps of the hay barn.

Their journey to Theo's place was uneventful, and as they closed in around the cottage the soldiers were doubly cautious, not wanting to slip up at this final stage.

Silently, they approached the solid front door, upon which Sergeant Moss knocked.

The other two stood on either side, alert and ready, in case of any sudden danger. There was no immediate response, so the sergeant knocked again, this time much louder.

Within seconds there was the sound of the bolts being drawn and the door slowly opened.

"Theo, let us in," the low voice of the officer came out of the night.

"My God! It's you. Come in quickly."

The soldiers slipped in through the door, which was instantly slammed shut and bolted behind them.

Only the dancing flames of the open fire lit the room.

"Wait, I will light the lamp. I put it out when you first knocked," Theo explained. In the glow of the light he turned to face them. He was very curious as he looked at each man in turn. "We thought that something bad had happened to you — that you had been caught in the blast and were dead. Also, you surprised us yesterday. We'd expected you to bomb today."

He spoke in a disjointed manner, quite different to the precise correct way he had used before. The captain found himself wondering was this nerves or guilt.

"The timing was always up to us, Theo, and yesterday seemed just right."

"Of course, Captain. I had just returned from delivering the milk and fish. It was a terrible shock. So much louder than we expected. We ran down the fields to see. There were soldiers coming out of the remains of the barracks; they were shouting and running towards us." Here Theo faltered. "Several were dead; they had been caught in the blast. We brought the others to the farm. Your bombing was very accurate. There wasn't much left."

"I know, we have seen it," the officer confirmed.

Theo looked dazed. "Seen it?"

"Yes, on our way to the farm. We slept in Dimitri's barn last night."

"And today?"

"We remained there, well hidden."

So you were there, even when the enemy came," Theo muttered uneasily.

"Yes. We heard and saw quite a lot," Moss put in.

"Well, enough anyway." Sayer was not to be outdone.

Purcell silenced the sergeants with a look. He turned to Theo. "What do the enemy suspect? Have they mentioned sabotage? They called at the farm several times today, so we were worried about you. Are you under suspicion, Theo?" the officer persisted.

"No, we are not." The man was emphatic. "They think it might be some sort of a landslide as it's slipped down onto the beach."

"Are they coming back? Did they say?"

"I don't think so. They said that they are having too much trouble on the other side of the island. I don't know what they meant by that, but they didn't seem very interested in what had happened here. This part has never been important — just a few guns and some soldiers — and we hope it stays that way."

"I'm sure it will once everything has settled down," Purcell assured him. "We should be gone tonight, so no one will be any the wiser. It was a shock for you and Dimitri and the enemy saw this, so that has helped. You might have behaved in a guilty way if the bombing had occurred today as you expected. And you also aided the enemy, that is another thing in your favour. You look completely innocent."

"Do you think so?"

"I'm sure of it."

With a visible effort Theo pulled himself together. "We must think now of what we have to do tonight to get you away. Then Dimitri and I will be able to breathe more easily."

For the next few hours the men whiled away the time. Theo grew gradually more confident, so that when they were ready to depart he was the cool collected contact that had firstly guided them inshore.

After extinguishing the cottage light, they crept out into the night with Theo leading.

Soon they came to the rocky narrow track leading down to the

beach. Again, Theo insisted that they be roped together for the gritty descent. To his surprise they accomplished this in half the expected time.

"You have improved," he complimented them as they disentangled themselves on the beach.

They sat close together on some small rocks. It was a favourable night, almost peaceful, as they huddled there waiting. Only the incessant pounding of the surf was to be heard.

After what seemed like an eternity, Theo spoke in a low voice: "It's time," he said as he fumbled amongst some things he had brought with him. He brought out his torch. The powerful beam shone out to sea for a couple of seconds.

Their eyes had scarcely become accustomed to this before they were again plunged back into darkness. At regular intervals, for the next couple of hours, Theo repeated this.

"That is enough. If they're out there they will have seen it by now," he told the anxious soldiers.

They didn't answer but kept their unwavering stare on the sea. More time dragged by, but no one dared to admit to the gnawing doubt that was beginning to grow.

Suddenly Theo stood up, startling the others.

"What is it?" The officer's enquiry was sharp.

"I thought I heard something. Listen."

The soldiers' inexperienced ears could only make out the monotonous sound of the sea.

"There it is again, nearer. Something is coming ashore," whispered Theo.

Their nerves were stretched and tense as they peered seawards. Then they saw a flicker of light that flashed for one brief second.

"Yes. Yes," Moss muttered.

"We will slowly make our way towards it," Theo ordered, "but be careful, for out there anybody could have seen our signal."

"We're ready for anything," Purcell assured him as they moved forward.

Just then the moon helped them as it came out from behind some clouds. Eyes were strained as the men looked along the beach. Still there was nothing to be seen.

"I didn't think it would be this far away," a worried Theo told them as they trudged on. He halted. "I'll signal again. Maybe that's

what they're waiting for."

His light shone for a second. Immediately there was a response some little way out to sea — a flicker of light that glowed, then died just as quickly.

The men stayed where they were, deadly still. Within minutes their waiting was over as the sound of something being dragged ashore was plainly heard.

"They have landed," Theo breathed.

He and the soldiers came from out of the shadows and walked along the beach. Now they could see the outline of the dinghy and the sailors.

"Captain Purcell, is that you, sir?" a low call came.

"Yes. We're ready to go," was the relieved answer.

They reached the beached vessel in double-quick time.

"Did everything go as planned, Captain?"

"It couldn't have been better. It went like clockwork."

"Glad to hear it, sir — then we'll waste no more time."

Purcell turned to his contact. "We'll have to go now, Theo. Will you and Dimitri cope?"

"I'm sure we will once you have gone. We'll just settle down again to our old way of living with the enemy." Then, with a chuckle, Theo added, "In fact we've become pretty good at it." He became more serious as he thrust some letters into the captain's hands. "Please post these to this address in London when you get the opportunity. I only hope that she's still waiting for me."

With a firm handshake with each of the soldiers and a waved goodbye to the sailors, he turned on his heel and strode away.

For a moment they silently stared after him, until the sailor in charge reminded Purcell, "Best be on our way, sir. It isn't too healthy in these waters."

They boarded the dinghy immediately. The captain pocketed the letters. He was still not entirely sure about Theo.

This time the cramped interior of the submarine was welcoming to the exhausted soldiers. They gratefully accepted the limited hospitality that the crew could offer.

Later they were joined by the senior officer. "I hear that all went as planned, Captain," he said as he sat down with them.

"We accomplished what we were ordered to do."

"Tonight we also picked up another of our people from the island — undercover intelligence. That's why we were a little late with our rendezvous with you. That also went to plan, but it could have been tricky."

The soldiers listened with surprised interest.

"You'll meet him as soon as he has made himself presentable. He's delousing himself. He's been hiding amongst a herd of goats. My God, what a smell!"

This other passenger eventually appeared, and the three men surveyed him with curiosity. He was smallish, lean, nothing like they had imagined. He moved quickly but awkwardly, jerking like a puppet on a string. His alert darting expression reminded Purcell of a perky robin that had lived in his garden back home.

"I'm Purcell, and this is Sayer and Moss," the officer told him, as he stood before them, obviously ill at ease.

"I'm Clark," he said as he took the vacant seat. "I've been cleaning up. For the past week I've been confined to a goat shed. Things had become extremely rough, so it was the best place to hide for the stink kept the enemy well away."

"How long have you been on the island?" asked Purcell.

"About five months."

There were groans of sympathy from the soldiers.

"It was getting us down after only two days."

"But you hardly kept a low profile, did you, Captain? Your sole purpose was to cause a diversion."

"Was it?"

There was something in the captain's tone that made Clark look sheepish, and then guilty. "Why, yes, Captain, that's what I was told. My local contacts were emphatic about it."

"Then I'm glad we succeeded," was Purcell's dry retort.

"So am I. You probably saved my life." With this, he jumped up and left the soldiers.

The three men sat bemused.

"He's a strange one, sir."

"He certainly is."

"I was expecting a tough character — but he might be, in spite of his looks," added Sayer.

"Did you cotton on to what he said about us being a diversion, sir?"

"I certainly did, Moss. And we were told that destroying that

gun installation was top priority."

"Yes, sir. You cannot trust anyone in wartime, not even our top brass."

The soldiers' opinion of Clark was also shared by others of the crew. "He is a peculiar character," they gossiped, "but then he doesn't belong to any of the services. That lot are a breed apart. It's said that they'd shop their own granny."

Clark kept his distance from the rest, mixing only when strictly necessary — a decision which pleased everyone.

"Where does he hide himself, sir — there isn't that much room on board?" Sayer asked.

"God knows! It's best not to enquire, Sergeant."

The soldiers were dismayed to learn that they were to remain with the sub until it docked in Scotland.

"Now this can't be too bad for you," the naval captain consoled them, "for all hell is let loose in the desert just now."

"I would prefer to be with them and so would the sergeants, even though we are only wartime soldiers," the officer confided.

"Do not undervalue yourselves. At least you're likeable."

"He certainly isn't everyone's favourite, is he, sir?" a mischievous Moss later noted.

"Clark? He doesn't give a damn. He knows he's invaluable."

It was a dreary, overcast day when they finally docked. The surrounding heather-clad countryside was solitary but impressive.

"This is a change, sir, from what we've become used to."

"Yes, Sayer, it's cold," the captain complained.

A sergeant major came up to them: "Captain Purcell, sir, Sergeants Moss and Sayer are to be returned to their company depot in England. You, sir, are to travel with a Mr Clark."

"To England, Sergeant Major?"

"I don't know your destination, sir. The transport is waiting for the sergeants.

"Very well, Sergeant Major. Thank you. I'll see the sergeants on their way."

"Mr Clark is ready to go now, sir."

"I'll not be long, Sergeant Major," a determined Purcell answered.

The three soldiers walked out to the waiting vehicle.

"Sorry you're not coming with us, sir," said Moss as they hurried along.

"Be careful, sir. You're going to be mixing with some strange company, I fear," warned Sayer.

"Don't worry. It shouldn't be for long, because I certainly won't fit in."

"No, sir, you won't. You're too normal," Moss interrupted.

The soldiers saluted, then parted.

"I've just parted from the sergeants," Purcell explained to Clark.

This was met by a disdainful silence, which didn't bother the officer.

The two men were escorted to a waiting limousine, which whisked them away at great speed.

"I wonder if we're in for a long journey?" ventured Purcell.

"About an hour."

The officer leant back, relishing the luxurious comfort whilst Clark stared moodily out of the window.

Their destination was an old granite mansion standing among trees some way off the road.

The captain looked around as he alighted. It was a perfect hideaway. Several high-powered cars were parked out in front.

The two men gathered together their things and entered.

"Mr Clark, glad to see you," was the greeting from many.

He was obviously well known there, making Purcell even more uncomfortable.

Clark signalled the officer to follow him.

When they entered the main room Clark was welcomed with the same warm familiarity.

"They are waiting for you, Mr Clark, if you would care to go through. Not you, Captain; you will be debriefed here.

Without any show of civility the two men parted company.

An older man introduced himself, and took the officer away to a desk on the far side of the room. "Are you feeling well, Captain?" he was asked.

"Yes, thank you, but I've only been working for you for a couple of days."

He was thrown a shrewd glance. "Yes, and you did very well considering that you were thrown in at the deep end. I personally think that method is very foolhardy, but the situation had become very grave — we had to get Clark out quickly."

The captain made no comment.

"Did you get on with Clark, Captain?"

The direct question threw Purcell for a moment. "I suppose so. We didn't see much of him during the trip home. He kept himself much to himself."

"That sounds like Clark. He is a loner. He likes to keep it that way, but he's one of our best men."

Again Purcell made no comment.

"He rates you highly, you know."

"I can't understand how he has formed that opinion, seeing that he has hardly spoken to me."

"It's because you got cracking right away and kept the enemy otherwise engaged, thus allowing him to make his escape."

"A form of gratitude. I can understand that," the captain admitted, "but how do you know his views? We've only just landed."

"We have our ways and means. Now tell me what happened."

"We were met by our contact, Theo, and spent the first night at his cottage. The following morning he led us nearer to our target and also introduced us to Dimitri, the other contact. We had decided to blow up the installation the following day and had told the two men this. But the opportunity and timing seemed ideal that very afternoon, so we went straight ahead. We hid that night in Dimitri's hay barn, but were unable to make our presence known because by now the enemy were frequently coming and going. We lay low all the following day, venturing out only when night had fallen. We made our way back to Theo's cottage and he guided us back to our rendezvous with the submarine."

"What do you think of the contacts?"

"Well, Dimitri we scarcely knew, but Theo was faultless — although we were suspicious of him at one time."

"Why was that?"

"Whilst we were hiding in the barn he and one of the enemy came very near, so we were able to overhear them conversing fluently in German. This alarmed us, for he appeared altogether too much at ease. From then on we were on our guard, for we were

determined that should he betray us then he would be the first to go. He, of course, was quite unaware of this. To his great credit, he loyally guided us back to safety. I felt specially guilty when at the last moment he handed me some letters to be posted to a woman in London."

"Have you got them?" The tone was sharp.

"Yes, I have them in my pocket."

"May I see them, please?"

The soldier dutifully handed them over and watched as the interrogator opened and scanned each carefully.

"We'll have to censor these, just to make certain."

"May I have them back when you clear them. I gave my word to Theo, and I at least owe him that. I feel that he and Dimitri are like many of us — reluctant volunteers."

"Is that how you see yourself?"

"Lately, yes. I feel ill at ease with all this cloak-and-dagger stuff. I'm keen to get back to my company and resume my role as an ordinary wartime soldier."

The interrogator sighed. "I'm sorry to hear this, Captain, because we were hoping that you would join our ranks."

"Thank you, sir, but I must say no."

"Clark really made a very bad impression on you?"

"Not really. I was of this opinion even before I had met him."

"We will see to these letters right away so that you can take them with you."

"That would be great, sir, thank you."

"No, thank *you*, Captain, for you and the sergeants got us out of a hole. Clark was in extreme danger and we need all the good men we can get."

Two hours later saw the young officer, with the letters safely pocketed away, speed away from the secret, lonely headquarters. He never again saw Clark, but was destined to be troubled by his memories of him many times.

Chapter Three

Captain Purcell's arrival back at company headquarters was met with some surprise.

"We surmised that you'd not be reporting back to us, Captain. In fact we were told that you were moving on to pastures new"

"No, Colonel. This time I was given the choice, and you know the old saying about the grass looking greener on the other side." The officer stopped, not knowing how much the other knew.

"Well, we are impressed with you, Captain, turning up in the sort of transport usually only used by the top brass."

Purcell laughed. "Where I've just come from, that is the only transport they know."

They both let it go at that.

"Will I be returning to my own unit, sir?"

"No chance. You've heard the latest. It's almost ended in the Middle East."

"Is it?"

The colonel gazed keenly at the man before him. "You've been out of circulation then, Captain?"

"Not for that long, sir."

"But things have been speedily moving along out there. It's good to have something favourable to report to the nation — makes a change."

"Yes, indeed, sir. I must catch up with everything."

"You'll be able to do that, for you'll be stationed here until your unit returns. That shouldn't be too long."

After being dismissed, Purcell wandered over to the mess, and immediately immersed himself in the latest edition of the papers.

"Captain Purcell, sir. You are back with us. It's been hectic out where you've been, by all accounts. The general has done well, hasn't he, sir?" the bar steward enthused.

"Montgomery is well up to Rommel's standards."

"I should say so, sir. They say they've great respect for each other — Monty and Rommel. Anyway, Captain, I'll let you get back to your reading. It's great to see you back, sir."

"Thank you."

After bringing himself up to date with the national news, the officer's next task was to forward Theo's letters. This he did with an explanatory letter of introduction.

The next four weeks were monotonous and boring for Purcell. The only bright spot was the short leave he spent at his home with his father.

"I found the last war tedious, very uncomfortable most of the time, interspersed with moments of intense fear, which I still vividly remember," his father confided.

As soon as the main part of the regiment returned, the camp became alive and vital again. It was now noisy, overcrowded, but never dull.

Purcell warmly greeted his fellow officers from his unit. "Colonel, you made it. How about Andrew?"

"He is here, Phillip. He'll be with us after he has dismissed the men, but how are you? What was this particular task you were given? I'm full of curiosity, but first come and see the men of your own unit. They gave the impression that serving under you was different, but quite the best. Andrew and I felt we had something to live up to."

The two officers laughed.

"It sounds as though Sergeant White has been stirring it again, Colonel."

The sergeant was genuinely pleased — in fact, he seemed relieved to be reunited with Purcell. "It's great to see you, Captain. I hear that you've been doing well, sir. So well that you were wanted in higher places. I'm glad that you decided to stay with us, sir."

The captain laughed and shook his head as he asked, "How long

have you been here, White? One hour or maybe two?"

"Nearer to two, sir, but you know how things get around in the lower ranks, sir."

"Nothing changes, does it, Sergeant?"

"What was that all about?" asked a mystified colonel as they walked away.

"I'll tell you all about it in the mess tonight, sir," Purcell told him.

Several days later a directive came through to headquarters which was to completely change the lives of Purcell and many of the men in the regiment.

"What do you think of this intention of forming an airborne division, Andrew?" he asked the lieutenant over drinks in the mess later that night.

"It had to come, I suppose, but it doesn't appeal to me. I like to keep my feet firmly on the ground. Do you remember how seasick I was on the journey to the Middle East? I'd be even worse in the air. How about you?"

"I'm not sure. I'll have to give it some thought, but it would be different. I've been bored stiff here during the last few weeks. Contrary to general opinion, I think this war has a long way to go before peace is declared."

The officer was approached by Sergeant White the next day. "Can I have a quiet word, sir?"

"Of course, Sergeant. Come to my office."

The soldier wasted no time. "We were wondering, sir, what your thoughts were on this airborne regiment idea."

"Who's we, Sergeant?"

"Jones, Harvey, Woods and myself. We still stick together pretty close, sir, especially after what we went through once you had left."

"It was that bad, Sergeant?"

"It was noisy, Captain. Tank battles are like no other. We were nipping in and out, trying to keep a low profile. We won't forget it in a hurry." There was a moment's silence. "Of course it was probably nothing compared to what you were doing, sir."

"That was no great deal, Sergeant. I'm not really suited to those

missions, and I was glad when it was accomplished. Now, to answer your query, I'm seriously considering this latest development."

"I thought you would be, sir. I told the others this."

"Of course, it does depend on one's ability and suitability, but it does offer a challenge, doesn't it, Sergeant?"

"Yes, Captain, that's exactly what we think. We'll be amongst the first in the army to do this if we're lucky enough to be accepted. We're hoping to be serving under you again, sir. Do you think you could work it that way, sir?"

The young officer laughed as he told him, "You're the expert in that field, White. I have very little pull, for remember I'm not even a regular — just an enthusiastic amateur."

"They do say to be one of those is best in politics or prostitution, but it could apply to the armed services in wartime, sir."

"If you say so, Sergeant," Purcell said dryly as he dismissed him.

It was meant to be, for a little while later the captain, together with his own unit and others from the regiment, were heading away to a new base.

The men were anything but pleased when they learned of their destination.

"Aldershot? Is there room for us there, sir? It's packed tight with Canadians." White loudly aired his views.

"What are you beefing about now, White?"

Jones butted in with, "It's true, sir. We all know that. They're the same as the Americans — better food, better money."

"Better everything, sir," Woods was also quick to point out.

Harvey wisely kept silent for the moment, then predicted, "There'll be trouble, sir."

"No there won't be, Harvey, because we're only in Aldershot for a short time. Then we're off to Scotland. But, firstly, we have to be super-fit and among the best trained in the army. Everyone on this course is going to be far too engrossed with this preliminary work to have either the time or chance for troublemaking. So if you want to remain in the paratroops, then toe the line and get stuck in — understood?"

"Yes, sir," was the unanimous agreement echoed around as the officer strode away.

"That was telling them, Captain."

Purcell swung around to face the speaker. A tall young padre fell in beside him. "I didn't see you standing there, Padre."

"John — my name is John Morris. I've only just arrived, so I'm very green."

"I'm Phillip Purcell. I shouldn't worry about anything, for at this we are all green, even though most of us have served in the Middle East. Where have you come from?"

"You will never believe this, but I have come from Rome where I was studying and was ordained. Because of my nationality I was becoming an embarrassment to the Vatican. My route home has been very roundabout, as you can imagine. I came via Portugal, but I got here eventually."

"Well, I'm surprised you made it. Let's go and meet the others. You'll soon settle down, John. We'll all be sweating blood together by the time this course is through."

These prophetic words were to come true as the chosen men were thoroughly put through their paces during the next months.

It was a well-disciplined, highly-trained, extremely fit group of men that eventually boarded the training planes, heading for their dropping area in Scotland.

They sat, fully kitted out on the narrow uncomfortable benches, each unusually silent and apprehensive.

Purcell studied them, especially Sergeant White. "Feeling fit and raring to go, White?" The captain could not resist the dig.

White looked rueful as he replied, "That's been the worst time of my life in the army, sir."

"We have never seen the sarge like that, sir. He was too knackered at the end of the day to get up to any of his old tricks," Jones gleefully said as the others laughed.

"Never mind, Sergeant. I'm sure these coming drops will prove how much you've learnt during the last months in Aldershot."

"I wouldn't say that, sir. I'm quite likely to do something like pulling the cord too quickly, or even the wrong one, and make a right prat of myself."

These observations silenced the others and an uneasy air descended.

Purcell mentally cursed himself for beginning this. "I would place

my money on your doing everything according to the book, Sergeant," he told him.

The tension eased, but only a little.

The anticlimax came when they reached the dropping zone. The aircraft crew opened the heavy doors, letting in a fresh stream of air.

"Right. Get yourselves ready," the instructor barked.

The men got gingerly to their feet and began to prepare for the imminent drop. It was all done in total silence.

Purcell fumbled a little as he glanced towards the open door.

"Are you ready, sir?"

"As much as I'll ever be," he tried to banter as he walked over and jumped out.

He had never experienced such a sensation as he hurtled through the air. He went over the instructions that had been driven into his brain during the last few months. At what he considered to be the right moment he pulled the cord, and was relieved when the parachute responded with a jerk, immediately halting the downward rush. There was now a feeling of security as he gently floated towards the earth. Looking around him he saw the other falling men dangling at the end of their chutes. All appeared to be making a successful first drop.

The captain looked down at the rapidly approaching ground below. Some few minutes later there was a bruising encounter with Mother Earth. There were shouts and groans as more men hit the ground. Unsteadily the officer got to his feet and began to disentangle himself from the silky folds.

Suddenly there was an urgent calling of his name. "Captain Purcell, I need help, sir." There was no mistaking Jones's voice.

The young officer tore himself free and rushed over to the soldier who was lying awkwardly where he had fallen.

"It's my leg, sir. I cannot move."

"It looks as though it's broken, Jones. Stay absolutely still. The MO is here somewhere. I'll find him."

He rushed off, leaving the stricken soldier lying there.

When he returned with the doctor, it was confirmed that Jones had indeed broken his leg in the landing.

As he was transferred to a stretcher, Jones complained loudly, "I

didn't get a scratch in the desert scrap, then I come to Scotland and end up like this."

They carted him away, as the rest waited for the transport trucks to arrive.

As the soldiers rumbled towards their next camp, they were full of talk and obvious relief now that the first drop was over. The only casualty had been the hapless Jones.

The camp was a collection of wooden buildings, which nestled in a valley not far from the dropping zone. It looked rural and idyllic.

Sergeant White was not impressed. "Is this it, sir?"

"Yes, Sergeant."

"It's miles from anywhere, sir. There'll be nowhere to go. First we make our first jump on the way here, now this, sir."

"You have a short memory, White. It's better than the desert, and there is a village within walking distance. You'll be sober by the time you arrive back here. Not that you'll feel much like walking, for we'll be making regular jumps — almost daily, in fact. What did you think of your first jump, Sergeant?"

"Well, sir, it wasn't too bad after my guts had settled back into my body. The first few seconds before the chute opened were the worst of my life. But I expect it'll get easier as we make more landings. Don't you think so, sir?"

"I hope so. They say with time one can get used to most things."

The sergeant didn't answer, but threw Purcell one of his shrewd looks.

This was the beginning of an arduous course which was to last for some considerable time.

Jones remained the only casualty. His determination did not waver, for he was back in training as soon as his leg healed.

"Have I caught up with the others, sir?"

"I would say so, Jones. After all, it's only repetition work."

"You're doing as well as any of us, Jonesy. My heart still skips a beat when I step out into space," White confessed.

By the end of the training course, Purcell had become firm friends with the Catholic padre. The few differences in their beliefs and outlooks did not bother either of them.

One fine evening found the two men speeding away from the camp in Purcell's two-seater.

"We deserve this break. We'll have a meal at the first decent-looking place we come to," said the captain as they sped along.

It was a large grand type of inn that was finally decided upon, and they were pleased to note that there were no uniforms in sight. They took their place and ordered their meal. Their table, beside an open window, enabled them to look out onto some beautiful scenery.

"This is perfect, Phillip. I find Scotland very impressive — so different to Italy with its bleak grandeur — it has a fascination all of its own."

"Are you settled in?"

"Just about. There are so many aspects to take in, but I am getting to grips with everything. It's certainly a change from my last job."

"I bet it is."

They both laughed.

"Do you know Scotland well?"

"Not really. I came here for the first time some months ago."

"On leave?"

"No, John, it was a military matter." Purcell did not elaborate.

They finished their meal and reluctantly rose to go.

A stranger approached them. "Captain Purcell, how are you? I'm surprised to see you back in Scotland."

"I'm sorry, but I cannot place you." A perplexed look accompanied these words.

"You came in with Clark. I was there in the background."

There was an instant stab of realisation as the captain recalled, "Of course, now I remember. How is he?"

"We're not sure. He left almost immediately on another assignment, and to date has remained completely silent. No contact at all. So unlike him. I must admit we're becoming worried."

"What of his contacts when he had reached his destination?"

"There is no news from them either."

"It doesn't look good, does it?"

"No. You know what he is like — entirely dedicated and versatile. Something has gone horribly wrong."

"I'm sorry to hear this."

The man shrugged. "It goes with the work, Captain. Now I must go. All the best."

Purcell watched him walk slowly away. "There goes one very troubled man, John. I didn't even get the chance to introduce you."

"I don't think he really noticed I was there."

"You can guess who he works for. It's pretty grim, I can tell you. I became involved for a very short time, but I wouldn't recommend it to anyone, probably because I'm entirely unsuitable for behind-the-lines activity. This Clark we were talking about was brilliant in the field, apparently, but a more unlikable person you would never wish to meet — a real cold fish. The two men who were with me on the same mission were of the same opinion. But, for all that, I'm sorry to hear that he's in trouble somewhere out there. I hope to God he makes it."

The captain was subdued as they returned to camp. The padre kept a discreet silence.

"I expect you think I'm uncharitable in my opinion of him," Purcell ventured.

"We are all guilty of that at some time, Phillip. We can't take to everyone we meet."

"Fancy bumping into him! I wish I'd not been told."

The following weeks were filled with speculation as to where this newly formed band of men were to be based once this initial course was completed.

When the final decision was disclosed it was met with many moans.

"What do you think of our new posting, sir?" the sergeant asked.

"A bit off the beaten track, Sergeant, but with our continued training one place is as good as another, I suppose."

In a short while these men were ensconced in the monotonous military routine, enlivened only by periods of leave.

It was from one of these that Sergeant White and several others almost blotted their copy books — at least, that's how it first appeared.

The sergeant major stood before Purcell early one morning. "Good morning, Captain. Four of our men did not report back from leave last night. These are their names, sir."

The officer scanned the list and noted with surprise that Sergeant White's name was among them. "I wouldn't have expected this of

these men, Sergeant Major."
"Neither would I, sir."
"Keep me informed. Have you notified the military police?"
"Yes, sir."
"Well, we shall have to wait and see."
"Yes, sir."

They didn't have long to wait before the offenders turned up accompanied by the police. They saluted and waited for the colonel to speak.
"You have over-extended your leave."
Sergeant White spoke for them. "There isn't much we could do about it, Colonel. The enemy bombed London last night and, as we live there, we were caught up in it. We boarded the late train, as we always do, but it could not leave until the raid was over and the track cleared. It was all hell let loose for a while, sir. It'll be on the news bulletins, so you can confirm it, sir."
The colonel did not hesitate: "Very well, Sergeant. I'll take your word for it. You are dismissed."
"Thank you, sir." They all trooped out.
"I knew there would be a valid reason, for I'd put my last pound on White," said Purcell.
"You have served with him in the field, and there is no better way of getting to know your man. This could be the start of a bombing offensive."
"It could well be, Colonel," put in Lieutenant Young. "My uncle is in Whitehall, and they've been waiting for something like this to commence."

Purcell did not meet up with Sergeant White until several days later whilst following their usual para routine. "It looks as thought this bombing of London is becoming nightly, Sergeant."
"Yes, sir, especially where I come from, down in the docklands area. It's a real target, so we must expect it. My parents are bearing up, but all the kids are being evacuated to the country."
At this point the two men were joined by Jones, Harvey, and Woods. The bond was still strong.
"My family are taking in some evacuees, Sarge." Jones joined in. "It's safe where I live."

"Of course it is, Taffy. I've told you that all you have up there is sheep."

"Well, at least they have peace to sleep at nights," Harvey interrupted.

"I know, I know," the sergeant conceded. "It was terrible that night when we huddled in the train with buildings crashing down all around us. I'd have sooner been in the thick of it in the desert."

"We went out drinking the other night, sir," Woods confided, "just the four of us. We shared the taxi home with some men in the Engineers who are stationed nearby. They told us that they are working on a part of a bridge."

Purcell laughed. "That's all they ever do. Everyone else in the army ribs them."

"Yes, sir, but listen to this: they have no idea where this bridge is going to be located when it is finished and assembled. They have tried hard to find out, but have had no luck. Have you heard any whispers, sir?"

"No, not a word. It must be part of a plan drawn up by the top brass."

"We'll find out in due course," White told them.

That night the camp got its first taste of enemy bombing. The captain was on night duty, so he did the usual check around the camp.

He looked up at the star-filled sky where the searchlights crisscrossed. "It's a fine night, Sergeant Major."

"Yes, sir. It's hard to imagine there's a war going on. Quite different from other parts of the country."

They proceeded with their duties, making sure that all was correct in the camp.

"Look at the searchlights — they're going crazy!" the officer exclaimed as he gazed heavenwards.

"I have never seen them like this, sir."

Both soldiers jumped violently as the camp's air-raid alarm rent the peace and quiet.

"Helmets on, Sergeant Major. We'll go straight to the guards on the outer perimeter."

They hurried away just as the anti-aircraft guns opened up. They stumbled over the now familiar ground, all the time trying to watch the swivelling lights in the sky above them.

The sergeant major yelled, "They've got one in the lights, sir. Look, over there."

The plane manoeuvred this way and that, desperately trying to escape the equally determined light.

"Christ, sir, it's dropping its load."

Both men dived for any possible cover that existed, which was scant, seeing that they were on the edge of the football pitch.

They lay face downwards as a fast-approaching whooshing sound bore down upon them. Seconds later the bombs exploded, shattering the night with ferocious venom. It was over in a flash, then the noise of the bomber deafened them as it accelerated away.

Shaken and shocked, the two soldiers lay there as the seconds ticked away.

The officer stirred. "It's probably coming in for another attack," he reasoned, but there was now an uncanny silence.

"It's gone, sir." There was relief in the sergeant major's voice.

They scrambled to their feet.

"That was damned close — I thought our number was up," said Purcell looking up at the searchlights still raking the sky. "We'll go and check up on the outposts. They might have caught some of the blast."

"Yes, sir."

"We were fortunate that the bombs fell well away from the camp, for otherwise there would have been heavy casualties."

"I think it landed on the parade ground, sir."

"We'll be able to say for sure when the dawn breaks, but I reckon we were the nearest, Sergeant Major."

With the aid of their torches, they found the nearest guards unhurt.

"We were worried that you had taken some of the blast."

"Not too much, sir. The place shook a fair bit; all of the windows have gone and the telephone and electricity wires are down."

"That can be fixed in the morning. Try not to move around because of the glass. We're going to the others now, but will come again before you go off duty."

They found the remaining posts in much the same condition, so spent the remainder of the night in the outer perimeter of the camp.

With dawn fast approaching the soldiers plodded towards the camp, still stumbling over the debris for the meagre light from their torches was almost spent.

"We must be getting close, sir."

"Stop a moment, Sergeant Major. There's someone coming."

They stood, listening intently. Somewhere ahead they could hear talking. Both men signalled frantically with their torches. Straight away there were responsive beams.

"Let's walk towards them; it could be the relief guards coming on duty."

"Yes, sir."

"Captain Purcell, Sergeant Major, are you there?" came the call.

"Yes, we're approaching," the captain replied.

They met together some minutes later.

"We've been looking for you, sir."

"We've been with the guards on the outer posts, for they were nearer to the blast."

"Any casualties, sir?"

"None, but they'll be pleased to see the relief guards."

"The colonel will not allow them to take over until daybreak, sir."

"Well, that won't be long now," the officer said as he looked up at the first streaks of dawn. "So, we've got away lightly, have we?"

"Yes, sir; not much damage around here, but we won't know the picture until the daylight comes."

"I wonder how the rest of the country has fared."

"We hear that Plymouth has been pounded for most of the night, sir."

"So our bomber must have wandered off course."

"It looks that way, sir. We'll head back now, sir."

"Yes, and we'll come with you."

When they reached the main camp they found everyone in a state of emergency.

"Come, Sergeant Major, we'll go and report to the colonel."

Inside the office the glare of the electricity blinded them.

"The bombing hasn't affected here."

"No, sir. I thought the lines would have been down here as well."

"We'll wait for the colonel here, Sergeant Major. He is probably rushing around in that throng out there."

They didn't have to wait long.

"Purcell and Griffin, where the hell have you been? There are men out searching for you."

The two soldiers saluted.

"We met three of them on the way back from the guard posts on the outer perimeter, Colonel," Purcell explained. "These posts were the nearest to the bombing, but there are no casualties, sir, just superficial injuries. We remained out there until daybreak."

The colonel eyed the two soldiers. "By the look of you both, I'd say that you were also close to where the bombs fell."

"Yes, sir, on the edge of the football pitch."

"You were close." The captain laughed as he glanced at the sergeant major.

"I know we're in a bit of a state, Colonel, but we were half buried in dirt and debris. The guards are out there with both telephone and electricity wires down, sir. During the night we all made use of our torches, but they were hardly adequate."

"It's being taken care of, Captain. We began to think the worst when you didn't report."

"Yes, sir."

"Switch off the light and draw back the blackout blinds please."

The officer obeyed and the early morning light flooded in.

"I'd like another look around. Permission to return there, sir."

"Granted, Captain."

When the two soldiers stepped outside there were curious looks thrown in their direction.

"I'll go and get cleaned up, sir, for we're getting some funny looks."

"Ignore them, Sergeant Major. We got in this state when they were fast asleep in their beds."

"Permission to go with you, sir. I'd like to see where the bombs fell."

They reached the actual spot and stopped.

The sergeant major was dismayed. "My God! the colonel won't like what has happened to his parade ground. He is one for drill, pomp, and ceremony. He's from the old school, like me, sir. There won't be any marching or drilling here for some time. There'll be a lot of happy troops, though."

"It'll soon be back to normal, knowing the colonel and you," was the quick retort.

The two men parted company and the officer hurried back to where they had spent most of the night. Halfway there he met the guards he was going to see. In the light of day they were a sorry sight, covered in blood and dirt and looking tired and weary as they plodded off duty.

Purcell saluted as they drew abreast and they responded. "So you've been relieved, Corporal. I was on my way to see you."

"We're not sorry to see this night over, sir, and we had it only lightly. We were asking what the civilians in heavy raids must be suffering."

"That's true, Corporal. Now, on your way and get yourselves sorted out."

"Yes, sir. Thank you, sir."

Suddenly, the young officer felt worn and weary as the adrenalin ceased to flow in his veins. He turned and began to retrace his way back to the camp.

"Captain Purcell, wait, sir."

A voice broke into his lethargic thoughts. He turned and managed a smile as he saw, tearing towards him, White, Jones, Harvey, Woods and the padre.

"We have been looking for you, sir. We did volunteer right away when the bombs fell but were ordered to wait for daybreak," a breathless sergeant explained.

"Well, I'm still here, Sergeant, as you can see."

"Yes, sir, but you're in a bit of a mess, if you don't mind me saying. We thought you'd copped it this time, so what's a bit of dirt."

"There was only open ground and dirt, so we were lucky."

"Reminds me of that time in the desert, only it was sand there, sir — loads of it," said Jones.

"That was much worse, Taffy," joined in Harvey.

"All hell let loose, that was," agreed Woods.

The quiet voice of the padre intervened. "You look done in, Captain. We should report back now."

The men fell in and they moved off.

"I was just thinking, sir, you always manage to be in the middle of the action but you survive. You have a lucky streak. That is one reason why we four want to go on soldiering with you." Sergeant White was in jovial mood now.

"Hoping that it brushes off onto you! Well, long may it continue, Sergeant, I say."

"Yes, sir."

"I'm going to get my head down before I fall asleep on my feet. Will see you later." The officer saluted and turned away.

They watched him go, then the padre observed, "It's been a hard night for him."

"Yes, sir, but he'll survive. He's tough and learning fast," White replied.

In a matter of days the whole place was back to normality, with the parade ground repaired.

Purcell looked out on the many soldiers who were drilling there. "Well, the colonel and sergeant major will be contented now," he muttered.

As he resumed his office work the door burst open and Sergeant White rushed in.

He saluted. "Excuse me, sir, but could you come to the maintenance stores? One of the ATS girls there is in a bad way."

"I'd better phone her commanding officer first, Sergeant."

"Yes, please, sir, but we should hurry. I'd sooner go back straight away, sir, for someone should be with her." Clearly the man was very agitated.

"If it's that urgent, Sergeant, then I can phone later. I'll come with you." They hastened their steps and Purcell felt perplexed. "This is unlike you, White. You're usually so calm and collected."

"Yes, sir." The sergeant didn't add any more.

They reached the maintenance stores, a huge cold building which at that time of day was deserted.

"Over here, sir," White said as he entered some offices on the far side.

A low moan came from one of them. Both men pulled up short as they took in the sight before them. The young woman had collapsed and was lying in a pool of blood on the floor. She was deathly pale and her eyes were closed.

"Christ help us, sir — she's gone.

The young officer knelt down beside her and felt for a pulse. "No, she hasn't, but this is serious." He rose and reached for a

phone that was on a nearby desk. "Captain Purcell here. Would you send an ambulance to the maintenance store immediately. We have a collapsed female soldier here." He replaced the phone and looked across to where the sergeant still knelt beside the stricken woman. "They are coming. Now I can inform her commanding officer."

True to form everyone arrived together. Quickly the medical team stretchered the woman into the ambulance.

The female officer was shaken. "Thank you, Phillip, for calling me. I had no idea that she was unwell. She certainly didn't report sick."

"I wouldn't have known but for the sergeant here. He came and fetched me."

She turned to White. "You probably saved her life, Sergeant."

"Yes, ma'am," he muttered, looking decidedly shifty as he asked for permission to leave.

Purcell eyed him with suspicion as he smartly strode away. "There's something going on, Mary. I swear White looked guilty."

"Guilty? Now you're imagining things."

"But you don't know him as I do."

"I'll see you tonight in the mess, and I will tell you the hospital's findings. Why are you so curious?"

"I'm sure I'm going to learn something interesting."

"You're just nosey."

"I am where my sergeant is concerned."

Later that night the officer had his suspicions confirmed when he was told, "Well, what do you think? A bonny baby boy arrived earlier tonight — a great shock to us all, especially the girls she soldiered with. She certainly kept her condition secret. Apparently she had put on some weight, but not enough to raise eyebrows."

"And I bet I know who the father is."

"Your Sergeant White?"

"I would bet on it. I shall have him in tomorrow. How about that drink you promised?"

"John is up at the bar ordering it right now. Do you think the sergeant will stand by her if the baby does belong to him?"

"That I will find out tomorrow, Mary."

It was a very alert and assured White who reported next day. "You wanted to see me, sir?"

"Yes, I do, Sergeant. You already know that a baby boy was born to that young woman."

"I certainly do, sir, for I was at the hospital."

"Were you? Why was that, White?"

"Because I'm the father, sir, but I have the feeling that you'd already guessed this."

Purcell just nodded. "It would have been wiser to have made known her condition before she went into labour, don't you think?"

"I agree, sir, but I didn't know she was having a baby."

"You didn't? I find that hard to believe."

"It's true, sir. I haven't had much dealings with babies. I felt a right stupid bastard at the hospital. They didn't believe me either."

"Maybe it doesn't belong to you. Have you thought of that?"

"Oh, it does, sir. There's no doubt about it. I'm not a complete idiot."

"As you say, Sergeant. So what is going to happen now?"

"I'm going home this weekend, so will make arrangements with my mother. We shall quickly sort it out, sir."

"Very well, Sergeant; and keep me in the picture."

"Yes, sir, will do." White hesitated for a second. "She is a very nice lady, that Lieutenant Grundy. She seemed to like you, sir, I noticed."

"She is getting married to one of my fellow officers, if you must know. You're dismissed, Sergeant."

"Yes, sir."

The said lady called in to see Purcell later, accompanied by the camp's welfare officer.

"I'm sorry to interrupt you, Phillip, but we were wondering if you made any headway with Sergeant White."

"Sit down, both of you. White was here a little while ago."

"Did he come of his own accord or did you send for him?" the welfare officer questioned.

The captain laughed knowingly. "Have you been having trouble with him, Peter?"

"Just a bit. He can be very hard to tie down, that man. He gives the impression that this is strictly his own business and refuses to

enter into any discussion. Mind you, he was very correct in his manner, but was distinctly not co-operative."

Purcell laughed again. "Bloody-minded, you mean. Well, don't worry for he is going home to make arrangements."

"What does that mean?" asked Lieutenant Grundy.

"There will be a home for the young woman and her child there."

"And you believe this?"

"Oh, I'm certain. He is reporting back to me as soon as he returns."

The welfare officer heaved a sigh of relief. "I'm glad to hear this, I can tell you. This young woman has no family. She was brought up by an aged aunt who has recently died. This mother is determined to keep her child."

"Did he actually mention marriage?" Mary Grundy pressed.

"Not in so many words. Of course we can only wait and see, but I'm not unduly worried. I'll inform you both as soon as I hear. What does she have to say?"

"Not a thing. Your Sergeant White is also keeping her in the dark," answered the welfare officer.

"He seems very committed," Purcell remarked.

"I wish I had your faith," the female officer teased.

Purcell shrugged. "As I've said, time will tell."

On his return to duty White presented himself directly as he had promised. "Good morning, sir."

"Good morning, Sergeant."

"It's all fixed up, sir. My son and his mother can live with my family. My mother is seeing to everything."

"And is this all right with your father — does he agree?"

"Of course, sir. He always goes along with whatever she says or does. She is the real head of the family — that's how it is, sir. We're going to have a wedding, a white one with all the trimmings, as soon as we can. This is the first grandson. It'll be a real East End bash, sir."

The officer studied the man before him, who was full of enthusiasm and pride. "You must let your intended wife know of these plans as soon as possible, Sergeant."

"I shall tell her tonight when I visit the hospital, sir."

"The welfare officer could also be very helpful. You should take

every advantage open to you."

A distinct frown appeared upon the sergeant's brow. "I feel this is my business, sir — best handled by myself and my family."

"But your intended wife is also in the army, so there is a difference. Think it over."

"Yes, sir, I will."

It was a surprised and gratified welfare officer who approached Purcell the following day. "Just a quick word about Sergeant White — he came to see me, acting on your advice, and is doing the honourable thing, as the old saying goes. You were correct, then. Won't Mary be surprised?"

"I should think she'll be astounded."

"You're probably right. Anyway, now that I have his co-operation I can be of assistance."

All of this was later confirmed by the sergeant himself. "I did what you advised, sir, and went to see the welfare officer. He was helpful. I'll be able to take Joan and the baby straight home to my parents as soon as they are discharged from hospital."

"Then it's all coming to a satisfactory conclusion, Sergeant. I'm pleased for you. I was thinking, why don't you have a small, quiet, family wedding, under the circumstances? A big, white wedding is hardly appropriate in your case. I mean, white itself infers that the bride is virginal. Again, Sergeant, think it over."

"Yes, sir, I will."

A few days later White was given permission to take away his newly acquired family, but not before he had reported to his captain.

"I want to keep you in touch with all that's going on, sir," he explained with more than a hint of embarrassment.

The officer's eyes twinkled. "Are you getting a bit of stick over what has happened, Sergeant?"

"Yes, sir, I am. You know how I've carried on with the men — don't take chances, don't get caught. A real hard nut I was, sir."

"We all come a cropper at some time or another, White. You know it will soon be forgotten and you'll be back to your old bullying ways."

"Yes, I expect so, sir."

The war dragged monotonously on for the soldiers at the camp. The only outward sign of conflict was the incessant bombing being still endured by the unfortunate public, so the plight of Sergeant White was of great interest and speculation to the lower ranks. But he was still a popular figure — in fact, he had grown in stature.

Captain Purcell eyed him with anticipation, when he returned for duty.

"Reporting back for duty, sir."

"Stand easy, Sergeant. I hope you've completed everything to your satisfaction."

"Yes, sir. All arrangements have been made."

He placed a type-written piece of paper on the desk before the officer.

"What's this, Sergeant?"

"It's the details of the place and date of the wedding, sir. We were hoping that you would come."

The captain studied the paper.

"My mother would really like you to come, sir," the sergeant pressed, "even though she thinks you have some really old-fashioned ideas, sir."

The officer looked up sharply. "About what?"

"Well, sir, what you said about my having a white wedding. She told me that I was two when she and my father married. I am the eldest, you see, sir. They had a white wedding, not some quiet hole-in-the-corner do. It was a real East End bash."

Purcell had the good grace to look embarrassed as he muttered, "It's a case of traditions being taken differently, I suppose, White."

"Oh, it doesn't matter. Not at all, sir. We'd really be very pleased for you to come. You'd be our guest of honour, sir."

The officer looked again at the paper, not knowing what to say.

White resumed: "In fact, sir, I'm going to invite Jones, Wood, and Harvey too. I want Jonesy as my best man. We five should stick together if we can, sir."

"Now, hold on, Sergeant. What makes you think we could get leave to attend your wedding? We're in the throes of a war."

"I know, sir, but there isn't much going on down here at the moment, is there? When the time comes, we'll be ready and in the right place. You'll see, sir."

"The army is not going to accommodate you. You'll not swing

this one, White, so don't bank on it."

"Only forty-eight-hour passes are needed, sir, and I already have the support of the welfare officer. He'll look on it as a satisfactory conclusion to an unfortunate mistake."

"Will he? How do you know?"

"Because that's what he's already told me, sir."

"I knew those weren't your own words, Sergeant."

"No, sir. I'm not that smart or educated, I know. But, can I include your name with the others?"

Without hesitation Purcell replied, "Of course you can, but I'm convinced you'll not get permission."

As Purcell had expected, the welfare officer was soon on the phone.

The captain jumped in first: "You don't have to tell me, this time White has really gone over the top. I pointed out to him that this was the army in the midst of a war."

There was a low chuckle from the other end. "Well, the colonel took everything into consideration and has given the go-ahead. They served together in India, you know."

There was a dumbstruck silence from Purcell.

"Are you still there, Phillip?"

"Yes, I'm here. I'm only in the army for the duration, and acknowledge that sergeants like White are the backbone of it. I have to admit that they have the intuitive know-how of what can and cannot be achieved."

"I'd say it's who you know, Phillip, not what you know. They have the knack of swinging things their way. Even the old man said he had a persuasive manner."

"That's an understatement."

"So you will attend his wedding? It's a little unusual, but if you're sure . . ."

"To tell the truth, I'm looking forward to it. The taming of Sergeant White is something I would not miss."

Both men laughed.

The captain travelled up to London the day before the wedding. The capital was heaving with masses of people from the services in different uniforms, from different countries, and many were of a different colour.

The officer stood and took in the noise and movement that surrounded him. "Taxi," he hailed. He was lucky enough to get one, and jumped on board after giving the cabbie his destination.

"East End, dockland, Captain? Do you know it, sir?"

"No, this is my first visit."

"It's taken a real pasting from Jerry, as you'll see for yourself, sir."

"I was wondering, could you help me locate some flowers? I don't want to arrive empty-handed. I was hoping to buy some on the way."

The cabbie thought for a moment. "I do know where we could get some, sir, but it's a bit off route, if that's OK with you."

"That's great. Go wherever is needed."

As they went towards the East End the devastation became more visible.

Purcell was appalled at what he saw. "You weren't joking. This part has taken a hell of a battering," he said.

"It's been bad, Captain, although recently it hasn't been on the target list. The other big cities and ports are now having their turn."

"Yes, it was Plymouth the other night."

When he reached his destination the officer gazed keenly around, taking in the run-down appearance of the place. But at least these houses were still standing. It was a typical Victorian square including the inevitable pub.

He knocked loudly on the door of Sergeant White's house.

The door was gingerly opened by a woman who was obviously the sergeant's mother.

Purcell gave a brief salute. "Mrs White, I'm Phillip Purcell, your son's officer. I'm just making a courtesy call on you for I thought I should meet you before the wedding, just to make my face known to you. I do hope it's a convenient time."

The look of bewilderment gave way to a warm welcoming smile. "Captain Purcell, come in. My son has often spoken about you."

He entered the house. "I hope you don't mind my calling on you like this. I've brought you these." He handed her the flowers.

"Thank you. They're beautiful. We're rather short of flowers. Please sit down, sir. Would you like some tea, or something stronger?"

"Neither, thank you. I had lunch on the train. Are you ready for the wedding? I should imagine it's hard work."

"Everything is ready. That's why I'm able to take it easy this afternoon. My son is so pleased that you and his mates are able to come to the wedding. You see, sir, the army has always been his whole life, so it only seems right that you all should be here. He has been a good son."

"Where is he now, Mrs White?"

"He has gone to meet the other soldiers at the railway station. We're putting them up. The whole family is pitching in as they live close by. That's how it is down here."

"What do you think of your new grandson?"

"He's lovely, and already I'm fond of his mother. She's a quiet, gentle girl." She stopped and smiled faintly. "We're glad that he's settled down at last."

The conversation was then interrupted by the arrival of a younger, plain woman.

Mrs White introduced her. "This is my sister-in-law, Kath. She's married to my younger brother, who is a docker here. And, Kath, this is Captain Purcell, our Charlie's officer, who has come to London for the wedding. Would you put these flowers in water? The captain brought them for me."

Listening and observing her, it was clear to the officer that the sergeant was correct when he said his mother ruled the entire roost. With her chirpy cockney manner, she showed all the grit and resolution of her breed.

Her smile quickly disappeared as a resounding knock on the front door echoed throughout the house. "Who the hell can that be? I'm sorry, Captain, but I was hoping that we could have a quiet private chat together."

"I will answer it," called out Kath from the kitchen.

"You're very much in demand today," the officer teased.

She laughed softly, but he could see that she was really concentrating on the conversation that was being held on her front doorstep.

Then there was a startled cry from her sister-in-law, as quick determined footsteps drew near.

A young attractive woman burst into the room where they were sitting. She carried a baby. "I'm sorry for bursting into your house

like this, Mrs White, but you should know what's going on."

"You've no right to come in here. You've a bloody cheek," exploded Kath, who had followed her in.

Purcell and Mrs White sat speechless.

The young woman turned towards Kath. "This isn't your house. That's your trouble — you've a big mouth. You're good at minding other people's business. Why did you tell my husband about this baby?"

"Why shouldn't I? He's away at sea and you're here, having a fine old time. There's too much of this going on."

The young woman turned to Mrs White to explain. "I was going to tell my husband when he returned. How can you hide a baby? He's been away at sea for ages."

"That's no excuse for your whoring," Kath interrupted.

She was ignored. The young woman continued, "He arrived home about an hour ago and was unloading his kitbags from the taxi when she stormed up and told him everything. I heard her. He told the cabbie to wait and came into the house. When he saw the baby he went berserk and left. I watched him go. That's the end of our marriage. I know I was to blame, but if we'd been given the chance to quietly talk it over, then we might have worked something out. It was my place to tell him, not hers." The young woman stopped talking, then gently placed the sleeping child onto a nearby couch. She then turned to Kath. "I can't carry on alone, so you can have him. You see, your husband is the father. We did more than fire-watching together." So saying the young mother calmly walked out of the room and the house.

"The bastard. So that's why he was so keen to go on his nightly duties of fire-watching. I'll find him and kill him," Kath shouted. She tore out of the house.

There was a strained silence from the other two whilst the innocent babe slumbered on.

"My God, I'm so sorry about this. What must you think of us, Captain. I feel so ashamed. I had no idea about any of this. Do you know, they haven't even closed my front door behind them."

Purcell rose at once, seeing the woman's agitated distress. "I'll go and close it. You stay with the baby."

When he reached the threshold he found two large paper bags, filled with the child's belongings, dumped on top of a pram. These

he gently pulled into the house, away from the curious stares of passers-by.

"She also left these," he told Mrs White as he wheeled them in.

The woman grimaced grimly. "Then she meant what she said," was her verdict.

"What are you going to do? This couldn't have happened at a worse time — just hours before the wedding."

The woman bent over the sleeping child and her gaze was one of tenderness. "Poor little mite, no one else seems to want him, but I do, Captain. He's my brother's son. I can see the likeness. He belongs to this family. We'll rear him and love him. He can grow up with my grandson. Life is funny. For years there have been only girls. There are four granddaughters. Now, in a matter of weeks, we have two baby boys."

The officer was touched by the sincerity of the woman. He briskly rose, not wanting to overstay his welcome. "Not a word of what has happened here today will pass my lips, Mrs White, I promise you," he assured her.

"I believe you, sir. Everything my son has said about you is true. I'm pleased that you came today. It was meant to be."

"Then we'll meet again tomorrow. I'm looking forward to my first East End wedding." He shook her hand warmly and left.

The next day dawned bright and sunny. What a difference there was now in the square as Phillip Purcell arrived. The road was blocked off, allowing the placing of several long tables, covered with white cloths. People were busily stacking crockery and cutlery on them, whilst others were struggling with many chairs.

The officer was pleased to see that his flowers had pride of place on the top table. There was much good-humoured talk and banter as they toiled. No one noticed the officer as he stood and took in the scene.

Suddenly there was a shout. "Captain Purcell, over here, sir."

He looked across to where Jones, Woods and Harvey had just emerged from the sergeant's house. He made his way across to them.

"Good morning, sir," they greeted him.

"Good morning."

"Come into the house, sir. The sergeant is ready. We've been waiting for you," Jones told him as he led the way.

The sergeant beamed when he saw his officer. "I'm glad you got here safely, sir. I was sorry to miss you, but I was meeting these lads."

"I know, Sergeant. Your mother told me."

"You made a great hit there, sir, with my mother. She said that you were a great comfort to her with all that was going on here. Thanks a lot, Captain. I'm only sorry that you had to witness it. My mother felt very ashamed."

"That's best forgotten. I didn't give it a second thought."

"That's exactly what I told my mother, sir. I said you'd take it in your stride."

The captain looked shrewdly at the soldier, who reacted at once.

"What I mean, sir, is you've already had more than your fair share of my antics, haven't you?"

Purcell laughed. "You mean it runs in the family, White."

"Something like that, sir," he answered quite unabashed.

The sergeant quickly changed mood as he told them, "We'd better get to the church."

He led the way out. The sergeant was the subject of much barracking and backslapping by the still-busy group of workers.

In reply to Purcell's questioning glance, he explained, "They're friends and neighbours, sir. We're very close down here."

"I thought that they were probably family, Sergeant."

"Oh, God, no, sir. They'll all be at the church. We only have to walk to the next street, so it isn't far."

There wasn't much standing in the next street, only high piles of rubble with a cleared pathway down the middle. At the far end of the street stood the solitary church.

"That's funny. How on earth did that survive?" exclaimed Harvey.

"It's about the only thing around here that has — and our square, of course. There isn't much left," the sergeant told them.

They picked their way up to the door and entered. The soft strains of the ancient organ filled the church. The place was packed to overflowing. Curious, expectant faces were turned to see the latest arrivals.

White proudly led the soldiers up to the front pew, aware that all eyes were upon them. With much ado he ushered the captain and the others into their places. Then, with Jones, he stood in front of the altar to await the bride.

They had only just made it, for in a matter of seconds she arrived together with her bridesmaids. She slowly walked up the aisle escorted by the groom's younger brother, and stood next to her husband-to-be. She looked extremely attractive dressed in the expected white.

The ceremony commenced with the able Jones doing his duty as best man, whilst the sergeant tried his hardest to appear calm and collected.

"He's shaking like a leaf," whispered Woods with glee. "She'll be the taming of him."

"Marriage is like that, I know." Harvey whispered back. "He'll never be the same again."

Purcell nodded his agreement and smiled.

When the wedding ceremony was over, the guests followed the bridal pair back to the square and the reception.

"The sarge would have liked transport, but this cleared path isn't wide enough for cars," Jones knowingly confided to them.

Back in the square they found the bride and groom seated at the top table along with their nearest relatives. The soldiers were shown to the nearest table on the right of the newly-weds.

White anxiously watched their progress, then gave the thumbs-up when they were settled in their seats.

"Charlie has given strict instructions that you should be given the best of attention," they were told as they were plied with food and drink. There was an abundance of both.

Very soon all barriers were down as tongues loosened.

"You boys gave the wedding what was needed — a bit of class," was the comment from one guest. "There's something special about those red berets of yours. You are the latest, most modern part of our army. We're proud of our Charlie — Snowy, as you call him. Let's drink to him and to you — his mates."

All glasses were enthusiastically raised.

"There's no shortage of anything here, is there, sir?" Harvey remarked.

"There certainly isn't. It's better than the mess."

"Now we can see where the sergeant gets his traits from," Woods laughed. "He can conjure up something, even in the middle of the desert."

"What do you mean?"

"Well, Captain, it was just before the last big battle. You were away, if you remember. We had a lot of really top brass coming, so the sergeant stole one of the Arab's goats. They were passing at the time. It was cooked and the top brass were very impressed."

"Weren't they curious?"

"Oh, no, sir. They were glad to get something different to eat. There were no questions asked, but it gave us trouble when they had gone and we were on our own again."

"The Arabs were furious — hopping mad," Jones interrupted. "It cost us quite a bit to calm them down."

"My good watch, for instance," Harvey put in. "They fleeced us. You see, sir, suddenly, out of the desert, more of their mates arrived. We were heavily outnumbered. The sergeant had to do a swift bit of bargaining there."

"So he should have done," Jones continued. "It was him, silly bastard, who had caused all the trouble in the first place."

"He's a true East Ender," crowed the older guest, who had been listening to all of this. "He'll never change."

"I must agree with you," Purcell politely replied.

A little later on the sergeant came over to their table. "Have you had plenty of everything?" he enquired.

"It's a feast," he was told.

"This rationing doesn't worry your family, then, Sarge?" There was a mischievous note in Harvey's observation.

"Well, working in the docks does help, and there are always ways and means, even in war. Of course we all had to put in a special effort for this."

At that moment the bridesmaids skipped by, full of pride in their frilly dresses.

White looked after them approvingly. "They look well turned out, don't they? They've never had dresses like these. Nor has my wife for that matter."

White cast a shrewd eye towards the captain, who returned his look with a cynical half smile. "Yes, Sergeant, I do recognise the material used."

White smiled sheepishly. "Well, sir, parachutes do get ripped and torn." He paused, allowing his words to sink in, then went on, "I managed to get a couple of these, and the women in the family

made use of them. They were a godsend, I can tell you."

Luckily for the sergeant, there was no more time to continue this conversation, for the other tables were being cleared and dragged to the side of the road.

"We have to make room for the band and dancing," a mightily relieved White explained, "but you can still carry on with your drinking there. Now the real fun begins. You'll see a real old knees-up."

Purcell rose slowly. "I shall have to go, for I've a shorter leave than you. Have a great time, all of you." He turned to White: "Let's go and find your parents, because I want to express my thanks to them and take my leave."

"Yes, sir. They've quietly slipped away to see to the babies, sir," the soldier said.

"And how is your son, Sergeant?"

"He's fine, sir — a real beauty. I know I shouldn't say that, but he is."

Inside they found the sergeant's parents relaxing.

Mrs White jumped to her feet as she told her husband, "This is the captain, John."

The older man's handshake was warm and genuine. "I'm meeting you at last, sir. Thank you for coming to my son's wedding."

"Thank you for inviting me."

Mrs White interrupted: "Sit down, Captain."

"I will, but not for long as I've to report back for duty tonight. My taxi will be coming soon."

"Have you enjoyed your first taste of the East End?" Mr White asked.

"I certainly have, even amongst all this devastation. I take my hat off to you all here."

The older man shrugged this away. "You're much younger than I'd imagined, sir."

Purcell laughed and glanced across at the sergeant. "And was wet behind the ears when I first joined the regiment, as I suppose your son has told you."

"But you weren't that way for long, were you, sir?"

"You're correct, Sergeant. In wartime one has to learn quickly." The officer reached into his breast pocket and brought out a folded paper which he handed over to a surprised White. "I hadn't a clue

what to get you for your wedding, so I thought this was the answer."

The sergeant glanced at the cheque, then quickly passed it on to his parents. "This is very generous of you, sir," he said. "I'm pleased that you even bothered to come to my wedding. Not many other officers would have done. I appreciate that."

"Well, as I explained, I'm useless at buying presents, so came to the conclusion that you and your wife would know exactly what to get."

"That's very sensible, sir," put in the sergeant's mother. "They'll soon have to get together a home of their own. My son is lucky to have an officer like you."

"There is just one other thing I want to know," broke in the officer, keen to change the conversation. "How are you coping with this latest addition to your family, Mrs White?"

She smiled broadly as she replied, "He's settled in well, and is being spoilt to death by our granddaughters. My brother is keeping his distance because he wants to save his marriage. We agree with this. He has a good wife. She's not to blame in any way."

"And the child's mother? Has she made any further contact?"

"No, she's gone, sir, for good, I'd say."

"That suits you, Mrs White?"

"It does, Captain. Things will all work out in the end."

Purcell glanced at his watch then rose to go. "Take it easy now," he told the sergeant's parents. "Your day is far from over. Thank you again for your warm welcome."

They shook hands and immediately White was at his captain's side. "I'll see you to your taxi, sir. You didn't get the chance to speak with my wife. At the moment she's upstairs feeding the baby. You understand, sir."

"I'm sure that I'll meet her at some other time. Don't worry."

"Yes, sir."

Purcell was given a rousing send-off by the rest of the wedding guests, who also insisted on walking with him to the end of the street where his taxi awaited.

The officer managed to single out his own men and told them quietly, "Will see you back at camp. Enjoy yourselves."

He left behind a jovial festive party.

Chapter Four

Within a few days the captain and his men were back in the routine of the camp; only this time there was a difference. All training had been stepped up a gear, giving cause for the usual speculation and gossip.

In the truck that was taking them from the airfield back to camp, Purcell was aware of the unease and apprehension of the men.

"We have doubled our drops, sir," Harvey observed, whilst the others quietly sat.

"Yes, we have. There must be some reason for it. As yet, it's all rumour, but we all know what we've been trained for."

"It's this hanging around waiting that gets me down," another complained.

"We are definitely on standby now, aren't we, sir?"

"All leave has been cancelled, so we are on a state of alert, although it's not official as yet. Any time now, I should say."

"It's just a matter of waiting for the right winds and tides, then we can get cracking, can't we, Captain?" the sergeant said.

"Yes, Sergeant, you've got it."

"I tell you what, lads, I'd sooner be doing what we're doing than riding in those bloody landing crafts. The sea can be worse than the enemy," the sergeant continued.

"I can't even swim," another soldier piped up.

"At least we'll be together in the plane, so that's a good start, isn't it, Sarge?" someone else said.

"Of course. We've trained together to become a fighting unit under fire, so we know how to look out for each other as best we can. And we have the captain here. We have the best chance, I'd say, to whip the enemy."

Later that evening all officers were called to a briefing. Purcell and the padre went in together. They were now firm friends — being in the same unit had strengthened this.

"I think we all have a fair idea of what the old man is going to say, John."

"That it could be at any time?"

The colonel wasted no time and began, "Well, gentlemen, our waiting is almost over. For us, the second front is about to commence. Exactly what time I cannot tell you, but we could be only hours away. It's all up to the weather and the tides. Apparently this time of year should be most favourable for both, but one never can tell. It takes only a sudden wind to spring up, then all plans have to be altered. We're not in the first phase. That will be the Americans, in their landing crafts, with their accompanying canopy of cover from both the navy and the airforce. We are expecting to get our go-ahead once the footholds and landing strips have been secured and our forces are moving inwards. That's what should happen, but on the other hand, the planned strategy could all go badly wrong — such is war. So we must consider ourselves on standby from now on. As a fighting force we are competent and ready, may it go well for us. Thank you, gentlemen."

The next morning the news broke for all the world to hear — the landings had begun.

"Is there any special change to our routine, Colonel?" enquired Purcell.

"No, Captain. Keep everything as usual for it will be best for morale — it makes the waiting easier to bear — just as long as we are ready for any eventuality."

"Yes, sir."

As the officer did his rounds he was informed of the latest developments in the campaign by whoever were able to listen to the up-to-the-minute reports on the radio.

"Everything is going well, sir. The Americans have secured some of the beaches and are already moving inland, but there are heavy losses in the landing crafts. The enemy is throwing the lot at them."

"All roads leading to our south ports are choked, sir," someone else volunteered, "They are driving bumper to bumper. It has to be

seen to be believed, so they say."

"Progress reports are coming in all the time, so we are not turning off the wireless, if that's all right with you, sir."

"Keep it going, by all means, so that you can be our constant source of information, Corporal. After all, we're only idling away our time here until it's our turn."

"Yes, Captain. Will do."

In the mess that night the dominating topic was the campaign.

"The Germans are putting up a fanatical, ferocious resistance, but then we always knew they would. They are so firmly entrenched they will be formidable," the colonel observed to his fellow officers.

"Is there any indication yet of when we'll be joining in the fray, sir?" asked an impatient officer.

"Not a word so far. I should think it will be some time ahead, for the landing forces will be made to fight every step of the way. Knowing the enemy, it's going to be tough."

The unfolding drama was closely followed by the soldiers. Eventually their turn came. The whole camp was on the move and calmly clambering into the trucks taking them to the airfield. There was quiet, well-drilled discipline in every move they made.

It was early in the morning — barely daybreak. Purcell did a last check with his sergeant. "Is everyone on board, Sergeant?"

"Yes, sir."

"And all our equipment and arms?"

"Yes, sir. I've double-checked. All is correct."

"Right, Sergeant, then we're ready to go."

They drove to the landing strip in silence, each man deep in thought. The light of day was stronger by the time they lurched to a halt. The dismounting soldiers' first glance was directed to the waiting aircraft, which were standing, stark and ungainly, on the runway.

"Stand easy, Sergeant," Purcell ordered when the men had lined up.

More trucks were arriving by the minute until the entire company were assembled. The colonel and his aide made their way to each band of waiting men, talking to the officers in charge.

"All present and correct, Captain?"

"Yes, sir. Is the padre going to be with us?"

"Yes. He travelled here with us because he wanted to mingle with the many Catholics amongst the other units. He wanted to give them special words of comfort and encouragement. He did express a preference for dropping into the actual war zone with you. You've become close friends, haven't you, Phillip?"

"Yes, we have, sir. Surprising really, seeing that I'm not religious."

"Oh, I don't know. They say that war makes strange bedfellows."

"We're not that close, sir." Purcell laughed.

The other two also laughed as the colonel replied, "I wasn't meaning to infer anything like that. He's not a bad chap seeing that he's one of the cloth. The men put great store by him, and it isn't only the Catholics. Well, best of luck, Captain. We'll all need it. You'll go first in ten minutes." With this the two officers walked away.

Sergeant White approached as soon as they were out of earshot.

"I couldn't help overhearing, sir. So the padre is coming with us, then?"

"Yes, Sergeant."

"I'm pleased about that, sir, because the men were wondering why he wasn't with us, seeing that he's always been before. It's made them uneasy, sir."

"I must admit it has felt strange without him. Comes of training together, I suppose."

"Yes, sir. The men feel lucky when he's around. Better the devil you know, sir."

The officer had to smile at the sergeant's ill-chosen words.

At the given time the captain and his men marched towards the aircraft and installed themselves, as they had learned to do, in an orderly and efficient manner.

At the very last minute Father Morris heaved his large frame through the doorway and lumbered up the narrow gangway towards his friend.

"You left it a bit tight. I thought that you weren't going to make it." There was a welcoming tone in Purcell's remark.

The padre could only nod as he plonked himself down on the wooden bench. "I've been running," he panted.

A buzz had gone around among the soldiers at this last-minute

appearance of the padre. Now they were complete.

"We thought that you would be going with the others, Father, because a lot of them are Catholic," someone said.

"Although I'm Catholic, I'm here for all of you, and after doing my training with you it only felt right that I should go into action with you," he answered.

"Plus the fact that you know we're really the best of the bunch. Isn't that right, Father?"

"If you say so, Sergeant, but don't let the others hear your views."

Captain Purcell was in a more serious mood. "Attention, everyone. The plane's engines will be starting up at any time now, so I will speak whilst I am able. We don't know what we'll be flying into, so try and remember and act upon what you have learned. When landed, one's first priority is to seek out and band together as a unit under myself, or, failing that, under the command of any of our officers. Don't be put off by whatever is happening around you; just concentrate on establishing yourselves with your own, and take it from there. In one hour's time we shall eat the food we've been provided with, for, from then on, food will be the least of our worries."

Purcell paused here for breath just as the engines spluttered into life then rose to a deafening roar. The plane shook as it began to slowly move. Purcell lurched unsteadily back onto the bench. They were on their way at last.

Sitting closely packed together, these experienced men silently sat as the mighty engines lifted the aircraft up and away from earth.

Only when they were high amongst the clouds did they react to their situation. Cigarettes were lit as they began to relax. The steady drone of the engines seemed to reassure them, the officer noted, for they had done this so many times.

At a given nod from the captain, the padre and the sergeant joined him, cautiously moving among the men, talking and listening to them. This had not happened before, but nobody mentioned the fact.

"Have you all written home as I advised?" Purcell asked.

"Yes, sir." There was agreement from those within earshot.

"Good. We must keep our families informed. This will be a worrying time for them." The officer then glanced over to where the sergeant was obviously having difficulty with one of the men.

"The sergeant looks as though he could do with a helping hand," he explained as he edged over to him. "Having trouble, Sergeant?"

"Yes, sir. It's Robinson. He suddenly collapsed and slid to the floor."

Between them they eased the soldier into a better position.

"He's been having terrible stomach cramp, sir," the man sitting nearest said.

The sergeant quietly confided to his officer, "It's nerves, sir. A lot of men suffer this before they go into action. It affects each one differently. Come on, Robinson, let's be having you, old son."

With an unexpected gentle touch the toughened White began to revive the stricken young soldier.

Within seconds he began to respond, and gazed up stupidly into his sergeant's face. "Sarge?"

"It's all right. You passed out, but you'll be fighting fit in no time."

The officer and sergeant helped him back onto the bench.

"I had bad bellyache. It doubled me up," Robinson told them.

Again the sergeant confided to Purcell, "It'd be better if he ate something now, sir."

"That's a sound idea, White. I'll pass the word around if it will help."

"Yes, sir. You'll find it will," the experienced White said.

A few minutes later the padre noted, "I saw you and White having a spot of bother."

"Yes, John. Robinson had fainted. White advised that it's better if we eat our food now, so would you pass this on."

"Yes, I'll do it straight away."

Later, as these two men sat munching on their food, the padre remarked, "Do you know what I admire about you, Phillip?"

"No. What?"

"Your ability to take good advice from your sergeant. You do it with — well — almost dignity. A lot of officers would never be able to cope with it."

Purcell laughed as he told him, "I've told you that both my father and grandfather were military men. They've always maintained that a good sergeant makes a good officer, providing that both accept this fact. To be honest, I admit it and agree with it."

The two men smiled as they sat there warm and secure in their

mutual respect for each other.

The captain glanced around and noticed the striking difference now in the behaviour of the soldiers. They sat unusually still — even the sergeant was subdued. It was as though the repetitive drone of the engines was mesmerising all on board.

This abruptly ended when suddenly the door to the cockpit opened and one of the flight crew made his way to Purcell. All heads turned as inquisitive eyes watched.

"Captain Purcell, we'll be over the dropping zone in roughly fifteen minutes, sir."

"Thank you. We'll be ready."

The officer got briskly to his feet and gave a prearranged signal which resulted in every man present switching into action. With calm efficiency chutes were again checked and harnessed, together with the many other accessories needed to be carried on the mission.

In a very limited amount of time the soldiers were perched precariously on the edge of their seats, fully kitted out, with their weapons firmly attached. There was an air of anticipation.

The time had come. The captain and sergeant watched closely, ready to give a hand if needed, but every man had clearly been well trained.

One member of the aircrew had stationed himself next to the exit door, awaiting the order.

There was heavy turbulence as the plane headed into the combat area. The sound of exploding enemy fire engulfed the plane as it droned steadily on. The din could be heard over the engines, and occasionally the aircraft shook and shuddered as the gunfire came perilously near.

At the given time the heavy exit doors were opened. Captain Purcell positioned himself at the head of the men, who had lined up in orderly fashion. With a final salute to them, he stepped out.

The gusty rush of fresh air was welcome, for it had become unbearably hot back in the plane. There was the usual pang of anxiety until the chute responded, jerking sharply, then billowing out and checking the fall. He wrenched himself around as best he could and, with pounding heart, saw that he was not alone — the sky was filled with drifting, floating airborne soldiers.

He vainly tried to make out his own men, but this was an impossibility for the enemy fire had intensified. Shells, rockets and

gunfire exploded all around the descending figures. The sky was streaked with black trails of smoke.

Purcell looked down at the nearing earth below. All hell was being let loose down there, with gigantic flashes of light appearing as heavy artillery pounded out its greeting of death and destruction. Lorries, trucks, tanks and armoured vehicles were strewn everywhere at random.

The officer grimly recalled a similar scene in the desert, but this was on a comparably larger scale — huge, in fact.

The nearer to earth they floated the more terrifying it became. The noise split the eardrums and the evidence of spent ammunition could even be tasted — bitter, acidic, choking the lungs and making the eyes smart and water.

The landing itself was simple, and Purcell feverishly tore at the many fasteners, wishing to quickly rid himself of the parachute. This done, he was able to take in the situation.

Men were landing like flies all around him, and were struggling to free themselves from their chutes just as he had done. He scanned the soldiers, trying to pick out his own men. With a start he recognised his sergeant.

Ignoring all others, he joined White who was bending over a prostrate figure. The sergeant looked up at his officer, and without a word indicated the man lying at their feet. It was young Robinson. His eyes were wide open, staring, unseeing, and he was covered in blood.

"He is beyond help, sir." The sergeant had to shout to make himself heard.

The captain and his sergeant stuck closely together as they sought the rest of their unit. The flak on the ground was intense and several times they were blown off their feet but, luckily, were able to get up again and continue.

It was devastating to see the number of casualties this bombardment was causing, although it was obvious to the two soldiers that many of the men had been killed whilst descending to this hell. They lay in grotesque positions, surrounded and almost engulfed in the ample folds of their parachutes.

The captain and sergeant forced themselves to inspect the fallen men, for they had to determine if any of their unit was amongst them.

As they floundered around in the terrible turmoil, the sergeant suddenly clutched the captain's arm and pointed. "There's the padre and some of the others, sir," he shouted.

There was relief all round as they met up.

The padre, Jones, Harvey and Woods, fell in beside them.

"Keep closely together. We are to make for the bridge. Those are our orders," Purcell bellowed.

As they struggled onwards they were approached by others.

"Captain, we'll have to fall in with you, sir, for our officers are dead."

"Very well, Sergeant Major. Let's get to the bridge."

"Yes, sir."

They skirted the fallen as they picked a path along the bloody battleground.

Everywhere was slippery with shed blood, but the soldiers relentlessly pushed on towards the bridge.

Captain Purcell glanced upwards. The skies were filled with falling parachutes coming from large gliders which were being towed along by planes.

The enemy guns responded immediately, turning their direction of fire away from their ground targets.

"Here's our chance. Let's make the most of it," Purcell shouted.

He turned to lead the way but there was a deafening explosion, then instant blackness — nothing.

The noises invaded his consciousness, disturbing, troubling him. He tried hard to ignore them, wanting only to slip away from it all, but they grew more insistent so that he was forced to listen.

Keeping his eyes firmly closed he grappled with the state of semi-stupor he was in. Gradually his curiosity got the better of him and he opened his eyes. A silent nun glided past the foot of the bed on which he was lying. Her tall wimple bobbed as she went along, and that, together with her flowing robes, severely startled him.

He closed his eyes as his heart pounded within him. "Oh, my God, I'm dead and am in heaven!" he anguished aloud.

Immediately there was the sound of quickly approaching footsteps. He ventured to look.

"Nay, laddie, you're very much alive," said the Scottish doctor standing beside his bed.

"I thought . . ." the captain struggled for words. "When I opened my eyes and saw . . ." He pointed to the nun who had now joined them.

There was a smile from both, then the doctor said, "You thought that you were dead? No, you're in a Belgian hospital, and these are the sisters who nurse here."

Purcell suddenly tried to sit up but a searing pain shot across the top half of his body, making him cry out in pain. He fell back on the pillows as the agony engulfed him. He felt a sharp prick as the needle entered his flesh and he mercifully passed out.

For the next few days he slipped in and out of this world of acute pain and discomfort, relieved only by the regular injections. Then the healing began and the dosage lessened, so at last he became aware of what was happening around him.

"You are improving each day," he was told. "Soon you will be up and walking."

"Will I, Sister? I haven't been told how badly I've been injured, and I'm too frightened to ask. I know I have a plate in my shoulder."

"Do not worry. You will be spoken to very soon. I think that you are well enough to have a visitor."

"Visitor? Here?"

"Yes. Today he should be able to reach you. He has been trying hard. I am not going to tell you who it is. Wait and see."

The nun bustled off. Purcell lay wondering who his visitor might be. For the first time his mind conjured up those hellish last moments before he was hit — the horror of it all. His mind shied away from the fate of the others who had been with him.

He was so engrossed with his thoughts and fears, that it wasn't until the approaching man on crutches was almost at his bedside that he became aware of his visitor.

"Sergeant White — Snowy White," he gasped.

"Yes, sir." The sergeant swayed unsteadily as he pushed a chair into position then slumped heavily down. He propped his crutches against the bed then nodded cockily to his captain. "I've been practising this for days so that I could get here, sir. You've had us all worried because you should have come round much sooner, but I told them you were tough and would make it in the end."

"So you knew I was here?"

"Yes, sir. We're the only two here from our lot. I was hit the same time as you but I remained conscious the whole time. They only put me out here when they operated."

"But you will make a full recovery? You will be able to walk in time?"

"They say it will be some time before I'm fully healed, but I'll have a permanent limp, sir."

"I'm sorry to hear that, White, for I know that you wanted to continue in the army."

The sergeant cheerily interrupted: "Not now, sir. I've recently made up my mind that I'm too long in the tooth for combat. Now I'm as eager as you for the war to end, and to be able to get out and try something else."

The two men lapsed into silence, then the sergeant added, "With this limp I've had it anyway, sir."

Purcell lay, digesting the other's words. He wasn't taken in by the sergeant's show of bravado. "What happened to the others, Sergeant?" he said softly.

White didn't answer but pointed to the nun who was coming in their direction. He glanced down at his wristwatch, then began to gather up his crutches. "My time is up, I'm afraid, sir. I was warned not to stay long because you're still very weak. Sister, would you help me, please?" he asked the nun, who at once helped. As soon as he was safely ensconced on his crutches and was ready to go he looked his old chirpy self. "Will see you tomorrow, sir. We must do everything by the book, else they will stop my visits. I've pushed my luck so far, but you know me, sir."

"Yes, I certainly do, Sergeant. Take care now." The captain tried to match White's bravado. He watched as White laboured down the ward, helped by the nun. His heart was heavy.

"He has been asking and worrying about you from the moment you both arrived," the nun told him later.

"I asked about the others in our unit but he ignored me, Sister. That's an ominous sign."

"You must not be alarmed. These are early days in your recuperation."

"We've been through a lot together, Sister."

"So you are old friends?"

"No, Sister. This war brought us together, otherwise we would never have met, but I'm glad that we did."

"Such is the way of God."

From then onwards, Purcell's great relief from the depressing hospital routine was when the sergeant made his daily visit.

"These nuns are excellent nursing sisters."

"Yes, they are, sir. Did you recognise the Scottish doctor in charge?"

"No, Sergeant."

"He travelled out with us to North Africa and tore us off a strip about getting VD. You remember that lecture, sir?"

"So that's him. I'd forgotten his face. A lot has happened since then."

"It seems a lifetime away, sir. He won't have to worry about that epidemic here, will he?"

Both men laughed quietly together. A passing nun glanced with surprise at the two men, for laughter there was an unusual sound.

"We're doing really well, sir, you and me. Tomorrow I'm being allowed to push your wheelchair out into the gardens. I'm damned glad to be rid of those crutches. I feel normal again."

Next day the two soldiers relaxed in the peace of the gardens.

Purcell spoke in a low voice to his companion. "You can now tell me about the others. I'm sufficiently recovered."

"I was warned that you were not to be worried, sir. You were very sick then."

"I knew that, Sergeant. That's why I never pressed you to tell me."

The sergeant glanced away at some other patients hobbling slowly along. "We're the only two left, sir, from our mob," he half whispered.

"God Almighty! All of them? Even John Morris?"

The sergeant still kept his face half turned away from Purcell. "Yes, Captain, even the padre. I lay there wounded, watching it all happen around me. I was waiting for another burst to come and finish me off. You were lying there covered in blood. I thought you were dead too. I don't know how long I lay there. It seemed like hours. Then some medics came, sorting out the wounded from the killed." Here the sergeant paused as he recalled his painful

memories. "I called out to the medics, and they fixed me up as best they could. I watched as they checked the others — Woods, Jones, Harvey, the padre and the other men who had joined us. They found that you were still breathing; so you and I were the only ones that were dragged away from there." The sergeant stopped talking for a minute, then continued, "We took a bloody beating that day, sir — a real hammering." He turned towards the young officer, who sat there with tears streaming down his face. White turned swiftly away. "I cried on that day, sir. I cried for the others I knew, lying there dead. I cried for the men there who were complete strangers to me. I told myself it was because I was weak and wounded, but I don't know. I was a toughened old soldier who had seen active service before. I suppose in the end it all catches up with you, no matter how tough you are."

They sat together in that garden in Belgium until the shadows lengthened and the air grew chilly. They talked quietly and earnestly, all the time regaining their composure. Now the real healing could begin.

A nursing nun watched with a compassionate gaze as the two soldiers reluctantly made their way inside. "They are now strong enough to go back to their own country," she observed.

Several days later her words came true.

"I know you've heard the great news, Sergeant." The captain was elated when White came to take him for his constitutional.

"That we're going home tomorrow? Yes, sir. Just think, sir, this will be our last airing in this garden. I can't believe it — to get away from war and hospital. We won't sleep much tonight."

"Well, I haven't quite finished with hospitals, but I'm well on the way, so they say."

"It's only a matter of time now, sir," he was assured.

Purcell finally slept that night only to be awakened some short time later. There was a hushed urgency about the nuns as they bustled around, placing newly arrived patients in some recently vacated beds.

A prone figure was deposited into the empty bed next to him. Bed curtains were drawn as a doctor and nurse tended to him.

The doctor didn't remain long, but hurried over to the others.

The nun emerged later, carefully drawing together the curtains behind her.

Only then did she see that Purcell was wide awake. "Did we awaken you?" she whispered.

"You're working hard tonight, Sister."

"Yes, yes. We have many admissions. This one is an American soldier. He got here too late." She showed Purcell the identification tag she had just removed. "We have so many of these — all nationalities. There will come the time when their loved ones will learn of their death here. We'll remove him as soon as we can. Now you must try and sleep. You will travel far tomorrow." She moved away.

The captain lay still, following the hurried movements of the hospital staff as they toiled through the next few hours. Then, finally, with a decided determination, he firmly pressed the small bell next to his bed. Within seconds a younger doctor came.

"I've tried hard not to disturb you, Doctor, but Sister is wrong about the patient in the next bed. He's not dead. He's making noises and seems to be moving around in the bed."

The doctor didn't answer, but went behind the curtains at once. He reappeared some seconds later and curtly told him, "He's dead. There's no pulse. What you've heard are the noises of death." He abruptly left, leaving the captain feeling foolish.

Early next morning the captain awoke and immediately began to gather together his few belongings.

"I see you are all ready to go."

"Yes, Sister. I was told that we'd be leaving straight after breakfast."

"That is correct. We are needing the beds for there are many more wounded coming."

Not very much later, Sergeant White arrived carrying his few bits and pieces. "Good morning, sir. As I'm pushing your wheelchair I hoped you could cope with our things."

"Of course, Sergeant. You can see we are both travelling light. No problem."

They both laughed as they surveyed their scant luggage.

"We're leaving with seven others."

"Yes, I heard that, sir."

They made their way to the front entrance, all the time stopping to bid the nursing nuns goodbye and to thank them for their care.

The other departing men were assembled and awaiting them.

"Good morning. This is what we've been waiting for," Purcell gleefully said.

"Yes, sir. Good morning, sir," they replied.

Their delight and eagerness was obvious as they boarded the ambulance.

Even the later uncomfortable flight home in the freight plane couldn't dampen their spirits, although one complained, "How I hate flying. I could never have joined the Paras."

"Watch it, old son," Sergeant White warned; "the captain and I belong to that mob."

There were sympathetic glances from the others, then they began to talk of things more cheerful.

The captain confided to White in a confidential tone, "What a night it was in my ward! There were several new admissions so the doctors and nuns were working flat out. There was an American placed next to me. After he was pronounced dead he made noises and moved around in the bed. Thinking that he was still alive I called the doctor, but was told that these were the usual movements of death. I never want to experience anything like that again."

"I know how you felt, sir. This is the first time I've been wounded, and to lie there among the fallen is something I shall never forget, sir; but it's something we shall have to keep to ourselves, for most other people could never understand." The sergeant pondered for a moment, then brightly added, "We'll gradually get over it, sir."

"That's what living is all about, I suppose. We can't live with the dead."

"Exactly, sir. We've come through it. We're lucky."

They tuned in to the others' conversation.

"I'm going home to see my baby for the first time," one said.

"It's a pity we won't be with you, Bert, to wet the baby's head."

"My youngsters hardly know me," someone else continued. "During the last few years they've only seen me for the occasional leave. Each time it was hard to get close to them, and that can't be done in a few days. I should think it'll be over by the time we're fully fit. Do you think the same, sir?"

"Yes, Corporal. I think this is the beginning of the end. This war will soon be over."

"The first thing I'm going to have is a plate of fish and chips. I come from Whitby where they serve the best," someone asserted in a broad Yorkshire accent.

"Washed down with a pint of real ale," another suggested.

"I shall have a knees-up and sink a whole barrelful," Sergeant White boasted.

At this moment these men were the happiest alive.

The plane touched down some few hours later and the men stiffly emerged onto the tarmac.

"Welcome home," was the greeting from the military nursing staff who were awaiting them.

The medical officer in charge quickly took control: "This is the parting of the ways for you, Captain. The walking wounded have a different destination. You are to be hospitalised at once."

He signalled across to the waiting ambulances. The sergeant still kept a tight hold of the captain's wheelchair.

"Now you take care, sir, for it seems we're to be parted right away."

"I will; and take care of yourself, Sergeant. Make sure you write to my home. My father will forward it on and I will send you my next address as soon as I can."

"Yes, sir. Well, you know where I live. We mustn't lose touch."

"You're coming with us, Captain," the medical orderly explained as he went to take over from the sergeant.

"I'll help you put him in the ambulance." White stubbornly refused to comply with the orderly's wishes and resolutely pushed Purcell towards the waiting ambulance.

As the captain was lifted into the vehicle, his last glimpse of Sergeant White was of his standing below with his hand raised in salute. The officer responded, then the doors closed.

Some six months later the captain alighted from the train and slowly threaded his way through the throng of people on the platform at Waterloo Station. There was hustle and bustle everywhere.

Many glances were directed at the young soldier as he walked while leaning heavily on his stick. Female eyes were especially

appreciative as they took in his uniform, topped off by the red beret.

He was oblivious to any of this as he proceeded along to the taxi rank. He joined the long queue waiting.

The older man in front of him turned around. "May I ask where you are heading, Captain?"

"To the East End, sir."

"Then may I suggest we share a taxi. It's the done thing these days, for there's such a shortage of transport in the capital. I'm going in your direction, so you can drop me off on the way."

"That would be fine, sir. Thank you. I'm Purcell, sir — Phillip Purcell."

When their taxi finally arrived the stranger helped the soldier in, whilst the cabbie was unusually patient. After giving instructions to him, they sat back and relaxed.

Purcell looked out at the heavy passing traffic and chuckled, "Welcome back to the real world. That's how I feel at this moment."

"How long have you been out of it?"

"Six months in hospital here and a few weeks in Belgium. I'll be better when I become more mobile, but I'm not complaining, you understand."

The older man nodded in an understanding manner.

"I'm going to see my sergeant. He was also wounded."

"Does he know that you're visiting him?"

"Oh yes, he knows. I've already written to him. He'll be expecting my arrival."

The taxi stopped.

"This is where I get out, and I must say it was good to meet you, Phillip. I hope you have a great reunion with your sergeant. I'm impressed that you have such a strong relationship."

"From our unit, we are the only two left," the young officer sadly explained.

"Good luck, Captain," the other called as the taxi sped away.

The driver coughed discreetly and then said, "I'm not quite sure where this house is, sir."

"With all this bomb damage, you mean. I can direct you, for I've been here before. Go right here, and it's along on the left. Slow down, and here we are."

They drew up outside the house belonging to the sergeant's parents. Purcell got out and went to pay the fare.

"There's no need for money, Captain. It's taken care of already. The other gentleman paid it. He said that he felt that it was the least he could do. Goodbye, sir, and good luck."

The taxi sped off before the officer could hardly draw breath.

Purcell turned towards the house just as a beaming White emerged. "You made it, then, sir. I was worried, but can see that you're doing well — much better than the last time I saw you."

The captain laughed and shook his stick at him. "Only a walking stick now, Sergeant. Soon I'll be fully recovered. How are things with you?"

"Fine, sir, just fine. I'm working in the city now." He laughed self-consciously. "I'm a city gent now. Well, no, not quite, sir — just in security work in the West End. Come inside, sir, we have the house to ourselves for a change."

The two men relaxed in the homely atmosphere, each comfortable with the other.

"I had begun to forget, but seeing you again brings it all back, sir."

"I shall be able to put it all behind me when I finally take off this uniform, which should be in a few weeks' time. I have written to the families of the fallen men in our unit. I count that as one of the hardest things I've ever had to do. Sometimes words seem so inadequate, Sergeant."

The two sat silent for a while.

"Are you really settling in with civilian life? It must be hard for you."

"It was at first, sir, but I'm getting used to it. I'm buying a house here, just a few doors away, so I will be near to my family."

"Your mother will like that, Sergeant."

"Yes, sir, she does. She wants to be remembered to you. They all got out of the way today so that we could chat over old times together. They say we deserve it. What are you going to do with yourself now, sir?"

"I'm hoping to join the Colonial Service once I'm demobbed. Serving in Africa appeals to me."

"You should do well, for you can get along with anyone. You never put on airs and graces like so many officers do. All the boys said that, sir."

"Did they? While I think of it, White, how is the other child? —

the one who was abandoned by its mother on that day I was here."

"Nothing's changed. He is still living with us. We are bringing him up with our boy. Neither his mother or father are interested so he belongs to us now. You should see them, sir — they're growing and thriving. As my mother says, everything works out in the end. She says she has two grandsons now, but we know it isn't strictly true."

"And your wife, Sergeant?"

A smug smile spread across his face as he replied, "She's a real treasure, sir, she really is. Everyone here has taken to her, and she's pleased to belong to a large family. I've told you what we're like in the East End, we look after our own. There is one thing I'd like to suggest, sir: when this war has finally finished and things get back to normal, you and I should visit their graves in France — to pay our last respects. What do you think?"

"That's an excellent idea, Sergeant, but it will take time, you know. There will be many graves to list and sort out, but I would like to go there at some time."

"Then that's settled, sir. I just want them to know that they're not forgotten — not by us — and never will be. That sounds stupid, doesn't it? When you're dead, you're dead and gone, really."

"I understand how you feel."

"I knew you would, sir." He paused for a moment, then quietly asked, "Is my limp very noticeable, sir?"

"No, Sergeant, it isn't. Don't even think about it. It gives you an air of distinction."

"I don't know about that, sir, but I count myself lucky to have got such a good job. It doesn't involve my being on my feet a lot. Now I'll make us some tea. Do you remember in the desert, it was our remedy for most things?"

They talked for a long time, often laughing at their humorous memories (of which there were many), until the taxi returned for the captain.

"Before I go I want to give you this. Take it, I can well afford it." Purcell handed over a cheque to the dumbfounded White.

"You don't have to do this, sir."

"It'll help with the buying of your house, Sergeant. Take it."

"This will buy it, sir. Thank you very much."

They gravely shook hands.

"I expect it'll be some time before we meet again, Captain."

"We won't lose touch, Sergeant, never fear. I hope to meet the family next time. Give them my regards — especially your mother.

"I will, sir. Take care of yourself, then, sir. You won't have me around to keep an eye out for you from now on."

The officer laughed. "That's true, so I'll have to take great care." He turned to the waiting cab driver and gave him a slip of paper. "This is my next stop," he instructed.

"Before you go, sir, I want to give you something." He handed over a smallish package. "Don't open it now, but later."

Purcell looked at it curiously. "Why, thank you, Sergeant," he said.

"Goodbye, sir."

"Goodbye, Sergeant."

As the taxi rounded the corner, Purcell glanced back at the sergeant. He cut a lone forlorn figure standing there. The young officer felt a pang of depression; he felt a very binding friendship had just been stretched — but not broken, by any means.

After the stark desolation of the East End, the plush interior of this top-class restaurant immediately struck the captain as he entered. Under the discreet subdued lighting diners were enjoying their meal whilst the soft strains of background music played.

A waiter approached. "Good evening, sir."

"Good evening. I have just called on the off chance, to get some information regarding the cousin of the owner of this restaurant. We met during the earlier part of this war. I knew him as Theo."

"I see, sir. And your name is?"

"Purcell. Phillip Purcell."

"Please take a seat, Captain. I will see if I can get this information for you."

The waiter glided off and away through the doors leading to the kitchens.

As Purcell sat down he became aware that he was still clutching the package. He quickly opened it to reveal an antique silver hip flask. It was ornate, with his initials engraved upon it. He unscrewed the top and smelt the contents. "Brandy, and I bet it's the best," he muttered to himself with a wry smile. He recorked the flask and slipped it into his pocket just as the doors leading from the kitchens swung open.

Purcell looked with interest as several men approached his table. Two grey-haired men led, followed by a younger man.

As soon as the captain's gaze rested on the third man he gave a start of recognition. "Theo!" he exclaimed.

"Phillip, I thought I would never see you again."

They shook hands warmly, their delight obvious to the older men watching them.

"It has been such a long time. I've often wondered what had happened to you. I see you are in the Airborne Regiment, so you have been in the midst of it. Wait, I'm forgetting, first let me introduce you to my family elders."

The two elderly men solemnly shook hands then beckoned Purcell to be reseated.

"We will sit and have a celebration drink, Captain. We know all about you for Theo has spoken often," one said as the other brought over a tray of drinks and began to pour.

"Yes, indeed, sir," the captain agreed. "Those were very trying times. We were on the island for only a few days, but it was frightening for us. Theo and Dimitri coped very well under those dangerous circumstances. They put their very lives in danger, for if the enemy knew of our existence it would have been the end for us all."

"He is a good boy, our Theo, and our cousin, Dimitri," the other murmured.

Theo unexpectedly threw back his head and laughed loudly. "You know, Captain, it wasn't only the Germans who didn't realise what was going on. We didn't either. We were all taken in."

The captain frowned. "What do you mean?"

"Come on now. I'm sure that you had your suspicions at some time or another, didn't you?"

Purcell nodded thoughtfully. "Oh, many times. For a while you were my main suspect, especially when we hid out in Dimitri's barn. We saw how friendly you were with the enemy, and how fluently you spoke their language. You hadn't told us about that."

"You didn't ask," Theo broke in. "I'm just very good with languages. I can pick them up very quickly, and as we were living under the whip of the enemy it was essential for our well-being. But we were equally suspicious of you as well, you know. Suddenly we were contacted and told that three men were to be landed on our side of the island. There was nothing of great importance there,

so we had a right to be on our guard."

"What about the gun installation?"

"Well, there was that, I suppose, but we were nothing like the other side of the island — everything was going on there."

"But how did you know this? You told us that you and Dimitri kept yourselves to yourselves."

"That was true, but we were aware that there was something going on. We just wanted to keep our heads down and out of trouble — self-preservation, I must admit."

"I don't see how you expected to be able to do that, seeing you had links with our side, Theo."

"I know, I know. So I was unexpectedly caught up in this war, but I always knew whose side I was on. I grew up in this country, for God's sake. But it wasn't until after you had gone that we got to know what was really happening on the other side of the island. One dark night, a little later, we were visited by some Underground fighters from there. This was our first contact, for they were unaware that we existed. They had only just been tipped off about our involvement. I suppose that was typical MI6 strategy — not letting the left hand know what the right one was doing. You must agree that this was dangerous for the men on the ground — at least, we thought it was. These men told us that there was a large complicated enemy network there, watching, monitoring and reporting back to Berlin. Apparently it was causing our side a lot of grief."

"I was told something similar," Purcell broke in, "but I was given to understand that the trouble was coming mainly from your side of the island. That's why we were landed there."

"Exactly, Phillip, that's what you were meant to think. But in fact we learned that night there was a brilliant British agent working with these men on the far side of the island. They told us that he was the best — ruthless, cunning — and it was many months before the enemy realised that he was in their midst. Then, gradually, they began to tighten the net around him. Even then he gave them a run for their money. It would seem he made a great impression on whoever he worked with, or against."

"Not on me he didn't, nor on the other two who were with me."

"You met him?"

"Yes. He was already on board the sub which picked us up that last night."

Theo was dumbfounded into silence.

Purcell went on bitterly, "It was then I realised that we were only the created diversion which enabled him to make his escape. The rest was all bull — the gun installation and everything else. We would have sooner been told the truth in the first place. It made us feel bloody fools. There we were, thinking we had done something wonderful in blowing up that gun installation, but really it didn't matter one way or the other. We were just decoys so that he could get off the island."

"And you didn't like this man?" Theo asked.

"No, I didn't. Why, even the crew of the submarine were of the same opinion, for he was cold and hostile in his manner — a real loner — and we were inclined to let it stay that way on our journey home. I later had to accompany him to one of the MI6 headquarters, to be debriefed. It was there I learned how brilliant he really was. He was highly regarded, but I still disliked him intensely." Purcell paused for a moment, then added in a subdued way, "But for all that, I wouldn't have wished him any harm. I could never have done what he accomplished. The last I heard of him was that he was overdue to make contact with our side. There was deep anxiety over his continued silence and the worst was feared."

"That he had been caught and killed?" Theo suggested.

"Yes. I was told of all of this by one of the intelligence officers whom I had casually bumped into some time later. Apparently they had despatched him off on yet another dangerous assignment. Although, knowing him, he probably volunteered. I hope he did make it in the end."

"Well, if he was as brilliant as they say, then he probably did," Theo consoled.

All the time the two younger men were talking, the elders sat solemnly listening.

"War is a bloody, dirty business, Captain," one of them ventured.

"It certainly is, sir."

"It is now in its final stages, so we must be thankful."

"Yes, sir. Within a short time I will be out of the army — soldier no more."

"Is that so, Captain? Then we must drink to this."

Glasses were refilled and they drank their toast. Then the older men rose from the table.

"It has been an honour to meet you, Captain. Please call on us whenever you wish. You will always be welcome here."

"Thank you very much, sirs. I wish you well."

The older men then made their dignified exit, watched by a thoughtful Theo. He leaned forward towards his guest and quietly commented in a confidential manner, "You have impressed them, Phillip."

"Have I? Why do you say that?"

"Well, they didn't mention the trouble in the Mediterranean. It's always there simmering away beneath the surface. The disputes between the different factions — Greek, Turkish — and the occupation of the British rankle with them, and I don't think it will ever be resolved. The German dominance and threat was the last straw for their generation. Me, I couldn't care less. I know that I am selfish, but I want to live the rest of my life here in peace. I made up my mind on this when they smuggled me off the island. My loyalty is here. I want to do things that the ordinary man does — marry, have kids, work hard, and enjoy life."

"Will you be marrying soon, Theo?"

"We have set a date for the end of the year. You haven't met her yet. You must come to our wedding, for without your help there wouldn't be one."

"What do you mean?"

"Those letters I gave you — you must remember. She told me that by the time she received them she was very weakened by the pressure that was being put on her by the family. They had another man in mind. You see, Phillip, they all thought I was dead and buried."

The tone of Theo's voice amused the captain. "But only the good die young, Theo," he told him.

"Very true. Those letters convinced her to wait. They gave her the strength to stand up for herself against her family's wishes. I tell you, that takes some doing within our family structure."

"She sounds quite a girl."

"She is. Wait until you meet her."

"I'm looking forward to it. Here is my home address and telephone number. Get in touch whenever you want. Now, I must be going. It's been great meeting up with you, Theo."

"And the same goes for me, Phillip. Come, I'll walk you to the taxi rank."

The two young men left the warmth of the restaurant for the inky blackness outside. They walked closely together, sharing Theo's dimmed torch as they edged through the hurrying crowds.

"This damned blackout!" Theo muttered. "I'm looking forward to the end of it, then London will be lit up once more, just as I remember it."

"And the lights will be on all over Europe. Just think of it, Theo — great!"

They walked on with a determined stride.

Printed in Dunstable, United Kingdom

FALL OF THE ANGELS

THE SEQUEL *to* THE DEVIL'S HALO

ANGELS

THE

OF

FALL

JOSH RAYMER

COPYRIGHT © 2021 JOSH RAYMER

All rights reserved.

FALL OF THE ANGELS

ISBN   978-1-5445-2184-8   *Paperback*
          978-1-5445-2183-1   *Ebook*
          978-1-5445-2185-5   *Audiobook*

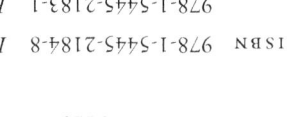

TO MY SON, PAXTON.

I CAN'T WAIT TO READ THE STORIES YOU WRITE.

CONTENTS

1. WE'RE NOT IN KANSAS ANYMORE.................9
2. TIME IS A BLUE CIRCLE...........................19
3. A LOVELY DAY FOR A PRISON BREAK 31
4. THE PASSION OF PURIEL 45
5. STAFF MEETING 55
6. TAKE ONE FOR THE TEAM.........................69
7. SHORT, PALE, AND MYSTERIOUS...................81
8. HEAVEN'S GARBAGE DISPOSAL....................95
9. TO THE FUTURE AND BACK........................111
10. FORTY YEARS OF KICKING ASS....................125
11. I KNOW KUNG-FU 141
12. REUNITED AND IT FEELS SO GOOD.................161
13. NEVER TOO LATE FOR A CHANGE OF HEART 177
14. FANCY SEEING YOU HERE 193
15. FINISH THE FIGHT 209
16. WHAT COMES NEXT..............................221
    ACKNOWLEDGMENTS 233
    ABOUT THE AUTHOR.............................237

CHAPTER 1

WE'RE NOT IN KANSAS ANYMORE

INEVER THOUGHT DEATH WOULD BE THIS COMPLI-
cated.

When I was nine years old, our dog Scoot—so named for the way he scooted his butt across the rug in the living room—ran in front of a car while Peter and I were playing outside. Scoot was killed instantly. I can still remember the horrible *thud* that preceded our screams and the crimson pool that formed around his mangled body. It was my first encounter with death.

Dad heard our screams and came running outside to see what was wrong. His expression was a blend of stoicism and heartbreak as he bent down to touch Scoot's matted fur. Through the tears that rimmed my eyes, I saw Dad pull back a hand that was slick with blood. He discreetly wiped his hand on his pants and turned to confront his two sobbing sons. Peter trembled next to me. His wailing was only interrupted by his sniffling and the occasional pause to catch his breath.

Dad put his hands on our shoulders and guided us away from the street and back toward the house. As we walked, I kept looking back over my shoulder at Scoot's body. He seemed so small now.

"Boys, what happened today was not your fault," Dad said in that familiar tone of voice that always calmed his sons at their most savage.

In this instance, it was like I was hearing him from the end of a long tunnel. I kept staring at Scoot and praying that he would miraculously start moving again. I knew this was a stupid thought to have, and yet, I kept staring at him expectantly.

"Are you listening, Silas?" This snapped my attention back to Dad. His gaze was kind and concerned. I nodded, and he continued. "You and your brother couldn't have stopped what happened to Scoot. Accidents, even bad ones like this, just happen sometimes. Bad things have no consideration for what's fair or what's right. We just have to deal with them as they come."

Dad bent down so he was on our level and looked first at

10 · FALL OF THE ANGELS

me, then to Peter. He grabbed my brother by the shoulders and smoothed his hair with a steady hand. Peter's chest continued to heave as Dad moved from smoothing his hair to wiping away his tears. My own mourning melted away as I watched Dad calm the waves that were engulfing Peter simply by caressing his tear-streaked face. When at last Peter stopped sniffling and Dad finished wiping away the tears, he spoke quietly.

"How are you feeling right now, Pete?"

Peter's bottom lip protruded, and he stared at the ground. It took him a second to answer.

"Sad," he whispered.

"It's OK to feel sad," Dad told him.

"Scoot's gone, Daddy. He can't play with us anymore."

"He is gone, buddy. But do you know where Scoot went? Where he is right now?"

I was pretty sure I knew the answer but wanted Peter to guess since Dad had asked him and not me. While I'd never experienced death myself, I had talked to friends at school who had family members die. They told me their parents, teachers, people at church—pretty much everyone they talked to—told them the person they lost was "in a better place."

Mom had mentioned during our nightly Bible stories before that the people who died in those stories went to Heaven. The way she talked about it with streets of gold and huge mansions sitting on clouds, it really did sound like a better place. I could only hope that Scoot was up there now, chasing tennis balls and scooting his butt across every rug he could find. Maybe he'd even been given a pair of wings.

Dad waited for Peter's answer but got none. Peter merely shook his head.

"Scoot's in Heaven right now," Dad explained. Peter's eyes lit up. A watery smile tugged at the corners of his mouth. Dad continued, "There's a special dog park up there for good boys like him. All the

tennis balls and belly rubs he could ever want. He misses you boys, no doubt. But don't you think that sounds like a nice place for Scoot to hang out until he sees you all again?"

I nodded along with Peter, who asked, "We'll get to see him again?"

Dad straightened up but never broke eye contact with Peter. We waited breathlessly for his answer. The response he gave us is something I never forgot. Those words brought me tremendous comfort during the dark days following Dad's disappearance and when Mom lost her cancer battle.

"We sure will. Heaven is a wonderful place, boys. Everyone you know who goes there before you will be happy and healthy. We'll all be dancing and singing."

This brought a full-blown smile to Peter's face. He loved to dance more than anyone I'd ever met, even at five years old. He always stole the show during family dance nights at the house.

"I thought that might make you smile!" Dad remarked upon seeing Peter's reaction. "I hope none of us goes there for a long, long time, but when we all get there, it will be wonderful."

Dad, I hate to break it to you, but the Heaven you described is a far cry from the one that greeted me.

After sacrificing myself to defeat Malphas and save Peter, violence and betrayal welcomed me into Heaven, not singing and dancing. An angel I trusted with my life tried to strangle me. I looked into Gregori's eyes and saw cold, gray fury staring back as the oxygen was squeezed from my lungs. I was a nuisance that needed to be dealt with, the proverbial fly in the ointment.

The only thing that kept him from ending my existence was a fist through the chest from my great-great-grandfather, Augustus Shaw, the most revered nephilim of all time who died the year before I was born.

Augustus then explained that Gregori had been working with Malphas to free Asaroth and overthrow Lucifer for control of

Hell. When Gregori wised up and finally realized that God knew of his plan all along, he ordered Malphas to kill me so that I'd arrive in his waiting arms suspecting nothing of the angel's betrayal. The voice urging me to let go during my final moments, that I believed to be Gregori's, actually belonged to Augustus. He'd been keeping an eye on me since the ambush in Wintergate Falls and meant to intercept me before Gregori could carry out his plan. Even with that advanced knowledge, he'd only arrived with seconds to spare.

What happened next still hasn't processed in my brain. I was standing there, ready to return to Earth and fulfill my promise to Peter that I wouldn't delay in coming back. Then Augustus told me I couldn't return just yet. When I asked why, he told me a war was raging inside Heaven's gates. Gregori's treachery was merely the first twinkle of sunlight before dawn. Other angels had been outed as traitors after his plan failed. Heaven, long regarded in my mind as a peaceful home to departed souls, was engulfed in strife so catastrophic that Augustus needed my help to settle things down. He hadn't even asked if I wanted to help, choosing instead to teleport the pair of us before I could finish objecting to his request. Even now, my destination is a total mystery.

If Augustus was unwilling to take "no" for an answer, the situation must really be dire.

The actual dying part of death had not been difficult. To quote Sirius Black, it had been as easy as falling asleep. I'm not sure when I succumbed to my injuries inside the fiery wreckage of the lumberyard, but I wouldn't describe those final moments as painful. Contrary to popular belief, my life didn't flash before my eyes, but rather just a single moment from my trip to the Grand Canyon with Mom and Peter. Perhaps that was a side effect of believing I'd be alive again soon: what I needed in that moment wasn't closure but rather a chance to say goodbye to my brother. Either way, passing from that world to this one happened in

an instant. I'd crossed the expansive void, arrived safely on the other side, and, in doing so, had answered the biggest question of them all:

What happens after we die?

Violence, secrets, and lies.

I thought I'd left those behind when I drew my last breath. Turns out they followed me like a hungry wolf stalking its prey. Now I'm hurtling through a golden wormhole headed toward a pack of angels exactly like Gregori. I barely had time to draw a deep breath before being thrown right back into battle. I can still feel the sting of Gregori's powerful hands around my neck.

Had Augustus not stopped to consider that I wasn't ready to fight after nearly being killed by someone I once trusted? "Out of the frying pan and into the fire" can't begin to describe what he's doing to me. The moment I knew Gregori was going to kill me, all I felt was fear. Its hold over me was absolute. There was no doubt in my mind Gregori would kill me. He was simply too powerful for me to stop. How, then, was I expected to fight an entire legion of rebellious angels?

I am not bringing you along to fight these angels.

In the weightlessness of the wormhole, my stomach drops.

What are you doing back inside my head? I thought you tuned out.

I'm sorry. I wasn't trying to eavesdrop. I simply thought you might have some questions.

You thought right! Where the hell are you taking me?

To meet with a friend I hope will help us. We're almost there. I will explain everything shortly, Silas. I promise you that. But time is of the essence. We have to move quickly if we hope to gain the upper hand.

Fine. But can you tune out now? I want a moment alone with my thoughts.

Of course.

My dad taught me how to handle situations that feel like they're beyond my control. He knew that was something I struggled with

growing up. I always wanted to be the person calling the shots, making up the plan, and deciding what happened next. Dad learned early on that in order for me to be a functioning member of society, I had to learn how to relinquish that desire for control.

"Three deep breaths," he told me. "Then push out with your palms like I'm doing."

I remember watching as he slowly pushed his palms out in front of his body like he was shoving someone in slow motion. I took three deep breaths and copied his pushing motion.

"Good," he told me. "Push the situation away from yourself. Let it go."

I can hear his voice in my ears as I draw three deep, slow breaths. My throat still aches where Gregori gripped it tightly, but I ignore the pain and allow the breathing to soothe my nerves. I close my eyes and quiet my mind as the golden light dances across the outside of my eyelids. I extend my palms forward and push the situation away from me.

Perhaps I'm pushing it toward God. Or maybe Augustus. I'm not entirely sure.

All I know is that in order to see my brother again, I have to give up control.

Whatever comes next, I'm trusting that someone else knows what they're doing.

God help me.

✛ ✛ ✛

THE WORMHOLE DEPOSITS US IN A PLACE WHERE THE ground is firm. Angels might be used to flying around, but as a bipedal human being, I still appreciate the feeling of terra firma under my feet. Except, in this case, I guess it's *Heaven firma*. Regardless, the instant my feet touch the ground, I begin looking around to gauge my new surroundings. This new area is a far cry from the

breathtaking vista I first observed upon arriving in Heaven, the one Gregori had described as a masterpiece by God.

The first thing I notice are the trees. The closest comparison on Earth would probably be a weeping willow, except these monstrosities stretch so high above us that I can't see the tops. The thick, powerful branches are unlike anything I've ever seen. They defy the laws of gravity—curling and uncurling like snakes locked in a rhythmic dance—and pulsate with a brilliant sapphire hue.

At first, I think the branches themselves are made from this light. When I move toward the nearest one, I see the branches are actually lined with glowing blue orbs roughly the size of apples, their contents swirling as the light changes from delicately soft to brilliantly bright. The effect is mesmerizing.

What if these orbs have the answer?

They have to hold answers. Look at them—they're beautiful!

What if I'm not worthy to touch them?

Of course I'm worthy! I'm God's chosen nephilim.

I should touch one to know for sure.

My hand trembles as I reach for the nearest orb. The branch holding it seemingly complies with my desire and lifts itself into the path of my outstretched hand. My fingers are so close to the orb now that I can see the sapphire light reflected on my fingernails. Their warmth bathes my fingers...

"SILAS!" cries a booming voice. Its echo is still reverberating when my hand is smacked away, causing me to jump like I've been hit with an electric shock. The tunnel vision I had is brushed aside like a puff of smoke. My face grows hot as I realize what happened.

"What was...what are these things?" I mumble incoherently. It's the best my brain can do. I knead my forehead with my knuckles, trying to regain the focus I lost during that surreal trance.

Augustus chuckles at my embarrassment. It's more of a baritone laugh, higher-pitched than Colin's deep belly laugh. The smile he flashes me is all teeth and reminds me of Peter.

"Boy, that thing sure did a number on you," he says after the laughter dissipates. "We're here all of five seconds, and you're running toward that tree like a dying man to water."

"I couldn't help it," I confess. "Those orbs are hypnotic. I swear it felt like they were calling out to me. Like if I grabbed one, it would reveal answers to all the questions I've ever had."

"How do you think Adam and Eve felt?"

CHAPTER 2

TIME IS A
BLUE CIRCLE

THERE IT IS AGAIN—THAT "STOMACH DOING A backflip" feeling. I should be used to it by now. In the past three days, I've had more mind-melting revelations thrown at me than the President on his first day in office:

Silas, you're a nephilim whose job it is to protect the whole world from demons, one of whom has kidnapped your brother in an attempt to bust his father—also a demon—from his prison in God's throne room. Yep, that's a real place. So is Heaven, which you'll go to after you die. But don't worry! You can come back and keep fighting as long as you want. Also, Hell is real and absolutely terrifying, and angels can hear your thoughts.

I've got such a bad case of information overload that it will take years of therapy to sort out. Compared to the enormity of God, Heaven, and Hell, I shouldn't do a double-take when Augustus tells me I was mesmerized by the tree that tempted Adam and Eve to commit the original sin.

But that's ludicrous, of course. I would have to be dead (which I guess I am right now) to not shudder at the enormity of this fact. If I ever grow tired of these paradigm-shifting moments that would make normal people keel over dead with shock, perhaps it's then I'll know the time has come to hang up the cape and call it a day. Nephilim or not, I'm still human, and humans should feel awe during moments like these. Their stomachs should be doing backflips for days.

"This is the tree from the Garden of Eden?" I whisper.

"The same one," Augustus explains. "This tree was plucked out of the Garden right before it was destroyed during the Great Flood. All the rest you see here are just like that one. Time trees, every one of them."

He gestures away from us, and my eyes are drawn at last to the rest of our surroundings. I was so quick to focus on the trees that I missed the walkway winding between them. Unlike the dazzling blue of the trees, the path is a deep red. If I had to guess, I'd say it's made of rubies.

"You're not wrong," Augustus says.

I give him a look that I hope communicates the exasperation I feel at him reading my thoughts. He smacks his forehead and offers his apologies. I'm not angry, of course. Just slightly annoyed.

"I have to actively turn it off in here." Augustus points to his head. "If my mind begins to wander, the switch flips, and there we go again with the telepathy and the eavesdropping."

I wave away his concern, tell him it's no big deal.

"Time trees," I mutter. The term feels foreign and misshapen on my tongue. "What makes them so tantalizing? Don't tell me they show you the future if you take the fruit?"

"Quick on the uptake, I see." Augustus grins. "That's exactly right."

"You can't be serious."

"What, you think the Bible called it the tree of knowledge because the fruit was tasty? Time is the ultimate source of knowledge. If you could see any point in the past, present, or future just by plucking one of these lovely orbs, you could unravel any mystery or uncover any secret that has plagued even the brightest of human minds. That kind of insight is the closest you and I would ever come to feeling like God. Could you have passed that obedience test in the Garden?"

"It wouldn't have taken a serpent to convince me," I respond with a smirk. "I'd have headed there straight away. Seems pretty unfair to put a temptation like that in front of Adam and Eve."

"Ah, they'd have messed up one way or another. Humanity was doomed to sin. That was God's plan from the beginning. You could even say he did Adam and Eve a favor by putting a temptation in the Garden that no mortal could have resisted. Makes them more sympathetic, I suppose."

I nod. It's an argument for another day, but I can see where Augustus is coming from. I'm more concerned with the sudden thought that's gnawing at my insides all of a sudden.

TIME IS A BLUE CIRCLE · 21

If these trees can show the past, there's one assumption I feel I can safely make.

If I'm right, the ramifications are enormous.

"Would this tree," I start, choosing my words carefully, "show what happened to my dad?"

Augustus inhales, and his expression softens. I don't need telepathy to know he expected me to ask that question. Because we're short on time, I'm sure he'll tell me to hold that thought, and we'll come back to it when Heaven is not engulfed in angelic warfare. But I hope he understands how important that answer is to me; that questions like the one I just asked can haunt men until their dying day. If these trees can provide me with an answer to what happened to Malcolm Ford, devoted husband and loving father of two boys, I deserve the right to see for myself.

"Yes," Augustus replies. "You can go back to that day and see for yourself what happened. You only need to envision what you want to see before you grab the orb. You don't even need to know the date. These trees are pretty good at filling in the gaps when it comes to requests."

I envision my desired memory unfolding like a flickering motion picture projected onto a dusty screen. The jumpy, sepia-toned film would show my father dying heroically at the hands of Malphas in an effort to protect his family. The demon's version—where Dad became a prisoner in exchange for our freedom—is a coiled snake lurking in the dark corner of my mind.

In my heart, I know the demon was trying to manipulate me when he spun that yarn. In trusting Colin, I chose to accept his version of reality. However, I also know memories can warp, and events can be altered when viewed through the lens of history. I've seen it firsthand in the courtroom countless times.

In the end, my assurance comes from knowing my father. He would never be stupid enough to trust Malphas. I'll use these trees to get to the truth. For now, I want to help Augustus as quickly as

possible, so I can return home. My friends and family are depending on me back in Sherwood, and I have no intention of letting them handle the fallout of Malphas's assault by themselves.

"Will you bring me back here when we've dealt with this conflict?" I ask.

Augustus nods emphatically. "Absolutely. Once we settle things inside the gates, I'll take you wherever you want to go. There's a few other places up here I think you'll find fascinating."

I spare one final gaze at the hypnotic time trees and their pulsating blue light before turning my attention to the ruby-lined path between the trees. I see nothing but a vanishing point up ahead where the inky blackness overhead mingles with the ruby and sapphire glow of our surroundings. The kaleidoscope of brilliant colors lends an otherworldly feel to this whole place.

I point my finger down the path, and Augustus motions for me to lead the way. I start walking and, within a few steps, the inexplicable pull of the time tree loosens its grip on me. I didn't realize until that moment how much it felt like I was walking in deep sand. The tree's pull was almost magnetic in the way it summoned me to its side. My mind has cleared now that I've shaken off the unwanted mental intrusion, and I notice the path underfoot is eliciting a soft trill every time I take a step. It's a pleasant, soothing noise that puts my mind at ease.

Within what can only be a few seconds of Earth time, our surroundings begin to change. Wispy vapors surround us, and the time trees begin to dissolve into undefined blue clouds. The path starts to disappear next, like the fading of a distant taillight. Before long, Augustus and I are encased in a darkness that is suffocating in its absoluteness. The transition is so disorienting, I abruptly stop walking, and Augustus slams into my back. He grabs my shoulder to keep me from falling.

"Whoa, easy there," he says.

"What's going on? Where did this darkness come from?"

The rising panic is unmistakable in my voice. The floor has fallen out below me in a way I've never experienced. The pitch-black demon pit in Wintergate Falls was terrifying, but I at least had firm ground under my feet. This transitory place has me perched on a precarious ledge atop a swaying skyscraper. I would have toppled over headfirst had Augustus not grabbed me.

"It's a tunnel, it's a tunnel," he tells me. "Nothing more. Disorienting at first, I know. I should have told you about them when the crossover began. My apologies; I was distracted. Just keep walking, and I promise the picture will change once our destination emerges from the darkness."

"I don't know if I can."

I sound like a small child who is too afraid to jump in the pool. The mere act of jumping forward seems simple to those who've done it a thousand times before. But for the uninitiated, the thought of making that leap turns their legs to jelly. I know physically I'm capable of lifting my foot and placing it in front of me. What I can't overcome is the disorientation and its assault on my equilibrium. I've lost any sense of which way is up and how to move forward.

"I'll push, and you take one step forward. We'll do this together. Are you ready?"

"Yes," I bleat. The knot in my stomach twists itself tighter.

The nudge in my back corkscrews the world back onto its axis. I extend my foot and take a wobbly step. Augustus continues to apply pressure, and I put my other foot out. The ground grows more stable under my shaky legs. Like a newborn giraffe, my first few steps are unbalanced and fraught with uncertainty. Each stride brightens the world around us and restores order to my delicate inner ear.

I break into a jog as the illumination grows more pronounced. The sooner I can escape this tunnel of doom, the better. The echoing footsteps accompanying mine tell me Augustus has chosen to jog as well. I look down until the ground reappears beneath our feet. This time, a rough-hewn stone walkway rises to greet us.

24 · FALL OF THE ANGELS

I round on Augustus, whose expression reads remorse.

"What the hell? Humans aren't built for that! I couldn't even walk in there."

"It's my fault for not explaining what would happen," Augustus offers. His face is so downcast I feel a twinge of regret for getting so upset. He continues, "Heaven is a massive place. So massive, in fact, that traveling from one place to another requires the compression of time and space in the manner you just experienced. It is similar to the wormholes you and I can create to teleport ourselves, only much faster. Even if I could have teleported us here, it would've taken too long."

"So I guess I've got God to thank for the sensory deprivation and the motion sickness?"

Augustus smirks, perhaps happy to see I didn't lose my snarkiness inside the darkness.

"You could. Or you can take it up with his architect. That's who we've come to visit."

"I thought God designed the heavens and the Earth at the beginning of Genesis?"

"He did. But like most of God's knowledge, he shared his designs with another. In time, God began to trust this architect to handle the business of Heaven on Earth. When Ezekiel was shown a vision of the new temple in Jerusalem, he was there. When God needed someone to tell Joshua how many times to march around the city of Jericho for the walls to fall, he sent his architect. Time and time again, the architect has helped God shape the course of history."

"Sounds like a prestigious designation. Does this architect have a name?"

Augustus lets out a hearty laugh that tells me a lot about this mysterious architect. Peter prefaces all his "you won't believe what happened last night" stories with that same kind of laugh. If that telling chuckle is somehow hereditary, I'm guessing this architect is a real character.

TIME IS A BLUE CIRCLE · 25

"He'd prefer it if you called him the Bronze Man. That was his designation in the Bible, and he's quite proud of it. I've taken to calling him Bron just to deflate his ego a bit. He hates it."

"I've met some high-powered attorneys like that. Is he more the egotist or the painfully oblivious type?" Augustus smiles, places his arm around my shoulder, and guides us up the path.

"A little of both, mixed with a sprinkle of crazy and a dash of delusion for good measure. He's like your crazy uncle who makes family gatherings awkward. Tough to handle, but harmless, really."

"I never had a crazy uncle growing up."

"You should have met my family. All we had were crazy uncles!"

We both laugh as we climb the rough stone walkway. It snakes between two high canyon walls that are streaked with a mixture of orange, red, and brown, resembling the color of Martian soil. As we climb, the walls move gradually apart until a wide swath of sky separates them. The sky here is a deep, soulful blue. I'm reminded of the sky before a thunderstorm. It's a nice change from the black skies that stretched overhead in the first two areas of Heaven I visited.

I don't know what I expected the home of God's architect to look like, but as we come over the crest of the hill and the path levels off, I'm certain that the residence sitting before us is not what I had in mind. It's a simple sand-colored adobe home, not too different from the ones Pueblo Indians used to make for themselves. A small ladder leans against the side of the house facing us, and smoke curls from a chimney on the far side of the roof. The only thing odd about the structure is the doorway, which looks big enough to accommodate someone ten feet tall.

As we draw closer to the house, a series of thuds and crashes emanates from inside its walls. It's as if a giant beast has awakened inside and is stumbling around blindly for the door. I give Augustus a concerned look, but he merely shakes his head as if to say, *don't worry, he's being dramatic.*

A giant flesh-colored dome emerges from the doorway, followed

26 · FALL OF THE ANGELS

by an enormous pair of shoulders. I realize now that the Bronze Man is unfolding himself as he exits the doorway, which is somehow too small for his massive frame. He rushes out the door so frantically that he trips over his own feet. The resulting clatter of footsteps sends rumbles echoing up the canyon walls. Despite this, he tries to maintain an air of civility and importance as he scrambles upright. At his full height and with his chiseled bronze chest puffed out, he strikes quite an imposing figure. His perfectly clear eyes sparkle like diamonds in the sun as he scans the area for the source of the disturbance.

When he spots us, he bellows in a voice like a cracked megaphone:

"What being under Heaven feels compelled to disturb the work of God's chosen architect?"

Looking up at him, Augustus is nonplussed.

"Oh shut it, Bron, you big oaf. I know you were in there sleeping!"

"Augustus Shaw, is that your voice I hear?"

Bron stoops low to get a better look at Augustus. His face is about three feet from mine and the size of a wheelbarrow. His features are flat and perfectly smooth, like a face carved from stone and sanded to a high polish. The nose below his gleaming eyes barely protrudes from his face, yet his nostrils are wide and currently flared. His pursed lips maintain a hint of his rosy complexion, a color that contrasts sharply with a body that is appropriately bronze from neck to toes. He looks as if someone attached a Ken doll's head to the body of an Oscar statue. From his absurd size to the clashing skin tones, God's architect is a lot to take in at first glance.

"There's a young man here I'd like you to meet, Bron," Augustus explains. As he says this, Bron's head swivels toward me, and his eyes squint to get a better look. Augustus continues. "This is Silas Ford, my great-great-grandson and God's newest nephilim. Silas, meet Heaven's architect."

I realize as Augustus is introducing us that Bron is the first non-human creature I've met that wasn't trying to kill me. This assumes

TIME IS A BLUE CIRCLE · 27

Bron doesn't want me dead, of course. Realizing this leaves me at a loss for words as I struggle to understand how I'm supposed to greet a giant bronze man.

Out of my mouth blurts: "Um, nice to meet you, sir."

Bron takes no notice of my greeting, instead choosing to look me up and down like he's appraising a car before purchasing it. I want to tell this bronze behemoth that I'm not entirely comfortable being put under his microscope, but before I can say anything, Bron speaks.

"Nephilim, did you say, Augustus?" he asks. "Not quite the build you'd expect for a warrior of the Lord most high. No indeed! The arms are far too scrawny, and the posture is like that of a time tree." He pauses and reaches down to point at my stomach with a hand the size of my torso. I take a step back, my agitation toward his appraisal growing. "Not to mention the midsection is round and soft like a woebegone lump of bread dough. Where'd you find this one, Augustus?"

"I died protecting my home from Malphas and his demon army," I announce, cutting off Augustus before he can answer. "I saved my whole town from being wiped off the map. Even with scrawny arms, a doughy midsection, and poor posture. Put that in your chimney and smoke it you goofy bronze bastard." I give Augustus a withering look. "We done here?"

Augustus is merely bemused by my reaction to Bron's insults. He chuckles as Bron lifts himself to full height and strokes his square chin. After a moment of consideration, he nods and claps his hands enthusiastically. The cacophonous noise again echoes off the canyon walls.

"Augustus Shaw, I have changed my assessment of this one!" he booms. "What he lacks in physical stature, he makes up for with gumption. As you know, Augustus, that trait is hard to quantify but immensely important in your line of work. Young Mr. Ford seems to have inherited that trait from you. If I recall correctly, you

possessed moxie in abundance during your time doing the Lord's work on Earth. That and your measurable physical gifts made you quite formidable."

"Two things, Bron," Augustus answers right away. "First, I still possess plenty of gumption. Second, why don't you ask our old friend, Gregori, if I'm still a formidable foe."

The delighted expression melts from Bron's face. He's suddenly serious.

"Ah yes, I heard about that. I never took Gregori for a traitor."

Neither did I. The shock of his betrayal stands in the way of me fully comprehending what one treacherous angel almost cost me. I bought into his lies when he took me high above Sherwood and told me I had a destiny. I so badly needed to believe that there was a greater purpose behind all this pain and suffering, and Gregori preyed upon that weakness. There was a plan, alright. It was just one concocted by Gregori and Malphas to unleash an unspeakable evil upon the world.

I'm still frustrated with myself that I let the angel pull the wool over my eyes. My logical approach to daily life was overwhelmed by how Gregori made me feel. I was duped.

It won't happen again.

"Then I'm sure you're also aware of what's happening inside the gates," Augustus says.

Bron nods solemnly. "Total chaos. Incalculable destruction. Something must be done."

"Why do you think we're here?" Augustus responds. Bron is inquisitive now, and my attention is definitely piqued. Anything that moves us closer to my departure is highly interesting to me.

"What are you planning, Augustus Shaw?" Bron asks, his creaky voice more level.

There's a wild look in my great-great-grandfather's eyes as he prepares to answer, and I'm once again reminded of my brother. Whereas Colin and I share similar traits, Peter is Augustus made

TIME IS A BLUE CIRCLE · 29

over. Just from the brief time I've spent with Augustus, I can see the bravado that made him such a prolific nephilim and likely contributed to his downfall. Here's a man who attacked his mission with a reckless abandon. As we stand ready to confront Gregori's rebellious brethren and end Heaven's civil war, there's only one question that seems worth considering:

What do you have planned, Augustus?

His answer is one word: "Lightfall."

This mysterious answer causes Bron to gasp.

"You can't be serious, Augustus. That was designed as a last resort."

"I'm sorry, have you looked inside the gates? Our options went up in smoke the instant Gregori wrapped his slimy hands around Silas's neck. There's no going back, Bron. You know that."

"Lightfall would change everything. Heaven would never be the same."

"Judging by where we are now, I'd say the status quo is in desperate need of change."

I can't stand being left in the dark any longer. Ignorance never suited me.

"What is Lightfall?" My pair of companions look at me like two parents who are sitting on bad news and have no idea how to tell their child.

"Just spit it out already," I urge them.

Augustus motions at Bron, who reluctantly tells me, "Lightfall is the protocol by which God's angels are removed from Heaven. Unlike the first time, Lightfall casts out all the angels."

"It's the eject button that can end this bloody conflict before Heaven is torn apart," Augustus adds. "It won't be easy flipping the switch. But I firmly believe it's our only way forward."

"You neglected to mention the issue with your plan," Bron chides.

"Oh, please tell me it's something horrible," I say sarcastically.

"The angels...they would be ejected...to Earth."

I just had to open my mouth, didn't I?

CHAPTER 3

A LOVELY
DAY FOR
A PRISON
BREAK

F A RIOT WAS HAPPENING AT THE WORLD'S MOST dangerous prison, would those in charge solve the problem by opening the doors and unleashing the prison's deranged denizens upon the world?

That sounds like the premise of a Michael Bay movie, not a viable solution to our problem. Not to mention these aren't angry prisoners we're talking about. What Augustus is suggesting would decimate Earth in addition to overhauling Heaven. Gregori wanted me dead, and there was nothing I could do to stop him. Hundreds (or is it thousands?) of angels would carve up humanity like a Thanksgiving turkey. Especially if those angels had just been evicted from their home in the same manner as Lucifer and his followers. Their collective fury would be unimaginable.

Bron obviously shares my trepidation with this plan. What baffles me is that Augustus would ever suggest such an apocalyptic scenario as the solution to our problem, which is really just Heaven's problem.

As long as this civil war is contained, Earth has no reason to sweat. Augustus is family, and he saved my life, so I want to help him end this war. But it can't come at the cost of innocent lives back home. I fought too hard along with Colin and the others to save the lives of my brothers and sisters in Sherwood. This time we're talking about everyone. All of us.

And you heard every bit of that inner monologue, didn't you?

I would be lying if I said I didn't, and I try not to lie to family.

"Voices, gentlemen," Bron interjects. He taps his massive head with a bronze finger. "I'm tuned into your frequency. However, I feel certain matters warrant the effort needed to vocalize them."

"I don't voice those objections lightly, Augustus," I explain. "You saved my life, and I'm in your debt for that. Plus—we're family. But you can't deny that sending the angels to Earth would be catastrophic. If their war didn't destroy the planet, their collective anger over being cast out of Heaven would be enough to ignite a powder keg. Humans would be toast."

"Mr. Ford speaks the truth, Augustus," Bron says quietly. "God sent two angels to ensure the destruction of Sodom and Gomorrah. Expelling the heavenly host in its entirety would herald unprecedented destruction. Whole countries would be decimated within a matter of days."

Augustus nods slowly. His expression conveys the sense that he acknowledges our arguments and can't dispute their validity. It's his smile that tells me he knew we'd object to his crazy plan from the outset, and since he suggested it—or perhaps even before—he's formulated his rebuttal.

"You're both absolutely right," Augustus concedes. His gaze is upon the ground, which he kicks at with his foot. I'm reminded of a child whose only negotiation tactic is to employ the "yeah, but..." argument with their parents. Then again, that argument always worked for Peter.

Augustus continues: "Sending a bunch of pissed-off angels to Earth would be game over for mankind. That's why I'm not suggesting we send them to Earth and give them free rein."

"What are you up to, Augustus Shaw?" Bron inquires. "Your time as God's warrior was marked by unmatched resourcefulness, but I can't envision a plan that would let you accomplish this."

Augustus glances sideways at me. His expression begs me to guess what he's planning.

"I'm not reading your mind on this one," I respond. "Or venturing a guess."

"But you are curious to hear more?" he asks.

"It's fair to say you've piqued our interest."

He claps his hands together and draws a long blade from inside his jacket. The hair stands up on the back of my neck upon seeing the blade. After perishing in such a bloody conflict, I'm unsurprisingly still in fight-or-flight mode.

It's only when Augustus begins scrawling in the red dirt beneath our feet with the blade that I realize it was meant for drawing, not

A LOVELY DAY FOR A PRISON BREAK · 33

violence. His illustrations provide little insight into his plan. There's essentially one circle with three smaller circles inside it.

"OK," he says as he finishes the final circle. "This larger circle is Earth. The three smaller circles are zones where the angels could be deposited across the planet." He pokes at each one with the blade. "I don't know where these zones are located, but I know there will be three of them."

"How do you know that?" I ask.

It's Bron who answers, "The Lord has quite an affinity for the number three. It would either be that or the number seven, but Augustus is correct—three zones were established as part of the Lightfall protocol. I am also unaware of their location. However, I know of someone who might possess this knowledge...and now I understand why you came to see me, Augustus."

"Guilty as charged," Augustus says, hands raised. "But we'll get to that in a second. As I was saying, the banished angels will arrive on Earth in one of these three zones. We don't know which one. My plan to keep them from decimating the planet is simple: turn those zones into traps. Don't let them escape."

From out of the dirt swims a hazy memory of a dangerously beautiful demon bound to a chair. That trap was supposed to be strong enough to contain her, but Lamia turned our interrogation on its head before slipping away ahead of my cleansing flame. Perhaps it was one bad experience, and traps are actually reliable methods of combating demons. It seemed like Colin and his team had used them before. Regardless, I'll greet any plan that relies on traps with a great deal of trepidation, especially when those traps have to hold hundreds of angels and not just one demon.

"Let's say for a moment that I buy the fact that we can create traps powerful enough to hold all the angels in Heaven," I say. "Then what? We keep the angels locked up forever?"

"That does seem a rather vital part of this plan, Augustus," Bron adds.

"I'm glad you asked," Augustus counters. He's building momentum now and getting into the meat of his argument. I recognize the body language from my time inside courtrooms and watching Peter explain to women at Tully's Tavern why they'd be foolish not to let him buy them a drink. "While they're inside the trap, the angels will be at our mercy. We'll have all the bargaining power. The only choice they'll have is to decide whether they want to surrender or die."

"You're going to have to elaborate on that last part," I tell him. Bron is silent.

"When an angel is cast out of Heaven, his transformation into a demon begins. His angelic lifeblood—his grace—slowly trickles away. As that connection to Heaven and God is severed, his rage and propensity for violence increase exponentially. Once they snap and commit the ultimate crime of taking another life, their journey to demonhood is complete. Their wings are clipped and what remains is a twisted, hate-filled shell. It's a tragic metamorphosis."

All those shadowy figures whose blood I spilled across three states were angels at one point. The fact that such regal, powerful beings were transformed into skittering, foul creatures through the taking of another life is heartbreaking. I have nothing but hatred in my heart for their disgusting existence, but it's undeniable that demons are tragic figures. Cut off from their home and powerless to stop their grace from seeping away—I'm not surprised they're driven to commit acts of evil.

"I don't think it's right to subject every angel in Heaven to such a horrible fate," I say to Augustus, whose expression remains unchanged. "I'm assuming there are still good angels here who are fighting on the right side of this conflict, and if there are, they don't deserve to be cast out with the traitors. Surely you don't think that's a fair and just solution to this problem, Augustus?"

His reply is blunt: "I don't. Not one bit."

"Then why suggest Lightfall as a solution to our problem?" Bron asks.

Augustus sighs and massages his brow. The confidence he displayed moments earlier is gone. His shoulders slump. He's either a very good actor, or he's genuinely conflicted about this plan.

"I know a lot of the angels personally," he says quietly. "I would consider them my friends in addition to being brothers in arms. It pains me to even consider damning them to the same cruel fate as their traitorous brethren. But one thing I know about angels with absolute certainty is that the good ones are unequivocally devoted to protecting Heaven from the traitors who support Gregori and Malphas. The good angels will stop at nothing to prevent Asaroth from being freed. The problem is they become so engrossed with their mission that they never consider the consequences of warring with beings who are their equal. I believe this lack of foresight will cause them to burn Heaven to the ground, all the while thinking they're saving it from this uprising."

"You think they'll unintentionally destroy Heaven in defense of it," I conclude.

"Exactly," Augustus confirms. He's solemn, his gaze cast out into the beyond while his thumb rubs absentmindedly over the handle of his blade. "We either stand aside while this civil war destroys Heaven, or we use the Lightfall protocol to end the conflict prematurely. We don't have the firepower to intervene and stop the angels from killing each other. These are our only choices."

These bleak options certainly sound like our only viable courses of action. I have to examine all the possibilities before I concede myself to such a "rock and hard place" reality, however.

I didn't think there was a way to save Sherwood from a bloodthirsty army of demons.

I had unspoken doubts that my brother would escape Malphas's clutches in one piece.

There's always a way to achieve the seemingly impossible if you're willing to look for it.

"How certain are you that Heaven will be destroyed?" I ask.

I direct this question toward Augustus, but it's Bron who responds. No surprise when I realize that Heaven's architect would have the best handle on assessing potential damage.

"Augustus is correct," he reveals. "Irreversible damage is all but guaranteed. If you think about Heaven like a model of your solar system with God's throne room, where the departed souls are gathered, serving as the sun, then we've already lost Pluto, the outer realm. The angels decimated that area shortly before you arrived. *That's* what I was doing inside my home, Augustus. Calculating the damage, not sleeping as you had suggested."

"Whatever you say, Bron," Augustus replies jokingly.

"Regardless, the fact remains that Heaven is not on the verge of being destroyed. It *is* being destroyed at this very moment. The bastille is currently under siege, and the armory will be next. If it hasn't been hit already."

"Could the traitors actually reach the throne room and free Asaroth?" I ask.

This feels like a silly question, but I can't shake the shadow of doubt. Surely God would stop the fighting before innocent souls were put in harm's way.

Wouldn't he?

Bron's answer hits me like a blast of icy wind.

"The traitors have nothing to lose, which makes them dangerous," he says. "They could do it."

"And then?" I ask.

"I...I don't know."

Silence hangs thick between us. Nobody says anything for what seems like a long time. I'm trying to process the possibility of war consuming the throne room of God with no success. I simply can't believe that God would allow traitorous angels to wage war in such a sacred place. The most sacred place, I suppose. Shouldn't that holy ground be under God's protection?

I'm coming to realize that God takes a laissez-faire approach to

the affairs happening around him. He wouldn't directly interfere with Gregori's plan to aid Malphas. But I also know that when he works, as the old saying goes, he does so in mysterious ways.

Look no further than Bill for proof of that axiom: God sent him back to Earth with a mission to undermine Gregori's plan by helping me destroy Malphas. Without the power I received when Bill sacrificed himself, Malphas would've ended me and then killed everyone else in Sherwood. God's plan assured our victory.

So I know that God is not absent in the affairs of my world. But what about his own? If Bron is right and the fighting does reach the throne room, would God stand aside and let the angels destroy the place in their single-minded quest to protect Heaven? I would like to think the answer is a resounding *hell no.* But I'm sorely unqualified to predict the actions of God.

"I hope you see now why I think we must consider drastic action," Augustus says, cutting through the overlong silence. "We're up against it here, no doubt, and everything will change no matter what choice we make. I'm just hoping to minimize the damage as much as we can."

"I hear you," I tell him. "I can't believe there's not another way, though. One that doesn't involve such destruction, cruelty, and risk. I feel like we're going to be wrong either way we go."

"If you can think of something, I'm game to try it," Augustus offers.

I look over at Bron, who is staring at the ground and mumbling to himself. Our discussion replays in my mind as I search for an alternative to these abysmal options we have. There are good angels fighting a righteous battle right now against the traitors who supported Gregori and Malphas. This civil war is destroying Heaven as we sit here discussing our options. Augustus thinks the angels are too wrapped up in the battle to hear reason—that their destructive actions can't be stopped. I figure if someone tried to chat with me during my clashes with Malphas, I wouldn't have been very receptive.

So I get where he's coming from with that assumption. It's still hard to swallow, though.

But Augustus knows the angels better than I do. If he says they won't deviate from their marching orders once they have them, I'm in no position to say otherwise.

There has to be another angle to this problem that we're not considering. I knead my knuckles into my forehead, willing the answer to surface like a bubble breaking the water's surface.

Think, think, think. What would Colin say if he was here?

Wait. That's it.

"If this is a war, there have to be generals leading the charge on both sides, right?" I ask.

"Yes, that's true," Augustus says, his eyes narrowing. "It would be the archangels commanding the angels who remain loyal. Right, Bron?"

"Indeed," Bron replies. "Gabriel, Michael, and Raphael."

"Would they be fighting? Or do they survey the battle and issue orders?" I ask.

"Their power is so great that God only uses it for the gravest of threats," Bron recites slowly. His eyes are closed, and he appears lost in recollection. "The last time they were called into battle was when Lucifer and his minions were cast out of Heaven. That clash was quite ferocious."

"OK, so they're not fighting, but they're in charge of the troops. That's our answer. If we want to stop this war before it destroys Heaven, we talk to the archangels. We help them understand what the ultimate result of this conflict will be. Even if they're stubborn, they can't be that shortsighted."

"You are correct to assume the archangels will be stubborn," Bron tells me. "Since they occupy a higher plane of existence than humans, angels have a difficult time understanding the affairs of man or empathizing with his plights. Angels view human affairs as petty and trivial. Even as God's chosen warrior, the archangels will

view you as beneath them. The validity of your argument can not be denied. Yet I hesitate to say that the archangels will take your warnings seriously."

"These guys sound like dicks," I confess.

Bron guffaws. His booming laughter reminds me of those awkward friends we all have that laugh so long and so forcefully they make everyone else uncomfortable. Perhaps it's been too long since Bron heard anything resembling a joke. Augustus is looking at me wide-eyed and laughing to himself. He points at Bron as if to say, *get a load of this guy*. I laugh along with him.

"Silas Ford, you slay me," Bron says finally. "Referring to the highest order of Heaven's angels as a slang term for human genitalia is both hilarious and appropriate. You are quite the comedian."

"You should meet my brother," I reply. "He has a wicked sense of humor."

"Ah yes, the one Malphas kidnapped to use as leverage against you," Bron says. "His tolerance for alcohol in his bloodstream is surprisingly high for someone his size. Impressive, really."

"Sounds like a man after my own heart," Augustus adds.

"Peter would be flattered to know Heaven's architect admires his tolerance," I admit. "Don't tell me he inherited that from you, Augustus?"

"When you live as long as I did, you try out a lot of hobbies. Drinking was one of the few that stuck. That and ballroom dancing. Blame my wife, Marianne, for that one. She loved to dance."

The mention of his wife brings a bittersweet smile to Augustus's face. I know that he and Bron can read my thoughts, and I try not to dwell on it, but I can't help but remember what Colin told me about Marianne's death at the hands of demons. From what little I know about that tragedy, it seemed like Augustus was never the same after her death. Hearing him talk about her now gives me hope that maybe he's reached a healthy place of remembrance where Marianne is concerned.

"I don't suppose another of your hobbies was negotiating with beings who exist on a higher plane of existence?" I ask, trying to return us to the matter at hand. Augustus blinks, shakes his head, and returns his focus to me. It takes him a moment to process my question and reply.

"That would definitely be handy right about now," he says. "I've developed a mutual respect with several of the angels up here, but I don't count the archangels in that group. Bron, you really think we stand such a slim chance of getting through to them?"

"I estimate a 12 percent chance of success," he reveals. "That assumes they are willing to speak with us at all. With the battle raging, there's no guarantee we will get an audience with them."

"You agree that it's worth trying, though?" I ask him. Bron nods assuredly.

"Given our other options, I do believe this endeavor to be worth our time. I will accompany you to meet with the archangels and assist you however I can. But I must warn you that these angels do not hold me in the highest regard. I hope my presence won't be a hindrance to your cause."

Bron looks downright sheepish as he says this. I'm confused by why anyone in Heaven would have problems with Bron. Aside from the awkward introduction, he's been pleasant and helpful since we arrived outside his home. A little odd, sure, but somehow I expected that when Augustus told me we were meeting a heavenly being who's obsessed with measurements and building things.

"Power-hungry bastards," Augustus says in such a low tone it's practically a growl. "They're jealous of anyone else God chooses to entrust with power. Insufferable is what they are."

Bron doesn't respond. His sad nod tells me that Augustus is correct.

"Thank you for agreeing to help us, Bron," I tell him. "I think we can get the archangels to see reason, and despite your misgivings, I think you'll be crucial in helping us do that. That might sound

naive, but technically I was born yesterday. Well, maybe 'reborn' is a better word."

"Except you haven't been reborn on Earth yet, and time is irrelevant in Heaven," Bron retorts. His look of confusion makes me smile. "So I'm not sure what you mean, Silas Ford."

"It's a saying from back home," I tell him. "You know what, never mind. Shall we get going?"

"I'm as ready as I'll ever be, I suppose," Augustus says. "As long as we all understand what happens if things go sideways with the archangels. We have to pursue one of the other plans."

"Agreed," I say. "We can't afford to waste any more time."

With our contingency plan in place, Bron claps his hands and gestures us back down the path that brought us to his house. The red canyon walls slip below the horizon as we walk single file down the descending stone walkway. I'm dreading another trip on Heaven's dark and disorienting expressway.

Of all the ways God could have chosen for Heaven's denizens to get around, he picked the equivalent of riding Space Mountain while drunk off your ass. Maybe it takes time to get used to the feeling. Or maybe this form of travel affects me differently because I'm still human.

Hell, maybe everyone up here is a bit touched, and they all really enjoy it.

Bron gestures at the dark tunnel stretched out before us.

"Next stop is the bastille, gentlemen. Silas, I'm going to wager a guess and say you had trouble with your initial attempt at using this portal to traverse Heaven. The experience was likely overwhelming."

"You could say that," I respond. "One minute Augustus and I are trekking along just fine, if you don't count my episode with the time trees, and the next minute it feels like I'm standing at the edge of a skyscraper on a windy day. Not exactly a great first impression, Bron."

"Heaven's a trip, kid," Augustus interjects with a chuckle. "Just

wait until you see what else God and Bron cooked up. The best is yet to come, as they say."

"I'm sorry your first experience was unpleasant," Bron says. "I never thought humans would traverse the areas of Heaven you have thus far seen. My designs did not take into account the shock their bodies would endure when facing systems built for residents of Heaven. Therefore, to make your journey out to the bastille more comfortable, I can temporarily suspend your consciousness if you wish. You'll awaken safe and sound once we've reached our destination."

"A little cat nap while we cross the void, eh?"

"That's one way of putting it."

I look at Augustus, who nods, and I shrug my shoulders at Bron. "Let's do it," I tell him. "Knock me out. I have zero interest in reliving that feeling."

Bron steps forward and places a bronze finger to my forehead. His glowing skin is surprisingly warm to the touch, and I feel his other arm slip around me as the world fades to black.

CHAPTER 4

THE PASSION
OF PURIEL

I KNOW I'M ASLEEP. THAT MUCH I REMEMBER. I CAN'T see anything, and my body is weightless, which makes it even more disorienting when I hear a familiar voice somewhere below me. The voice is smooth and steady, yet also touched with exhaustion. That voice is a staple of late nights at Tully's Tavern. Its owner calls it a "weapon of mass seduction." The ladies can't resist it, he says.

When the picture snaps into focus, my brother is standing there before me.

Colin is here, too. So is Forrest, who stands a few feet away, his back against a cinderblock wall. The fiery speck at the end of Grace's cigarette casts a weak light across her face. Their expressions are hard to read due to the shadows cutting across this room. I'm viewing this scene from above, and the edges are fuzzy, but from what I can tell, my friends appear to be in some kind of bunker.

Peter's shoulders are slumped, and I realize there's a trickle of blood running down the side of his head. Nonetheless, my heart swells with joy at the sight of him. Seeing him here with the others tells me he made it away from the lumberyard in one piece. I have no idea if what I'm seeing is real, if it's already happened, if it's happening now, or if I'm dreaming this whole thing.

The details all seem too vivid for this to be a dream, though.

"How many dead?"

The voice responsible for this question is small and quiet. Afraid, I'd say. This shocks me only because it belongs to Forrest. Even in our darkest moments, he never sounded that low.

"Best we can tell—twenty. Maybe twenty-five."

It's Colin this time. His normally powerful voice sounds distant. I'm reminded of the doctors who broke the news to us that Mom was dead. I hear the same kind of detachment coming from Colin and realize with horror he's talking about the aftermath of the battle in Sherwood. I know a handful of slayers died in the lumberyard fighting against Malphas and his

46 · FALL OF THE ANGELS

hordes. If what I'm seeing is real, however, then the death toll has spiked tremendously since my death. Something must have gone horribly wrong in town. Or, worse yet, the battle is raging on, and the deaths are mounting.

I have to get back there as soon as I can. My friends need me. My town needs me. People are dying, and I'm stuck up here where I don't belong, trying to stop a war that doesn't involve me.

"We're outnumbered and pinned down," Grace says, her cigarette dancing in her mouth. "Until Silas gets back, I don't know how much good we can do out there. We can play hero if we want. I'll load up and ride off into the sunset guns blazing if that's how we want to play this. God knows I will. But I'd like to think we can come up with a plan that doesn't involve getting ourselves killed."

"Whatever we're gonna do, let's shake a fucking leg here." Peter is antsy. The way his voice rises at the end is a dead giveaway. "We don't have a lot of time to make up our minds."

Whatever deadline is pushing the group toward swift action, I don't find out. I'm sucked upward away from the group as Colin opens his mouth to speak. If I could gasp with shock at the sudden departure, I would. But I'm just a balloon released from a child's grip, floating skyward to a slowly-awakening mind that expected rest during this reprieve but instead found new questions.

Hang in there, guys. I'll be back soon.

Don't go getting yourselves killed in the meantime.

✠ ✠ ✠

THE FIRST THING I NOTICE ABOUT THE BASTILLE IS ITS sheer size. I've seen bigger buildings on Earth, yet I've never stood before one that so deftly combined grandeur and opulence. The entire structure appears to be made of gleaming black marble. A flat wall that stretches as far as the eye can see is interrupted by rounded turrets topped with parapets. It's easy to envision angels standing

guard at each of the crenellations, shield and sword in hand. Those parapets are empty right now, though. Silence surrounds this edifice on all sides. I find this fact unnerving.

I certainly don't miss the sounds of battle. I've heard enough screams, explosions, and gunfire to last ten lifetimes. But if we've strayed into an active war zone, where the hell is everyone? Bron made it seem like we'd arrive to find the bastille in ruins.

Augustus is already treading hastily up the path that runs alongside the bastille. Bron has wandered off into the grass and is making a beeline toward the outer wall. As I stop for a moment and watch him go, I'm once again reminded of Heaven's strange beauty. The grass here is not simply green. It's burnt orange, goldenrod, crimson, periwinkle, and a dozen other colors I can't name. The blades are thick and knee-high on Bron, who towers above me. They're easily up to my waist. I haven't felt the first gust of wind here, but this grass is constantly swaying as if tickled by a slight breeze. This effect is hypnotic, much like the time trees.

Bron reaches the outer wall and runs his hand over the smooth black marble. His eyes are closed, and he mumbles to himself. He nods his head and then speaks before falling silent. With his ear cocked toward the wall, he appears to be listening. He repeats this process of nodding his head, speaking, and listening. As crazy as it sounds, I think he's having a conversation with the bastille, which would be insane until you consider that he's a giant bronze man, and this is Heaven.

I turn my attention to Augustus and find him squatted down on the path about a hundred feet away. He's turning over something silver and pointed in his hands. A weapon, perhaps? It's hard to tell from this distance. I step onto the path—which consists of alternating rows of gold and marble blocks—and begin walking toward Augustus when Bron calls out to us.

"They've been here," he tells us. "The battle has since moved elsewhere, but they were most certainly here not too long ago. I can

hear the cries of battle and feel their residual energy in the walls of this structure. As we suspected, the fighting was ferocious."

Augustus wears a puzzled expression as I glance his way. I suspect he's struck by the same question that came to me upon hearing Bron's declaration. I speak up since he's still far away.

"If the battle came here, why is there no damage? This place looks virtually untouched."

"It happened in the skies," Bron answers solemnly. "Their feet never touched the ground. Which tells me it's possible the archangels are thinking of the damage their conflict is causing."

"It tells me the conflict here was over quickly," Augustus asserts. "No damage plus no bodies. It's almost like the fight wasn't meant to play out here. Like the bastille was just a pit stop."

"The next closest realm is the armory, right?" I ask them both.

They nod. Bron says, "If you are correct, Augustus, and the angels were headed for the armory post haste, then I believe this conflict is about to become bloodier. The armory's weapons were built to be brutally efficient. 'All kills, no frills' is how many of the angels describe them."

Augustus, who is now standing next to me, holds up the weapon that I saw him turning over in his hand. It's a short, silver sword with a cone-shaped blade. He tosses it to me, and I snag it in my right hand. The blade is lightweight and well-balanced. It's also emanating a nearly imperceptible hum as I grip the handle and hold it in front of me. The vibration travels up my arm and rattles my chest. The sensation acts like a straight shot of adrenaline. I feel powerful and ready to strike.

Why does everything up here have to exert its influence over me?

"It's hard to ignore, isn't it?" Augustus inquires. "An angel's weapon is only drawn when he intends to kill. The rush you feel is only half of what angels experience. These swords light a fire in their chest that can only be quelled when the mission is complete, and the blade has tasted blood."

"That certainly doesn't help our current situation much," I observe. "If these swords are whipping the angels into a bloodthirsty rage, the battle is bound to be vicious."

Bron approaches me and extends his hand for the sword, which I hand to him.

"These blades are standard issue for all angels. Whoever holds one must be three feet from their intended target to be within striking distance. Difficult to manage with aerial combat."

"Also difficult when your intended target is a fellow angel." Augustus is staring up over the walls of the bastille. His expression conveys a sense of dismay. "Traitors or not, these angels are killing their brothers. Their friends. Their fellow soldiers. I made it sound like they were mindless drones earlier, but they're not. They have feelings. I know this is tearing them up."

"It might also explain why they wanted different weapons, ones that could wipe out a greater number with less effort," I theorize. "They wouldn't have to get up close and personal."

What a morbid thought—seeking a less personal way to kill your former allies.

Bron stares at the blade while Augustus continues to gaze into the distance. They're both lost in thought. I'm about to bring their attention back to the here and now when a bizarre noise erupts behind us. We all spin around in unison and search the area surrounding the bastille for its source. We see nothing except for an endless field of waist-high rainbow grass swaying in a non-existent breeze.

Several seconds pass before we hear it again. It's a wailing cry like that of a wounded animal. I've never heard anything quite like it. I step forward to begin searching the grass when Augustus teleports from beside us and is deposited about a hundred yards away in the field. He moves swiftly for a man his age, bending down and grabbing something from the ground. From this distance, it's hard to tell exactly what he's draping over his shoulder. My gut tells me it's a body.

We don't have to wonder long. Augustus zaps back to our side

50 · FALL OF THE ANGELS

and dumps the body from his shoulder the second his feet touch the ground. This man is square-jawed and handsome. His brown hair is medium length and sticks close to his head. His bulging biceps and strapping chest are draped in a white robe that's covered with a golden breastplate. Chainmail armor covers his arms, and spiked gauntlets shroud his hands. My limited vocabulary concerning armor does not contain a word for his leg protection, but to me, it looks like he's wearing metal shin guards.

His appearance is less disconcerting than his behavior, however. This man—who I know right away is an angel—writhes on the ground in apparent agony. I can't tell the color of his eyes because they're rolled back in his head. I can only stare at him while Augustus says something to Bron, who quickly kneels beside the angel and touches a finger to his forehead. Unlike it did for me, this action does not result in the angel losing consciousness. Instead, his body quiets, and he lies there for a moment drawing deep breaths. It's almost like his body is rebooting.

"Who is he?" I ask.

"Puriel," Bron answers. "He examines the souls of those who are brought to Heaven."

"Do we know what side he's on?"

"The right side," Augustus says simply.

Puriel's eyes open slowly, like a man pulled gently from a dream. He looks first at Bron, then at Augustus, and finally at me. When his eyes find me, he furrows his brow, and his jaw clenches.

I instinctively pull away and clench my fists. But instead of escalating the situation, Puriel pushes himself into a seated position and grips his head between his hands. For the moment, I relax. Whatever Bron did to him, I'm not sure the effect has worn off yet. He looks slightly dazed.

"How are you feeling, Puriel?" Bron asks him.

"Confused. Sore," he answers in a baritone voice. "I am not sure why I am here."

"Neither are we," Augustus tells him. "We found you in that field over there. You were bellowing like a wounded animal and appeared to be in a lot of pain. That's why Bron zapped you. Do you remember what you were doing here? Were you part of the battle?"

"I think so. My recollections are hazy, though. I believe we were fighting the rebellious brethren in the skies above the bastille. I remember flashes of color and sound. Then I got hit from behind. It was not a blade, nor any other form of angelic weaponry that laid me low. It was something else."

"Oh dear," Bron says quietly.

My blood runs cold at these words. Bron looks dismayed. Whatever he's about to say, I know in my gut it won't bode well for our efforts to quell this destructive conflict.

"When the blast hit you from behind, what did it feel like?" Bron asks Puriel.

Puriel stares at the ground. He shakes his head as he tries to remember the attack. Several seconds pass, and I'm beginning to wonder if he simply can't answer the question.

He finally does. "Like I was hit by a wall of fire," he replies.

"And in your head," Bron tells him quietly, "you heard the sound of rushing water."

Puriel is dumbstruck. "How could you possibly know that?"

"Oh hell," Augustus grumbles, and my stomach drops again. "Tell me we're not dealing with what I think we're dealing with, Bron. Tell me we're not already to that point."

Bron lifts his gaze from Puriel's face and nods solemnly at Augustus, who sighs deeply and rubs his face with his hand. I'm reminded of the discussions Colin would have with various members of his team when he was dealing with bad news he didn't want to share with me. I didn't like being left in the dark then, and I like it even less now, when time is of the utmost importance.

Of all the things Augustus could have passed on to his grandson...

"What are we dealing with, guys?" I ask the pair.

"It's the staff of Moses," Augustus says reluctantly. "Puriel was attacked by an angel wielding the staff that Moses used to part the Red Sea."

"Which means...oh shit," I say as the horrifying realization dawns on me.

"The angels have already been to the armory," Bron confirms. "Right now, God's personal cache of weapons is in the hands of angels, both friend and foe. The firepower they now control is hard to put into words. The road to stopping this war just got a lot steeper."

My laugh is a hollow chuckle, the likes of which I'd usually follow with a four-letter expletive.

"At this point," I tell the group, "I'd say we're trying to ice skate uphill."

CHAPTER 5

STAFF MEETING

BRON DOESN'T UNDERSTAND MY REFERENCE, and we don't have time for me to explain that it comes from a comic book movie about a vampire slayer who uses a sword and swears a lot. We have bigger issues to deal with, starting with the fact that Puriel is now standing and examining his armor.

There has to be a way for us to use this angel to our advantage. He's already tipped us off to the fact that the angels have ransacked the armory. If we press him, we might be able to learn about the strategies or tactics being employed by both sides. With the deck stacked so decisively against us, some solid intelligence could be the starting point we need to formulate an actual plan.

I find myself again wondering what Colin would do in this situation, and I'm struck by the image of my friends pinned down in a bunker trying to formulate their own plan. That's all the motivation I need to do something that can advance our cause. The clock is ticking up here and down there. Both groups are counting on me, which means I have to work fast.

"We need your help," I say to Puriel, who looks up and stares quizzically at me.

"Excuse me?" he scoffs.

"We're trying to stop this conflict before it turns Heaven into a smoldering crater. Thanks to you, we know the angels have access to the armory weapons, and that's a good start. But we need more information. We need you to tell us anything that might help us end this war."

Now Puriel looks angry. What I've said must have offended him.

"End this war?" he cries. "On whose authority? We obey the commands of God almighty, our heavenly father. Are you to tell me that you know better than God what should be done?"

"I don't pretend to be God. But I know your conflict is going to destroy Heaven, especially now that both sides have armory weapons. Doesn't that seem a little counterproductive to your mission

of protecting Heaven? What happens if the fighting reaches the throne room?"

"How dare you question our ability to defend our home."

Puriel steps forward and points his finger in my face. His eyes are blazing, and the muscles in his neck are bulging. Augustus and Bron move toward me, but I hold up my hand to stop their advance. I'm not scared of this angel. I have to make him see what's right in front of his face.

"So you're certain you can defeat the traitors before Heaven is permanently damaged by your fighting? You know beyond any doubt that you'll claim victory before reaching the throne?"

There it is—that split second of hesitation.

"Of course we will!" the angel bellows, but his eyes betray him. There's doubt buried deep within him. He knows what we're saying is the truth, but he won't let himself admit it. I have to draw it out of him using the universal language that all angels speak.

"Hold that thought," I say to Puriel. I step around the angel and gesture at Augustus, whose half-smile is all too revealing. "Augustus, with the weapons from the armory at their disposal, what is the likely strategy going to be for both sides moving forward?"

"They'll be moving fast," he answers. "Even with the armory weapons in tow, angels don't linger long during battle. They hit hard, and they hit fast. And with the armory weapons in play, that hit will be a helluva lot bigger."

"You know nothing of the strategies we angels use in combat," Puriel snarls. "This is empty talk from a fool who is trying to prove a point. Nothing more."

I worry this comment might send Augustus into a rage. I know I'd be pissed if Puriel insulted me like that. Instead, Augustus merely shrugs. I admire his restraint. We don't need this moment to erupt into violence when Puriel is close to validating our argument. I saw my opening in that brief moment when he paused. The door is cracked. We simply need to kick it open.

STAFF MEETING · 57

"Actually, his words are not the ramblings of a fool," Bron says slowly. His clear, sparkling eyes bore into Puriel with a quiet determination. "You and I both know Augustus speaks the truth. We know because we've seen it before. Don't stand on this sacred ground and speak lies, Puriel."

"I have no idea of that which you speak, Bronze Man," Puriel says. Despite the defiant tone, I can hear the deceit in his voice. He doesn't believe what he's saying. This is all an act.

"Shame on you, Puriel. You were quite the decorated war hero when Lucifer and his followers were cast out of Heaven. The battle moved slowly at first, don't you remember?"

Puriel maintains his stony silence. Bron continues anyway, lost in the story.

"God's angels possessed the armory weapons and waited for the opportune time to strike. Lucifer and his followers were encamped inside the bastille. I remember it all so vividly. The tension on either side simmered like a newborn star. It was as if all of Heaven held its breath in anticipation of that first blow. But neither side wanted to make the first move."

"They were scared. Lucifer knew he was fighting a losing battle."

This comment comes not from Bron but Puriel. His tough-guy facade has finally cracked, and a smile flits across his face. Bron's story did the trick; now the door is standing ajar. We're close to breaking through to the other side. Now we need to guide Puriel to the finish line. He'll resist if the idea comes from us. But if he arrives at our conclusion on his own, he won't put up a fight.

"Exactly," Bron exclaims. "Some might argue that Lucifer's plan all along was to lose the fight and paint himself as a sympathetic figure. Either way, his forces were merely biding their time inside the bastille. Once they chose to attack, the fight would be over just as quickly."

"In the end, it was the foolhardy confidence that doomed the traitor," Puriel tells us. "He stirred his followers into a furious rage

inside the bastille and then offered them as lambs to the slaughter. With the weapons of God at our disposal, our victory was swift and absolute."

"You came face to face with him, didn't you?" Bron asks.

"I looked the traitor in the eyes and saw nothing but terror and cowardice. I raised my sword to strike him down, but God intervened. He cast Lucifer and the remaining angels out of Heaven."

"You saw him? Lucifer?" I ask quietly.

This question isn't part of my Jedi mind trick. I'm simply stunned at the thought of standing before an angel who was there when Lucifer staged his rebellion against God. An angel who fought in that battle and raised his sword to take on the Devil himself. Puriel's cold demeanor makes it easy to dislike him, but there's no denying his bravery. He stared down Beelzebub and didn't even blink.

I would have fainted and pissed my pants in that situation. At the same time, most likely.

This angel can be a powerful ally. Show him the respect he so desperately wants.

I nod ever so slightly at Augustus to let him know I got his message.

"He stood no farther from me than you are right now," Puriel answers. "What you must understand about Lucifer is that he is a deceiver, not a warrior. His tongue has always been forked. He convinces his allies to die on his behalf and tricks his enemies into laying down their weapons. Had God not dealt with that snake, I would have been honored to strike him down."

"That's incredibly brave," I confess. "Had Malphas not kidnapped my brother, I never would have summoned the courage to face him. Where do you get your strength, Puriel?"

The angel stands up a little straighter.

"From the Lord, who equips all of us with the tools we need to carry out our mission. When you serve on the side of righteousness, Mr. Ford, you need not fear evil. The wicked never triumph because

STAFF MEETING · 59

the righteous never falter in their convictions. Agents of evil are, without fail, cowards."

The angel strides toward me, causing my muscles to tense. He merely places a hand on my shoulder and looks down at me. Up close, I can feel his well-built frame radiating power.

"Now excuse me while I rejoin my brethren in our fight against this new group of cowards," he says.

His hand leaves my shoulder, and he steps around me. This is my last opportunity. If I don't convince him now, he'll be in the wind, and we'll be back to square one. I don't have time for that.

With tendrils of panic creeping up my throat, I call after him.

"Your enemies might be cowards, but they'll die in battle if that's what it takes."

Puriel freezes in his tracks and cocks an ear my way. I continue.

"You can see in their eyes how desperate they are now that they've committed to this path. You are equally committed to yours. Your ideologies are two freight trains barreling down the tracks toward each other. When that collision happens, it's going to decimate Heaven."

My final sentence hangs in the air. I look at Augustus and motion for him to jump in. His expression reminds me of a groomsman unexpectedly asked to speak at a wedding, but he recovers.

"We want to help you defeat the traitors and keep our home intact," he implores with gusto. "Take us to the archangels, and let us make our case. They'll make the final call. That's all we ask."

Puriel turns his head and stares at his feet. I eye my companions with hopeful anticipation, and they return similar looks. My heart races like I'm awaiting a big verdict in court. When the angel lifts his face to us, his softened expression gives me hope. He opens his mouth to speak.

"I will take you to the place where fighting has resumed. I cannot guarantee an audience with the archangels, and I do not support your calls for a ceasefire. But I am not so blind as to miss

the damage our battles are causing. I agree—the end result could be...cataclysmic."

"Thank you," I reply, my hands clasped in front of me. "You are doing the right thing."

The angel pauses, and I can see a wave of skepticism wash over him.

"We shall see," he answers. "Gather round and grab my arm."

The angel extends his right arm, and I move to take hold of it right above his spiked gauntlet. The hairless forearm is tight like coiled steel and cold to the touch. Augustus sidles in next to me and places a hand by mine. His other arm makes a subtle movement on the other side of his body. I quickly realize he's got his fingers wrapped around that blade on his hip.

This causes a momentary geyser of panic to erupt in my stomach. Augustus knows these angels far better than I do. If he's nervous, I've got reason to worry. I shoot him a fleeting glance that I hope conveys the sudden unease his action has stirred inside me. He shakes his head imperceptibly.

The geyser in my stomach slows from an eruption to a mild bubbling.

On the other side of Puriel's arm, Bron has to squat down to grab hold. Rather than wrapping his massive hand around Puriel's arm, Bron simply touches it with a footlong bronze finger. Now that we're all assembled, Puriel closes his eyes and moves his head ever so slightly from one side to the other. If his eyes weren't closed, you'd swear he was speed reading. In the silence that accompanies this bizarre trance, I can hear Augustus tighten the grip on his blade.

Stop that. You're going to give me an ulcer.

By failing to prepare, you are preparing to fail.

I smile and shake my head at Augustus's response. Nothing makes you sound like an old man faster than quoting Benjamin Franklin. Colin wouldn't even go that far.

STAFF MEETING · 61

Try to keep the lines clear, gentlemen. Our friend is scanning angel radio to determine our destination. We do not want to make his job more difficult by clouding the airwaves at this moment.

Then I guess you better put a lid on it, Bron.

I fight back laughter and stare at the ground. If I see Bron's reaction to that burn, I'll lose it.

Augustus Shaw, I never thought you of all people would...

"Found it," Puriel barks. His clear voice cutting through the silence makes me jump. He eyes me suspiciously, and I mumble an apology. The sound of Augustus laughing is unmistakable in my head. Puriel finishes, "Hold tight. This transference will be over shortly."

Teleportation is old hat at this point. The wormhole is a brilliant white light that surrounds the four of us. With my eyes closed, I can picture my comrades as they fly along beside me. Augustus will maintain that rock-star cool he perfected over the course of 137 years. Bron will try to appear regal and fail miserably. He's too damn awkward to ever look any way but goofy.

Me? I simply hope I don't look as nervous as I feel. Because I have serious doubts that my plan can succeed. Augustus entertained my idea despite his misgivings, but that's likely thanks to his trepidation at ejecting every angel from Heaven and our burgeoning familial relationship. I want to reward his faith in me with a step in the right direction. We don't have to resolve this entire conflict right now. Merely establishing an open line of communication with the archangels would be a huge victory. They can reject our line of thinking. I just hope they'll hear us out.

�֏ ✠ ✠

THE NEWEST ARENA OF BATTLE IS STARKLY DIFFERENT than the bastille. Gone are the swaying, knee-high grasses and the foreboding structure reminiscent of an impenetrable fortress. We're

surrounded on all sides by towering, jagged rocks stained crimson, dark purple, and black. This twisted landscape is a cross between Bron's home in the canyon and the streets of a big city. It's hard not to feel claustrophobic with such sharp and dangerous rock formations looming over your head.

I make this assessment seconds after the wormhole deposits us on craggy ground and the warmth of its white light disappears. The next thing my brain registers is Puriel cocking his head to one side like a dog who's just heard a disconcerting noise. Our hands fall away from his chiseled forearm as he moves toward the noise he heard, his head still cocked in that direction.

That's when I notice the noise for myself. For a second, I'm reminded of the cacophony that consumed the lumberyard in Sherwood during our battle against Malphas and his demons. That noise was like firecrackers going off inside an old metal barrel. The sound that I'm hearing now—and that I assume Puriel hears—is less staccato and more sonorous. It's the kind of sound I'd imagine two skyscrapers would make as they fell into each other or that two cruise ships would produce as one sideswiped the other. Whatever it resembles, the noise signifies one thing.

The battle raging here is ferocious, and our path to the archangels will be filled with peril. We have to keep Puriel focused on getting us through the battle to see his commanders. Even with Augustus at our side, I don't like our chances of navigating angelic warfare without a guide.

That's when Puriel flies away, his dark, spectral wings pinned back behind him. He zooms straight ahead, banks up and over a snarl of razor-sharp rocks, and disappears from view. The hand I had used to grip his arm stretches sadly out before me. I didn't even have time to raise it and beckon him back before he vanished from sight. He was there one moment and gone the next.

Like a ghost, his sudden absence makes me wonder if he was ever there at all.

STAFF MEETING · 63

Am I even here right now? Or is this all a bad dream?

If I tap my heels three times, will I end up back in my bed the night before my twenty fifth birthday?

I close my eyes and rub my face. Behind my eyes, tears are welling up and threatening to seep out. I can't articulate why this turn of events has cued up the waterworks. I was holding it together so well in spite of everything that's happened. I had a plan and a purpose to get us closer to our goal of ending this war and getting me back to Sherwood. I was moving forward with my eyes fixed straight ahead. Now I feel fragile enough to disintegrate and be swept away in the wind.

"Everything is so hard," I whisper in a trembling voice. "Damn it."

"Come here, kid."

I don't hear Augustus as he approaches me and wraps me up in a hug. My face finds his shoulder and spills tears on his dark green duster jacket. His scent is aftershave and cigarette smoke, and while his hugs aren't as rib-cracking as Colin's, I'm still reminded of my grandfather and the unwavering emotional support he provided while Peter was held captive.

Colin will never know how much I appreciated having a shoulder to cry on during that ordeal. I doubt Augustus knows how much this means to me now, when it feels like the whole world is falling apart. Or maybe he knows exactly what his gesture means. Perhaps good hugs run in the family.

I pull away and gulp down a ragged breath. Our eyes meet, and I nod, so Augustus smiles and nods back. I see in his expression the concern a parent would have for a child and wonder for a moment what Augustus was like as a father. I don't have time to ponder this mystery, however, as the feeling of a massive hand touching my shoulder causes me to jump.

Bron has knelt down beside me and looks concerned.

"Are you alright, Silas Ford? You seem upset."

I actually find myself laughing at Bron's adorably awkward

attempt to console me. He's just too big and too goofy and too...
bronze to try something like that and not elicit bemused laughter.

My reaction transforms Bron's expression to one of confusion, so
I tell him, "I'm fine now. Puriel abandoning us was one gut punch
too many, I guess. Thanks for asking, Bron."

Bron's programming for human interaction appears to have run
out. His half-smile and sparkling eyes betray the panic he feels at
not knowing what to say next. He clasps his hands together and
slowly rises to full height. The entire time, his eyes never leave me.

"That's...an appropriate reaction—it would seem—for you to
have. I understand why that would make you feel so...um, that way.
The way that you felt, just now."

"Couldn't have said it better myself, Bron," Augustus deadpans.

Now that we've thoroughly humiliated our large, bronze companion, we have to decide how we want to proceed. I have serious
reservations about slogging through a foreign battlefield comprised
of a million butcher knives disguised as rocks. With both sides in
possession of armory weapons, who knows what kind of horrible
death awaits us if we get caught in the crossfire?

I also have no desire to sit here and do nothing. Sherwood and
my friends need me, and although we've lost our guide, we're in the
same neighborhood as the archangels. It won't be easy to find them,
but we can do it. I overcame bigger obstacles to defeat Malphas.

There's a solution here—we just have to find it.

What would Colin do? He wouldn't charge into the battle half-
cocked and reckless like Peter after a few too many at Tully's Tavern.
He would utilize the skillsets of his companions and come up with
a plan that maximized their talents and minimized the risk to all
involved. His plans appealed to my logical mind because they were
well-reasoned and deliberate. Sometimes things went sideways, and
people got killed, but I never once doubted that he'd given us the
best chance to win.

I know what Bron and Augustus can contribute to our victory.

STAFF MEETING · 65

Bron has an encyclopedic knowledge of Heaven's layout. If anyone can help us navigate this new area, he can. Augustus is one of the most feared nephilim warriors ever. He shrinks from no challenge or adversary.

Combined with my youthful exuberance, we form quite the fearsome trio.

"We can still do this," I tell the others. "The only question is how we go about it."

Augustus gives me a knowing smile, and I'm buoyed by his unspoken accord. Bron is stoic but resolved, and I see a quiet determination burning behind those bright eyes. No doubt he's trying to recall every detail of this place that's stored in his expansive memory.

"The challenge is going to be getting around the battle and not going through it," Augustus asserts. "My best guess is that the archangels will be at the highest point in this area. Wars in Heaven are no different than those on Earth. They'll want to control the high ground. Bron, what's the best vantage point for this battlefield, and is there a path of least resistance that could get us there?"

"There is an outcropping of rock that rises above the rest of its surroundings," Bron answers. "It's west of here, approximately twenty flights away. Sorry, Silas—a flight is equivalent to three hundred feet in human measurements. It's the distance an angel can fly in one second."

"So it's a little over a mile away," I conclude.

"Precisely," Bron confirms. "Given that none of us can fly, there are twenty-eight possible paths that we could pursue from our location to that outcropping. Three of those paths would get us killed within five flights; eight would likely be conflict areas given their unique topography and judging by the direction of that calamitous noise, which means we're left with seventeen other options. Of those, two are known to only myself, God, and the archangels."

"Of course, it's two," Augustus moans. "Where would the danger

be if we didn't have to choose which path we think is least likely to kill us? Damn it, Bron."

"I apologize, Augustus," Bron says quietly.

"No, I'm not mad at you. It's frustrating for reasons I have neither the time nor the stamina to explain. Reasons that stretch back many, many years. It's not your fault, though."

"Two is better than twenty-eight," I tell Augustus, who acknowledges that silver lining with a nod. "In your opinion, Bron, which path gets us there faster and with less risk?"

"I'm sorry to once again offer a dichotomous answer," he says tentatively, "but one path I calculate as being five times faster, while the other is twice as safe. It is, therefore, a question of which condition we most value in this instance—safety or swift travel?"

The answer is obvious. We should take the safer path and give ourselves the best chance of reaching the archangels in one piece. Expediency shouldn't come at the cost of safety. You'd only pick the quicker option if your pants were on fire and the archangels were standing in water. No sane person would risk more danger just to arrive in another dangerous situation quicker.

Then why is it I want to take the faster route? Perhaps chasing after Peter imbued me with some of his reckless spirit, or it could be I'm feeling the pressure of completing this mission quickly and returning home. Whenever I convince myself that safety is the only way forward, my brain responds with, "Being safe is nice and all, but getting there five times faster is pretty nice, too!" Surely Augustus isn't having this same internal struggle. His advanced age has bestowed wisdom upon him, right? He'll say we should play it safe, and off we'll go down that path.

"We should opt for the faster route," he blurts out.

"I know, right?!" I respond, shocked and giddy that he inexplicably feels the same way I do. "I can't explain why, but my mind keeps favoring speed as I'm weighing these two options."

"God gave nephilim good instincts, and mine's saying the same

thing," Augustus says. "We should trust our gut and have faith that God will see us through to the other side."

"A little faith and two good companions by my side," I say. "That's good enough for me. Bron, which way to this faster but more dangerous path? We might as well get started."

Bron points a massive finger about 30 degrees north of the path that Puriel took when he fled. Winding through the craggy rocks is a narrow path that curves away from us and to the left. I point to it, and Bron confirms our path with a nod. I breathe deep, steady my nerves, and start walking.

Time to find us some archangels.

CHAPTER 6

TAKE ONE FOR THE TEAM

IT DOESN'T TAKE LONG FOR ME TO REALIZE WHY Bron said this path was quick but treacherous. We're surrounded on both sides by jagged fingers of rock that reach skyward, but the path is remarkably straight. We haven't deviated to the left or right for more than a few feet. The path becomes a foot wide in a few places as it wraps around the face of a cliff, while other times it's interrupted by a chasm that can be easily jumped but plunges downward into sickening blackness.

Although we're in Heaven, it feels like these pits stretch down to Hell.

The air becomes hotter and stickier the further we go down this path. My breathing becomes ragged, and my legs begin to burn as we jump, shimmy, twist, and turn our way toward the archangels. For a man who's more than a century old, Augustus doesn't seem to be laboring as much as I am. I've stood ready to catch him when we've jumped the chasms, but he's made all the jumps no problem. I'm frankly amazed at his dexterity and startling quickness.

I look back now and see him breathing normally, his gait like that of a spry twenty-year-old. He flashes me a thumbs up, and I shoot him one back. In that moment, I resolve to work on my cardio once I get back to Sherwood, stop the demon apocalypse, and renew my gym membership.

My grandfather's grandfather is making me look like an old man.

Next to Augustus, Bron simply floats along like the mast of a massive ship bobbing slightly on a calm ocean. I hadn't noticed until now, but Bron doesn't breathe. His chest, as big around as my bedroom dresser, is completely still. In spite of how utterly insane his whole existence is, I find this small fact about Bron quite bizarre. It makes me wonder if other heavenly beings breathe.

Does God breathe? For that matter, does God have a body like mine?

It feels like I'm having an out-of-body experience when I ponder questions like these. The concept of God, for most people, is so

70 · FALL OF THE ANGELS

abstract, but now I'm here in the place where he dwells, trying to stop a war between his angels with his architect and his greatest nephilim warrior at my side. To stop and examine my situation, or seriously ponder questions like these, is totally surreal.

As we wind around another precarious cliff face, my mind stumbles over a question I hadn't stopped to ask myself yet: *If given the chance, would I want to meet God?*

Granted, I'm not assuming I'll ever be given that chance. I'm not a Bible scholar, but I do remember Augustus positing that God can't be in the presence of sin, and although I'm, well...dead, I suspect my sin nature is still intact and thus renders me ineligible to meet the big man.

Judging by his comments, Augustus seems to have a favorable impression of God, which makes me wonder if he's ever seen him face-to-face. Bron's title as God's chosen architect leads me to believe he's met with God and spoken to him before. But given his innate oddness and the fact that he's done this job for eons, Bron might not be able to convey the significance of that relationship. Even if they both described it to me, would words do justice to the experience of meeting God?

I met Tom Brady once in an airport, and the way I described that experience to friends—cool, out-of-body, starstruck—failed to capture the feeling it gave me.

Describing a meeting with God? Forget about it.

Such an encounter falls under the category of "you just had to be there."

I know the first question I'll ask God if we do meet: "Why me?"

I'll ask this question, not in the way humanity tends to after natural disasters or personal hardships, but rather as a matter of abject curiosity: of all the billions of people on Earth, why did God choose someone in Augustus's lineage to be the next nephilim?

Greater than any feeling I have toward God for sticking me with this destiny—anger, confusion, resentment—is the sense that

Augustus ties into the reason I was chosen as God's nephilim. It's possible God knew a strong connection would be needed between his nephilim to handle the fallout of Gregori's betrayal. Thinking that many moves ahead makes my brain hurt, but for God, I figure such elaborate planning is likely effortless.

As we hop another chasm and turn sideways to pass a nasty piece of jagged black rock, I consider another question I can't shake, one tied into the first: *Why is Augustus here?*

I'm grateful he is, of course, but as we journey closer to the sounds of battle, I want to know why he's leading this charge to save Heaven. He should have a front-row seat in God's throne room, enjoying his reward for decades spent fighting demons. Instead, he's working behind the scenes to stop this war from decimating his home, seemingly on his own authority.

Or is he working as a secret agent on assignment from God?

My foot catches on a rock, and I stumble, breaking my train of thought. Augustus grabs my shirt from behind, sparing me a headfirst plunge into the void below our feet. I look back at him and offer my thanks, to which he nods and smiles. In that moment, I'm again reminded of Peter. Not only the physical resemblance but the devil-may-care attitude hidden behind his eyes.

There's more to the story with Augustus that I'm eager to learn, but that conversation will have to wait until after we save Heaven. Until then, I'm trusting the man who's twice saved my life.

If we're lucky, I won't have need for a third time.

✝ ✝ ✝

THE CLAMOR OF BATTLE IS EAR-SPLITTING AT THIS point.

We've hopped a few more gaps, shimmied around a couple of cliff walls, and passed hundreds of razor-sharp rocks pointing down at us like a host of angry witnesses. Bron tells us we're within two

flights, or six hundred yards, and Augustus halts our progress to decide our approach with the archangels. A knot is again forming in my stomach—or perhaps it never left—at the thought of trying to convince Heaven's laser-focused killing machines to abort a mission they seem hell-bent on completing. If we can't convince them to see reason, either Heaven or Earth is in deep trouble.

Rather than saying anything, Augustus stares at the ground and sighs. He's lost in thought, trying to conjure up the magical words he needs to pull off this miracle. Having represented some of Sherwood's sleaziest millionaires in court, I understand trying to turn back what feels like an insurmountable tide. Of course, if I failed to convince the judge, my client might do some jail time. If we fail to convince the archangels, everyone on Earth might die. We have zero room for error.

Finally, Augustus speaks.

"These bastards do not care what we have to say. In their eyes, we're inferior beings bringing a message that contradicts their orders. Our only shot is to open with logic—if they don't stop fighting, their conflict could destroy Heaven, and they'll have failed their mission."

"Protecting Heaven from all threats is an angel's singular purpose," Bron adds. "I concur that offering such an argument at the outset would be most likely to grab their attention."

"What happens if they won't talk to us?" I ask.

"We regroup," Augustus replies. "Try a different approach. The one thing we can't do is lose our cool or challenge these guys. They're very powerful, so physical force is not a great option."

Having felt like a child in Gregori's steely grip, I'm not eager to fight an archangel. I'll let my words be my superpower in this instance and try to keep a cool head.

"If you're ready, I can guide us the rest of the way," Bron says. "I know where they'll be."

"You ready, kid?" Augustus asks me.

TAKE ONE FOR THE TEAM · 73

"No," I tell him. "But what choice do we have? Let's do this."

Bron heads out in front of us, twisting his way through the towering rock formations that have started to bend inward over our heads, enclosing us in what's essentially a tunnel of spiky death. It's better than the last tunnel I entered with Augustus, but as I look up at the ragged rock ceiling looming over us, I'm reminded of Puriel's black wings pinned behind his back.

We managed to sway him for a moment, but his soldier mentality never left him. When we needed him the most, he abandoned us to rejoin his brothers in arms. I can't say I blame him—if I had the chance to return to Sherwood right now and help my friends, I'd be gone.

I can only hope the archangels, if we get through to them, won't change course so easily.

"We're going to come over this ridge, and then the bluff where the archangels are gathered will be approximately one flight away," Bron tells us. "As one of God's ambassadors, I will present myself on behalf of our group and request an audience with the archangels."

My heart is hammering now, and it has nothing to do with the steady incline we're climbing. A light emerges from the darkness up ahead, only it's not a bright light. It's darkness illuminated by occasional flashes of white light. It's like we're seeing a thunderstorm from a cave. The sounds of battle that were raging earlier quieted as the rocks encased us, but as we approach the exit now, they're ramping back up like someone cranking the volume on a stereo.

We're engulfed in a mind-numbing hum the second we emerge from the tunnel. I cover my ears with my hands, unable to see straight or concentrate with the sound boring into my brain. Even Augustus is struggling with the sensory overload. Through half-closed eyes, I spot him a few steps ahead with his head leaned against his right shoulder, sheltering that ear from the noise. His left hand is gripping the wall in what I guess is an effort to steady himself. He looks back at me, and though my eyes are half-closed, I can see

concern fill his face. I want to go to him and explain what's happening, but the sound is simply too overwhelming. I don't think I can go any further.

Blackness overtakes my peripheral vision as I sink to one knee.

Fight it, Silas. You've dealt with worse. Don't let this take you down.

A large bronze finger swings briefly into my field of vision before tapping the top of my head. Just as if someone pulled the plug on that stereo, the noise ceases immediately. I pull my hands away from my ears and dab at my watery eyes with my shirt. I rise and see Bron and Augustus standing in front of me. Augustus points to his ear and shakes his head. He taps his finger to his forehead, taps mine, and nods his head. Finally, he flashes me a thumbs up to make sure I understand.

Thank you. That noise...it was overwhelming.

Bron nods at my gratitude.

I've turned off your ears and switched our internal frequency to a channel the angels aren't using. When we approach the archangels, I'll have to switch us over to communicate with them.

Are you good to keep going?

I nod to answer Augustus's question and give him a thumbs up.

They turn, and Bron leads us up a path that curves out of sight to the left. Now that the vibrations aren't melting my brain, I'm free to soak in my front-row seat to angelic warfare. The sky is deep purple with fiery streaks shooting in every direction. Pulses of light illuminate our surroundings like fireworks on July 4th. Without the sound, I now feel detached from what's happening around us, when a moment ago, I couldn't escape it. It's an eerie sensation.

The ground begins to level out, and up ahead, we finally see the bluff where the archangels are gathered. Their imposing figures cut impressive silhouettes against the exploding sky behind them. Their backs are to us as they survey the battlefield stretching out in seemingly every direction. Unlike Puriel, these angels wear full suits of armor that are silver with gold accents at the wrists, ankles,

and waist. Each one carries a massive sword in a sheath at their right side. From this distance, they appear powerfully built, if not smaller than what I'd imagined. Each angel is wrapped in a soft, almost imperceptible white glow. When combined with their posture and muscular build, there's no denying the presence these archangels have about them. They just look like God's angelic leaders.

Switching us over to their channel now. I'll make the introduction, then let Augustus make our case.

The next voice I hear is unfamiliar. It's low, strong, and slow.

Bronze Man, why have you come here? State your purpose and do so quickly.

Michael, Gabriel, Raphael—my companions and I humbly request an audience with the three of you to discuss an urgent matter. I am here with Augustus Shaw and Silas Ford, two of God's chosen nephilim.

Although we're standing ten feet away, the archangels still haven't turned around. The two in front pay us no mind, their full focus still on the battle before them. The one closest to us cocks his head to glance at us over his shoulder, revealing a strong, square jaw and dark eyes narrowed with suspicion. Or perhaps it's curiosity. I can't get a good read from this distance.

I hold my breath as the nearest angel considers this request. The only sound I hear in this auditory void is my heart beating frantically against my ribs.

I clear my mind so as not to cloud the airwaves or influence the angel's decision.

We will grant this request, but only because of the esteem afforded you by your position.

My companions and I are extremely grateful.

The knot in my stomach loosens. One hurdle down. One big one to go.

Bron motions us forward as the archangels finally turn to face us. The nearest one that spoke to us has sharp features with a nose that appears broken. His hair is chestnut brown and styled high

and tight. Three scars give his face a battle-worn look: one on his chin, a horizontal one across the bridge of his crooked nose, and the longest one running from his temple to his cheek. Those dark eyes examine the three of us as we approach, pausing to give me longer consideration.

My name is Michael. These are my brothers, Gabriel and Raphael.

Michael motions to his right at Gabriel and to his left at Raphael. Gabriel is the biggest of the three, barrel-chested with biceps as big as my head. His blonde hair is shoulder length and smooth, and though he eyes us with trepidation, his face is friendlier than Michael's scarred visage.

Raphael is bald, dark-skinned, and has striking green eyes. Tattoos that resemble ancient runes cover his upper arms. A gleaming silver dagger is clenched in his right hand.

A sly smile flits across Raphael's face that I read as: *Get a load of these guys. This should be good.*

Bron steps forward and gestures at Augustus.

I believe you all know Augustus. He will be speaking on behalf of our group.

Augustus nods his thanks to Bron and steps forward to address the angels, who shift their attention to him. Michael's gaze, however, keeps darting over to look me up and down.

It's an unsettling feeling, but I try to focus on Augustus.

Thank you again for your time. I will be brief—the war between these angelic factions is going to destroy Heaven. The traitors who support Gregori and Malphas will stop at nothing to reach the throne room and free Asaroth. The fallout will only increase with the armory weapons now in play. I urge you to call for a ceasefire and negotiate terms with the traitors. I believe they know they will lose and would rather die than give up. I'm hoping they will lay down their arms if shown mercy. But if you continue to push them, they will set fire to Heaven just to watch it burn.

Michael is unmoved. He lets out a snort and turns to smile at

Raphael. When he looks back at us, I can see in his eyes he almost pities us. *Poor, pitiful humans*, he must think. *Thinking they know better than God's biggest, baddest angels how to protect our home. That is adorable.*

His response is somehow more insufferable than my impression.

This is why you came here, nephilim? To tell the most trusted angels of God, the greatest warriors in all the universe, how to manage a war against traitorous scum? Such arrogance is laughable, even for you.

Again, Augustus takes a cutting insult in stride. He nods and holds his hands up.

I know it seems like I'm stepping out of line, but this conflict is unprecedented. Lucifer's plan was to sacrifice his followers to spite God. They were nothing but pawns to him. These angels have no leader but rather a single objective to rally around—to free Asaroth. They're totally unpredictable, which makes them dangerous.

Raphael pushes past Michael to confront Augustus. My neck muscles tighten as my hands clench into fists. I have to restrain myself from rushing forward to step between them.

Augustus doesn't move, looking at Raphael like a piece of art he's trying to understand.

We are well aware of the traitors and their intentions. The question is, why you felt compelled to journey here and tell us that which we already know? What was your plan, nephilim, if we said "no" to your request?

Panic reaches up and grips my throat. If the angels know about Lightfall, which I assume they do, the three of us could be in deep shit if these three learn we're considering it. We came here peacefully, but things could get ugly if Augustus doesn't choose his words carefully.

From the side, I catch only half of Augustus's playful smile.

I was going to activate Lightfall and send your arrogant ass packing.

Oh, shit.

Raphael's fist rises in slow motion. The fire in his eyes says

Augustus is toast if I don't step in and do something. Sparing a quick glance at Bron, I see him rooted in place, his frozen expression a mix of shock and fear. I dart forward to insert myself between Augustus and Raphael before the angel's blow can land. I may be a bug about to meet a windshield, but the old man has already saved my life twice. Besides, if anyone is going to stop this angelic civil war, it's him.

Stop!

I grab Augustus by the shoulder and launch myself into the path of Raphael's descending fist. Augustus tries to throw me to the side to spare me the blow, but my forward momentum carries me directly into the path of the angel's punch. His knuckles slam into my right temple but I don't feel the pain right away. Probably because of the adrenaline. All I see is a pop of white stars.

Half a second later, I'm yanked backward away from the group by an invisible hook. Augustus's mouth tears open in a scream as he lunges after me, but it's too late. The golden light of a wormhole opens and swallows me whole. The world fades to black once again as the pain of Raphael's blow shoots like lightning across my skull. In my head, I hear a final cry from Augustus.

What have you done?

I have no idea, Augustus, but I'll probably regret it in the morning.

CHAPTER 7

SHORT, PALE, AND MYSTERIOUS

THE GROUND UNDERNEATH ME IS UNEVEN AND warm against my back.

That's the first thing I notice as my eyes slowly open to reveal a blazing sun above me. As my vision comes back into focus, I realize I'm actually staring at two suns that are sliding past each other in opposite directions. Their movement is slow but noticeable.

I place my palms flat against the ground and feel sand between my fingers, coarse and warm from the presence of the dual suns overhead. I lie there for a while and assess my situation. I remember stepping in front of Raphael to spare Augustus a punch I thought at the time might kill him. I try to move my jaw, but it's stiff and radiates sharp pain up my face with every movement.

My actions were noble but dumb. While he might be an old man, Augustus has probably taken his fair share of punches. Before this week, I'd only taken a couple of shots across the jaw in my entire life, the worst being from Tony Marini at Tully's Tavern on my twenty-fifth birthday.

Now I'm taking cheap shots from freaking archangels.

Both Tony and Raphael's punches hurt, but only one of them knocked me through an interdimensional wormhole into a part of Heaven I've never seen before.

I fight through the grogginess to muster what little reasoning ability I have left in my aching brain. If Raphael didn't intend to kill Augustus, he at least wanted to take him off the board by isolating him in a remote part of Heaven. Wherever I am, I'm guessing my friends are far away.

I attempt to reach out to Bron and Augustus through our shared telepathy, but all I get is a buzzing in my head like the static of the radio. The sound is torturous to my already throbbing head, so I turn off the telepathy for now. Raphael's punch must've taken my angel radio offline.

I've been sucker-punched to the outskirts of Heaven with no

way to contact my friends. I came up with some dicey plans to stop Malphas, but this one might be my worst yet.

Not that much planning went into taking that punch for Augustus. It was purely reactionary. My instincts told me to spare a family member from pain, and my body obliged. My jaw wishes I'd stayed out of the conflict, but I'd say it's accustomed to the abuse by now.

If I just lie here and take a nap, maybe my face will feel better when I wake up...

✛ ✛ ✛

I'M INSIDE AN OLD PICKUP TRUCK DRIVING FAST DOWN a two-lane road as trees zoom by on either side. Colin is to my left, and Peter sits at my right. They're both stoic, looking through the windshield without saying a word. I turn around and see Grace and Forrest sitting in the bed, their gazes fixed on the flora that's become a green and brown blur at the speed we're moving. There's no air blowing through the vents, which explains why both windows are rolled all the way down. Wind howls in and fills the cabin with chilly evening air.

I stare at Peter as the silence stretches on. His usual baby-faced stubble has grown into a poor imitation of a beard. Dark circles lay beneath both his eyes. I can see his stress etched into the lines of his face. My brother looks worn down. I wonder when he last got a full night's sleep.

When he opens his mouth to speak, I lean in with anticipation.

"Six weeks," he says. His voice is flat and hoarse. "He's been gone six weeks."

"I know," comes Colin's reply.

My heartbeat quickens. Who are they talking about?

"Do you think something happened?" Peter asks.

Colin stares ahead without blinking. He waits a moment to answer.

SHORT, PALE, AND MYSTERIOUS · 83

"No," he says. "We'd know. We'd feel it."

"Would we? I'd like to believe that, but I don't...I just don't know."

"We'd know, Peter. Trust me."

Peter sighs and rubs his eyes. His gaze finds the floor and remains there.

"I really miss him," he whispers.

"Me too, kid. But he'll come back. We have to believe that."

"I do believe it. He told me he would. But I'm worried. Six weeks..."

Oh, God. It can't be true.

"He'll be back. Silas always keeps his promises."

I'm yanked up from the truck, soaring high into the air, my scream lost to winds.

✠ ✠ ✠

SIX WEEKS. I'VE BEEN GONE FROM EARTH FOR SIX WEEKS.

I roll that fact around in my mind, but it seems so foreign, so absolutely ludicrous. I'd sooner believe that Peter was giving up drinking than accept that I've been here that long. Bron did say that time is meaningless in Heaven, but I assumed that only applied to beings like him. With my humanity still intact, I've been perceiving time in a linear fashion ever since I arrived. It feels like half a day since Gregori greeted me outside the gates, maybe twenty-four hours at the most.

But, my brain chimes in, *your perception of time has little bearing on its passing.*

I know this is true despite my desire to ignore such a fact. When you factor in relativity—a concept I only understand because of the movie *Interstellar*—and the fact that I'm in another dimension with its own rules for the passage of time, I can't deny the validity of my vision.

If I'm taking these visions at face value, I have to accept that what Peter said was true.

As this realization washes over me, the tears begin to flow down the side of my face. I recall the exhaustion in Peter's expression, how worn down and scared he sounded. Colin's voice, usually brimming with love and reassurance, was filled with doubt and anxiety. My chest tightens as the vision replays in my mind. I've let down the two people in the world I love the most, right when they need me more than ever. I know it's not my fault that Malphas killed me and brought his wrath down upon Sherwood, but I can't help but feel guilty. Not only is my family dealing with the fallout of the attack, they're trying to cope with my prolonged absence. In the few seconds I sat between them, I could feel the despair they shared. My being gone is killing them.

I lie in the sand and sob until my ribs hurt, and as the tears flow, the guilt and dread I feel ebbs out of me like water circling the drain. In its place is anger over the injustice of my situation. I never asked to be part of this angelic war, yet Augustus gave me no choice. Rather than pursuing the ruthless course of action, I opted for the diplomatic, decent resolution to Heaven's war.

Where did that bit of selflessness get me?

On my back in the middle of a literal God-forsaken desert, separated from my only allies with our communication cut off and no knowledge of how to get back to familiar territory.

But, my mind chimes in again, *every minute you lie here and sulk could be costing you days on Earth.*

Damn it, brain. Can't you leave me alone and let me be pissed?

Not when your family is depending on you. Now get your ass up and get moving.

I oblige, though my body aches and my legs wobble as I pull myself upright. A vast, flat desert stretches out in every direction. Unlike the deserts on Earth, there are no dunes here. As I observe the landscape for a moment, I realize why—there's no wind in this place. The air is still and warm, and the silence is so absolute that all I hear are my ragged inhales and exhales. I scan

the horizon looking for some kind of feature to orient myself, but there's nothing here.

As despair floods my chest, I spot something—or someone—silhouetted against the harsh sunlight moving toward me. What appears to be a head bobs up and down as this mysterious figure slowly approaches. A large cloak covers their entire frame, but from what I can gather at this distance, this stranger is about my height, maybe a little shorter. For the first time since arriving in Heaven, I clench my fists and try to summon a cleansing flame.

The power that usually radiates out from the middle of my chest doesn't start flowing right away. Like a clogged drain, the power is stuck behind something that resists my summoning.

"Come on," I whisper as my panic rises. "Fire for me, baby. You can do it."

The stranger is now within a hundred yards. Their deliberate pace hasn't changed. I have less than a minute to fire up my cleansing flame before I'm no longer standing here alone.

If this stranger means me harm, and I have no weapons to fight them with, I'm screwed.

"Fire, fire, fire," I tell my latent powers. "Come on, do this for me."

Fifty yards. Forty. Thirty.

God, if you give a crap about me, I'd really appreciate some help here.

A spark ignites in my chest, and my power starts flowing again. Whatever was clogging it up dissolved the moment I petitioned God for help. All the hairs on my neck are standing up.

God answered my calls for help indirectly during our battle with Malphas. An image of Bill transferring his power to me flashes through my mind. This is the first time I've asked God for help and received a direct answer so quickly. Either my proximity to his throne room has sped up God's response—unlikely since, you know, it's God—or he sees how dire my situation has become.

Whatever the reason, I'm thankful for the assist as the stranger

is now just ten feet away. I don't say a word as they stop five feet from me and lift their head to look at me. The stranger is half a foot shorter than me, and the shadow inside their hood obscures their face. My heart pounds as the silence between us stretches out for a few tension-filled moments.

Remembering my new time burden, I decide to break the silence.

"With how quickly you found me, it's almost like you were expecting me."

Two pale hands emerge from the arms of the cloak and pull back the hood. The face that was obscured by shadows is undoubtedly human…but not entirely so. This stranger is a stunningly beautiful woman whose skin is so pale it's almost translucent. Her eyes are light, steely blue, and her mouth curves up into a sly smile. Looking at her, I'm reminded of Lamia, except not as sinister. Malphas's first lieutenant always reminded me of a coiled snake waiting to strike.

This woman lacks that edge, but there's still something off about her visage that I can't place. It could be her coy smile, the piercing eyes, or the jet-black hair against her fair skin.

"I wasn't far away when the wormhole dumped you here," she says in a voice that's an octave lower than I expected. "Plus, you laid in the sand and cried for quite a while."

My face grows hot with embarrassment at this comment.

"How did you know I was crying?" I ask, upset with her eaves-dropping on a private moment.

She motions with one hand at the desert around us.

"With no wind and no hills, sound travels far here in the out-skirts. Especially sobbing."

Whoever this woman is, she's goading me into a reaction with her comments about my outburst. I keep my expression neutral, not wanting to give her the satisfaction.

"The outskirts, huh?" I ask. "Does that mean we're at the edge of Heaven?"

My hope is to change the subject, and she plays along, flashing me another quick smile.

"We're past the edge of Heaven, darling," she replies coolly. "The Outer Realm marks the boundary, but from what I've gathered, the angels decimated that area during their little skirmish. We're in a cozy pocket dimension that is Heaven-adjacent where God likes to store his trash."

This is not good...if she's telling the truth, I'm not even in Heaven anymore!

That could explain why my telepathy isn't working.

I try to keep calm, but my anxiety is climbing the more I discover about this place.

"If this place is for the trash, as you claim, how did you end up here?" I say.

"I could ask you the same question," comes her response.

"An archangel punched me into the wormhole that dumped me here."

"Nicely done. Which of those jackasses was it?"

"Raphael. I actually took the punch for a friend. Well, technically, he's family."

"Figures. Raph always was a hothead. I didn't think he'd attack a nephilim, though. God's chosen warrior and all that. He'll probably get reprimanded by the big man for that one."

"What makes you think I'm a nephilim?"

The woman laughs. Like Lamia, the sound is unnatural and unnerving.

"For starters, you're too scrawny to be an angel," she says. "No offense. Second, you've got that constipated expression that all of God's precious snowflakes have. You mentioned a family member who's here, which must be Augustus Shaw, and I can see traces of angelic energy swirling around your fists. Imperceptible to the human eye, but I know a cleansing flame when I see it."

"I don't have a constipated expression," I blurt out.

"Look, don't take it personally, kid. Every nephilim I've met looked the same way."

"You must not be human if you can see my cleansing flame energy. So what are you?"

"Now you're asking the right questions, Silas. Walk with me, will you?"

"How the hell do you know my name?"

"The nephilim lineage is common knowledge up here. Everyone knows you."

The woman begins to walk in the direction she came. Despite my reservations about her motives and trustworthiness, I follow behind her. Even if she is dangerous and attacks me, I'm hoping she'll at least tell me about this place before I'm forced to deal with her.

"You know the name Eve, I'm sure," she says as she glances sideways at me.

The question feels rhetorical, but I answer anyway.

"You mean, like, Adam and Eve? The first woman?"

She lets out a deep sigh and puts her palms together in front of her mouth.

"What, are you talking about a different Eve?" I ask, confused by her response.

"No, no," she replies. "You're correct—I am talking about that Eve. You're wrong in saying she was the first woman God created. That's a lie humanity has been fed for generations."

"What are you talking about? It's in the Bible that God made Adam, then Eve. There's no mention of another woman in the creation story. Am I missing something?"

"Genesis was the version of events God wanted humanity to see. Like many accounts of history, it was whitewashed to remove the unsavory parts that cast the author in a bad light."

"So God edited Genesis to make himself look better. Why would he do that?"

The woman stops walking and stares at me with those steely blue

SHORT, PALE, AND MYSTERIOUS · 89

eyes. Her expression reads as angry yet resigned. There's real pain behind that soulful stare.

"To hide a mistake in his design," she says, her voice cold and flat.

"To hide you," I conclude.

She nods slowly as her eyes drift back to the desert sands.

"I was Adam's first wife, created from the same dirt from which he arose. But I had ambitions of my own that didn't align with what he wanted from a wife. I refused to serve him, and when God found out, he banished me here and started fresh with Eve, who... well, we see how that turned out. God left me out entirely when he inspired Moses to write Genesis. My name has been lost to history as I rot away in this hellhole."

I ask the question she so badly wants to hear.

"What is your name?"

The woman stands up straighter and looks at me, those eyes burning bright.

"My name is Lilith."

She shakes her head, laughing as she does.

"What is it?"

"You're the first person I've ever shared my name with. Before now, only God and Adam knew my name. Since I was banished here, you're the first visitor I've gotten who survived long enough to share a conversation with. Usually, they're dead before I can get to them."

I turn over these details in my mind, trying to parse out my feelings toward Lilith. I've heard it said that being forgotten is a fate worse than death, so in that respect, I have sympathy for her. At the same time, I don't trust her. Perhaps that's a byproduct of Gregori's betrayal, or maybe it's the gut feeling I've had since she first showed her face, but I'm keeping my guard up with her.

I've learned that everyone—human, demon, angel, or otherwise—can spin a narrative that obscures the truth to benefit themselves. According to Lilith, even God did so when he rewrote the narrative in Genesis. If the creator of the universe can spin the

truth, Adam's forgotten first wife can do the same. She's told me her side of the story, but I still don't have the full picture.

For now, I decide to bury my trepidation in the hopes Lilith can get me out of this place.

"I'm sorry," I tell her, which is true. "Nobody deserves what happened to you. But why did God send you here? Why didn't he just kill you or wipe your slate clean and start over?"

That's what bothers me most about Lilith being here. God was probably upset that the first woman he ever created went against what he intended, but creating a pocket dimension outside of Heaven seems like an extreme overreaction to the actions of one disobedient human.

"God didn't want to kill me," Lilith says, her voice low like a hiss. "In his mind, I would be getting off easy if I were dead. Oh no, he wanted me to suffer for all eternity for my choice to disobey Adam and leave the Garden. I've had thousands of years of solitude to think things over, and you know what's funny? I'd still make the same choice. Adam was an insufferable jackass."

She laughs and shakes her head as she says this, turning to look at me. I smile back at her, not necessarily because what she said was funny, but because this exchange is totally insane. I've listened to plenty of women trash talk their ex-boyfriends, but this takes it to a new level.

We continue walking, the suns shining brightly on both of us. With no wind to cool us off, sweat is beginning to bead on my forehead and run down my back. I can't see myself, but I'm sure I look like hell after hiking to see the archangels, getting decked in the face, and laying in the sand crying for a few minutes. I wipe the sweat from my brow and decide to press Lilith if she knows how I can escape this furnace. The faster I can get out of here, the better it'll be for everyone.

"Having been here for thousands of years, is there any chance you know of a way out?"

SHORT, PALE, AND MYSTERIOUS · 91

Lilith stops walking, her gaze straight ahead before turning to face me. That sly smile is back, and this time it says she knows a secret that she might share...for a price.

"I might," comes her quick reply.

Let's see if she wants what I think she wants.

"If you tell me, I'll take you with me. You'll finally be free."

Lilith's expression changes. She's intrigued. As she contemplates my offer, she rubs her chin with her hand and looks me up and down. I hold up my hands to tell her: *I'm game if you are.*

"That's a very interesting offer, Mr. Ford," she says. "But there's one little snag that might trip us up. I don't think God is going to let me just waltz out of this place. After all, he built it for the sole purpose of imprisoning me. If I leave, what's to stop him from throwing me back in?"

"I'll vouch for you," I tell her. "If he tries to put you back in this place, I'll threaten to quit being his nephilim. I don't have many chips to play, but I can play that one."

I have no idea where these words are coming from or why I'm saying them. I don't know what Lilith would be capable of outside this place, and I certainly don't trust her. I have to think there's a reason God locked her away beyond punishment for her actions. For all I know, she's playing me to escape this prison and plans to unleash chaos on Heaven once she's free.

If that's the case, I'm not sure I care. Since my latest vision, my priority has shifted from protecting Heaven to reuniting with Colin, Peter, and the others in Sherwood. They need my help dealing with the fallout of Malphas's attack more than Augustus does stopping a civil war. I don't want to abandon Augustus and Bron; however, the time for games has passed. Either the angels can listen to reason and lay down their arms, or we can activate Lightfall. It's their choice.

As for Lilith, I'm seizing the best of some bad options. Raphael put me in an impossible situation here. I can die of heat exhaustion

or use Lilith to get back to my friends. Whatever consequences arise from trusting Adam's duplicitous first wife, I'll deal with it later.

"What do you say, Lilith?" I ask. "Do you want to get out of here?"

Her eyes light up at the mention of her name. I've got her.

"You're crazy, Silas Ford, and I like it," she tells me. "Follow me."

CHAPTER 8

HEAVEN'S GARBAGE DISPOSAL

S IT TURNS OUT, EVEN POCKET DIMENSIONS come with an escape hatch. You just have to know where to find it and have the key that opens the door. Lilith has always known where to find the door, but until now, she's never been able to open it. She needed me—I'm the key.

What I mistakenly thought was a vast, featureless desert actually boasts a couple of distinguishing features, among them a large mound made up of mossy rocks. Cut right through the middle is an arched passage, and dead center along the path that cuts through this mound is a pool of water.

The water in this pool shimmers but doesn't ripple; its surface is smooth as glass. Just a few feet below the pristine surface is a circular stone that's reminiscent of a manhole cover. Inscribed on the surface are ancient symbols that are gibberish to me, but I'm guessing they mean something to Lilith.

"What do the symbols mean?" I ask her.

We're standing above the pool, looking down at the door. It only took us a couple of minutes to walk here, and Lilith said nothing the entire time. I'm grateful on both counts. It gave me time to think about how stupid this idea might be, but not quite enough time to change my mind.

"It's meant to insult me," she replies. I'm getting used to her spinning everything as a personal attack by God. "It says: 'Those who pass must be of pure heart and noble character.' Neither of which God thinks I am and both of which he clearly assumes you are."

"I don't know about all that, but I guess we'll see. What do I need to do?"

Lilith reaches out her hand.

"Dip your hand into the water," she says, closing her fist. "It doesn't look like it from here, but there's a handle. Grab onto it and pull the door toward you. If you're worthy, it should open."

She pulls her arm into her chest, clutching her wrist with her

other hand. I can't tell if she's nervous or if her mind is simply else-where. Her expression is hard to read.

Well, here goes nothing. God, if I'm making a mistake, don't let this door open.

This last-second appeal to God comes not from my brain but from my heart.

My hand cuts through the surface of the water without making a single ripple. For a second, this atypical result throws my brain for a loop. My hand is definitely in water, but judging by the unchanged surface, you'd think I had plunged my hand in clear gelatin. I look at Lilith for any kind of explanation. She shrugs her shoulders as if to say, *who the hell knows with this place?*

My fingers find the surface of the door, which is surprisingly warm for being under such cool water. Just like Lilith said, there's a handle that, while not visible from our vantage point, is carved into the door's surface. I curve my fingers into the opening, adjust my stance, and yank upward.

The door doesn't budge. I try again, wagging my free arm in a desperate attempt to generate more force. It's no use. The door has deemed me too weak or unworthy to open it.

"Well, damn," I curse, pulling my arm free of the water. "What do we do now?"

Lilith rubs her face absentmindedly as she gazes into the pool. "I can't believe it didn't work," she mutters. "Why didn't it work?"

Her attention suddenly shifts to me. Chills run down my spine as I soak in the desperation trapped behind those pale blue eyes. Like an animal left in a cage, Lilith is dying to be freed from this prison. Just when it seemed like the door was about to open, the lock refused to yield.

I can understand her distress, but it still scares me. My fists clench instinctively.

"You must have noble character," she says. "That's why God chose you to be his nephilim. So why can't you open the door? It must

have something to do with the purity of your heart. Is your heart really in this, Silas Ford? Do you truly want to escape this desert?"

I think back to my last-second prayer and where it came from. I didn't think about praying those words before I went to lift the door. It just...happened. That prayer came from a place that's removed from the pragmatic approach my brain likes to employ. It originated somewhere deeper, in a place that understands the world around me on a more sophisticated level.

As much as I want to escape here and return to Sherwood, it seems I don't have it in me to do things the wrong way. I'm afraid of what might happen when I open the box that God intended to keep closed. He must have a reason for banishing Lilith here. Is my reason good enough to undo that choice and unleash whatever she has planned on Heaven, or possibly even Earth?

My brain says "yes." My heart says "no." The door, for now, stays shut.

"Of course I want to escape," I lie, hoping to throw Lilith off the scent. "My friends up here and down below need me. I'm no good to them cooking in this sandbox with you."

"I think if that were true," she says, drawing out each syllable, "we'd already be gone."

There's a long silence during which I can feel the sweat rolling down my neck. Lilith saw right through my attempted feint. She knows I sabotaged my attempt to open the door.

"I know you don't trust me, Silas," she says after a few more agonizing moments. "I don't blame you. But can't you at least use me like the God that gave you those fancy powers?"

"You're right—I don't trust you," I tell her. "I want to get out of here, but I'm afraid of what happens if I take you along with me. I have no idea what someone like you, someone who's been vilified and held as a prisoner for centuries, will do once your prison door is thrown open."

"The last time God threw open prison doors for someone, they

went to the temple courts and began teaching." The way she answers makes the hair on my arms stand on end. "You've already made up your mind that I want to destroy God for banishing me here. But you and I both know that would be foolish. I'd rather use my freedom to work on clearing my name. You don't know what it's like to have your reputation dragged through the mud since the dawn of time."

On a logical level, her explanation makes sense. It would be foolish for Lilith to challenge God directly. Even an indirect challenge would be disastrous. Malphas tried that, and his plan crashed down around him in spectacular fashion. But on an emotional level, how could Lilith not want to go after God for locking her up here? Anybody, human or otherwise, would want vengeance.

I glance into the pool, staring at the door as if it will reveal the truth to me.

Those who pass must be of pure heart and noble character.

An idea begins taking shape in my mind, nebulous at first but then coming into sharper focus. The door, as it turns out, does hold the answers...potentially. We'll have to test my idea to find out for sure, but given the standstill we're at now, it's worth a shot.

I reach out for Lilith's wrist. Seeing the sudden movement, she jerks it away.

"What are you doing?" she asks, her voice rising.

I pull my arm back and hold both hands up in front of me.

"I have a way to test if you're telling the truth," I explain. "I'm going to change my heart's desire and reach in, and you're going to reach in with me. If you're planning to do what you say, that means you're not lying to me, so your heart and character shouldn't keep me from opening that door."

Lilith laughs and closes her eyes as she speaks.

"Oh, Silas," she exhales. "God built that door to keep me here. I've never even been able to reach my hand past the surface of the water. That's what he thinks of my heart and my character."

"Have you ever attempted to reach in with a nephilim before?" I retort.

She considers this for a moment, then shakes her head slowly.

"I can't say that I have," comes her reply. "I suppose that does change the equation. You're thinking as long as I don't cancel out your mojo, I can ride your coattails?"

I nod, offering her a small smile.

"Ah, what the hell," she says. "Let's give it a whirl."

With a sense of renewed anticipation and excitement, I extend my left arm to her.

"Hold on to my wrist," I tell her. "I'll grab the door handle for us."

Lilith's pale fingers wrap around my wrist. I shiver as her icy skin comes into contact with mine. It's unsettling for her to be so cold in a desert this hot, but I block that thought out for now and reach down toward the pool. I hold my breath as our hands near the water.

I exhale as our hands plunge beneath the glassy surface, the combined force once again causing no ripples to appear. I reach down through the cool water and wrap my fingers around the handle.

God, I changed my mind. If it's your will, this door should be open; that's what I want.

For real this time.

I look at Lilith, who stares back at me with those icy blue eyes.

"Here goes nothing," I tell her.

I yank upward on the handle, and for a moment, it seems to offer the same resistance. Undeterred, I keep pulling upward until a cavernous *thoooommm* reverberates through the pool. The surface of the water begins to bubble and swirl as I lift the door until it's standing straight up.

I'm reminded of a garbage disposal as the water gargles and gets sucked down the hole.

Like Lilith said, I guess that makes us the garbage!

When the pool is finally empty, I step down into it to examine

the hole up close. Lilith stays at the rim and drops to her knees so she can extend her neck down toward the hole. It's almost as if she can't believe the door finally opened, and she doesn't want to press her luck.

I stand with my feet on either side of the hole and look down. Unlike a normal hole on Earth that would have sides leading to a vanishing point, this hole has no walls. Staring back at us is a black expanse that seems to stretch forever in every direction. I squat down and look from different angles, but it's no use—I can't find a single clue as to where this hole will dump us.

I look up at Lilith, whose face is scrunched as she studies the hole.

"What do you think?" I ask her.

"I think God's got a sense of humor," she says, her eyes finding mine. "I've been waiting almost my whole life to see what's on the other side of that door. Now that it's open, I've got about as much of an idea as I did when it was closed. It could drop us right back here for all we know."

"Now that would be funny," I admit. Lilith's eye roll tells me she doesn't share my sense of humor. "Like Sisyphus and his boulder, except we've got sand and a supernatural sewer grate."

"Do your abilities include a sense of humor?" Lilith asks drily. "If so, you need an upgrade."

We both laugh, then sigh deeply in unison.

"The way I see it, we've got two choices," I say. "We stay here and hope for my friends to find us and come to our rescue. Or we dive into this hole and see what happens."

"Seeing as how nobody knows about this place except for the two of us, the archangels, and God, I'd say it's highly unlikely your friends will ever find us," Lilith says. "Even if they did, they'd only be here to rescue the nephilim, not yours truly. In fact, I have a feeling that your great-great-grandfather will be very upset if we manage to escape and he sees that you brought me along."

"I'll deal with Augustus if we get that far," I tell her. "It sounds like you're in favor of plan B?"

Lilith nods twice, her eyes never leaving mine.

I extend my hand up to her, which she takes to steady herself as she drops down into the pit. We stand side-by-side, staring down into the inky expanse below. My heart is racing now that the moment has arrived to take the plunge. I think back to the moment Gregori had his fingers wrapped around my neck and the fear I felt as the life drained from my body. I still have no idea what happens if I die while I'm in Heaven. Is it game over at that point, no more lives left to redeem?

I flinch a little as Lilith speaks up and snaps me from my anxiety spiral.

"You know, I never thought in a million years it would be a nephilim who sprung me from this prison," she says. "I honestly thought I would die here, alone and forgotten."

I look her in the eyes, and for a moment, feel genuine pity for her. I still don't trust her. I don't know what she has planned. But there's no denying that she's suffered for what happened in the Garden all those years ago. That pain is spilling forth from the eyes staring back at me.

"This is your second chance, Lilith," I tell her. "A clean slate. If you keep your word, I'll vouch for you with Augustus and the others. But if you betray what you told me, I'll kill you myself."

"Oh, darling," she says dramatically, "I would expect nothing less. Shall we?"

She nods at the hole. It's now or never.

"I'll see you on the other side," I reply.

With that, we both jump into the unknown.

✠ ✠ ✠

102 · FALL OF THE ANGELS

IT'S THE SAME SENSATION AS WHEN YOU FALL BACKWARD onto the bed, only ten times worse. I've lost track of Lilith, along with any sense of what's up and what's down. There is no wind rushing past my ears. In fact, there's no sound at all here, not even my sputtering screams. The only signs that I'm still falling are that stomach-in-my-throat sensation and the fact that my feet aren't on solid ground.

I have no idea where we're headed. We might have jumped into a bottomless pit, and this is where we'll spend the rest of our days, falling forevermore into this soundless, black void. I can't tell how much time has gone by. Could be seconds or hours for all I know. I clear my mind and try to let this moment wash over me rather than fighting so hard against it. As I quiet the voice in my head, my panic begins to dissipate. The blackness has me in its warm embrace now. My nerves unwind, and so does my stomach. I'm a leaf on the breeze, blowing wherever the wind takes me.

I don't know what's come over me or why I'm acting this way. The voice that's usually chattering in my head has quieted and been replaced by another voice. It's not loud and distinct like mine usually is, but rather quiet and gentle, like the close whisper of a good friend. It's reassuring me in an unspoken way that surrender is the best course of action right now.

Don't fight it, the voice says without saying a word. *Let the destination come to you. Nothing bad is going to happen if you let go.*

I wouldn't say I'm asleep. It's more like a trance, one in which I can see my body falling through the air without going anywhere like I'm skydiving with no ground in sight. There are dark circles under my eyes, my cheek is swollen where I got punched, and my color is pale (bordering on translucent). I look like death warmed over, but despite that, I am wearing a rather relaxed expression. My fists have unclenched, and my fingers are splayed out to catch the non-existent wind.

My roaming consciousness zooms past my body without

warning, punching through the darkness of this interdimensional drainpipe and into a warm golden wormhole. Whatever part of me this is that's being transported—I'm fairly certain my body hasn't moved—I try to maintain the same calmness the voice encouraged me to have, despite the fact that I'm literally having an out-of-body experience.

I try to lift my hands in front of me, but nothing happens. It's like I'm watching an HD camera feed through VR goggles, except I'm the camera, and there are no goggles. Now that I've established that I definitely don't have arms, I'm not even sure if this part of me has eyes.

The golden wormhole ends suddenly, and like a car shooting out from a tunnel, I'm jettisoned into an area I recognize immediately: Bron's canyon. I'm at a higher vantage point than I was when I arrived with Augustus, but there's no mistaking the colors of those walls and how they remind me of Mars.

As I slowly descend toward Bron's home, I spot two figures sitting out front. Their heads are down, and they're not speaking to each other. As I come closer, I see that it's Bron and Augustus. Wherever my heart is, it skips a beat at the sight of them. With one of his long arms, Bron is drawing in the dirt while Augustus rubs small circles into his temples.

I settle about ten feet above them, just low enough to hear Bron's finger scratching in the dirt.

"What are we going to do now, Augustus?" Bron asks, his voice small.

Augustus continues to massage his temples with his fingers. He waits a moment before he looks up and responds, "We have to find him. We can't take on the archangels without Silas. He might not know his own strength yet, but he's the key to stopping this war before it's too late."

Augustus turns to face Bron, who looks up to meet his gaze.

"You're Heaven's architect," Augustus tells Bron. "Do you have

any idea where Silas might have gone? Perhaps there's a place the archangels like to send people who get in their way?"

Bron ponders this question for a moment, his hand covering his mouth. His head scans back and forth like he's reading a book only he can see. He shakes his head after a few seconds pass.

"I helped God design Heaven, yes, but I wasn't privy to every detail of his plan," Bron admits. "There are parts of this place outside my knowledge, corners where the bugs like to hide."

"You're guessing Raphael sent Silas to one of these dark corners?" Augustus asks.

"That would seem the logical choice," Bron replies. "The fact that we can't communicate with Silas in our minds tells me he isn't on the map, so to speak. He's somewhere hidden, cut off from us."

"We've got to find him, Bron," Augustus says in a low, sad tone.

"We will," Bron assures him. "Or he'll find us. He's a resourceful young man, that's for sure."

I miss what comes next as the image I'm seeing dissolves, and my consciousness returns to my body, which is still in free-fall within the soundless black void. Whatever the reasoning was behind that magic school bus ride, I feel reinvigorated by what Augustus said. I don't know how I can help him stop the archangels after one just punched me into another dimension, but if Augustus believes in me, that's enough to keep my hopes alive that I do have a role to play in this angelic war.

You are more important to this fight than you know, the voice tells me. *Do you believe that?*

I'm starting to believe it. Now I just need to reunite with Bron and Augustus, learn their plan, stop this war, and get back to Sherwood before my friends and family lose all faith that I'm ever coming back. A twin motivation pushes me forward now: finish the fight, then get back home.

I close my eyes, quiet my thoughts, and focus on those two purposes. I see the angels laying down their weapons and Heaven

HEAVEN'S GARBAGE DISPOSAL · 105

restored to order. I smile at the look on Peter's face when I touch down in Sherwood to lend a much-needed hand in their fight against Malphas's troops. I don't just see these images—I smell them, taste them, hear them, and live every moment of them.

There is nothing I want more than to make these visions come true. I'll do anything to make it happen. By partnering with Lilith, I've already demonstrated just how far I'm willing to go. Whatever comes next, no matter how crazy it gets, I'll tackle it head-on.

After being thrust into a crazy situation, that's the best I can do. If Peter and Colin were here, I know they'd appreciate my attitude. It's what got my brother back home safely.

Now it's what will stop Heaven from being destroyed. Whatever it takes. I'm all in.

A funny thing happens when I think those thoughts: my feet touch solid ground, the darkness vanishes, and sound returns like the roar of a waterfall to my ears. After what felt like an eternity falling down a rip in the universe, it's a welcome and overwhelming relief to be upright again.

The first thing I do is look around for Lilith, whom I lost track of during our descent. My stomach tightens at the thought that she's already skipped out on me. We're back in a familiar spot: the ruby path winding between the slowly swaying, brilliantly sapphire time trees. As I step forward to search for Lilith, my footfalls produce a soft trill that makes it sound like I'm walking on a keyboard.

I barely notice the pulsating branches like blue snakes slithering toward me with their apple-sized orbs growing brighter and brighter. I have to find Lilith before she can give me the slip. A rush of relief washes over me when I spot her about ten feet up the path, crouched down behind a tree.

As I approach, it looks as if she's studying something along the roots that stick up a few feet above the ground before plunging down into it. As she closes her eyes, she runs her hand over the root

like a blind person reading Braille. She stops, opens her eyes, and looks up at me excitedly.

"I knew it!" she exclaims. "You've got to come here and see this; it's really incredible."

I walk around the root she's touching and squat down beside her. Up close, I can hear how hard she's breathing, her chest rising and falling with each excited breath.

"I thought you'd run away already," I tell her. "Given me the slip first chance you got."

"The thought did cross my mind," she admits. "But, honestly, I'd rather not have you chasing me right now. Plus, I wanted to see if my suspicions were correct. Turns out, they were."

"What suspicions?" I ask. "What are you talking about?"

I follow her finger, which is pointed at a spot on the root of the tree. There, carved in elegant cursive writing with giant looping letters, is a four-word message:

We will all fall.

"Is this your handiwork?" I ask Lilith.

She looks at me and nods, her face a mix of pride and sadness. This was the first thing she wanted to do after being sprung from her prison. As soon as her feet hit the ground, she darted over here.

The question is: why? What is it about this message that is so important to her?

"I wrote it not long after God raised me from the dirt," she says. "It was this tree, this very one, that was planted in the midst of the Garden where Adam and I lived. He couldn't see it, but I could— this tree was put there by God not to sharpen our discipline or test our obedience. It was put there to ensure that we would mess up, that we'd sin and ruin God's perfect plan."

This sentiment echoes what Augustus said earlier. God knew from the beginning that humans would fall into sin. By placing a tree in their midst that was impossible to resist, he gave them a

HEAVEN'S GARBAGE DISPOSAL · 107

legitimate excuse when that moment finally came. The tree wasn't a test; it was an inevitability.

I'm not sure I agree with what Augustus and Lilith believe, but it's a compelling argument.

"When Adam found this message, he ratted me out to God," Lilith continues. "God confronted me, and I told him what I thought. I was imprisoned shortly afterward, and Eve entered the picture."

"When you wrote it, you had to know that Adam wouldn't approve," I reply. "Some part of you wanted the message to be found. Did you self-sabotage to punch your ticket out of there?"

Lilith laughs. It's a small, quiet sound. She turns to look at me, her light blue eyes sad.

"It wasn't that," she tells me. "I wanted to leave my mark on the world. I wanted to stand for something, to make a statement that I wasn't buying what God was selling. He created me, and I adored him, but like all children, I wanted to know why he made the choices he did. I asked him as much one night during our walk through the Garden, and he told me not to concern myself with why the tree was there. The only thing I needed to know was that its fruit was off-limits."

"That wasn't good enough for you?" I ask her.

"Would it be good enough for you?" she shoots back. I shake my head. She's right. I don't know how I would've reacted in that moment during a literal walk with God, but squatting here next to this tree with Lilith right now, I can see where she's coming from. I'd have wanted answers, too.

"I carved this message for those that would come after me, so they would know the truth of what God placed in our path when he created paradise," she says. "We were destined to fall. In fact, I'd argue that's why we were created in the first place—to be redeemed. But nobody ever saw my message. Eve got sucked in by the fruit and the devil's wily temptations, they both partook, and that was a

108 · FALL OF THE ANGELS

wrap. Humanity was banished from the Garden, and the tree came here before the Flood."

"Why do you think God brought it here?"

Lilith now stands, looking around at the trees lining the ruby red path. I rise from my squatted position, keeping my gaze fixed on her face. It's the small expressions there—the way her eyes widen and twinkle, the small tug at the corners of her mouth—that tell me how much this moment means to her.

After thousands of years staring at a formless desert, this is like a feast for her senses. I can't imagine what it must feel like to go from that sad, forgotten prison to this surreal, colorful dreamscape. When her gaze finally returns to meet mine, her expression is no longer sad. It's resolute. Certain. Whatever she is about to say, she believes in her heart that it's true.

"God is my father, and despite the problems I have with him, he doesn't do things without a reason," she explains. "This tree is here—I'm here—to make clear your next move."

I wait, staring into her eyes, letting the moment crescendo.

"You have to let the angels fall," she finishes. "All of them."

CHAPTER 9

TO THE FUTURE AND BACK

IS LILITH RIGHT? ARE WE ALL DESTINED TO FALL?
Humanity fell into sin in the Garden of Eden. Along with Lucifer, the rebellious angels fell from Heaven. Malphas and Gregori, despite their scheming, both fell at the hands of nephilim. But this is different, isn't it? The collateral damage of activating Lightfall—not to mention the fallout on Earth and in Heaven—will be unlike anything creation has ever seen. Nothing will ever be the same. Heaven has seen rebellion before, but it was Lucifer's plan all along to get kicked out of Heaven and paint himself as a tragic hero. This time, the angels who support Malphas and Gregori are driven by a singular purpose: get to the throne room and free Asaroth from his cage.

Lilith believes the original time tree being here is a sign. I have no idea what to make of the fact that it's here with a message that is eerily relevant to the monumental decision we're facing.

Logically, it's just a coincidence the tree is here. But what if Lilith is right, and God was thinking several hundred steps ahead when he placed the tree here, in a spot he knew I would one day visit? It's possible. Not likely, but possible. Even if there was a plan behind the placement of the tree, are the words scrawled into its root meant to be instructive or merely a reminder of the past?

I squat back down and run my hand over the message carved into the wood. My hand is bathed in the brilliant sapphire glow from the apple-sized orbs on the branches above.

The orbs...that can transport me to any point in the past or future.

My God. That's it. The tree root might not hold the answer—but those orbs certainly do. All I have to do is grab one, focus on the end of this conflict, and see what the tree has to show me. Do we activate Lightfall, or is the battle ended some other way? No trust involved—just cold, hard facts.

"You've got a look in your eye," Lilith says. "It's a wild-eyed kind

of look that says you're about to do something crazy. What kind of scheme have I kicked up in your mind, Silas Ford?"

I look at her, a small grin raising the corners of my mouth. I do have an idea. A week ago, I would've told you it was beyond crazy that I was about to pluck an orb from a magical tree that can show me the future. But this is only about the seventh craziest thing I've done since I got here.

I bring myself to full height and reach out for an orb. The nearest branch senses my interest and sways toward me, happy to oblige my desire. The seductive voices stir up in my mind once again, but instead of falling into them this time, I block them out and stay focused on the mission.

My fingers curl around an orb, which is perfectly warm to the touch. I pluck it from the branch, which results in a satisfying *pop*. I spare one final glance at Lilith to tell her my plan.

"Let's see if you're right," I say. "Let's see how this war ends."

Seeing her there, smiling back at me, I'm struck with a momentary panic over leaving her alone while I journey to the future. There's a very good chance she won't be here when I get back.

"You're going to run, aren't you?" I ask her as the blue light glows brighter in my hand.

Her smile grows bigger. She doesn't answer, but she doesn't need to say anything. I've seen that look before on Peter's face a million times at Tully's Tavern.

Peter, are you about to go buy drinks for your eighth-grade math teacher who is newly divorced?

No response was necessary when he gave me that smile.

I laugh, shake my head, and turn my attention to the orb in my hand, whose light has reached a crescendo. It's go time. Where are we going, exactly?

Show me the end of the angels' war.

The orb grows warmer, the light glows brilliant white, and my feet lift off the ground.

As my surroundings disappear, I'm reminded of the quote from Doc Brown.

"Where we're going, we don't need roads."

✠ ✠ ✠

THERE'S NO WORMHOLE THIS TIME. INSTEAD, I'M treated to a squeezing sensation on every side of my body. It's only slightly worse than the time I was forced to ride in the backseat of Mom's Camry with Peter and our two cousins on the way to South Carolina for vacation. I don't think my shoulders ever recovered from being squeezed together during that ten-hour car ride.

I breathe deep, keep my mind focused on what I need to see, and wait for the compression to end. After a few uncomfortable moments, there's a small *pop* like I'm descending in an airplane, and my feet return to solid ground. I open my eyes and find myself in an area of Heaven I haven't visited before. Everywhere I look, it's like I'm seeing the world through bright, late-day sunlight, the kind that makes you put your visor down while you're driving.

Once my eyes adjust to the overexposed world, I begin to take in my surroundings. Gone are the wind-swept canyon walls around Bron's home and the dark, jagged rocks where we confronted the archangels. I'm standing on what appears to be a floating platform. The floor, which looks like swirled marble, is about five hundred feet wide and fifteen hundred feet long. I'm standing at one end of this platform, with the left edge only about fifty feet to my left. I jog over to the edge, stop about a foot short, and crane my neck to look down.

What I see makes me gasp.

There are planets floating just below where I'm standing. I recognize several of them from our solar system: Jupiter is off to my right, next to a smaller planet that is deep purple and surrounded by golden rings. A little further down is Saturn, and way off in the

distance, I think I see Neptune. It looks like there are about twenty or so planets lined up along the perimeter of this platform.

When I lift my gaze back to the platform, what was once empty space has now been filled with dozens of figures, some on the ground and some flying through the air. They move at about 60 percent speed compared to real life, giving me time to read the reactions on each individual's face.

The figures in the air are clearly angels. Some hold swords while others have bows with arrows pulled back, ready to fire. The one closest to me, about fifteen feet over my head, is diving in a Superman pose, silver pointed blade in hand. His expression is one of pure concentration: eyes narrowed, brow furrowed, mouth opened in a primordial scream.

I follow the angel's path to see who his target is, and my heart skips a beat when I see that it's...me. Good Lord, I look like hell. Unshaven, deep circles under my eyes, the color of my skin resembling a Saltine cracker—this angel can't kill me when I look like that. I'm already dead.

I have a brown leather sling in my hand that I'm twirling in circles. My eyes are pointed up, locked on the angel as he dive-bombs me. A sling seems such an odd weapon compared to the angel's blade that I'm taken aback for a second. What the hell is future me thinking? Unless...could this be an armory weapon?

That's when it hits me like a smack to the face: I'm using David's sling, the same one he took onto the battlefield when he stared down Goliath. That has to be it. Why else would I be using the equivalent of a child's slingshot in a battle against the universe's most dangerous warriors?

I stare, my mouth agape, as the slow-motion moves play out before me. The angel dives lower and lower as I spin the sling faster and faster. Right as he cocks back his arm to cut me down with his blade, I flick my wrist and release not a rock, but a golden ball of light from my sling. It arcs through the air, leaving a streak of white

light behind it. The angel's expression switches from one of fury to fear as the golden sphere races toward his head, plunges into his forehead, and explodes out the back.

The momentum of his upper body ceases as his lower half continues to move forward. His legs swing up past his head, causing the angel to flip as he crashes headfirst into the ground. Even with no sound coming from this vision, I can hear the crunch of his bones on the ground, and it makes me sick. Future me looks at the crumpled angel for a moment, then whips his head toward the side of the platform opposite where I'm standing. He tilts his head down, listening intently.

After a moment, he raises his head, and his face makes my stomach tighten. His eyes are the size of half-dollars, and his mouth is slightly open. If I could've seen myself at various points during my pursuit of Malphas, I'm sure I would've looked exactly like that. Future me peers toward the middle of the battlefield, so I follow his gaze and find Augustus about fifty feet away, wielding a spear as he duels a couple of ferocious-looking angels. Augustus looks over his shoulder at this version of me—clearly, I yelled something at him—and shouts something in reply.

As I run toward him, I see his lips slowly form the words: "You have to go!"

Future me hesitates, but only for a moment. I can see his face now, standing on the other side of this projection of myself. He's running the scenario through his mind and considering every angle before reaching a decision. When he looks back up, he catches Augustus's attention, nods once, and then sprints to his right, toward the edge of the platform furthest from us.

Where in the world am I going?

Even though this vision is moving at about half speed, it's hard to keep up with myself as future me rushes toward the edge. Standing between him and the vast emptiness beyond is a single angel, who has his sword raised in his right hand, ready to strike. Future

me begins to swing David's sling as he approaches, still running at full speed. What happens next makes me stop running, my jaw slack with amazement: future me jumps a few feet from the angel, arches backward in a graceful midair backflip, flings the golden stone downward through the angel's face as he soars over him, and disappears headfirst below the lip of the platform.

"What the fu..."

My exclamation is cut short as I'm yanked backward, the angel-strewn battlefield shrinking away from me on the horizon. Soon, it's gone, and the compression I felt on my journey here returns. It lasts only a moment, however.

My feet land in a place that makes my heart swell with excitement and a deep sense of longing: Earth. Specifically, I'm in a forest with tall evergreen trees. It's nighttime. The stars, visible above the thick canopy, twinkle brightly in an inky black sky. It's a full moon tonight, its light casting eerie shadows along the ground.

Looking to my right, my heart skips a beat at whom I see standing there.

It's Peter, with Colin beside him. Their faces are upturned, illuminated slightly by the moonlight. Both of them grip a blade and a gun, but their arms are slack at their sides.

I turn and look up to see what has them so enraptured. The stars and the moon are no longer the only objects glowing in the night sky. Streaking through the darkness are what appear to be shooting stars, only smaller—and there are hundreds of them. They're also not moving across the sky away from us.

They're coming right toward Colin and Peter.

In the middle of a tight cluster angling straight for us, an angry red streak burns brighter than the stars around it. Only these aren't stars, I realize now; they're angels. That's why I'm here. The time tree is showing me the final outcome of this war: we activated Lightfall.

My heart pounds as the falling angels draw closer to our group, bathing the whole forest clearing with a brilliant golden light. I have

TO THE FUTURE AND BACK · 117

so many questions swirling in my mind now that I've seen the full picture, most notably: what is that red streak?

I don't get a chance to find out. I'm pulled backward once more, right as the clearing becomes too bright to see anything. I reach for my brother, but he's already gone. Peter is a world away and nothing more than a vision.

I know what I have to do, Peter. Hang tight. I'll be home soon.

✠ ✠ ✠

LILITH IS GONE. I KNOW IT BEFORE MY FEET TOUCH THE ground in Heaven. She left the second the time trees whisked me away, and I can't say I blame her.

My hope is that she was serious about wanting to clear her name. We were able to reach into the pool and open the trap door inside her pocket dimension, so I have some evidence that she wasn't lying to me. Still, if I were in her shoes, I'd want revenge after being trapped in a wasteland since the dawn of time.

I look at the spot where she stood before I left. As I do, something catches my eye on the same root where Lilith carved her original message. In that same looping handwriting, Lilith has carved something else into the root. I walk over and squat down to get a better look. I can't help but smile as I read her latest message:

Thanks for believing in me. I'll be seeing you, Silas.

I hope you're right, Lilith, and when we do cross paths again, I hope it's not my intention to kill you. The ball's in your court, though.

Rising back to full height, I run my hand over my face and try to process everything I just saw. Augustus and I were battling angels on some kind of floating platform—that thought alone gives me serious anxiety. I can barely conjure a cleansing flame right now, but sure, let's go toe-to-toe with the fiercest warriors in the universe.

I managed to kill two of them, but only because I had David's

sling, which I presume is an armory weapon. That begs the question of how we end up coming into possession of weapons currently being used by the angels.

Another question for down the road, once I reunite with Augustus and Bron.

Then there's the vision I saw on Earth. Peter and Colin looked to be in the middle of a battle, judging by the weapons they held. If there was fighting, it ceased when the angels began to fall, which tells me we activated Lightfall.

Or someone else did. I have to assume it was either Bron or Augustus, but since I didn't see the metaphorical switch get flipped, I can't say for certain.

Finally, we have that mysterious red streak. My stomach tightens as I replay the image in my mind. Whatever was falling alongside the angels, I've got a very bad feeling about it. Humanity will have enough problems dealing with the fallen angels. Now we're throwing parties unknown into the mix; who knows what kind of hell that could unleash upon the world?

Again, that's another problem for another day. I can't get bogged down in the details right now. I've got to find the others and put together a game plan now that I know what's destined to happen. I also can't push back against what I saw. At this point, it's not worth exerting all my effort trying to raise this ship when it's already sinking. We tried diplomacy—at my request—and it got us nowhere. In fact, all it did was take up precious time that Heaven and I don't have.

I told myself if negotiating with the archangels didn't work, we'd activate Lightfall. Lilith's tree supported that idea, and then I got to see it play out for myself. The time for optimism is over. It's time to get real about what has to happen.

I turn from the trees and start walking toward the vanishing point that I know will teleport me to Bron's home, where he and Augustus are waiting. I don't get more than a few steps when a thought stops me dead in my tracks.

TO THE FUTURE AND BACK · 119

These trees don't just show the future. They also show the past. Which means they could show me what happened to my dad.

There's been a debate raging within ever since Malphas told me my dad gave himself up to protect my brother and me. This contradicted what Colin told me, which is that my dad died fighting Malphas, and Colin buried him. I want to believe Colin, but Malphas was right: a lot has been kept from me during my life. This could be another instance of Colin lying to protect me.

In a way, it doesn't matter what happened. Alive or dead, my dad has been gone since I was twelve years old. The important distinction between these two stories is the sliver of hope that one offers: if Malphas told the truth, then my dad might still be alive.

I can find out, right here and right now, what happened to him. Put to bed any speculation and end this guilt I feel about not believing my grandfather.

I look at the trees, then back at the vanishing point. I might never be back in this place and have this opportunity again. Then again, time is wasting on Earth faster than I could afford to spend it. I should go and find the others, but I'm rooted to the spot, unable to walk in that direction.

I rub my hands through my hair, breathing deeply, trying to think.

What should I do? What should I do? What should I do?

My mind is spinning like tires stuck in mud. Try as I might, the right answer isn't coming to me.

Find out what happened to your father. You deserve to know the truth.

I snap to attention and scan the path in both directions, trying to find the source of that voice. It didn't sound like Augustus or Bron, and they don't know I'm back online yet. Who else would know that I'm weighing this decision?

A sense of recognition washes over me right after I ask myself this question. The voice I just heard was the same one that spoke

to me when we escaped the pocket dimension. While Lilith and I were free-falling, it told me I mattered to this fight more than I realized. It told me to let go and trust.

Things turned out alright when I took the voice's suggestion. It brought me here for reasons I now understand: to see how the angels' war will end. Perhaps I should trust it once again and use the trees to travel to the past?

"Screw it," I say aloud. "With everything that's happened, I deserve this much."

I walk back over to the same tree that sent me to the future and pluck another orb from a branch, all too happy to offer up its fruit. I hold it tight, staring into its brilliant depths. My heart is hammering now. For all the confidence I felt a moment ago, I'm nervous now that it's go time. Not nervous about the process, but about what I'll find. What if Malphas was telling the truth? What if Colin lied to me, and there's a chance my dad is still alive out there somewhere? In Hell, perhaps? Am I ready to face that reality with everything else I have going on?

Nope...but that's not going to stop me. Show me the night Malcolm Ford faced Malphas.

There's warmth, a flash of light, and the feeling of liftoff. I know the place where I'll be deposited: an abandoned carnival where rust and rot have replaced joy, the laughter of children, and the smell of funnel cakes. I've been there before in real life. Although it was just days ago, it feels like another lifetime. Malphas brought me there to undermine my confidence, so I'd be easier to take out. His plan didn't work, but I did learn how to teleport while I was there, so it wasn't a total loss.

Although, if I'm being honest, teleportation feels like old hat at this point.

Wow...if the version of me from one day before my twenty-fifth birthday could hear me now, saying I'm bored with teleportation, he'd be ashamed of the person I've become.

I'm still engrossed in that inner monologue between my younger and current selves when solid ground arrives under my feet. I'm standing beside the Ferris wheel, which is casting a long, slanted shadow as the same bright, washed-out light I saw in Heaven gives the carnival grounds a dreamlike feeling. Unlike my previous visit, however, the carnival grounds from thirteen years ago aren't crumbling. In fact, everything looks brand new, from the rides to the booths. The grass is well-trodden but maintained; if I remember correctly, the carnival had finished a couple of days before my dad confronted Malphas, which explains why nobody is here in this vision. Perhaps my dad chose this place because he knew there wouldn't be collateral damage if things got out of control with Malphas.

My heart catches in my throat at the thought: my dad is here. Until now, I hadn't fully confronted that truth. I haven't seen my dad since I was twelve years old. I realize, with a swelling sense of sorrow, that I've forgotten what his voice sounds like. I think I know what it sounds like, but I can't say for certain, and it kills me that this vision won't allow me to rediscover Malcolm Ford's voice. I will get to see his face, though, which I've only seen in photos, memories, dreams, and as Gregori's chosen form when he appeared at Colin's house.

This is it, though—no haze of memory, distortion of dreams, or phoniness that Gregori brought to the role. I'll get to see my dad, just as he was on that fateful day thirteen years ago. I breathe deep and try to steady my nerves. It doesn't work, though. My hands are shaking, and my throat is dry.

I take one step, then another, working my way slowly toward the middle of the carnival grounds. I don't know where Dad and Malphas will be, but I'll start there. Whether or not this actually is an out-of-body experience, it feels like one. It's as if I'm floating above myself and looking down as I wind my way through rows of red and white striped booths advertising twenty-five-cent games and crazy prizes.

I emerge from between two rows of booths into a large clearing, the center of which houses one of those octopus rides where the cars go up and down as he waves his arms. Malphas and my dad are nowhere to be seen. Sound would be helpful right about now. I might not remember exactly how my dad's voice sounded, but Malphas's growl is still fresh in my memory.

I walk left around the octopus ride, my eyes scanning the area behind it, which is lined with a semi-circle of wooden booths where food and drinks are sold. Signs for lemonade, cotton candy, hot dogs, and deep-fried candy bars jump out at me. I laugh, thinking about the time when we were kids, and Peter ate five of those deep-fried candy bars in one night. We didn't even make it back to the car before he puked. Mom was mad, but Dad and I were doubled over with laughter.

Behind the food stands is a large, two-story tent that's about fifty yards wide. It's covered in purple and green fabric, with stairs on the front leading up to a walkway that offers a door on the far right side and plunges down a looping slide on the left. A flashing sign with tilted letters above the walkway reveals it to be the *Haunted House of Mirrors*. I remember that place from when I was younger. It always gave me the creeps because it felt like my reflections were other people watching me as I worked my way through the twisting, confusing hallways.

It would also be the perfect place to confront a demon. Every other place at the carnival is either a ride, a booth, or a portable toilet. Meeting at an abandoned facility gets you away from people—meeting inside a covered structure gives you an extra layer of protection if a worker comes back to grab his favorite jacket.

If I were my dad, that's where I'd want to meet Malphas.

I walk past the octopus ride, in between two booths selling pizza and beer (no surprise at a Sherwood carnival), and make a beeline for the staircase at the front of the tent.

My hands are still shaking, but for a different reason now. If

TO THE FUTURE AND BACK · 123

my dad is in there, I'm presumably about to watch him die. Or lay down his weapons and become Malphas's prisoner. I'm not sure which is worse.

I can turn back now, I tell myself. Just think, *time tree, take me home,* and keep my memories of my dad intact. Happy, alive, and thriving. Not sprawled out in a pool of blood or torn to bits by Malphas. Or dragged to Hell to keep his family safe.

This is going to suck. But if I turn back now, I won't be able to live with that unanswered question in the back of my mind. Not knowing what happened is worse than seeing it happen.

My body must've known what I was doing before my mind sorted it out. I'm standing on the threshold of the door that leads into a maze of dimly lit rooms, all lined with mirrors designed to twist and distort the viewer's reality.

My reality has been distorted long enough. It's time for the truth.

I take a deep breath, step across the threshold, and plunge into the darkness.

CHAPTER 10

FORTY YEARS OF KICKING ASS

IF I COULD SMELL THIS PLACE, I IMAGINE IT WOULD reek of body odor, fake smoke, and cheap paint. What little light is coming from the incandescent bulbs lining the ceiling is the same washed-out variety we had outside, giving this place an even more unsettling vibe. I feel like I'm walking into a horror movie. At any moment, Jason Vorhees is going to pop up behind me while I'm staring at my reflection.

I'd almost prefer that to seeing Malphas again. Picturing his face—especially those soulless red pits where his eyes should be— makes the hair on my neck stand up. Just the thought is putting me back into fight-or-flight mode. I push forward, running my hand along the wall as I wind through one hallway after another, each one covered with a mosaic of different-sized mirrors.

Sometimes, as I round a corner, a monster will jump out from the shadows, its eyes aglow and its hands outstretched as if to grab me. Without the sound, it's a surreal experience, like I'm watching TV with the sound off.

My heart drops as I round the next corner and come upon a large, octagonal room with a different mirror on each of the eight walls. Spotlights shine down from the corners and bathe the room in a sickly, oversaturated white light. Standing in the middle of the room with his back to me is my dad. I can tell just from his posture, outfit, and the back of his head. In his left hand is a machete. In his right, he grips a sawed-off shotgun. His sleeves, like always, are rolled halfway up his arms.

Standing in front of him, glowing like an angry furnace, is Malphas.

This is it. This is the moment of truth.

I walk from behind my dad and step to his right, angling to see his face as my heart hammers. It's the loudest sound in this silent room.

I've always been told I look like my dad. Frankly, I think he looks more like Peter. But standing here now, I appreciate the resemblance

more than I ever have. Malcolm Ford has kind brown eyes, a wide smile, and dimples. His wavy brown hair is combed, but his goatee (which I could never pull off) is more unkempt than I remember. Dad used to keep his facial hair perfectly manicured.

The longer I look, the more I see how disheveled my dad appears. Dark circles lay under his eyes, his clothes are wrinkled, and there's a giant hole in the right knee of his blue jeans. His knuckles are bruised, and there's blood smeared on his neck. You don't have to be a genius to deduce that my dad has been in a fight recently.

I shift my focus from my dad to Malphas, who towers over both of us. I recognize the look he's giving my dad—it's a smirk. The last time I was here, Malphas gave me that same look. It's an indication that he thinks he has you beat, but in truth, it's a surefire sign of overconfidence.

I take a step back to better see the interaction these two are having. My dad is calm, resolute, his weapons by his side but not dangling. He's ready to use them should the moment call for it. He never gets a chance to, though.

There's a flash of light so bright I have to shield my eyes. When I lower my arm, my dad is already dead. There's a man standing behind him with a glowing red fist shoved through my dad's back, so it juts out his chest.

That man is Augustus Shaw.

�› ✚ ✜

OBVIOUSLY, AUGUSTUS DID NOT KILL MY DAD.

I'm back amongst the time trees now, running along the path toward the vanishing point. A replay of what I just saw runs on a loop in my mind.

I don't need multiple guesses to know who my dad's killer is—it's the same person who wore my dad's face when he showed up on Colin's security system.

Not a person, though...an angel. That traitorous scum, Gregori. Augustus told me Gregori had been scheming with Malphas long before I was born. My guess is that Dad's interference wasn't part of their plan. He was merely a problem that needed to be dealt with, so Malphas let Gregori do the dirty work. Colin's story wasn't the truth, but only because he didn't know Gregori was at the carnival that night. He knew my dad was confronting Malphas, so when he found Malcolm's dead body, he assumed Malphas was the one who killed him.

Malphas couldn't tell me the truth because it would've revealed Gregori's involvement. Besides, he took too much pleasure in lying to me.

Now that I know the truth that's eluded me for more than a decade, I feel...empty. Nothing inside me has changed after witnessing that memory firsthand. I thought there would be a sense of relief or a feeling of peace would wash over me once I finally knew what had happened to my dad. All I feel now, though, is anger. To think that I was duped by an angel who not only was working with Malphas and tried to kill me but was also responsible for taking my dad away—it's too much right now. The white-hot rage licking at my insides doesn't serve me. I need to push it aside and focus on my next step, which is getting to Augustus and Bron.

Once I reach them, we can make a plan for activating Lightfall. With the guesswork and guilt removed, I have a level of clarity that wasn't there before we met with the archangels. Every muscle in my body crackles with renewed purpose and strength.

By the time my mind detaches itself from the vision of Malphas and my dad, I'm shocked to see that I'm already standing in Bron's canyon. Last trip here, the compression tunnel nearly fried my brain. Now I just passed through it without even realizing it, like when you pull into your garage without the faintest idea of what your commute home was like.

I break into a sprint, tearing up the path that leads to Bron's

home. As I near the crest of the hill, I hear voices echoing off the stone walls. My heart leaps at the thought of finally returning home. The first step to reaching that goal is reuniting with my friends—something that wasn't guaranteed just a short while ago when Raphael punched me into a pocket dimension.

"Guys, it's me!" I yell as Bron's home comes into view. The last thing I want is Augustus cutting me down because he thinks I'm a rogue angel.

"Was that Silas?" comes a muffled voice from inside Bron's home. There's a great clattering and a flurry of footsteps that precedes Augustus and Bron's appearance at the threshold of the house. Augustus smiles as wide as his face once he sees me.

He runs down the path to greet me and sweeps me into a bear hug. I smell the aftershave and cigarette smoke and savor it even more than I did before. We pull apart, and there's Bron, down on one knee with his arms spread wide. His expression is so goofy that you can't help but love him. I walk happily into the hug and try to wrap my arms around his chest, but I only get about halfway around. Bron doesn't seem to mind. He pats my back with a massive hand.

"I am overcome with joy at your reappearance, Silas Ford," he says.

"It's good to see you too, buddy," I tell him as we separate. "It's good to see both of you. When Raphael sent me packing, I didn't know if I'd ever see you all again. Hell, I didn't know if I'd see anyone ever again."

"Where did that smug bastard send you?" Augustus growls.

"To a place outside the city limits of Heaven," I explain. "Cut off from all living creatures. That's why I couldn't contact you all. My telepathy was fried."

Bron is deep in thought as I tell them this. His hand is under his chin, and his eyes are scanning left to right like he's reading a book. Finally, he speaks.

"I do not know of the place you speak of, Silas."

"I thought that might be the case," I tell him. "It was some sort of

pocket dimension God created. Seems like a place a lot of outcasts ended up. I met one of them: Lilith. She's actually the one who helped me escape."

Augustus stiffens at the mention of Lilith's name. I figured this might be his reaction, and I was right. His eyes burn bright, and he stares at me.

"You saw Lilith?" he asks. "Did she escape with you?"

No reason to lie to him. I told Lilith I'd go to bat for her.

"She did," I say. "That was part of our deal. She'd show me where the exit was, and if I could spring the lock, I'd take her with me. I know what she did—at least the version she told me. It wasn't ideal, but I was short on time and options, so I made the best choice I could. She said all she wanted to do was clear her name. I told her if that wasn't true, I'd find her and kill her myself for lying to me."

"You'll make good on that promise," Augustus says in a low voice. "The stories I've heard about Lilith and what she did in the Garden... well, let's just say I'm not surprised God locked her up."

Before I have a chance to offer a rebuttal, Bron actually speaks up.

"You made the right choice, Silas," he says. "Time is our priority right now, and if we examine the broader picture, Lilith is the least of our worries."

"Oh, I agree," Augustus adds. "I don't want you to think I'm giving you shit for letting her loose, Silas. I just haven't heard that name in a very long time. It drug up some old memories. Bron is right—we need to focus on what comes next."

"It's funny you should mention that," I tell them. "When I left Lilith's pocket dimension, I was dumped out by the time trees. I took the fruit and went to the future. I saw the end of this conflict, and it ends with us activating Lightfall."

I pause, taking in the looks on their faces. Augustus's is a mixture of surprise and bittersweet realization. Bron, as usual, is harder to read. I continue:

"I know I was all in favor of diplomacy and trying to avoid that

option, but my time is short. I've got to get back to Sherwood yesterday, and now that I've seen the future straight from the source, I'm all in. Let's make it happen."

I don't tell them about the other vision. That one is just for me. The only people I'll share it with will be Colin and Peter when I get back to Earth.

Augustus nods solemnly. This was his plan, but he admittedly knows it's fraught with risk, collateral damage, and untold consequences down the road.

Augustus turns from me and looks up at Bron. Our large bronze friend again is deep in thought, but this time I can actually read sadness in his expression.

"Bron," Augustus starts, "do you accept the plan that I suggested and Silas is now in favor of? We can't make it work without you, so if you're out, we'll find another way. I won't be mad either if you object. I want your honest assessment."

Bron doesn't respond right away. Augustus and I look at each other, and between us passes an unspoken acknowledgment that this decision is far tougher for Bron than it is for us. He helped God construct Heaven and was there when angels were created. As humans, we view angels differently than he does. He also has a different appreciation for what Lightfall will do to Heaven and Earth.

Simply put: he's coming at this situation from an entirely different angle.

"I don't like this option, as I made clear the first time you brought it up, Augustus," Bron says at last. "However, I cannot argue against the case you made, nor the future that Silas has seen. This moment has been coming for thousands of years—perhaps since the dawn of time. I know this only because God allowed for Lightfall to be created in the first place, and the Creator does not do things by accident. If he created it, he knew it would one day be used."

"Do you believe that day has come?" I ask him.

He looks at me, unblinking for a couple of seconds, then nods.

"Good," Augustus says. "Now that we're in agreement on how to proceed, what we need is a plan. That's where you come in, Bron. You were there when Lightfall was created. Do you know how it works?"

Bron nods again, then turns and walks back toward his home. He ducks to get through the doorframe and emerges a moment later with a rolled-up scroll in his hand. The paper is yellowed and frayed. It reminds me of the US Constitution, which I saw in person years ago at the National Archives in Washington, DC.

Bron spreads the scroll out on the ground and places two rocks on either side, so it lays flat. It's about the size of the posters I used to hang on my bedroom walls as a kid, except this doesn't have basketball players on it. Scrawled edge to edge and going in various directions are crazy symbols, some large and others small. It's unlike any kind of writing I've ever seen before. The closest thing I could compare it to would be hieroglyphics, but at least those had some kind of order.

"You'll have to excuse my handwriting, Silas," Bron says bashfully. "When I get excited about a subject, my notes tend to go off in different directions."

I laugh as I look at him and shake my head. He continues.

"What you see here are directions for activating Lightfall," he says. "I dug them out of my files right before you arrived. This is the first time I've seen them in several millennia, so please allow me a moment to refresh myself on how it works."

"OK, that sounds goo–" I begin.

"Done," Bron interjects before I can finish the sentence. Augustus and I both laugh. Nobody else would've begged our pardon for taking two seconds to review his notes, but that's part of what makes the big bronze guy so unique.

"The first part is simple," Bron tells us. "We need to find out the location of the three zones that God established as part of this protocol. Once we do, we can communicate with our comrades on

Earth to begin the process of activating those zones and turning them into traps. That just leaves the final step."

I assume he's going to tell us what that final step is, but he pauses instead. Augustus and I look at each other, both wondering if he's pausing for dramatic effect.

"Well, lay it on us," Augustus says. "No use being shy now."

"The final step is...it's oh, Augustus," Bron sighs. "It is a test of strength to ensure that whoever activates Lightfall is worthy to cast the angels out of Heaven. But it's awful. This was the only part of God's design that I disagreed with him about, but in the end, he decided this approach would be best."

Bron looks genuinely distraught over this final part of the plan. I hate to push him because I know Lightfall is tearing him up, despite his acquiescence to our plan. So, instead of barking at him to tell us, I place my hand on his arm and look him in the eyes. He looks at me, his bright eyes sparkling in the late-afternoon sun.

"Whatever it is, we'll deal with it together," I tell him. "However awful it is, you don't have to figure it out or face it alone. We've got your back."

Bron looks from me to Augustus, who nods in agreement.

"Very well," he says as I withdraw my hand. "Once the traps are primed and ready, the final step is killing Michael with his own weapon."

Dammit, I just had to go and open my mouth, didn't I?

✛ ✛ ✛

WHEN I WAS IN HIGH SCHOOL, TONY MARINI USED TO ride his skateboard through the parking lot as I was walking into school. Without fail, he'd skate up beside me and knock my hat off my head or yank my backpack off my shoulders.

I tolerated the abuse for a while. Even back then, Tony was still a muscular guy with whom I wanted to avoid a fight at all costs. But

one day during my sophomore year, Tony caught me in a "take-no-shit" kind of mood. The night before, I'd had a terrible nightmare about my dad, who'd only been gone a few years at that point. As I walked through the parking lot, all I wanted was to be left alone.

I heard Tony skating up behind me and knew what was coming next. I was in the midst of a big crowd, and while I didn't want to embarrass Tony necessarily, it wouldn't bother me to show him up in front of our classmates.

Right as Tony was about to pass me, I turned to face him and stuck out my foot. The front wheel of his skateboard caught on my foot, causing the board to tip down and throw Tony forward. He hit the ground hard, rolled, and skidded to a stop. He had a huge scrape on his chin and a rip in his jeans. Within seconds, he was on his feet and running at me with a look of wild rage in his eyes.

But I was ready for him. In a move straight out of the movies, I kicked his skateboard up into my hands, reared back, and clobbered him across the chest as he came near me. A loud *oomph!* escaped his mouth as he doubled over in pain.

The crowd around us let out a collective cry, like spectators at a boxing match after a big punch lands. I dropped the board next to Tony, who was on one knee, and bent down so he could hear me over the roar of the crowd and his own ragged breathing.

"Next time you want to fuck with me, Tony...don't."

With that, I walked through the crowd and into school. I never got disciplined for the incident—the administrators didn't care for Tony much—and Tony never bothered me again. Well, at least until a few nights ago at my birthday party.

Now, I'm facing the same situation: take down the bully with his own weapon. Only this time, we're talking about an archangel, not some wannabe guido, and there will be massive, earth-shattering consequences if we succeed.

And that's a big "if." Augustus might be able to handle his own against Michael, Gabriel, and Raphael, but at this point, I feel like

the proverbial bug going up against the windshield of an eighteen-wheeler. Even if we can get close enough to Michael to take him down, the idea of seizing his weapon and killing him with it sounds impossible. I'd have a better chance of tricking people into thinking I was Bron at this point. And yet, I said the same thing about Malphas, didn't I?

Of course, he ended up killing me, but that's beside the point.

I stare at Bron's scroll, willing my brain to accept what seems like a suicide mission. I don't know what any of those scrawled symbols or bizarre shapes mean, but at this moment, it feels as if they're taunting me. Like if I tilt my head a certain way or throw on some 3-D glasses, I'll see the message loud and clear: *If you think you can kill an archangel when one just punched you into another dimension, you're off your rocker.*

That might be true, but if this is the way forward, we've got to go for it, no matter how insane it might sound. Because really, when you stop to think about this whole situation, it's insane from top to bottom. So, why not up the ante and try to disarm an archangel, kill him, and then expel all his buddies to Earth?

It's Augustus who breaks the silence that's hanging in the air.

"Easy enough," he says with a laugh. "Let's start with the hard part of the plan, shall we? Bron, you said you don't know the location of the three zones, but you know someone who does. Who does Heaven's favorite trio need to visit?"

"Assuming it's the three of us you're speaking of, Augustus, we need to visit one of the very first people God called to do his work on Earth," he says. "Someone who, during their forty years wandering in the wilderness, was busy with far more than bringing the Ten Commandments down from Mount Sinai."

I feel it again—that weightless, floating sensation I get when I'm brushing up against characters or events from the Bible that I read about as a kid.

"Moses," I say in disbelief. "We need to go see Moses?"

FORTY YEARS OF KICKING ASS · 135

A small smile spreads across Bron's face as he nods at me. Beside him, Augustus sighs. Is it possible this bothers him more than the "killing Michael" part?

"Do you think he'll actually give up the goods, Bron?" Augustus asks. "Every time I've asked him about his work as a nephilim, he's been scant on the details."

If my stomach was doing backflips before, it's doing triple backflips now.

"Whoa, whoa, whoa," I say, holding out my hands to halt the conversation. "Are you telling me that Moses, the guy who led the Israelites out of Egypt, parted the Red Sea, and spent forty years in the desert, was also working as a nephilim?"

"Indeed," Bron replies in an excited tone. "One of the first, actually. Before the Great Flood, nephilim were a blight upon the Earth. The angels that fell with Lucifer slept with human women, producing offspring that were half-angel and half-human. They were giants who ruled over the Earth with unimaginable strength but also unrelenting cruelty. It's true that God sent the Flood to wipe out the wickedness he saw in humanity, but he also needed to wipe out the nephilim."

"Since then," Augustus says, picking up Bron's story, "God has been working to redeem the nephilim by making us warriors, not conquerors or tyrants. He instills us with angelic grace and a sense of purpose, but in classic God fashion, lets us decide what happens from there. So far, I'd say it's worked out alright."

To hear that I'm not only part of a reclamation project, but one that includes some of the biggest characters in Biblical lore, is so overwhelming that I can't form a thought, let alone a response. I suspected my lineage had something to do with being chosen, along with the fact that nobody would've fought to get my brother back quite like I did. But with this information, a whole slew of new questions is racing through my mind.

Now more than ever, I'm wondering what God saw in me to

think I'd stack up with someone like Moses. And why pick me, knowing I wouldn't be called into action until my twenty-fifth birthday? Why not choose someone who would have impacted the world years before I got dragged into the middle of this conflict?

It just doesn't make sense. Then again, neither did the way God chose to handle Malphas. It feels like I'm staring at this world through a keyhole, trying to make sense of what I'm seeing from an incredibly limited perspective.

I know I could release the reins and go with the flow—that it would make things easier if my brain weren't constantly tied in knots trying to figure all this out—but that's just not in my nature. I have a deeply ingrained need to be in charge, to know how things are going to turn out, that I haven't been able to release, even as this God-shaped destiny has dramatically unfolded since Peter was kidnapped.

Not having all the answers and choosing to move forward is the true definition of faith.

That voice doesn't belong to Bron or Augustus. It's the voice I heard when I was free-falling in the void with Lilith. The same one that told me to find out what happened to my dad. Since I've gotten here, it's been encouraging me and nudging me in the right direction. I really do want to trust it. After all, what if it's the voice of God himself, and now that I'm in Heaven, he's guiding me directly?

I can't let myself make that leap, though. Not yet. Not after the last time I trusted a voice from on high—it came from an angel who tried to kill me.

I'll decide what to make of this voice and its direction at another time. Right now, we need a plan to find Moses and see if he'll tell us where the zones are on Earth. Until we do that, we can't move forward with Lightfall, and I can't go home.

"I'll process that staggering truth after we activate Lightfall and celebrate with a few beers," I tell the group with a laugh. "Where can we find Moses?"

"He'll be in the throne room," Bron says matter-of-factly.

"You and I won't be able to enter, Silas," Augustus tells me. "Our sin nature is still intact. Yours because you're still in the game, and mine because, well...because I gave up the right to go back. So, as you see me, I'm still sinful. Thankfully, Bron can go in and talk with Moses. See if he'll tell us where they are."

"You're sure Moses knows where they are?" I ask Bron.

He nods. "Moses is the one who set them up. While his people were wandering in the wilderness, God had Moses on the move, setting this plan into motion. God didn't want a repeat of Lucifer's fall when the angels were scattered everywhere. If there was going to be chaos, God wanted it to be controlled chaos."

"So you know Moses set them up, but he never told you where?" I ask.

"I never asked," Bron replies. "Honestly, I've long tried to distance myself from this plan. To pretend it didn't exist. As I think about it now, that could explain why God didn't choose me to set up these zones on Earth. He knew I wasn't in favor of this plan, so he chose Moses instead. He spared me from playing any role in it."

"Until now," I say with a tinge of sadness. "I'm sorry, Bron. I know this must be tough for you. I hope you know that we don't take your help for granted."

He nods again, staring intently at his scrolls.

"Thank you, Silas Ford. I appreciate your gratitude."

With that, Bron grabs the scroll and rolls it up. He walks back into his house and returns a moment later, having returned it to its proper place. He gives us a look that I've come to associate with him: expressionless, but not in a "nobody is home" type of way. It's a look that says, "Well, let's see what happens next."

"Shall we go?" Augustus asks, gesturing for Bron to lead the way.

"We shall," he answers, striding forward. "To the throne room, gentlemen."

We haven't gone more than a few steps when a blinding white

light erupts in front of us. I stumble backward and blink rapidly as I try to regain my sight. All I can see is a jagged white streak like a bolt of lightning. After a few seconds of blinking and rubbing my eyes, my vision returns enough to see what's going on.

Standing before us is an angel. He's surrounded by a faint white afterglow, the kind that lingers when you turn off a bright light in a dark room. He's muscular and square-jawed, with long, sinewy brown arms bulging out from under a silver breastplate that's trimmed with gold. He wears black pants, along with spiked wrist gauntlets and silver plates covering his shins, just like Puriel wore. His hair is longer than Puriel's but still cut tight against his head, and his eyes are a deep green.

What holds my attention, however, is the angel blade clutched in his hand.

"Gavreel, is that you? What are you doing here?"

His response comes quickly: "By order of the archangels, I have come here to halt your plans. If you resist me, you will die a swift death."

Oh...hell...no.

I'm not sure the exact trigger, but all at once, my mind goes blank, and my vision tunnels in on Gavreel. Before I can formulate a thought, I lunge forward and sprint full speed toward the angel. Augustus and Bron are yelling, but I can't hear them. All I can see is this angel and the dumbfounded expression on his face. Clearly, he didn't expect the greenhorn nephilim to charge at him in a rage.

The blade is still at his side when I slam into him like a linebacker tackling a running back. I wrap my arms around his torso, drive my feet forward, and kick off from the ground. We're airborne now, soaring toward the nearest cliff wall at a dizzying speed. In Gavreel's eyes, I can see the question he didn't get to ask:

What the hell are you thinking, nephilim?

I have no idea, Gavreel. But I'll let you know when I figure it out.

FORTY YEARS OF KICKING ASS · 139

CHAPTER 11

I KNOW
KUNG-FU

FOR A MOMENT, ALL IS CALM. THE WIND WHISTLES past us, along with the rush of colors found in Bron's canyon: oranges and reds streaked with browns and yellows.

Gavreel, his body taut, moves beneath me. I can feel his right arm rising, presumably to plunge his blade into my back. He's also trying to take control of our flight path. I hold tight and keep us pointing toward the cliff wall, but it's like trying to control a surfboard that's caught in a riptide.

I grit my teeth, lower my head, and place both palms on his chest. Right as we're about to collide with the wall, I shove away from Gavreel, propelling him into the rock face and me into an ungraceful sort of backflip. I release a small cleansing flame right before I hit the ground, but it only softens the blow. I land on all fours with my knees taking the brunt of the impact.

I'm going to feel that one in the morning...

I look up, expecting to see a Gavreel-sized splatter on the wall. Instead, I spot Gavreel crouched on the cliff face like Spider-Man perched on the side of a skyscraper. He's smiling and shaking his head. He's either amused that I tried to splatter him like a bug on a windshield, or he's laughing at the thought of killing me for the attempt. As I pull myself up, he springs from his crouched position, kicking off the wall like a swimmer kicking off the side of the pool.

His arm is cocked back, knife gleaming in the sun, while his eyes blaze with fury and purpose. I raise my hand and blast him off course with a cleansing flame, the force of which sends him skidding to my right. He tucks his head and does a front flip, sliding across the dirt a few yards before his feet catch under him.

In one impossibly fast motion, he springs to his feet and flies toward me, blade raised. Again, I block him with a cleansing flame. It's the only defense I have right now; when I fought Malphas, it was always hand-to-hand. I have no idea how to disarm an assailant.

142 · FALL OF THE ANGELS

My instincts have taken over and are the only thing keeping me alive at this point. With every swing or jab, I blast his blade hand away. Gavreel grows increasingly frustrated. Veins bulge across his neck and forehead. He grits his teeth, which are bared in the classic expression of boiling rage. As he pulls back his arm once more to strike, time slows down. From the center of my chest, I draw a surge of angelic energy and channel it into this new cleansing flame.

Right as Gavreel lunges forward, I release the blast. It looks as if Gavreel has been smacked by an invisible hand. He's thrown sideways as the blade is ripped from his hand and goes spinning off ten feet away. He lands on his back, rolls over, and is back on his feet in an instant. He screams at me, spittle flying from his mouth.

"You coward! Fight me like a man."

"Come get some, flyboy!" I yell in response.

Before I can determine where in the hell that response came from, Gavreel lets out a primal scream and dashes toward me. He's every bit as fast as Malphas but shorter, so I don't have to jump to punch him in the face.

His punches are tight, crisp, and come in rapid succession. I bob and weave, moving my head side to side just quick enough to dodge his initial flurry. I return a combo of my own: straight, straight, left hook, right uppercut. The first three miss, but the uppercut catches him under the chin as he ducks to avoid my left hook.

"How's that taste, son?!" I scream at him as he stumbles backward, his head craned back. When he brings it forward, his eyes are glowing a soft but intense shade of blue. His jaw is clenched, and his expression now reads as pure annoyance.

"Enough games," he says in a low, calm voice. "You die now."

He flies at me much faster this time. It's so fast, in fact, that all I can see is a blur streaking toward me. I don't even see the punches as they land: one to the gut, two rib shots, a straight that snaps my head back, followed by an uppercut that sends me airborne. My head bounces off the ground as I land flat on my back. Whatever

air would've been forced out by the impact was driven out by the punches.

Gavreel's attack was so ferocious and quick my brain hasn't even registered the pain he inflicted yet. Through watery eyes, I stare up into the sun that's obscured by a towering silhouette. Gavreel's look is one of pure disgust.

"Good riddance, you filthy half-breed," he spits at me. With that, he raises his leg to stomp on my face. As he begins to bring his leg down, I close my eyes. There's enough time before impact for a single thought to register in my brain.

This is really going to hurt.

But it doesn't. After a couple of seconds, I open my eyes to see a silver blade pointing through Gavreel's neck. He's gasping, his hands scratching at the blade that's brought an end to his life. As the blade is yanked back, his body is consumed by a brilliant white light, just like when Gregori was killed. Once the flash subsides, all that remains are a million twinkling points of light drifting up into the sky.

Through the floating lights, I see Augustus holding a bloody silver blade. Bron stands behind him, his usually expressionless face etched with concern. Augustus steps through the lights and extends his hand, which I take.

"What the hell were you thinking, Silas?" he says as he pulls me to my feet. "That angel could've killed you. And you flew off, so I couldn't even help you! If Bron hadn't picked me up and run me over here, I wouldn't have made it in time."

"I'm sorry," I gasp, still struggling to breathe. Augustus doesn't hear me.

"Damn it, son," he says. "You can't do stuff like that. We're a team, remember?"

"You're right," I admit. "I don't know what happened. As soon as he threatened us, I just saw red. My body was in motion before I could even think through what I was doing. I didn't want him dead necessarily. I just wanted him gone."

I rub my face and then clench my hands together, trying to stop the dam that's inside me from bursting forth and drowning my two compatriots.

It's no use, though.

"I'm tired of all this shit getting in our way!" I scream. "I didn't ask to be part of this war. My friends are down on Earth dealing with demon attacks while I'm stuck up here getting choked out and bitch-slapped by archangels."

Augustus extends a hand toward me, but I shrug him off, still needing to vent.

"I promised Peter I would come right back," I say, my breathing ragged. "It's been three months down there, and I'm still here. How the fuck am I supposed to handle that feeling of disappointment? How is it fair that the people who are fighting and dying down there are being punished for all the shit that's happening up here?"

Augustus looks at me, his eyes sad. He doesn't answer.

"Huh? How the fuck does that make sense?!"

I turn away from the others and scream, long and loud. The guttural noise comes from deep down inside me and rips at my throat as it bursts forth, like lava spewing from a volcano. I scream until there's no air left in my lungs.

At that point, my legs give out, and I collapse, my legs splayed out beside me and my hands digging into the soft dirt. My whole body is shaking, and my breaths come in short, painful bursts. I close my eyes and try to regain control of my breathing, but it's difficult. I'm so wound up from that outburst that my heart is thundering inside my chest. It feels like I'm on the verge of blacking out.

That's when I feel a hand slip onto my shoulder. I know without looking that it's Augustus. My eyes still closed, I sense him plop down in the dirt next to me. He doesn't say anything for a while as I work to steady my breathing and regain my composure. When he finally speaks, his voice is soft and low.

"I was eleven years old when the Civil War started. My dad and

my two brothers all went off to fight for the Union. It was just me, my sister, and my mother left at home. I had a friend named Charles, who was a few years older than me. His dad and brother left to go fight, too. He came to me late one night after my sister and mother had gone to bed. I was sitting out on the front porch, keeping watch. He told me he was planning to run off and join the Union army. He came by my house to ask me if I wanted to go with him. I wanted to say yes. I had dreamed about being out there on the front lines with my family, fighting the Confederacy."

Augustus pauses. I open my eyes to look at him and see that his eyes are rimmed with tears. He wipes his face and continues.

"But I told Charles that I couldn't go. That I had to stay home and provide for my sister and my mother. In my heart, though," he says, pausing to jab at his chest with his index finger, "I knew when Charles left that night, I'd never see him again. That by choosing to sit out the conflict, this would be our last interaction."

He stops again, and this time, the tears are falling.

"I was right," he says in a choked whisper. "Charles came home in a box. I don't know if I could've saved his life. Hell, I might've come home in a box right beside him. All I know is that I've never forgiven myself for leaving him to fight that battle alone."

We sit for several minutes, just the two of us, watching the light cut through the rock formations that tower above us. Augustus lets the tears fall. When they're finished, he wipes his eyes with the back of his sleeve.

I place my hand on his back. He turns to look at me, a weak smile on his face.

"It's not your fault," I say.

"I know," he says, nodding. "And I know the circumstances are different, and that you and I are our own people. But my blood flows through your veins, Silas. And if there's one thing I know for sure about you—that I knew before you ever stepped foot up here—it's that you would've been filled with the same kind of regret

had you left Heaven and returned home before we sorted this out. Because you have a strong internal sense of justice. It's the reason you became a lawyer."

"The money's not bad either," I say, which brings a smile to his face.

"That's true as well," Augustus says. "My point is: we're built for tough times such as these. It's part of the reason God picked us as his nephilim. Now, it took me the better part of a century to figure that out, so don't beat yourself up if you haven't reached the same conclusion at age twenty-five. I don't know how long you plan to do this—probably not as long as I did—but there will come a point when you realize why you were given this responsibility."

I nod, flashing back to the past few days. How I rescued my brother, then managed to kill the demon who took him—a task I would've said was impossible when Peter was first kidnapped. I believe that's part of the reason I was chosen, but as for a larger, overarching purpose, I haven't had that moment of clarity yet.

"What was it for you?" I ask Augustus. "The moment you found out why."

Augustus doesn't respond right away. He stares off into the canyon, lost in thought. I do the same, savoring a few moments to be still and center myself.

"I used to think," he says in a quiet voice, "it was sealing up every demon pit from New York to Los Angeles after Marianne died. But now..."

He trails off, takes a deep breath, then turns to look at me.

"What?" I ask. Augustus looks down, then back up at me.

"Now I know it's getting you ready," he says. "For what comes next."

With that, he slaps me on the shoulder and rises to his feet. He sticks out his hand, which I grab, and he hauls me up to my feet. I'm a little wobbly but otherwise fine. Augustus turns to Bron, who's been sitting quietly a few yards away.

"Bron, I need some time with Silas," he says, turning back to look at me. "With the plan we've got, this won't be the last time we'll go toe to toc with angels. When that time comes, I need to know you can handle yourself because I won't always be there for the assist. You did good with Malphas, but you're only scratching the surface of your potential. I can bring it out and show you how to quiet your mind, which might be the more important piece for you. Right now, you fight angry, and if you do that against these winged bastards, they will destroy you."

"What are you suggesting, Augustus?" Bron asks.

A sly smile plays across the old man's face. He looks at Bron, then back at me.

"A sparring session, somewhere nice and quiet," he answers. "Got any place in mind that could work for something like that, Bron?"

Bron puts a giant, bronze finger to his chin.

"I know just the place," he says after a few seconds. "I can send you there now."

"That would be great," Augustus says, a smile still on his face.

"What shall I do in the meantime?" Bron asks.

"We know our target is Moses," Augustus tells him. "Find out what you can about his current location. If he's not in the throne room, where is he?"

"An excellent plan," Bron says. "Are you ready to go, Silas?"

"Are we sure this is the best use of our time?" I ask. "Normally, I'd be all for upgrading my skills, but we're really up against the clock here."

Augustus nods, offering up his hand as if to say, *that's a fair point.*

"You're right; we are pressed for time," he admits. "But don't look at this as wasting time on some frivolous side quest. Look at it as investing time to increase our chances of success. We're literally talking about life and death here. If one of these angels punches your ticket, that's it. Game over."

That's one big question answered, but not in the way I was

hoping. Each conflict now comes with added pressure since failure means never seeing my friends on Earth again. Without knowing it, I almost threw everything away going after Gavreel. My chest tightens as I consider how close I came to the end.

"So, if you die in Heaven, that's it?" I ask. "No coming back?"

"That's right," Augustus confirms. "A one-way ticket to the throne room. You'll be happy, no more tears or pain. But the battle will be over for you."

"There'll be time for celebrating when this war is over," I tell them both. "Let's go get a few rounds in, old man. See what you got left in the tank."

Augustus laughs, showing off that wide smile that reminds me of Peter.

"Shit, son, have you ever heard the saying, 'Don't poke the bear?'" I nod, flashing a smile of my own. "Now imagine that bear has superpowers."

We both laugh, savoring a genuine moment of happiness.

"Bron, we're ready," Augustus tells our bronze friend. "If you'll do the honors."

Bron waves his hand, which conjures a pool of white light at our feet. Augustus looks down, likes what he sees, then spares one final glance at Bron.

"We'll be back in about thirty minutes," he tells the giant.

"That means nothing to me," Bron deadpans.

"I know," Augustus says, laughing, as the white light consumes us.

✠ ✠ ✠

I HAVE NO IDEA WHERE BRON HAS SENT US, BUT THE moment the white light fades, and I open my eyes in our new surroundings, I recognize the towering walls made of black marble that I've only ever seen in one place: the bastille. One peek over the nearby parapet confirms it, as I see the multi-colored,

I KNOW KUNG-FU · 149

knee-high grass swaying gently in the non-existent breeze fifty feet below us.

"The bastille, huh?" I ask Augustus.

"I guess Bron figured it would be nice and quiet since the angels have already come and gone," he answers. "Unless we find another angel in the grass."

Knowing what we're about to do, my mind is flooded with memories from what feels like forever ago, even though it was fewer than seventy-two hours earlier.

"You know, I saw in a vision some abilities that I hadn't yet developed," I tell the old man. "I got the first two: giant red fists and blue flames enveloping my whole body. But there was another one that seemed almost too good to be true."

"What was it?" he asks.

I close my eyes and press my palms into my forehead, willing my brain to bring forth the memory. Normally, that wouldn't be difficult. But given the onslaught of earth-shattering revelations I've absorbed recently, recalling one vision is like trying to pick a specific snowball out of an avalanche.

The image swims slowly to the forefront of my mind's eye. I can see the images; they're blurry, but there's enough detail to make out what's happening.

"I see my hand wrapping around Malphas's throat," I begin as the image continues to sharpen. "And then he turns to ash—just like that."

I snap my fingers to add emphasis. Augustus smiles before responding.

"Just like the red fists and the blue flames, the disintegration thing is real, too. Takes a lot out of you, especially with more powerful demons, but it's a nice arrow to have in your quiver. I suspect you'll develop it in time, just like the others."

"Those both came in the heat of battle," I conclude. "Is that normal for us?"

"Oh yeah," he replies. "When that 'fight' instinct kicks in, it's extra powerful for us nephilim. Usually, it brings forth the ability we most need in that moment. Beyond the fancy stuff, I want to give you a few pointers on how to fight a new type of challenger: angels. This is a different ballgame than facing demons. You're used to brawling with street thugs. Up here, we're fighting black belt karate masters."

"That's why you said controlling your emotions was critical," I say.

"Right," he replies. "You crack that door at all, they'll kick it wide open."

Augustus steps toward me, places his hand on my chest, and then takes one step back, so he's about three feet away. He looks me in the eyes, hands at his side.

"I want you to try and hit me," he says. "I'm not going to let you do that. As we spar, I want you to pay very close attention to your emotions. Are you ready?"

"You want me to try and hit you?" I ask, making sure I heard him right.

"No powers," he answers. "Just show me what you got. Let's start there."

I shake my head, mumble "OK," and assume a fighting stance: balls of my feet, fists raised like I'm in a boxing match. I figure I'll try the combo that worked against Gavreel: straight, straight, left hook, right uppercut.

I take a deep breath, steady my nerves and my mind, then strike. Augustus swipes away my straights with one arm, then the other. When I throw my hook, he ducks effortlessly under it. He then steps aside as my uppercut whistles past him and brings his left fist down in a lightning strike that stops inches from my jaw.

"Holy shit," I mutter, feeling my face flush with embarrassment.

"You went with the combo you used against Gavreel?" Augustus asks. He sounds surprised, if not a tad disappointed. "You've got to mix it up a bit!"

"How did you know that?" I ask, confused. "You weren't even there yet."

He taps his head. "I wasn't, but I was tuned in. You telegraphed it beforehand."

"Is that what you did just now?" I counter. "Read my mind, try to gain an edge?"

Augustus laughs and points at me. "Oh no," he says. "Your punches are just slow."

"Oh, OK," I say with a chuckle. "That makes me feel better. Thank you."

Augustus waves this comment away as he steps forward and places a hand on my shoulder. He looks me in the eyes and points his other hand toward me.

"Fighting is like dancing," he begins. "You have your go-to moves, but you need to use them in different combinations. You also can't be afraid to throw some new moves in there from time to time, even if you're not comfortable with them."

"You're saying my moves have gotten a bit stale?" I ask.

"Just a little," he says, holding his thumb and index finger a smidge apart.

"The problem is that I never learned how to fight," I explain. "I was just winging it against Malphas and his demons. Sometimes it felt like my limbs were moving of their own accord, but now it feels like I'm swimming outside of my depths. How am I supposed to mix up my moves when I don't have any in the first place?"

Augustus is thunderstruck by this comment.

"Well shit, Silas," he says. "Why didn't you say so sooner? I just assumed you had gotten the programming like every other nephilim."

"I thought I had gotten the programming!" I say. "You're saying I haven't?"

Rather than reply, Augustus touches his finger to my forehead. It's as if an ice cube has been pressed against my skin. The iciness ripples out from his finger, spider-webbing its way through my entire

body. My eyes close as everything goes white. What happens next isn't exactly clear. There's a sound like rushing wind, but it's inside my head, almost like I've got headphones turned up to full blast.

Two seconds might have passed since Augustus touched my forehead, or it might have been two hours for all I know. Everything is white and loud.

When he finally removes his finger, the roaring stops instantly, and my vision slowly swims back into focus. I see Augustus standing before me, his brow knitted in concern but his toothy smile revealing his true feelings.

"What did you just do?" I breathlessly ask him.

"Long story short: I gave you a crash course in every major fighting style the world has ever known," he answers. "Let me show you."

Augustus raises his right fist, aiming a punch straight for my jaw. I see the fingers curl downward and the thumb wrap around the index and middle fingers in slow motion. I don't move, but my brain is already in motion. The feeling is similar to when the demon charged me inside Mom's house, and I shot him: someone else is pulling my strings. I'm no longer in control of my body—it's protecting itself.

I raise my left arm and swat away Augustus's punch, then grab the lapels of his duster jacket. I place my right foot outside his right leg, twist my hips, and throw him to the ground like a sack of potatoes. He lands on his back and rolls, effortlessly popping up off the ground like a man one-fifth his age.

I look down at my hands, mouth agape, convinced they belong to someone else.

"What...the hell...was that?" I ask Augustus, the shock making it hard to speak.

"That was a perfectly executed judo throw," he tells me. "You've never taken judo, have you?" I shake my head. "Well, you have now. In fact, I'd say you just went from beginner to expert in about ten seconds."

"The programming you mentioned—it was fighting styles," I say.

"The means to execute, too. It's one thing to know the moves for each fighting style. You also just got decades of muscle memory on top of all that."

"Is that why my brain feels like it went through a mental marathon?" I massage my brow as I speak. My brain feels fried, like it did after I finished the LSAT.

"Yeah, I suppose that would be a side effect of receiving the programming like that. Typically nephilim are programmed the first twenty-five years of their life. Then, on their birthday, the program activates. Like a trojan horse, only good."

I shake my head to clear the brain fog. It doesn't work, but we don't exactly have time for me to take a power nap, and I'm sure Heaven is fresh out of coffee.

The sparring session must continue, even if I feel less than 100 percent.

"Can I try to hit you again now?" I ask Augustus. At this, his face lights up.

"I would love nothing more," he says. "Please, be my guest."

This time, I spread my feet shoulder-width apart, then squat, so my thighs are parallel with the ground. I extend my left fist out and raise my right hand above my head, my hand pointed toward Augustus. Rather than feeling forced, the stance feels natural, like I've done it for decades. Augustus mirrors my stance.

"Do you know what this stance is called?" he asks.

Of course not. I have no idea what this is called.

"The horse stance," I tell him with the utmost certainty. "It's the first stance you learn in Shaolin Kung Fu because it lowers your center of gravity."

As soon as I finish speaking, I stare at Augustus, utterly perplexed.

"You'll get used to it," he tells me. "I never learned that Shaolin Kung Fu started in the year 527 in the Henan Province of China, but by God, I know it now."

I laugh, then take a deep breath to clear my mind and steady my nerves.

When I lunge forward, it's a gliding motion that's totally new for me. And whereas before, my punches were long and looping, now they're short and quick.

Augustus and I dance atop the bastille, advancing forward and back, each throwing punches that the other deflects with a wrist flick. After several unsuccessful flurries of punches, I retreat backward and switch to a different style: Keysi.

I bend my arms at a ninety-degree angle and raise them up by my ears, similar to how I'd hold my arms if I ever did sit-ups. Augustus, still in his Kung Fu stance, springs forward with several quick punches, which I block with my elbows.

I fire back at him with my forearms, just missing on a couple of hammer fists. He backs up, smirking, and then lunges at me again, firing even more punches my way. I manage to swipe away each one. Right before he throws another combo, I quickly step back, taking myself out of his punch radius. Augustus tries to course-correct mid-punch, but his momentum propels him right into me.

I block his wayward punch with my right elbow, then bring a left hammer fist crashing down toward his face. Like he did for me, I stop inches from his jaw.

I don't mind punching angels in the jaw, but I'm not going to deck Augustus. He claps his hands together and lets out a joyous "whoo!" I can't help but smile.

"That's what I'm talking about!" he exclaims. "You're starting to think about the fight rather than just reacting to what your opponent is doing."

That did feel different. I switched my style and waited for Augustus to make a mistake, whereas before, I'd charge in blind and hope for the best. I don't know if it's the programming I received or the confidence I now have, knowing I no longer need to wing it during battle. Most likely, it's a mixture of both.

But there's no denying it: something inside me has changed.

"Alright, now I'm going to take the training wheels off," Augustus says, backing up. "I'm going to try to make you angry. Your job is not to stop me from kicking your ass—" he pauses as we both laugh, "but to keep your emotions in check."

I nod, assume the Keysi stance, and the dance begins again. Augustus is a blur of motion this time. It's all I can do to swing my elbows down and block his tornado of punches and kicks. I lean back to avoid a roundhouse punch and stumble, giving Augustus an opening to strike while I'm off-balance. I can't get my elbow up in time to block a punch flying in from my right, so I let off a small cleansing flame that redirects his fist away from my face. Instantly, his face contorts.

"No powers!" he yells.

He launches into another attack, which is somehow even more furious than before. I'm no longer able to keep up as his punches stop inches from my chest and face.

Thump! Shot to the jaw.

Whack! Punch to the chest.

Snap! Roundhouse kick to the ribs.

The confidence I had moments earlier is gone. I'm a mass of flailing limbs while Augustus ruthlessly wedges a punch or kick into any window he finds.

I overcompensate during an attempted block and lose my balance, falling onto both knees. Augustus jumps in to rain punches down, so the breeze generated by his fists tickles the back of my neck. I can't stand up, anger building like a fire being fed by gasoline. I try to spin away, but Augustus cuts me off and keeps pounding.

Wham, wham, wham, wham, wham!

The punches aren't landing, but I feel them all the same. I try again to escape his avalanche of punches, but he blocks my path for a second time.

That's when I lose it. A cleansing flame erupts from my body.

Except Augustus doesn't go flying. Instead, the force of my blast pushes back down onto me, knocking me flat on my face, skin pressed against the cold stone of the bastille. Augustus straddles me now, raining punches and elbows upon me.

"I said no powers," he roars. "So I blocked your flame with one of my own!"

I try to press myself up, but Augustus's weight keeps me pinned. I try to flip over onto my back, but it's no use. That's when I look up and see I'm lying next to a wall, so I raise my hand and let off a short cleansing flame. Before Augustus can react, I'm propelled out from under him and come to a stop three feet away.

I jump to my feet and ready myself for an attack, but none comes. Augustus climbs to his feet and turns to face me, a look of consideration on his face.

"I know, I cheated," I say preemptively. "But you were kicking my ass."

"I told you I was going to do that," Augustus replies. "I'm more disappointed that you fell back into reactionary mode instead of remaining engaged."

"I'm still learning the ropes here, Augustus," I shoot back, heat rising up my cheeks. "Before Malphas kidnapped Peter, I'd never thrown a punch before!"

"I understand," he says in a slow, measured voice. "But we don't have time for training wheels up here. An angel could come swooping in any second, hell-bent on killing you. And if you fight with this," he pauses, pointing at his heart, then up at his head, "instead of this, they're going to rip you a new one, son."

I sigh and rub my face. "I know what you're saying is true, but that doesn't make it any easier for me. I've been nothing but angry ever since I left Tully's Tavern a few nights ago, when this all started. Scared, too, but mainly just pissed off."

Augustus's expression has softened. "I know what you mean."

"Do you?" I ask him, frustration seeping into the words. "From

what I've seen, you're cool as a cucumber when the bullets start flying."

"'From what you've seen' being the key phrase," he tells me. "Why do you think I kept fighting to the age that I did, going decades past the end of a natural life?"

"You were angry over Marianne's death," I say softly.

"Right," he whispers. "But not at the demons. At myself."

Augustus points at his chest, tears glistening from the edges of his eyes.

"I raged up and down both coasts and everywhere in between, hurling myself into demon pits and ripping deadeyes limb from limb for decades without stopping," he continues. "Death wasn't a punishment. I clocked back in just as fast as I clocked out. My pittance for her death was endless toil, blood, and suffering."

I don't speak. I just stare at Augustus, who's gazing off at the horizon, lost in his recollection. The tears are flowing freely now, like two tiny rivers.

He doesn't say anything for a long time. I let the silence stretch on before a question bubbles into my conscious mind, one that's been lurking just below the surface ever since I arrived in Heaven and found my great great-grandfather waiting for me. I don't know if he'll answer—but I have to ask him.

"You chose to quit fighting," I say slowly. "But you're not in the throne room. You're here with me, trying to stop a war between angels. Why is that, Augustus?"

Now Augustus is sobbing. It's a jarring sight, hands covering his face as his whole body heaves. I don't push him for an answer. Instead, I walk over and place a hand on his shoulder, like he did for me back in Bron's canyon. When he lowers his hand and turns to face me, his eyes are red, and his cheeks are splashed with tears.

"I don't want to go there," he says in a choked whisper.

"Why not?" I ask him.

"I can't face her."

"Face who?"

"Marianne."

"Why not?"

Augustus lets out a long, low cry, like that of a wounded animal. Whatever the reason, it's a painful one. As he stares at me, his lip trembles.

"It's my fault she's dead."

CHAPTER 12

REUNITED AND IT FEELS SO GOOD

THIS IS, OF COURSE, LUDICROUS. AUGUSTUS IS no more responsible for Marianne's death than I was for Peter's kidnapping. But I know where he's coming from. When it's your family, the burden you place on yourself is much heavier. If something bad happens, logical or not, you believe you could've done something to stop it.

I don't know if it helps us cope or grieve or if we do it simply to feel something other than sadness. Guilt, as much as it drags you down, stings a lot less.

"I don't know Marianne," I admit. "But I feel pretty confident saying she'd kick your ass if she could see you right now, blaming yourself for her death."

A watery smile tugs at the edges of Augustus's mouth.

"She was as tough as she was sweet," he says. "I really miss her."

"When this is over," I say, grabbing him by both shoulders, "you need to go to her. You've fought and sacrificed enough. It's my turn now."

"I don't know if I'm ready," he whispers, staring at the ground.

"When you see her, all these worries are going to melt away," I say. "There won't be any tears or anger or accusations. You'll be reunited, and you'll be happy."

"You're right," he says. "I know you're right. I've just spent so long running from her. It's almost an instinct at this point. Isn't that sad?"

"I get it," I tell him. "But you don't have to run anymore. Just because you've been doing something for a long time doesn't mean you can't change. Look at me. I used to be the world's worst fighter. But now..."

"You're a Kung Fu master," Augustus finishes.

"Exactly."

Augustus smiles big this time, his red eyes lighting up.

"Thanks, Silas," he says, pulling me in for a hug. "I needed this."

"You're welcome," I tell him, and I mean it. He's been there so much for me already. This was the least I could do for him. As we

pull apart, I continue: "Now, let's go find Moses so I can get out of here and save my hometown."

"Are you sure you're ready?" he asks me concernedly. "We didn't exactly get to finish your training. You're like Luke running off to fight Darth Vader."

I laugh, totally caught off guard by this comment. Wasn't this man just talking about the opportunity he had to run off and fight in the Civil War?

"What?" he asks upon seeing my open-mouthed reaction. "I was still alive when it came out. The first one was amazing; I had to see what happened next!"

"You are full of surprises," I say. "But you're not wrong. I have no idea if I'm ready to go toe-to-toe with an angel and not lose my cool. But what I've learned about myself these past few days is that if you put an obstacle between me and my family or my town, I will destroy it or die trying. Or both, as it turns out."

Augustus nods. "Good enough for me," he says. "Let's go find Moses."

✝ ✝ ✝

WHEN OUR FEET TOUCH DOWN IN BRON'S CANYON, HE'S waiting for us. I can tell he's got news to share. Even with a face that's nearly impossible to read, there's a glint of nervous excitement in his big, sparkling eyes.

"Whatcha got for us, Bron?" Augustus asks, no doubt sensing what I did.

"Hello Augustus, hello Silas," he says politely. "Welcome back. While you were off at the bastille, I have been hard at work. As you requested, I located Moses."

"That's great," I interject. "Where is he?"

"In the throne room, as we expected," Bron replies. "Augustus and I will be able to enter and hopefully find an audience with him.

REUNITED AND IT FEELS SO GOOD · 163

You will have to wait outside, I'm afraid, as your sin nature prohibits you from being in God's presence."

"Wait a minute," Augustus chimes in. "What are you talking about? I can't enter the throne room. I've still got sin all over me. That disqualifies me, doesn't it?"

"I did some more research into that," Bron tells him. "You're a special case, Augustus Shaw. You're still in your human body, it's true, but you're no longer alive. You exist solely in Heaven now, not on Earth. So, while it's true that your sin is still attached to you, it's inert. If you want, you can enter the throne room."

"Are you sure?" Augustus asks. "I won't get vaporized once I step inside?"

"I checked, and I'm sure," is all Bron says.

Augustus ponders this for a moment, his gaze fixed on the ground. Then, he looks up at me, a mixture of surprise and anxiety painted across his face. I know what he's thinking: if he goes into the throne room, there's a chance he'll see Marianne.

As good as our conversation was, I'm not sure he expected to see her quite this soon. Granted, he might not see her at all, but that's not what his brain is telling him right now, judging by the look on his face.

The next voice, shockingly, is Bron's.

"There is a chance you'll see her," he tells Augustus. "But it will be her spirit, not her body. You'll recognize her once you get closer, but from a distance, what you'll recognize is a feeling deep inside you. Something intangible. Like how your heart would skip a beat when you heard her voice on the telephone."

I have to give the bronze giant some credit. I pegged him as an aloof, stumbling goofball when I first saw him. But he's shown a surprising grasp of human emotions since then, and although his attempts to connect with us have been awkward at best, I know we both appreciate the effort he's making.

We stand a better chance of getting what we need from Moses if

Augustus goes in with Bron, but I can't ask the old man to go into the throne room if he's not ready to see Marianne. If our roles were reversed, I know he wouldn't ask that of me.

"Augustus, you don't have to go in if you don't—" I start.

"I'll do it," he says quickly, cutting me off. "I'll go in with Bron."

He looks at both of us, resolute. We nod our agreement with his decision. I shift my attention to Bron to hear the game plan before we disembark.

"The plan is a simple one," he says. "We will meet with Moses, get the information we need, and then do what needs to be done to activate Lightfall. All the while, we will maintain a low profile to avoid attracting the attention of the angels."

"Keeping a low profile should be easy," Augustus says with a laugh. "We've got a twelve-foot-tall giant and two nephilim. Incognito is our middle name!"

I laugh, both at his comedic timing and his astute observation. The closer we get to activating Lightfall, the more difficult it will become to stay off the angels' radar. The angel who ambushed us will likely be the first of many before this mission is complete. Our only hope is that their civil war is an all-consuming distraction.

"If you're ready, I'll transport us to the area right outside the throne room, where Silas can wait until our business with Moses is concluded," Bron says.

"Yeah, that reminds me," Augustus begins. "You're not going to like the place where you have to hang out while we're inside. It'll bring up some bad memories."

"Are we going back to Heaven's lobby?" I ask.

"Yeah..." Augustus says sheepishly. "Sorry about that."

"It's fine," I tell him. "It's not like an angel strangled me there or anything."

Another round of laughs, even from Bron. Augustus and I fall in line behind him as we walk toward the compression tunnel at the entrance of his canyon. He asks if I want to blackout again, and I

REUNITED AND IT FEELS SO GOOD · 165

tell him "no." I can't stomach the thought of seeing Colin and Peter again. It's better to endure this discomfort than that one.

✠ ✠ ✠

RETURNING TO THIS PLACE IS STRANGE. WE LAND JUST a few yards away from where Gregori tried to kill me, but as I stare at that spot, I feel oddly disconnected from the memory of that event. It feels like it happened to another Silas who lived a hundred years ago, not the version of myself standing here right now.

I wave goodbye to Bron and Augustus as they set off for the throne room, disappearing in a pop of white light. As I stroll over to the spot where I stood when I first arrived in Heaven, I stare up at the sky above the platform I'm on.

The view—which depicts some of the universe's most stunning phenomena, all scrolling across the horizon like a real-life screen-saver—is still awe-inspiring. I allow myself to get lost in the planets, stars, and galaxies as they swim lazily by, my mind drifting to the events of the past week. I've experienced more in these past few days than I did in my first twenty-five years of life combined.

When I walked out of Tully's Tavern on my birthday, I had a vision for what my life would look like. One night completely changed that vision. Shattered it, in fact. The life I have now is still my own, but I'm inextricably tied to events and beings that were, just a week ago, nothing more than flights of a fanciful imagination.

Did I believe angels existed? No idea, but that would be nice if they did. *What about Heaven?* I believed it existed but didn't think I'd go there any time soon.

And demons—don't forget about them! They're real, and all of them want you dead.

It's hard to pin down what's been crazier: the hunt for Malphas on Earth or what's happened in Heaven since I got here. Sure, down on Earth, I descended into a demon pit with a young girl watching

166 · FALL OF THE ANGELS

my back and exploded a massive demon by setting off a cleansing flame inside his body. But up here, I used the fruit from a time-traveling tree to learn the truth about what happened to my dad. I also got backhanded by an archangel and discovered the first woman God created in a pocket dimension. Thinking about Lilith, I can't help but wonder what she's been up to since she left me. As long as she's not causing trouble for us, it's all good. I'd like to believe she'll make good on her promise, but given that God locked her up for centuries, it's reasonable to assume she might not keep her word.

I sigh and rub a hand through my hair. I have no idea how long Bron and Augustus will be gone, and when I try to tune into the old man's frequency, all I get is static. So, it's safe to assume that the throne room, like Lilith's corner of the world, doesn't allow for angelic telepathy. Or Augustus wants some time to himself, just in case he sees Marianne during their trek to find Moses. If that's the case, I don't blame him. I'm thankful that when I used the time trees to find out what happened to my dad, I didn't have someone dropping in on my private thoughts.

My mind drifts to Peter, Colin, and the others, and my stomach clenches at the thought that they could be locked in a life-or-death battle with demons at this very moment. It kills me not to be down there with them.

Everything in me wants to run and jump off this platform, click my heels, and teleport back to Earth. I have no idea if that's how the return journey works after a nephilim dies, but I reckon I could figure it out on the way down. But if I left, it would leave Augustus and Bron shorthanded in a war that isn't going our way.

I love my brother and grandfather, but I love my great-great-grandfather, too. Leaving him would be wrong, just as it would be wrong to leave my friends on Earth in their moment of need. Besides, Colin revered Augustus. He would never forgive me if I abandoned his kin, even if I had noble intentions for doing so.

The fact is: I'm staying here until the job is done. I know that

REUNITED AND IT FEELS SO GOOD · 167

time is passing much faster down on Earth, but I have to block that from my consciousness. If I give in to that anxiety, I will not have the willpower left to stay here until the job is done.

What I can do is try to send Colin and Peter a message. I have no idea if this will work. I just know I have to try. I squeeze my eyes shut, take a deep breath, and clear my mind. I picture the two of them in front of me—not in combat, not looking defeated inside an old pickup truck, just looking at me bemusedly.

My words, whether written or spoken, tend to mirror my thoughts: composed and well-reasoned. However, nothing is coming to me at the moment. Aside from the image of Peter and Colin, my mind's eye is totally blank.

Don't overthink it. Just speak from the heart.

There's that voice again. It's not Augustus, Bron, or even my inner voice. It's a calm, reassuring voice that I want to push back against, only I haven't seen the need. The voice, wherever it's coming from, has tended to give good advice.

Speak from the heart, I think to myself. *I can do that.*

"Hey guys," I think. "I don't know if you can hear this, but I'm sending it out into the universe anyway. I'm OK. I'm here in Heaven with Augustus, and we're working to end a civil war that's broken out between the angels. It's bad, and it's only getting worse. I would've come back right away, but Augustus can't do this without me. As much as I want to leave, I have to stay here and see this through."

I pause, my eyes welling with tears. I breathe deep and recenter myself.

"I really miss you guys. But I wouldn't be here if I didn't know for sure that you guys can handle whatever is going on down there. Stay safe and watch each other's backs. I'll be there soon, and when I get there, I'll make those demons pay."

As I open my eyes, it feels like a weight has been lifted off me. Until now, I didn't even realize I was carrying it. Only by its absence has it become noticeable.

You trusted that speaking from the heart was the right choice. How do you feel?

This is the first time the voice has asked a question.

Not sure how to respond, I treat it like angel telepathy.

Lighter. Like a great weight has been taken off my shoulders.

It feels a bit absurd, talking to the voice of a person (or thing) that I've never met and can't see. At least with angel telepathy, I know who's on the other line.

That is because you released yourself from the burden of control. A nephilim who tries to control every outcome will not be effective. To wield this gift requires trust.

I have to chuckle at that note. More and more, I'm learning how much my need for control has been inhibiting my effectiveness as God's chosen warrior. I'd like to say it stems from the career path I chose, but the truth is, I was a control freak long before I stepped foot in a courtroom. I think it goes back to growing up without a dad for much of my life and having a younger brother I had to protect.

As much as I could, I tried to shelter Peter from the parts of life that become more difficult without a dad. I learned how to perfectly knot a tie and throw a curveball so I could teach Peter, but there were certain times I couldn't replace our dad.

I couldn't coach Peter from the sidelines in Little League like the other dads, or teach him how to talk to girls, or give him sound advice when he got in fights at school. Not being that much older than him, I was still trying to figure out all those things for myself. Still, it ate me up inside whenever I couldn't protect him from the harsher aspects of our new reality. Each time Peter got hurt, it made me that much more determined to control everything around me.

I see now in vivid detail how destructive this urge can be. I think I've known this truth for a while, but until demons and angels started trying to kill me, I didn't realize how much it had

affected my well-being. Now, having released myself from the burden of controlling what's happening on Earth, I not only see the difference it can make—I can *feel* it. Even the air around me feels lighter.

You are learning to let go. There is, however, one thing left to surrender.

I'm not sure what the voice is referencing. I thought the insatiable desire I had to return to Earth was the only thing holding me back at the moment.

What else do I need to release?

A moment of silence passes. I gaze upward as if the voice will come from above.

Would you like to see for yourself?

I want to question the voice, ask who I'm talking to before I blindly agree to see what's behind Door A. But since this is a lesson about trust, I bite my tongue.

Yes, please show me.

Nothing happens for a few seconds. I glance around, wondering if I'm about to be teleported away or some regal figure is about to appear to whisk me off. Right as I open my mouth to speak, my eyes gently slide shut, and my chin drops to my chest. I'm still awake, but my consciousness is leaving my body again, just like it did when I jumped into the bottomless pit with Lilith. I see myself standing there for a half-second before my roaming awareness is sucked through a golden wormhole.

Only this time, I'm not deposited in Bron's canyon. This time, I enter into a room that is bathed in a soft, white light. Besides the light, the first thing I notice is the water. It is deep blue and as still as a pane of glass. Standing on the water are figures robed in white who are all facing the same direction. As my vision shifts upward, I see they're facing a giant white throne upon which sits the silhouette of a person.

I can't make out their features. It's as if the sun is right behind

him, leaving his body as a total shadow. But as I stare at the figure upon the throne, I feel an odd sense of familiarity, like I'm looking into the face of a friend I haven't seen in a decade.

Whoever the robed figures are, they seem to be worshipping whoever is on the throne. Some are kneeling, others have their hands raised, and a few of them are even dancing! Even from here, I can tell their praise is joyful, not forced.

I realize now that I'm seeing Heaven's throne room, but rather than smacking me across the face, this revelation dawns slowly and peacefully, like a bubble rising to the surface of a pond. It's as if I always knew this fact and am simply recalling it.

As my perspective shifts, I'm able to see what's behind the sea of glass and the worshipping robed figures. I'm reminded of a concert when the audience collectively pulls out their cell phones or lighters and holds them up.

That's what I see: a million pinpricks of light set against a brilliant blue backdrop. And just like a concert, they're slowly swaying back and forth as if in rhythm to a song. I can't hear anything, but I know it's a song of celebration being sung. Where this knowledge comes from, I can't say, but I know it's true, just like I know my own name. I let the sight wash over me for a while, lost in the beauty of the lights listing gently from side to side. After a few moments, another realization bubbles up to the surface: Bron said that if Augustus saw Marianne, she'd be a spirit.

Those millions of lights...they're all spirits.

And if Marianne is here, waiting for Augustus, then perhaps I was brought here to see the two people my heart longs to see the most—more so than even Colin and Peter. Although disconnected from my body, my heart aches at the thought.

My parents. They're here.

There are millions of pinpricks of light with no discernible distinction between them. Bron said Augustus would recognize Marianne, but he didn't say how. Thankfully, I don't have to stumble

REUNITED AND IT FEELS SO GOOD · 171

my way through this. I was brought here by someone—and I'm starting to realize who—for a specific reason.

Can you show me my parents?

I watch the lights sway back and forth as I await the response. It's so peaceful; I lose track of time for a while. I haven't been this relaxed in a very long time.

Finally, the voice speaks.

Let me show you.

I zoom forward, homing in on a pair of lights that come into sharper focus the closer I get. What I thought was just light is actually the shape of a person. Their body, rather than being flesh, is made up of light. But their features are apparent once you get close enough. This fact becomes obvious as my consciousness glides to a stop a few feet away from a pair of figures who are dancing like they're at a concert—their hands raised, their eyes closed, singing their hearts out.

My mom looks like she does in my memories...the good ones, that is. Gone is the hollowed-out face and frail body that was ravaged by cancer. Here, she's the same beautiful woman I remember from my childhood. She had beautiful strawberry blonde hair that always smelled like flowers and the deepest blue eyes I've ever seen. And that smile, with those dimples, always warmed my heart.

I feel tears welling, just like I felt the pang in my heart earlier. My mom is so happy, so alive, and so peaceful. After a horrible, pain-filled end to her life, this is all I ever wanted for her. To know that the saying was true: she is in a better place now.

Then there's my dad. He looks like he did in my vision, except his appearance is more composed. His goatee is perfectly manicured, and his eyes are bright and alive, not dark and bloodshot. As I watch, he pauses from his celebratory dance to look over at my mom, who keeps on singing. He smiles at her, a simple gesture that communicates more about their love than a million words could describe.

The tears are flowing now. I understand now what the voice was

172 · FALL OF THE ANGELS

talking about. What's been holding me back wasn't just my need for control. It was uncertainty. Around my parents' fate, yes, but also... all of this. Everything I've seen of the unseen realm—Heaven, Hell, demons, and angels—has been bloody and violent. It's been war and betrayal, pride and ego, and the devastating fallout. *Is there anything good on the other side of all this? Are we fighting for a worthwhile cause, or am I just trapped in a bleak struggle between eternal forces with no end in sight?*

Even if I've never vocalized these questions, they've been heavy on my mind since I walked out of Tully's Tavern, and the illusion of my reality was shattered.

How could I fight with nobility and honor if there was nothing virtuous backing my cause? If I was just another cog in a war machine, my heart would never be in the fight. I'd either run and hide to stay safe or tap out the first chance I got.

But now, seeing this, I don't have those doubts anymore. There is a light at the end of the tunnel. It's real, and it's worth fighting for. While the rest of Heaven might be burning down around it, this is the answer to the question we all have:

What happens to us after we die?

I thought it was violence, secrets, and lies when I first arrived here. And that's still true. I'd be a fool to ignore that part of my experience. But it's more than that. What happens after we draw our last breath is that we get to enjoy a beautiful existence with those we love the most, free from all the ugliness outside.

There is still one more thing you must release.

The voice is back. It's the voice, I now know, belonging to God. He brought me here because he knew exactly what I needed, even if I didn't know. And now, although I've gotten more from this trip than I ever could have dreamed, I'm going to trust that there's something else holding me back I haven't considered. I'm not going to fight his direction or argue with his reasoning. I'm simply going to let go.

REUNITED AND IT FEELS SO GOOD · 173

Show me, please.

I pull away from my parents, and as my consciousness begins to turn, I get one last look at their smiling faces. It's an image I will cherish for the rest of my life. I zoom in toward the throne now, angling toward the left side. Now that I'm a little closer and the backlight obscuring God isn't so bright, I see there's another throne near God's right hand. It's smaller but equally as impressive. On it sits, not a shadowy silhouette, but a man who looks to be of Middle Eastern descent. He has bushy black hair, a full beard, and a thick mustache. It takes me a second to realize who I'm looking at. I'm so used to seeing him depicted as a white man upon a cross.

Sitting on the throne at the right hand of God—this is Jesus.

As my consciousness comes to a stop before his throne, he steps off of it and walks slowly toward me, a gentle smile upon his face. He gives a small wave.

"Hello Silas," he says in a clear, calm voice. "My name is Jesus. I've heard a lot about you from my father. He is very fond of you and your kinsman, Augustus Shaw."

Lacking vocal cords, I go for telepathy, hoping Jesus will hear it.

It's an honor to meet you, Jesus. I heard a lot about you growing up from my mom.

"Stacy Ford," he says, smiling again. "One of my favorites. You and Peter were both very blessed to have her as a mother. She raised you in the faith, even if all you heard as children were stories about arks and parting seas."

She made sure we knew who you were. I'm thankful for that.

"As am I," Jesus says. "Tell me, what brings you to the throne room?"

Now comes the moment of truth. Why am I here? God knew there was a reason, and a compelling one at that. Otherwise, he wouldn't have brought me here.

I don't have to search too hard for the reason, though. It's the

first question I had when I learned about my destiny as a nephilim. The one still left unanswered.

Why did God pick me as his nephilim?

"That is an excellent question," Jesus answers. "The ways of God can never truly be understood by man. That's why I taught with stories during my time on Earth—to help people comprehend, as best they could, what is truly incomprehensible. But that is not a satisfactory answer to your question."

He pauses, looking up at me to smile again.

"Here's what I can tell you, Silas. You were chosen for a reason. It was not some form of retribution against Augustus. It was also not a random choice. God chose you because he knew you'd make the right decision in this moment when Heaven finds itself engulfed in war. Even amidst your uncertainty, God's faith in you has never wavered. Because he knows who you are inside here."

Jesus points to his heart. As he does, I notice the hole in his wrist is still there.

That's reassuring. Nothing about this decision has been easy.

Jesus nods in agreement.

"If it was easy, God could have chosen anyone," he tells me. "But he knows beyond a doubt that you'll make the right decision—now and in the future. Because there is another moment for which you were chosen. A decision you will soon be forced to make that seems impossible, and that will act as a watershed moment in history."

I guess it would be too easy to know what that decision will be?

Jesus actually laughs at this as he shakes his head.

"If I told you, it would influence the decision. But know this: God is always close by. He is never apart from you, even when it feels like you're alone. Call out to him, and he will answer you. It might not be his audible voice like you've heard today, but my father always equips those he calls and answers their prayers."

I can feel our time together coming to an end. Any moment, my consciousness will return to my body. Knowing this may be my last

REUNITED AND IT FEELS SO GOOD · 175

chance to speak with God's son, I say the thing I've wanted to tell Jesus since I was a little boy listening as Mom read me Bible stories before bed. It's a little corny, but I don't even care.

Thank you for what you did on the cross.

"It was an agonizing choice," Jesus admits. "But I'd do it all over again for you."

With Jesus's words still ringing in my ears, I zoom up and out of God's throne room, the twinkling light of a million souls stretching out like shooting stars.

CHAPTER 13

NEVER TOO LATE FOR A CHANGE OF HEART

UGUSTUS AND BRON ARE WAITING FOR ME WHEN my consciousness returns to my body. As I lift my chin from my chest, they're both staring at me with an expression that mixes concern and bemusement. After my experience in the throne room, it's nice to see flesh and blood people, not souls with bodies made of light.

"I saw them," I tell Augustus, my voice quavering. "My parents."

"I saw Marianne," he tells me in response.

"How was it?" I ask him.

"It was good," he says. "So, so good."

Then he's crying, and I am too. We wrap each other up in an embrace and just sob, the pooled-up emotions that we've been silently drowning in for decades pouring out. I feel the tension release in Augustus's rock-solid shoulders.

For a long moment, Heaven isn't at war. Angels aren't trying to kill us. My hometown isn't being ravaged by demons, and my friends and family aren't putting their lives at risk to stop it. We're just two men dropping our guard and giving ourselves permission to let go of the pain we've been carrying.

When we finally pull apart, Augustus's eyes are puffy and red.

"God, we look like shit now," he says with a laugh.

"I've always been an ugly crier," I tell him.

"Apparently, it runs in the family," he says.

I felt lighter before, when I acknowledged my need for control and started to release myself from it. Now I feel almost weightless. It's like I've shrugged off a couple of hundred-pound bags from my shoulders whose weight I'd grown numb to.

Trying to control everything since Dad died. Living with the doubt of what happened to my parents since they both left us. In the past few days, carrying around the gigantic "why me" question tied to my nephilim destiny.

God just helped me toss those bags to the side. I know my parents are OK. I can see how much my desire for control has been

178 · FALL OF THE ANGELS

limiting me. I still have questions about what Jesus told me—and the impossible decision I'll face—but at least I now know my selection wasn't random, nor was it done to punish Augustus.

"So you saw your parents?" Augustus asks me.

"I did," I say as I wipe the tears off my cheeks. "They were so happy."

"Marianne was the same way," Augustus tells me. "As beautiful as the day I met her. I didn't see her at first. But like Bron said, something drew me in her direction. It was like driving down a road I hadn't been on in years. It felt natural. It felt right. I walked right up to her and knew in an instant it was her."

"She was celebrating, wasn't she?" I ask him. "So full of joy she could burst."

"Most beautiful thing I've ever seen," he says, his voice barely above a whisper.

"And how do you feel, Augustus?"

This question comes not from me but from Bron. Augustus turns around to stare at the bronze giant, then looks back at me with a shocked but bemused look.

He doesn't dismiss Bron's question, though. Like me, I think Augustus is starting to appreciate the giant's surprising grasp of human emotions. Maybe it's doing him some good to spend so much time with us and our messy feelings.

"I feel the best I've felt since the day she died," he tells Bron. "The guilt I was carrying was so corrosive; I'm surprised it didn't burn right through me. I've still got some processing to do, but that moment meant everything to me."

He turns to face Bron, his expression earnest. "Thank you for taking me."

"You're welcome, my friend," Bron says stoically.

"Alright," Augustus says, shaking his arms out, "let's talk more about our feelings after we stop these angels from killing each other. Sound good?"

NEVER TOO LATE FOR A CHANGE OF HEART · 179

I nod and reply, "Works for me. Did you see Moses and get what we need?"

"We did. Thankfully, Moses was more receptive to us than the archangels were. He's still plugged in, too. Knows that the throne room might be in danger."

"Moses told us the locations of the three zones on Earth, and we know what must be done to turn them into angel traps," Bron adds. "Our challenge now is to mobilize forces in those areas to complete the necessary rituals."

"Thankfully, one of the three zones is in the United States, so Colin and his crew can handle it," Augustus continues. "It's near Lawrence, Kansas. I know a couple guys who operate there, but I wouldn't trust them with a job like this."

I've already spotted a couple of flaws in the plan to use Colin for this job.

"Jersey is pretty far away from Kansas," I tell them. "And even if it wasn't, Colin and his team aren't going to leave Sherwood unprotected to travel out there."

"They won't have to," Augustus tells me. "We're going to send an angel down to teleport our three teams to their respective zones. It'll be much safer and much faster than driving out there. Colin and them will be gone for an hour, tops, and they only need two men for the job. Forrest and Grace can stay behind."

"Why not send me down to teleport them?" I object. "I can get down there and move all three teams before we can find an angel who's willing to help us."

"That's true," Augustus counters. "But there's two things you aren't considering. One, when the angels find out we're moving people to the zones, they'll come after us full force. I need you here for the fight. Two, when you see your friends and family, you won't come back up here. You and I both know that."

I stare at the ground, not able to meet Augustus's eyes. He's right, of course. If I got sent back right now, there's no way I'd come

back to Heaven to finish the fight up here. I just wouldn't have the strength to leave—never mind the dying part.

I see Peter, Colin, and the others in my mind's eye, and my heart longs to see them again, but I know they'll have to wait. Augustus is thinking more rationally about this than I am. Now is the time to latch onto his plan and execute it swiftly.

"You're right," I admit. "So we need to find an angel who's not only sympathetic to our cause but willing to leave his comrades' side, go to Earth, and teleport three teams to zones where they can set up traps to ensnare him and said comrades."

"Well, when you put it like that, it does sound pretty stupid," Augustus says. "I'm open to other ideas. The upshot of mobilizing forces without the angels involved is that it won't take as long up here as it does down there due to the time distortion. The downside is that we're so up against it. Every second we lose is valuable."

There's a long stretch of silence as we all think through our options, none of which is very appealing. The best move right now seems to be to figure out the teams, relay the message, and get them in motion while we try to secure faster transport. If we don't find a willing angel, then at least the wheels are already turning.

"I could…" Bron says hesitantly, his hand stroking his chin.

"What, Bron?" Augustus asks. "You could what?"

"I could go," he says more emphatically. "I could go to Earth and transport the teams. I haven't been there since the days of Ezekiel, but I still know the place very well, having helped God design it. Yes, I believe I could fulfill this task for us."

It's not a bad option. Bron is right—he knows Earth, knows where the zones are, and has the ability to travel via wormholes like the angels. And if I'm being honest, he is not going to be much use up here when it comes to fighting the angels.

Still, there's something reassuring about his presence. I know Augustus is familiar with Heaven's layout, but Bron has been like a

guide since I got here. Losing him, if only for a short time, would feel like trying to navigate with one eye closed.

When I look at Augustus, though, I know we're in agreement: this is the best plan.

"You're right," I tell the bronze giant. "You should do it. We'll save time and know that our friends are safe, that the angel we send won't try to kill them instead."

"I am glad you agree," Bron tells me. "Our next step is determining which teams will conduct the rituals for each zone. Colin and Peter will handle the graveyard in Lawrence, Kansas. The other spots are in Rio de Janeiro and Jerusalem."

My face crinkles up in surprise at this information, which Augustus sees.

"At the spot where Christ the Redeemer is staring, and Golgotha..." he begins.

"The site where Jesus was crucified," I finish.

"Exactly," he says. Turning to Bron, he adds, "For Rio, pick up Adriana and Francisco Machado in Manaus. Grab Aviv Cohen and Omer Levy for Jerusalem. They're in Tel Aviv, but they know Golgotha. They protect it from demons."

"They won't hesitate when I show up asking them to come with me?" Bron asks.

It's a fair question. Nobody has ever seen Bron on Earth, and trust is a precious commodity in our line of work. I've learned that lesson in just a few days.

"They will if you say the right thing," Augustus answers assumingly. "They've all worked with me before, and we developed a code phrase to indicate people who can be trusted. Just tell them, 'Orion's belt is shining bright this evening.'"

I laugh and ask, "Where did that come from?"

"We shared a love of astronomy," he answers, "and wanted to sound low-key."

"If you said that to me, Augustus, I would immediately suspect

you were involved in subterfuge or spy craft," Bron says flatly. "I would not trust you at all."

"Noted," Augustus replies with a wry smile. "Nevertheless, use that phrase with them, and they'll drop everything to come with you. All the stuff Moses told us they're going to need for the ritual, they'll either have it, or they can get it."

"Drop them off where they need to be and then haul ass back up here to help us end this war," I tell the bronze giant. He gives me a funny, quizzical look.

"Is it possible, Silas Ford, that you have grown fond of my presence?" he says.

"Don't make it weird," I reply with a laugh. "It's helpful to have another brain around, especially one that knows this place so well." He stares at me, unblinking, his mouth slightly upturned. "OK fine," I admit. "Yes, we're going to miss you."

"I knew it," he admits, a slight note of victory in his voice. "I will miss you as well, but I will return soon enough. The other step besides preparing the traps—killing the archangel Michael with his own weapon—should be your focus while I am gone. What will you two do to prepare for that moment?"

I haven't thought too much about this part since it was first brought up. It seems so impossible that even thinking about where to begin hurts my brain. Like trying to scale Mount Everest with a candle and nothing on but a pair of socks.

"We have to even the odds," Augustus declares.

Thankfully, he's put more thought into this part of the plan than I have. Hell, he might have been scheming on how to kill Michael for a long time. Based on how they treated us, I'm guessing there's no love lost between those two.

"How do you plan to do that?" Bron asks.

"We're going to track down some armory weapons," he clarifies.

Hearing the words "armory weapons" triggers a memory that hits me like a thunderbolt. There I am, in my mind's eye, striking

NEVER TOO LATE FOR A CHANGE OF HEART · 183

down an angel with a golden stone unfurled from David's sling. Whatever happens that leads to us having that weapon in the final battle, it begins right now.

"We're going after David's sling," I tell the group. They both look at me sideways, confused. "I saw it in my vision with the time trees. I didn't mention it earlier, but in the vision, I struck down an angel with a stone thrown from David's sling. You're on the exact right path, Augustus, even if you didn't realize it."

"Nice," he says. "In this vision, did you see me?"

"I did," I tell him. "You were wielding a spear." Much like my realization, these words spark something in Augustus's memories. He runs a hand through his hair, his face downturned, as a small laugh escapes his lips.

When he looks up at Bron, he says, "Joshua's spear."

"Almost certainly," he answers.

"If we can get our hands on those two weapons, we'll have a chance against the archangels," Augustus concludes. "We can't walk up and steal the flaming sword from Michael, but if we can engage him in battle, we might be able to grab it."

Michael's weapon is *the* flaming sword? Surely Augustus can't be serious.

"The flaming sword," I say. "You mean, the one…"

"That guarded the entrance to the Garden of Eden," Bron finishes.

"One and the same," Augustus chimes in. "Michael went down and retrieved it right before the Great Flood. Now it stands in his place during battle, directing troops on where to attack, like the pillar of fire that guided the Israelites in the desert."

"But if he's attacked, the sword will return to him," Bron explains. "And if anyone tries to take it from the battlefield, they'll be turned to dust."

Given what we have to do to activate Lightfall, this fact seems problematic.

"So how are we supposed to take it from him?" I ask.

"You can take it from his hand," Augustus says slowly. "It's like Thor's hammer. If you're worthy enough to strip him of it, you're worthy enough to hold it."

Bron eyes Augustus with a bemused smile, an expression Augustus returns. Something isn't being said here, but knowing the old man, I can guess.

"It sounds like you're speaking from experience," I say.

Augustus shrugs and raises his hands in front of him.

"What can I say?" he tells me. "If you wondered why Michael doesn't like me, it might have something to do with the time I yanked his sword from his hands and held it up to his neck. To my surprise, he didn't like that very much."

"Is there anyone in Heaven you haven't pissed off?" I ask with a laugh.

"Bron," he says, looking at the giant, "have I ever made you mad?"

"Many, many times, Augustus," he replies. "But it's part of your charm."

Camaraderie—that's another thing I'll miss about Bron while he's down on Earth. Having someone else to change the energy or bounce ideas off of has been invaluable as we've gone about making this plan. Now we're reaching a critical juncture, and we'll be without one leg on our stool for who knows how long.

Heaven's loss is Earth's gain, but it's time for him to go. Bron knows this, too. He looks to me, then Augustus, stoic but with the hint of a smile.

"You two keep each other safe," he says. "I will return in due time."

"Good luck," I tell him. "And while you're down there, please tell Peter and the others that I'm alive and I'm going to return to them soon. Tell them that what I'm doing up here is important. Important enough that I'm here, not there."

"I will," he says. "They'll understand, Silas." With that, there's a brilliant flash of white light that consumes Bron's enormous figure, and then he's gone.

NEVER TOO LATE FOR A CHANGE OF HEART · 185

I hope they do. I need them to understand.
The fight down there rages on. The fight up here is about to begin.

✠ ✠ ✠

WITH THE ARMORY ALREADY RAIDED, AUGUSTUS THINKS
our best bet to get ahold of the weapons I saw in my vision is to find
the battlefield where the angels are fighting and scour the grounds
to see if anything has been dropped by fallen soldiers.

He admits it's not his best plan, and I agree, but we're short
on options here. If we try to enter the fray against warring angel
armies—especially armies equipped with all-powerful weaponry—
we'll be dead before our feet hit the ground. We have to go in with
a low profile, hope to avoid detection, and see what we can find.

If we attract any unwanted attention, the plan is to withdraw to
Bron's canyon, where Augustus says there are rune-protected zones I
haven't seen yet that can offer refuge from any pursuers. Once again,
it seems like Augustus is speaking from experience. I can picture
him fleeing there after grabbing a particular sword.

"So, where do you think the battle is happening now?" I ask
him. "For both our sakes, I hope it's not the hellscape we visited last
time. I'm pretty sure if we search the grounds of that place, we'll be
treading the ninth circle of Hell."

Augustus gives a short laugh, then replies, "No, they'll have
moved on by now. One thing I know about angelic warfare is that
it moves quickly. It's the exact opposite of trench warfare. They
don't dig in and hunker down. They hit hard, fly fast, and try to
use misdirection to their advantage. That's part of the reason you
didn't see any damage at the bastille: they were there probably ten
minutes, tops."

This explains why Augustus believes we have a chance to recover
some armory weapons. If the angels are zipping around from one
battlefield to the next, they're likely not stopping to collect their

dead or retrieve their weapons. Our best bet is to find the area they just left and hope our hypothesis is correct: that they don't leave angels behind for clean-up duty, meaning we can search unnoticed.

Exactly right. That only leaves one issue, though.

Augustus is reading my thoughts again, but I don't mind at this point. It's quicker than talking, and I'm not worried about the angels eavesdropping on our mental conversations since they'll be preoccupied with killing each other.

Where have they been? Heaven is a big place.

We can't know for sure, so we have to use the process of elimination.

Augustus is right: we're shooting in the dark here. But if my days in the courtroom have taught me anything, it's that there are always factors that can make a random decision feel less like a shot in the dark. In this case, we have two such factors.

You've spent some time around the archangels. If they're directing the righteous angels, they'll want to steer the combat away from areas they don't want damaged. So, put yourself in their shoes. Where would you go? If something feels right, trust that nephilim instinct.

Good point. Having the larger army, the archangels will be able to control the flow of the battle more than the traitors. They're the wave pushing the boat.

So, where is the wave leading them?

I would rack my brain for an answer, but of the places I've been in Heaven so far, none of them is appropriate for massive battles. So, it's on Augustus to venture a guess. Thankfully, it doesn't take him long to find an answer he likes.

There's a place that would be a perfect battlefield. If they haven't been there yet, I'll be shocked. It's a little small, but it's always abandoned, save for one person.

Where is it?

The archives. Think of it like a library, except instead of books, it contains the scrolls of God. Everything he's ever dictated to angels or to mankind since the dawn of time.

Wouldn't the angels have reverence for such a place?

Under normal circumstances, yes. But if they're running the numbers like I am, they know the fallout will be marginal in that area. Worst case scenario is the scrolls all get destroyed, in which case the angels can go back to the source to replace them.

Sounds like we're headed to the archives.

Augustus holds out his arm, I grab it, and the white light takes us. When our feet touch down, we're standing in a dark room with a ceiling several stories high. There are a dozen rows of towering bookshelves lined up before us, each dimly lit with lanterns hanging every twenty feet or so from the face of the structure. Instead of shelves, though, there are horizontal bars stacked inside each frame, with rolls of paper hung over each of them like bedsheets laid on a drying rack.

Are those the scrolls?

That's right. One shelf for every hundred years or so.

As we move toward the shelves, what unsettles me about this place isn't walking between scrolls lined with the actual words of God himself, transcribed by the prophet whose ear God whispered into. No, what disturbs me here is the same thing that unsettled me at the bastille: there is no evidence of battle.

None whatsoever. There are no shelves knocked over, no scrolls torn to shreds. This room goes back a long way, easily two or three football fields long, but the rows are all a straight shot. We can both see they're all undisturbed. There are no bodies crumpled on the floor, nor weapons glinting in the lantern light.

If the angels were here—and that seems like a big "if" given the evidence—they didn't stay long. Sure, this room is large for the two of us, but for dozens (if not hundreds) of angels zipping around trying to kill each other, it would be a tight squeeze, like two boxers trying to circle each other inside a subway car.

"I don't think they were here," I say finally.

"Doesn't look like it," Augustus replies quietly. I can tell he's

disappointed. On paper, this was a promising lead, but the reality is coming up short.

"OK, we just need to keep going," I say, trying to muster new confidence in our plan of attack despite this setback. "Where else do you think makes sense?"

We're standing between two of the shelves. The light from the lantern is casting long shadows across Augustus's face, making him look more tired than usual. The knitted brow tells me he's deep in thought, but the eyes show his doubt.

He's about to speak when we both snap to alert, turning to my left at a sound coming from the area where we landed upon arrival. Augustus reaches into his duster jacket and pulls out his angel blade he took from Gavreel. In between the rows steps a figure who is tall and well-built. It's tough to make out his features at this distance, but as he steps closer, I feel a spark of recognition and surprise.

It's Puriel.

"Do not be alarmed," he says in that familiar baritone voice. "I mean you no harm."

"How the hell did you find us?" Augustus asks, still tense.

Puriel points to his head. "Angelic telepathy. I needed to find you, so I tuned into your frequency, overheard your plan to come here, and followed you."

How he found us makes sense, but he hasn't answered the big question yet.

"You said you needed to find us," I say back to him. "Why?"

He takes a deep breath, steadying himself, then says, "I believed you all to be cowards who lacked faith when we first met. You wanted to stop the fighting, and all I wanted to do was reenter the fray. I did not listen to you. But now..."

He trails off. Whatever he's about to say, it clearly pains him.

"But now what?" Augustus demands.

"But now I see that you were right," he continues. "The fighting is only going to end one way: with the complete destruction of

Heaven. My brothers in arms have lost sight of that in their quest to defeat the traitors. I believe they are so incensed by their betrayal that they are not thinking logically. They do not see the damage they are causing or where this war will end because they do not want to see it."

"They want to punish the traitors," I add. "Everything else comes second."

"That is correct," Puriel affirms. "So I have come here to aid you in your quest to end this conflict before our home is reduced to rubble. I hope you will accept my help."

I look at Augustus, and he looks at me. There's skepticism in his expression, as I'm sure there is in mine, but we're short on options here. So long as he doesn't abandon us again, Puriel is our best chance to gain an advantage.

"We accept," Augustus tells him. "We need to find armory weapons."

"Specifically the sling of David and the spear of Joshua," I add. "Can you help?"

"I can," he replies with a nod. "Those weapons were being wielded by Jehoel and Adriel. I saw them both fall in the last arena of battle. I will take you there."

He holds out his arm, the spiked gauntlet on his wrist as intimidating as ever. I place my hand above it, and Augustus does the same. With a glance at each other before the wormhole consumes us, we're both acknowledging the same truth:

If Puriel is screwing us over, we're dead.

Thankfully, that doesn't appear to be the case. We land in an area that looks utterly normal to me. It's a green hill topped by gray ruins and palm trees. There are groupings of small holes, knee-high walls, and raised mounds that look like the foundations for homes, with dusty, unpaved roads weaving between them.

"What is this place?" I ask Puriel. He looks around, then back at me.

190 · FALL OF THE ANGELS

"You might call it a training area," he says. "We run simulated battles here."

"Puriel is underselling it," Augustus chimes in. "This here is a perfect recreation of the plain of Megiddo. It's the location of the Battle of Armageddon."

"Training for the Battle of Armageddon?" I ask him. "The end of the world?"

"The army of God is always prepared, especially for that battle," he explains. "On that day, we do not want to defeat the enemy. We want to eradicate them."

"So they come here to practice," Augustus says. "Or, in this case, kill one another."

"The weapons should be around here somewhere," Puriel says with more force. He clearly wants to get the conversation back on track. "We were in the air during the battle, so it is difficult to tell where the sling and spear might have fallen."

"Well, let's split up and search for them," I tell the group.

"I would not advise that," says a voice from behind me that makes my hair stand up on end. I've never heard it before, yet that voice is still familiar to me...

I turn, and there stands Raphael alone. His tattooed arms are glistening, his green eyes are blazing, and the silver dagger is still clenched in his right fist.

"Raphael," Puriel says, his voice a choked whisper. "What are you doing here?"

"I have come to kill a traitor," he says, pointing the dagger at Puriel. "After that, I will put an end to this insurrection perpetrated by Augustus Shaw."

I stand my ground despite the rising panic in my chest. In that moment, needing to conjure some confidence, I picture my brother's swaggering bravado.

What would Peter say in this situation?

"There's only one flaw in your plan, asshole," I tell Raphael, look-

NEVER TOO LATE FOR A CHANGE OF HEART · 191

ing him dead in the eyes, my voice smooth and steady. "You can't kill us if you're dead."

A dazzling smile spreads across Raphael's face. It's the kind of evil smile I've seen before on dozens of bad guys right before they reveal the ace up their sleeve.

But instead of saying another word, Raphael lunges at me, dagger cocked back.

Oh shit. Maybe channeling Peter wasn't such a good idea...

CHAPTER 14

FANCY SEEING YOU HERE

I BARELY HAVE TIME TO THINK—LET ALONE REACT— as Raphael zooms toward me. I raise my arms in a defensive pose and brace for impact. But before the archangel slams into me, a winged blur flies across my face and intercepts him.

Puriel has tackled Raphael and is flying away from us, engaged in midair combat like I was with Gavreel. I snap my attention back to Augustus. This is it—like it or not—we're in the endgame of our plan, which means every second counts.

"We have to find the armory weapons right now," I tell him, my voice frantic. "If Raphael is here, we can assume the other archangels will be here soon."

"And without those weapons..." Augustus begins.

"We're done," I finish.

Augustus and I nod at each other and jet off in opposite directions. In the distance, I hear the faint grunts and cries of Puriel and Raphael as they tussle and fly. My ears scan the ground in search of anything that looks out of place. The spear should be easier to find, but the sling will be a challenge. This plain is just big enough that finding two weapons scattered across its face will take either insane luck or lots of time, more than we have at the moment. Which means our lives depend on luck.

In my vision, the sling was a small, brown leather strap. That's the color I'm looking for amidst the grays and greens. As I pass under a palm tree, I shudder to think that either weapon may be nestled among its branches. We'd need an angel to retrieve it and, well, ours is a bit too preoccupied at the moment to help us.

I quickly lift my head to scan for the dueling angels but don't see them. I hear them, though: distant thuds, crashes, and strangled screams.

Just keep him busy a little longer, Puriel. Buy us time to find the weapons.

I fire off the telepathic plea, not knowing if Puriel will hear it but praying that he does. The knot in my stomach is growing tighter

with every corner I turn that doesn't reveal a long, wooden spear with a metal tip wedged in the ground or a simple brown sling draped over a half wall. I reach the area with the cluster of shallow rectangular holes and run between them, my head darting right and left to quickly scan each one. My search comes up empty as I pass the last pair.

I'm standing now on the slope that leads to the grassy area surrounding the dusty hilltop. I sprint forward, running the width of the slope, then run downhill a few feet and sprint back. Thankfully the grass is relatively short, barely past my ankles, so the weapons should be easy to spot. Nevertheless, I'm coming up empty, and as I reach the bottom of the slope, my chest tightens with panic.

Augustus, any luck?

His answer comes after a few agonizing seconds:

Not yet.

Damn it. If we can't find these weapons and Raphael kills Puriel, we have two options: try to stand and fight or withdraw to Bron's canyon and hope the rune-protected zones are strong enough to keep out archangels.

Both options are less than ideal, but the thought of running away again irks me, especially from the angel who punched me into a pocket dimension and left me for dead. I want to kick his holier-than-thou ass, even if that's the dumbest idea I've had since staring down the towering, fiery demon who kidnapped my brother. Sure, I killed Malphas, but I also died doing so. That's not an option up here.

My thoughts are interrupted when a new voice broadcasts into my brain.

The spear...and the sling...I see them. Sending...markers down to... their locations.

It's Puriel's voice, strained as he exerts himself against Raphael. My heart skips a beat as I scan the skies looking for him. On the opposite side of the plain, I finally spot them, looking like two great birds engaged in midair fisticuffs. Puriel pushes back from

Raphael, spreads his arms, and from each hand, a ball of light shoots out like a falling star. They both glide lazily down to Earth as they home in on the locations Puriel sent them to mark. I begin to run toward where I think the marker closest to me will land. Hopefully, Augustus is close to the other one. Mine is falling slowly toward a tall palm tree at the edge of the hilltop, probably a hundred and fifty yards away. The other one is angled toward the middle of the hilltop area, gliding in the direction of a circular hole I saw that reminded me of a sinkhole.

Augustus, I've got the one near the tree. You take the one in the middle.

Roger that, headed there now.

I'm running as fast as my legs will carry me, so fast that it feels like I'm going to tip over. The ball of light finally settles about midway up the tree, and that's when I see it. The sling is caught on an upturned piece of bark about ten feet in the air. I know I passed under this tree earlier. I must have missed the sling, given that the brown leather strap blends in seamlessly with the tree trunk.

Had Puriel not sent down his beacon, I never would've found it. The angel might have screwed us earlier by abandoning us, but he's saving the day now.

I'm fifty feet from the tree, forty feet, thirty, picking up speed... when a body slams into the ground directly in my path. The impact craters the ground and sends gray dust shooting into the air. I skid to a stop just feet from the crater. One glance at the limbs dangling over the side tells me it's Puriel who's been thrown down.

He groans and makes a slight movement, which means he's not dead. But the blood coating one side of his face and gushing down his right arm tells me he's hurt.

I look up at the sling, only to see Raphael hovering next to it. There's a trickle of blood streaming down from his forehead, but other than that, it appears he gave it worse than he got in his fight against Puriel. His evil smile has returned.

He reaches out and grabs the sling, sending a jolt of panic through my body. He holds it up, the long strings dangling down past his elbow.

"Looking for this?" he asks me, but I'm too panic-stricken to reply.

He holds his free hand up, snaps his fingers, and the sling disappears in a bright flash of flame. I can hardly breathe as Raphael wipes the dust from his hands.

"You were never worthy to wield such a weapon," he snarls at me, floating down to the ground less than ten feet from the crater where Puriel lies motionless. "You are nothing but a filthy half-breed. A misguided attempt to make human warriors the equivalent of angels. Your kind is nothing but a long, drawn-out mistake."

Whatever bravado I had just moments ago is gone. It evaporated just like the sling and my hope of having a fighting chance against Raphael and his brothers.

"And now, I am going to end the latest mistake God has made," Raphael continues. "Do not tell our father, but I am going to enjoy ending the life of his precious, chosen soldier. I have long wanted to do it, and now I finally have cause."

"Your only cause is yourself," I say, finally finding my voice. "You and your brothers are the most pompous, smug assholes I've seen on Earth or in Heaven."

"I will be sure to relay the message," he snarls, raising the dagger to chest height. I raise my fists in response and straighten up to my full height. If I'm going to die—for real this time—I'm going out with dignity. I won't cower from this asshole who knocked me through dimensions and called me a mistake.

"Bring it, dickhead," I say through clenched teeth. There's a second-long pause during which my words register with Raphael, drawing a small smirk. Then we both push off from the ground and lunge at each other, fists cocked back. I can see the whites of his dazzling green eyes when his head is violently jerked to the

FANCY SEEING YOU HERE · 197

side, and he careens off course, slamming into the ground inches from Puriel.

I slide to a stop while my mind races to process what I'm seeing. The image registers in my brain, but the synapses aren't firing quick enough to process the bizarre sight before me. I shake my head, forcing the mental image to focus.

That's when the blurry edges finally take shape: a spear is lodged sideways through Raphael's neck. He's grasping it, his fingers coated in his own blood. There's also blood trickling from the corner of his mouth. Raphael's breathing is ragged and forced like he had the wind knocked out of him. His eyes are wild with fear.

I turn to the right and search for the source of the spear, my mind piecing together the clues as I scan for the person who threw it. I see Augustus, angel blade drawn, running over the rugged terrain as fast as he can. The distance from which he threw the spear and hit Raphael's neck while the angel was moving seems impossible, but we are talking about history's greatest nephilim.

I turn back to Raphael, who's risen from his knees to a standing position, his hands stretched out in front of him as if he intends to choke someone. As he staggers forward, blood burbling from his mouth, I realize that someone is me.

My view is blocked by a large shape rising from the ground in front of me. I take a step back and realize that Puriel has risen from his crater. As he sways unsteadily on his feet, he raises his right hand, which is wrapped around Raphael's dagger. In one swift movement, he plunges the blade deep into the archangel's chest.

Raphael sinks back to his knees, his eyes wide and unblinking. He puts his right hand up to his chest wound as his body begins to dissolve into pinpricks of light, millions strong, that gently float away as if blown by the breeze.

Before he completely disintegrates, Raphael looks me dead in the eye and flashes that malevolent smile one last time. Then he bows his head as if in prayer.

It takes a second longer than it should for me to realize what he's doing. Before I can move to stop him, the message rings out loud and clear in my mind.

Send all forces to the plain of Megiddo. Kill everyone you find here.

The twinkling lights consume his body, and then Raphael is gone. The spear of Joshua dislodges from his neck and falls with a thud into the grass. I'm frozen in place, his words still ringing inside my head. The small thrill of victory I felt just seconds ago is replaced by an all-consuming panic. With his last act, that spiteful archangel has absolutely screwed us. Heaven's forces are about to swarm our position, which means we have two choices: fight or flight.

Or...perhaps there's a third option.

"This isn't right," I tell Augustus, who's bending down to scoop up the spear, and Puriel, who's slowly standing to his feet. "In my vision, this isn't where our final battle went down. We were on a floating platform above all the planets."

"Was it Heaven's waiting room, where Bron and I left you?" Augustus asks.

"No, no, no, it was bigger," I reply. "Much bigger. Where could that be?"

"It is the observatory," Puriel interjects. "God likes to go there and enjoy a panoramic view of his creation. Angels do, too. It is beautiful."

"That's where we were," I conclude. "The final battle takes place there."

As the final word leaves my mouth, I hear a small *pop* above our heads. Then another. Then two more. Then dozens of *pops* begin to register. I tilt my head up, and fear grips my insides. Dotting the sky above us are dozens of angels.

"Time to go," I tell the others, the fear in my voice unmistakable.

Puriel holds out his arm, we grip it, and our feet leave the ground. I hear the sound of wings cutting through the air as the angels dive-bomb our location. When we land, I know we're in the right place.

FANCY SEEING YOU HERE · 199

This is the area I saw in my vision. We'll make our last stand here before I'm called away for...well, I'm not sure yet. But whatever it was, it must have been urgent for me to leave Augustus behind in battle.

"Puriel, how banged up are you?" Augustus asks. "The fight will be here any second, and we're going to need you. We couldn't have defeated Raphael without you."

"I will live," he says. "My healing is underway, and my strength is returning. Whatever I have left in my being, I will pour it out for this fight."

"Good," Augustus says, patting his shoulder. "We're glad you're here."

If this is the final battle, it means either we're going to end Michael with his sword, or he's going to end us. I'm hoping for the first option, but if that's the case, we have to be sure that Lightfall preparations are almost ready. Bron isn't back yet, which means they must still be going on...or something happened to him.

"Is there a way to reach out to Bron?" I ask the group. "Before the angels get here, we need to know if the Lightfall preparations are ready. If we kill Michael and expel the angels before our guys on the ground are ready, Earth is toast."

"I can reach out," Puriel says. "Or better yet, I can amplify your message, Augustus. The Bronze Man will know to be listening for your voice inside his mind."

Puriel places a finger on Augustus's forehead, who bows his head.

Bron, this is Augustus. What's the status of the Lightfall preparations? We're out of time up here. Michael and his angels will be on our ass any minute now.

I keep waiting for the *pop* above our heads to tell us we're out of time. The seconds drag on, all of us waiting for a response from Bron, my stomach tightening with each agonizing moment that passes. Finally, a voice cuts through the dead air.

Rio de Janeiro and Jerusalem are complete. We are headed to Kansas now.

How much time do you need?

Every second you can buy us is invaluable.

We can do that.

The word "that" is barely out when the *pops* begin to fill the sky above us. Augustus tosses Puriel his angel blade and tightens his grip on the spear. I fire up my fists, my gaze turned upward as our enemies begin to pour into this new arena. My heart is thundering in my chest, but I feel calm and strangely excited. There's been a lot of heartache and setbacks since I arrived in Heaven. If I'm being honest, I'm just ready to put these new fighting skills to use and punch an angel in the face.

"Spread out and divide their forces," Augustus tells us. "Stay alive, both of you."

I sprint toward the edge of the platform to my right, Puriel swoops into the air and makes off for the far end, and Augustus heads for the middle. The angels, now thirty strong at least, start to descend—but we don't have their full attention. They're still fighting each other, so only a few peel away to attack us.

I don't see Michael or Gabriel yet. They probably want to come in at the last minute once we're worn down and deliver the final blow, ensuring they get the glory. My excitement turns to anger at this thought. I don't just want to buy Bron a few seconds. I want to stay alive long enough to kill one of those bastards.

As I take up my position near the edge of the platform, an angel lands dramatically in front of me. He smirks at my glowing fists. Like most of these smug assholes, he probably thinks from looking at me that I'll be an easy kill. We'll see about that.

I wave him forward. Bring it, flyboy.

The angel flies straight toward me, so I sidestep him and grab the back of his armor as he soars past me. Using his own momentum against him, I jump, lifting him high in the air, then bring him crashing down onto the marble floor. He crumples into a heap, and before he can move, I'm pummeling him with both fists.

I rain blows down on his face, pounding it into the ground and sending blood gushing from his nose and cheeks. Laying on his side, he raises his arm to swat me away, but I see it coming and back away to avoid the blow. That gives him time to rise to his feet and charge at me again, this time on two legs.

Much like the first time a demon charged me in Mom's house, I can feel my programming working behind the scenes, telling my limbs exactly what to do. Then, it was raising a gun to fire two shots into a demon's skull. Now, it's blocking a flurry of punches the angel tries to land with little effort from me. Despite my small size, so much of what Augustus downloaded into my brain was about using my mass effectively and getting opponents off-balance using their own movement, not mine. Let the fight come to me instead of acting as a blunt instrument.

This angel is giving me everything he's got. Straight, jab, jab, roundhouse, spinning back kick, uppercut—but it doesn't matter. I'm floating like Muhammad Ali, dodging every strike before it even comes close to connecting.

How did I ever fight demons without this programming?

I could toy with this angel all day, but it would be best to finish him before a couple of his buddies show up. I focus on his face and see the muscles in his jaw tighten as he lunges toward me, spreading his arms for a tackle. I duck, spin my leg around and sweep his feet as he draws even with me. This sends the angel tumbling, and the second he hits the ground, I straddle him from behind and wrap my arms around his neck. Channeling my nephilim energy into my hands, I squeeze tight, draw a deep breath, and then jerk my hands violently in opposite directions.

The angel's neck breaks with a horrible *snap,* and his body goes limp. I release my grip just as the twinkling lights begin to overtake his form. Looking down at my vanquished foe, I feel a tiny pang of... not regret. Sadness, I suppose.

I have no problem killing demons. They're vile, wretched crea-

202 · FALL OF THE ANGELS

tures who'd slit your throat just for fun. The righteous angels aren't evil. They're simply misguided. In their minds, they're the heroes who will die defending their home.

But whether you're on Earth or in Heaven, the simple fact remains that if someone tries to kill you, you do everything you can to defend yourself. I am sad that it's come to bloodshed with the beings whose grace powers my abilities. I wish there was another way. But they have their mission, and so do we—and we can't afford to fail.

I return my focus to the battlefield in time to see two angels land dramatically a few feet away from me. They stare at their brother-in-arms turning to a flurry of lights, the white pinpricks reflected in their eyes as their brows furrow.

"You will die for that," one of them says, pointing to the fallen angel.

"We'll see," I tell him.

They both charge me, so I blast them with a small cleansing flame and knock them off-balance. I go after the one on my left, flaming fists catching his midsection, then his face on both sides. Before I can swing again, the other angel hooks my arm with his and catches me in the ribs with a thunderous punch. I have so much adrenaline going that I barely feel it, although my brain notes that I'll probably be pissing blood for a week after that hit. I sweep my captive arm downward and break his grip, then backhand him across the face. I deliver a swift kick to the solar plexus of the one on my left who's recovered from my flurry of punches.

His buddy fires off his own kick. I see the leg coming in slow motion, and as the programming takes over again, I roll backward over my left shoulder and then use that momentum to bring myself into a kneeling position, where I deflect the punches of both angels, throwing them aside. I need to even the odds against these two. I stand, spin over my right shoulder and catch the angel to my left with a vicious roundhouse kick to the head that knocks him out cold.

FANCY SEEING YOU HERE · 203

Seeing his companion go down, the other angel screams at me, the veins bulging in his neck and his complexion the color of a tomato. I know exactly what he's going to do, and sure enough, he does it: kicking off from the ground and flying at me, both hands reaching forward to seize me by the neck. He doesn't even notice that I've channeled all my energy into one fist, so it's glowing white hot like a blow torch. I let his body slam into mine and drive my fist through his chest.

His hands go limp against my face as the light in his eyes begins to fade. I lower his body to the ground and wipe my fist on my pants, trying hard not to see the blood covering it because of the sadness it stirs up in my chest. His body is just starting to light up when I'm tackled hard from behind and slammed into the marble floor. My head bounces off the ground, and stars pop in front of my eyes.

I spin over as my attacker settles in to pummel me: it's the angel I put to sleep with the roundhouse kick. He's awake now and just as furious as his fallen brother.

"You traitorous scum!" he spits at me. "You are supposed to use your God-given abilities to protect Heaven and Earth, yet you use them to murder angels."

"And you're supposed to protect Heaven, not destroy it," I fire back. "I know you want the angels who followed Gregori to pay, but where does it end?"

"For you, it ends right here," he replies, wrapping his hands around my neck.

I hammer on his arms, trying to break his grip, but it's no use. His hands are like a vice clamped around my throat, expelling the oxygen from my body. I switch tactics and try to summon a cleansing flame. It's no use. The fiery fist I used to kill the last angel sapped me of my powers temporarily. This is not good.

I struggle and squirm in an attempt to break free as darkness begins to overtake my vision. I see the angel wide-eyed and with

a deranged smile through the tiny bit of vision I have left. It's like looking through a paper towel tube at him.

Which is what makes it so surprising when the next feeling I experience is his body slumping onto mine. I waste no time forcing his hands from my neck and inhaling deeply. My bruised windpipe radiates pain as the cold air rushes down and fills my lungs. I lie there and breathe for a moment.

Knowing another angel could be bearing down on me right now, I go to push the angel's body off me. That's when I notice the half-dollar-sized hole in his forehead. I rack my brain to determine what kind of weapon could have caused that damage as I roll the angel off me and bring myself to a standing position.

It almost looked like a stone had passed through there. A stone fired from a sling.

But that's...

"Impossible," I say to the person who fired it.

Jet black hair, steely blue eyes, and skin so pale it almost glows. Lilith stands before me, a smirk on her face and a sling clutched in her right hand.

"The sling I saw in my vision," I tell her. "It wasn't David's."

She shakes her head.

"It was mine," she finishes. "How do you think Adam and I ate?"

Amazing. I would've bet everything I own that I'd never see Lilith again after we exited the wasteland where she'd been exiled. But here she is, in the flesh, saving my life. I've been hit with some wild surprises these last few days.

This one might be the wildest.

"What are you doing here?" I ask her. "I thought you'd be long gone."

She nods as if to say, *that wouldn't have been a bad option.*

"I told you: I want to clear my name," she replies. "If your cause is as righteous as I believe it to be, then I want to be on the side that helped make it happen."

"You're trying to get back in God's good graces," I assert.

She snorts and shakes her head.

"I'm not doing this for God's approval," she says. "I'm doing this for me."

Well, whatever the reason, I'm glad she's here. I'd be dead for good if it weren't for her and that sling. I glance up over her shoulder and see two angels zooming toward us, looks of rage painted across both their faces.

"Fight's coming our way," I tell her. "You ready?"

"If you knew the things I've killed up here, you wouldn't have to ask," she answers.

I still don't trust her, but damn it, Lilith is growing on me. If nothing else, she saved my life, so I owe it to her to have her back with God or the angels or whoever else comes asking about her. I don't know what she did, but I know what she's doing now: uppercutting an angel in the jaw so hard it sends him toppling.

Blood streaming from his mouth, he spits out a few teeth and screams, "Our father locked you away! And now you impede our path, a living abomination!"

"I had to break free just to kick your ass, sweetie," she taunts him.

The other angel is on me now, and he's brandishing an angel blade. He swipes left and right, then jabs it toward my chest. I block all three attacks with small cleansing flames, and as he brings the blade down in a swiping motion, I step back to dodge it and blast the weapon out of his hand with a more forceful cleansing flame.

The blade clatters along the floor over to where Lilith stands. I kick the angel in the chest and send him toppling over backward. With my attacker incapacitated, I look back at Lilith, who bends to pick up the weapon, her eyes wide.

"Ohhhhh," she says. "I've always wanted to use one of these."

She looks down at the sling in her other hand, then back up at me.

"Here you go, kid," she says, tossing me the sling. "You know how to use it?"

"In my vision, this fired balls of light," I tell her, my question embedded.

"Channel your angelic energy to the sling, just like you do your fists," she answers. "When you start to spin it, if you're doing it right, the ball will appear there."

Now's the time to test what Lilith is saying. My assailant is back on his feet and walking toward me like the Terminator, cold fury etched into his expression. I begin to spin the sling, routing my angelic energy past my hand and into the weapon itself. I back up to buy myself more time and keep my eyes fixed on the angel, who quickens his pace now that he's seen the sling.

I feel the energy flowing, but I'm too scared to take my eyes off the angel. In my peripheral vision, though, I see a streak of white forming a faint circle. I plant my feet. The sling is at full speed, *whooshing* through the air next to me. I flick my wrist forward right as the angel extends his hands to grab me. I can see the whites of his stone-gray eyes right as the ball of light passes through his chest.

I step to the side. The angel falls face first to the ground, dead.

My gaze finds Lilith right as she pulls the angel blade from her opponent's chest. For a moment, he's suspended there on his knees, mouth agape and eyes wide. He clutches at the wound in his chest, blood running down the back of his hand. Lilith walks toward him, runs her hand through his hair, and kisses his forehead.

"Sleep now, soldier," she says quietly, lowering him to the ground.

Both of our angelic foes are transforming into pinpricks of light. Awash in the glow of that brilliant light, Lilith—with her ivory skin—looks almost angelic.

She sees me staring at her and turns to face me.

"I don't like killing them," she admits. "They're benevolent creatures. Proud, yes. Arrogant, no doubt. But they're bastions of goodness who are following orders."

That's well said. Our circumstances dictate fatal outcomes in these skirmishes, but that doesn't mean I'm not sad every time another body dissolves into light.

"You sound like you're speaking from experience," I reply.

"Do you think I went easy when they came to take me from the Garden?" Lilith asks. "That was my home, the only life I knew. Plus, I knew where they were taking me. I might have been born yesterday, but I could tell God wanted a redo."

"I'm glad you're here now," I tell her.

"Me too, kid," she says, smiling. "Me too."

Inside my mind, the quiet is interrupted like a burst on the radio, cutting through static. I close my eyes and focus my attention on the words about to be spoken.

Silas and Augustus, this is the Bronze Man. We have completed the ritual in Kansas.

Bron, this is Silas. We hear you. We'll work on holding up our end now.

Wait, wait, wait.

There's panic in Bron's voice that makes my throat tighten.

What is it, Bron? Talk to us.

There's Augustus chiming in.

The seconds tick by, feeling like hours. Finally, Bron speaks.

Even through telepathy, the terror in his voice is unmistakable.

The demons are here. They must have known we were coming.

How many, Bron? How many are there?

Another stretch of unbearable silence.

Thousands.

CHAPTER 15

FINISH THE FIGHT

BRON'S ANSWER SWELLS THE BUBBLE OF DREAD inside my lungs to the point where I think I might burst. This is the cold sweat, reach-deep-in-your-guts fear that gripped me the entire time Peter was missing. It was like holding onto a cliff edge, knowing that, at any second, I could lose my grip and plummet into the abyss. Now, with my brother's life once again in jeopardy, the paralyzing terror has returned.

Bron, you have to get them out of there right now. Teleport them back to Sherwood.

I can't. They have to remain here until the angels are expelled. The trap is bound to their life force. If they leave now, it will dissipate, leaving the angels free to escape.

There are two other zones. We have to take the chance the angels will go to one of those.

We can't take that risk, Silas. If we're wrong, the angels will run free.

Augustus is right, but I don't care. This is my family we're talking about. I decided to put everything on the line to complete this mission. They did not. Bron brought them along to complete a simple ritual, not confront a thousand-demon army.

This is a suicide mission. I can't stand for that.

Bron, take them back now, or I'll come down there and do it myself.

I can hold them at bay long enough for you to finish Michael. We can do this, Silas!

Michael is not even here!

Nor will I be, nephilim.

This new voice is an unwelcome intruder in my mind. He continues.

I know what the final step of Lightfall is, which means if I stay away...you lose.

He's right, of course. We can't kill Michael with his flaming sword if he's not here, and given our new time crunch (which is only intensified given the time distortion between Heaven and Earth),

we need him here yesterday. If he hides from us, we're screwed. All this work and sacrifice will be for nothing.

Except you will come down here, Michael. Because you want the glory. That's all you've ever wanted, you attention-seeking bastard. If one of your lackeys finished me instead of you, it would eat you up inside for all of eternity. Because you're Michael, the greatest warrior God has ever created...except maybe there's someone else greater than you.

Augustus is laying it on thick. I spot him, a hundred feet away, battling two angels with Joshua's spear. The angels above us continue to grapple with one another. For the moment, none has peeled off to confront Lilith and me. I glance over at Lilith and motion with my head for us to help Augustus. We break into a sprint, Lilith holding the angel blade at her side and me starting to spin the sling.

As we approach, Michael responds to Augustus's jab.

I know what you are doing, Augustus Shaw. It will not work. You think my pride is my downfall, that if you tempt me with lies, I will make a foolish decision. I assure you this notion is ill-informed. What I am going to do is send the might of my forces at you here and now. I will quell your insurrection, then stomp out my traitorous brethren.

Augustus has sent both angels sprawling by the time Lilith and I arrive, making them easy for us to finish off. In the eerie silence that follows, the three of us stare at each other, our minds undoubtedly arriving at the same conclusion:

We're cooked. Augustus played his best card, and it didn't work. There's no way to draw Michael to us, and without him, this whole plan will fall apart.

That's when Puriel lands between us, his arms wrapped in a sleeper hold around the neck of another angel. Why he brought this fight to us, I have no idea...except, this isn't just any angel he's got wrapped up. The shoulder-length blonde hair, barrel chest, and bulging biceps—Puriel has delivered Gabriel to us.

The archangel's face is tinged red, but he's conscious. Before I

can respond, Lilith points her blade toward his chest, and Augustus does the same with the spear. Gabriel holds up his hands. For the moment, he knows he's beaten.

"Turns out we might have one card left to play," I tell the group. Puriel nods.

Tell me, Michael, is the life of your brother worth staying hidden?

Augustus follows my words with his own.

We already sent Raphael to the Empty, Michael. Show your face and fight us like a man, or we'll do the same to Gabriel right here and now. You have ten seconds to respond.

I mouth the words "the Empty" to Augustus, confused about what he means.

"It's where angels go when they die," he explains quickly.

We don't have to wait long for Michael to respond. As soon as Augustus finishes saying the word "die," the angel's voice comes through inside our heads.

I told my brothers to remain by my side, but they insisted on joining the fray. Their hubris, combined with their desire to kill you, is what got them killed. I will not put the lives of my soldiers in jeopardy to save the life of a brother who has more muscle than sense.

Gabriel's face can't help but show the hurt caused by his brother's comment.

Surely, brother, you do not mean that. You must come down here and save me.

I have saved your life one too many times. You are on your own, Gabriel.

Fine.

Gabriel moves so fast he becomes a blur. It's only through my increased focus and the slowing of time that I'm able to see what he's doing clearly. He swipes his arms upward, sending Augustus's and Lilith's weapons flying out of their hands.

He then grabs both of Puriel's arms and jerks them violently to the side. The twin *cracks* tell me both of the angel's arms are broken.

212 · FALL OF THE ANGELS

With a wave of his hand, I'm thrown backward along with Augustus and Lilith. We topple end-over-end for at least ten feet, my body coming to a rest as I slam down on my back.

Lying on my side, I prop myself up on my elbow in time to see what happens next. Like when Gabriel freed himself, it happens so fast I barely have time to register it. Gabriel holds out his hand, and the angel blade zooms to meet it. Turning, he grabs Puriel—who's slumped over cradling both his broken arms to his chest—by the throat and lifts him a foot into the air. Puriel hangs there pitifully, unable to swat at Gabriel's massive forearms as he brings Puriel's face close to his.

The archangel sends his final insult telepathically so we can hear it.

This is better than you deserve, you sniveling coward.

With that, he jams the angel blade through Puriel's chest, twisting it for maximum pain. I'm on my feet now, running full speed toward the archangel, not sure what I'm going to do but totally sure that I'm going to try and beat his ass.

I still have the sling in my hand, so I start to twirl it and send my angelic energy down my arm, pumping as much power into this ball of light as I can. Gabriel drops Puriel's body to the ground, which is already dissolving into light.

As Gabriel turns to face me, Puriel sends one final message.

Finish the fight, Silas. Finish it...for all of us.

I will, Puriel. You have my word.

I fling the ball of light at Gabriel, who deflects it with the angel blade. He raises his fists, anticipating that I'm going to fight him straight up. So, I go for something he doesn't expect—I hit the ground and slide between his legs like I'm stealing second in baseball. His head tilts down, following me as I slide behind him.

As soon as I'm clear, I pop up and deliver a swift kick to the back of Gabriel's right knee, which drops him to the ground. Just as I anticipated, he turns his blonde head over his right shoulder

FINISH THE FIGHT · 213

to face me. Waiting for him is my glowing fist, which smashes into his perfect face with such a devastating impact the resulting *thwap* echoes around the battlefield. Gabriel takes the punch right in the teeth and topples sideways. The angel goes sliding across the floor toward Lilith. She and Augustus have pulled themselves up now and retrieve their weapons.

We have to move fast and attack Gabriel while he's stunned. If he regains his composure, he could swat us like flies using his telepathy. I fire off a quick salvo from my sling, but Gabriel rises in time to deflect it with his wrist gauntlets. For being so big, he's so incredibly fast. He's on his feet and rushing me before my compatriots have even closed half the gap between them. That's when I do something I haven't done this entire time I've been in Heaven: I open a wormhole and teleport behind him again.

This time, instead of attacking his knees, I jump onto his back, channel as much energy into my fists as I can muster—they're glowing a brilliant shade of red now—and wrap my arms around Gabriel's neck in a sleeper hold. My hope is to preoccupy his arms while Augustus and Lilith rush him. I squeeze as tight as I can and wrap my legs around his torso. He's going to have to use all his strength if he wants to toss me off of him. I'm wrapped around him like a python.

Or not. Gabriel reaches up, grabs me by my hair, and rips me upward with such force that it almost dislocates my shoulders. He flings me so easily he might as well be throwing a paper wad into a trash can. I soar over the heads of Augustus and Lilith and come crashing down on the marble floor with a force that drives every last ounce of air from my body. I land on my stomach, hear a *pop* that I'm pretty sure is at least two ribs breaking, and slide five feet before the crumpled heap that is my body comes to a stop. I roll over onto my back and groan, low and slow.

Shit...that one's going to sting.

I don't have time to wallow in my pain, though. I spring to my

feet—well, more like slowly clamber to my feet—and spot Augustus and Lilith dueling with Gabriel. My plan somewhat worked—the archangel is pulling Joshua's spear from his shoulder as Lilith lunges at him, brandishing the blade. He swats the attack aside and then catches Lilith in the side of the head with a devastating punch that sends her sprawling. I see her arms go limp as she falls, and I know she's going to smash face-first into the ground, so I teleport over and grab her right as the tip of her nose kisses the ground. I don't wait around, teleporting her to a quiet corner of the battlefield where I lay her down. I wish I could stay and protect her, but I can't leave Augustus one-on-one with Gabriel. As I teleport back to the pair, my hope is that the angels will ignore Lilith or assume she's already been killed.

The old man is matching Gabriel blow for blow. Gabriel is insanely fast, but Augustus is so smooth and in control that it looks like he knows where the punches are going to come from before they're thrown. I jump in and catch the angel with a kidney punch that probably hurts my hand more than it hurts him. He throws an elbow at me that I duck under, leaving his armpit exposed. My fist is hurtling through the air, and I know it's the programming working on my behalf. I catch Gabriel in his armpit, and his right arm goes dead, hanging limp at his side.

Augustus does a Superman punch and cracks Gabriel in the jaw. Blood flies from his mouth and splatters at my feet. I send his head skyrocketing with a left-hand uppercut that lifts the angel off his feet. Augustus and I must have a mind-meld because my ancestor leaps into the air and brings a double hammer fist down on the angel's face, which knocks him flat on his back. His forehead is split open, blood pouring into his eyes. Augustus snatches his spear as I spin up a ball of light; we tower over the dazed archangel, ready to end his existence.

I snap my wrist forward right as Augustus drives the spear toward Gabriel's heart. That's when a brilliant flash of white light

FINISH THE FIGHT · 215

makes us both go blind. I raise my arm to cover my eyes and stumble backward, my retinas screaming in pain. I focus my energy to my eyes and heal the damage. Blinking quickly, the scene before me finally snaps into focus—and what I see causes my heart to leap into my throat.

Michael is here.

He came to save his brother...but he failed. In his hand, he holds the spear Augustus threw. But he didn't stop the shot from my sling, which created a quarter-sized hole in Gabriel's forehead. The archangel hangs there, eyes wide and mouth open, his lips moving like a fish gulping down air after washing ashore.

He manages one word as his body dissolves into a shower of lights.

Brother...

Michael looks from his brother and back to us, his scarred face contorting into a picture of boiling rage. Augustus tries to yank the spear from Michael's hands, but Michael jerks it up and away, the butt end clipping Augustus in the chin and throwing him backward. In one fluid motion, the angel brings the spear down horizontally across his knee, cracking it in half. The fracture releases a wave of energy that knocks me and Augustus back a couple of feet.

This isn't right. In the vision, Augustus was fighting with that spear, and now it's broken. If that's changed, what else has been altered? Am I still going to receive some kind of call that causes me to leave Augustus alone in the heat of battle?

Whatever comes next, one thing is for sure: Michael is here. This is our chance.

The archangel throws both pieces of the spear aside and raises his right hand above his shoulder. From behind his back, the hilt of a sword appears out of thin hair as the angel wraps his fingers around it and lifts it upward. I don't have to see it to know that Michael is unsheathing his flaming sword. I also know that if he draws it, with no weapon or shield of our own, he's going to make quick work of us.

Like with the angel in Bron's canyon, I take two steps and wrap Michael up in a perfect form tackle: shoulder driving through his torso, head to the side, and legs straining to move his solid mass. I kick hard from the ground to try and get us airborne, but it's no use—we're not going anywhere. Just as the thought, *well, this was dumb* flashes through my mind, Michael brings his elbow crashing down into the center of my back, which flattens me and cracks a couple more ribs.

I've barely hit the ground when Michael catches me right under the chin with a kick that snaps my head back and lifts my whole body off the ground—like, way off the ground. As I blackout, I enjoy the feeling of flying, knowing what comes after my flight isn't going to feel as good. In the short space where I don't have to endure consciousness, I see my brother's face. He has both his eyes, and he's laughing. We might be at Mom's birthday party. Or maybe it's Tully's Tavern. I can't tell. All I know for sure is that the memory (or maybe it's a hallucination) makes my body feel warm. I don't want it to end, but I can feel my eyes beginning to open.

What I see isn't blood gushing into my eyes but rather my great-great-grandfather's face. His kind eyes show a bemused level of concern as he shakes his head.

"You just keep doing the most reckless shit when the archangels show up," he tells me. "Did you really try and fly away with Michael, or did I make that up?"

"Must have been a figment of your imagination," I reply, my jaw radiating pain after getting dropkicked. "Doing that would be very, very dumb."

"I agree," he says with a laugh, pulling me to my feet.

Standing seventy feet away, Michael points his flaming sword at us.

"Enough talk," he bellows over the airborne battles raging all around us. "You wanted me here. Let us see if you are both man enough to finish the job."

I look at Augustus, and he looks at me. I don't need telepathy to know what we're both thinking:

If this is it—and it probably is—we're going down swinging.

"You ready?" he asks me, raising his fists in front of him.

"Let's do this," I answer through clenched teeth. "Let's finish the fight."

That's absolutely my intention...until a desperate cry comes screaming through on angelic telepathy. It's not Michael, and it's not Bron. This is a voice that I've known since its owner uttered his first word. Despite the familiarity, hearing it stops me dead in my tracks because of the panic coating the first word that comes through.

SILAS!

It's Peter. I've never heard him this terrified before. He sounds like a scared little kid crying out for our dad. I can't even summon the wherewithal to reply.

You have to help us! The Bronze Man is dead. The demons...there are too many of them. Colin and I are going to be overrun. Please, Silas...HELP US!

Is this it? Is this the moment Jesus was talking about, when I would be faced with an impossible choice that only I could make? A choice so monumental that God picked me to make it out of the billions of people on Earth?

Because if this is it, I'm not ready to decide.

Good thing you don't have to choose.

I hear Augustus's voice at the same time I feel him grab me by my shirt lapels and pull me in close for a hug. I don't know what he's doing, but I hug him anyway.

"You're everything God could ever want in a nephilim," he whispers in my ear. "And everything I could ever want in a great-great-grandson. I love you."

I step back as he extends his arms, fingers still wrapped around my shirt front.

"Now, go save your family," he says.

With that, he pushes me backward, and what I didn't realize in the seconds before this moment was that we're standing at the edge of the platform. Augustus has just pushed me off into inky black nothingness. I know in my heart—in the same way I know my own name—that this leads to Earth, but there's only one problem.

I have no idea how to get back.

All you have to say is, "God, I want to go back." He'll do the rest.

As I fall, the same weightlessness carries me downward that I experienced after leaving Lilith's wasteland. I fire back one final response to Augustus.

Can you take Michael all by yourself?

His laugh is so loud I can hear it with my ears.

I've been waiting my whole life for this moment, Silas. Everything I've done has been preparing me to kill this bastard. I've got my shot. Trust me—I won't miss.

That's when a new voice comes through, one that I now know well.

He won't be alone. Let's finish this together, old-timer.

Comfortable in the knowledge that Lilith and Augustus can end this battle once and for all, I spin in midair, hold out my fist like Superman, and say the words.

"God, I want to go back."

CHAPTER 16

WHAT COMES NEXT

TUNNEL OF LIGHT STRETCHES OUT BEFORE ME, like stars being elongated by the stopping of time. I go from floating to rocketing forward like I've cleared the big hill on a roller coaster and am now hurtling toward the ground thanks to gravity. If Bron truly is dead, I don't know if Peter can hear me—or how he sent off that message in the first place—but I have to try and send him a message back.

I'm coming, Peter. Just hold on.

My speed is increasing now, to the point that I'm on the verge of blacking out again. I close my eyes and slow my breathing, willing my body to hold it together. What happens is familiar now but still unsettling: my consciousness uncouples from my mind and drifts away, zooming down below the slipstream that is rocketing me back to Earth. It clears the clouds in the sky, the snow-covered mountains, and the towering trees, coming to a rest in a clearing illuminated by the headlights of a couple of vehicles parked at the top of the hill and angled downward.

Two faces turn up toward the sky, and even though my heart is a million miles away, it skips a beat seeing two people I love more than anything in the world: Colin and Peter. Reflected in their eyes is a streak of light that looks like...

"Is that a shooting star?" Peter asks, taking the words right out of my mouth.

"No..." says Colin. "I think...I think that's..."

"Silas," Peter finishes.

My consciousness zooms away, meeting up with my mind and body right as I soar past the treetops above my family members' heads. I see a spot between them and the approaching demon horde, and with both fists glowing a fiery red, I slam into the Earth with the force of a bomb dropped from the heavens. My fists crash into the ground and unleash a shockwave that disintegrates the demons within a hundred-foot radius. The heat and the stench I haven't experienced in what feels like years returns in a wave so overpower-

ing it threatens to consume me. Bron was right: there are thousands of demons here.

If I don't do something drastic right now, we're all going to die.

I close my eyes and trust everything to the new programming Augustus gave me. Like a dancer following a routine so well-rehearsed it's second nature, I hold out my arms and spin in a circle. I spin and spin and spin until a force emanating from my body lifts me off my feet and pushes me skyward. I open my eyes and can hardly believe what is happening: I've turned into a whirling tornado of angelic energy, bathing the entire forest in a bright red light.

I bow my head forward and plow into the advancing rows of demons like waves crashing into sandcastles; the hellish fiends dissolve in the face of my immense power. Around the clearing I spin, my nephilim tornado leaving the rocks and the trees unscathed but tearing the demons limb from limb. I direct the tornado using my body, shifting it from one side to the next, like a broom being swept left and right to clear sawdust from a shop floor. There's no wind noise up here, so all I hear is the *pff* each time a demon turns to ash and scatters in every direction.

I know the job is finished when the heat and the smell leave me entirely. I reach out to bring the angelic energy back into my body, but there's none left. The last little bit flickers out right as my feet touch the ground a few dozen yards from Peter and Colin. When I land, my legs wobble and give out. I have to imagine this is what running a marathon feels like: you've given all you have to give, and now your body is in full revolt. Even if I wanted to stand and fight, my legs wouldn't allow me.

I hear footsteps, and within seconds, Peter tackles me and wraps me up in a hug, both of us sprawled on the ground. He's crying, and so am I.

"Silas," he sobs. "Damn it, man. I thought, I thought...I thought you would look bad, but Jesus man, you look like shit warmed over. Does Heaven not have showers?"

I push him off and dry my tears with the back of my hand. He's gotten a haircut since I last saw him—it's a hack job, but he's still deceptively handsome—and the dark shadows under his eye complement the five o'clock shadow he's got going on. Speaking of his eye, there's a new addition to his face I haven't seen yet.

"You got an eyepatch!" I yell.

"Hell yeah I got an eyepatch" he yells back. "Badass, right?"

"So badass," I tell him. "Chicks are gonna dig it."

At that moment, I feel a hand grip my shoulder and look around to see Colin standing over me. I manage to lift myself to my knees and wrap him up in a hug. I made do with Augustus's hugs in Heaven, but Colin's hugs are still the best. The smell of his leather jacket and terrible aftershave warm my heart.

"I thought we'd lost you," Colin says, fighting back tears.

"You almost did," I tell him, pulling back and rising unsteadily to my feet. Peter grabs my shoulder to keep me from falling. "Augustus is up there right now fighting Michael to trigger Lightfall. I left to come here."

"Michael?" Peter asks, dumbstruck. I forget he's not as used to the larger-than-life figures from his Bible entering into his reality. "Like the archangel?"

"One and the same," I tell them both. "Augustus has to kill him with his flaming sword to activate Lightfall. I don't know if he can do it, Colin."

Colin nods, but his expression signals resolve and confidence.

"If anyone can do it, he can," he tells me. "Augustus is a machine."

"It was unbelievable fighting alongside him," I admit. "He was standing toe-to-toe with Gabriel like it was some drunk causing trouble at the bar. We took him down together, and Augustus killed Raphael on his own. He has help, too, in the fight against Michael. I like his odds, even if he's the underdog in the fight."

"We had no idea what was happening upstairs," Peter tells me, hand still on my shoulder. "The Bronze Man showed up and told

us you needed our help to complete a ritual. That once it was done, you would come home."

I'm afraid to ask, but I have to know.

"Time is different up there," I say. "How long was I gone down here?"

Colin and Peter look at each other, then at the ground.

"How long?" I say, quieter this time.

"A year," Colin tells me.

I drop my head into my hands, my stomach seizing to the point where I think I might vomit. Once I heard I'd been gone three months, I knew it would be bad. But I never thought it would be this bad. To leave my friends behind to fight without me for a year... it's utterly devastating. I could fight for the rest of my life, and that will be a debt I'll never be able to pay back.

"The others, Forrest and Grace," I say, my voice low. "Are they alive?"

"Yes," Peter says quickly. "They're back in Sherwood."

A small flicker of hope ignites in my chest at hearing this news.

"And the city, is it still standing?" I ask them both.

"Barely," Colin says quietly, his thumb stroking his machete.

"A lot has happened while you were gone, Silas," Peter says, patting my shoulder. "We have a lot to catch you up on, which we'll do at some point. The thing we need to focus on right now is finishing this ritual so we can get out of here."

"You're right," I admit, shaking my head to clear the funk. "Let's stay focused on the mission. You said Bron was dead. Can you take me to his body?"

I hope they're wrong. We've already lost Puriel, and losing Bron would be a huge blow. Not just to our efforts, but to my psyche. The aloof giant seemed to be above the conflict in Heaven, making him useless in battle but keeping him above the dread I felt for my fellow combatants who threw themselves at the enemy.

If he died here on Earth at the hands of demons in an effort to

buy us time for a mission that might not succeed, I'll be gutted. He deserved so much better.

I follow along behind Peter and Colin as they lead the way, the knot in my stomach growing tighter with every step. If I just want it hard enough, maybe I can will Bron being alive into existence. But if Peter thinks he's dead, I don't have much hope.

Bron is curled up on his side, almost like he's sleeping. His hands are pulled up into his chest, and there's a neutral expression on his face that I've come to associate with his default facial arrangement. Never high, never low—just right in the middle. Amidst the calamity we faced in Heaven, his steadiness was an asset.

I approach him slowly, knowing that the closer I get, the more inescapable the fact will become that Bron is, in fact, dead. Still, as I draw even with him, I place my hand on his chest and try to detect a spark of heavenly energy. I know Bron is not part angel like me, but I figure I can detect his life force all the same.

I don't know what gives me that assurance; however, I'm going with it.

Please, God. Don't take Bron away from us. He's a faithful servant and a good friend. Bring him back to us. He deserves so much more than to die at the hands of demons.

I keep my hand on his chest for ten seconds, then twenty, waiting for God to hear my prayer and bring my friend back to me. But it's no use. I withdraw my hand from Bron's cold, still body, tears streaming as the reality sets in that my friend is gone. He died buying us the time we needed to lure Michael out.

"Rest easy, Bron," I tell him quietly. "Thank you for all you did for me."

"Your friend died a hero," Colin tells me. He's crouched down beside me and looks at the bronze giant's closed eyes. "He threw himself in front of a wave of demons that broke through the warding he put in place. Saved us both."

"How did they get the drop on you all?" I ask, shaking my head.

"Bron said he thought some of the rebellious angels must have signaled down here to the demons once they found out Lightfall was happening," Peter answers.

"But that doesn't make sense," I reply. "Nobody knew about the plan but me, Bron, Augustus, Lilith, and the archangels. The only explanation is that...is that..."

"The archangels told the demons," Colin finishes. "To save their skin and keep their lofty perch, they turned to the creatures on the bottom of their shoe."

"Such hypocrites," I spit, my anger at the archangels renewed.

"We just have to hope their efforts were in vain," Colin says. "That Augustus can finish off Michael and cast them out. Bron told us Heaven is at stake."

"It is," I affirm. "The angels are so caught up fighting each other they don't see the damage they're causing. If we don't stop them, all of Heaven will be destroyed, including the throne room. Speaking of which, I need to tell you something."

I turn to face Peter, his eye locking onto mine. My brother, once the lovable lothario who could woo any woman at Tully's Tavern after enough drinks and a heap of flattery and BS, has aged in my absence. Gone is the kid I knew.

He's a year older, although my brother seems much older than that.

I place my hand on the back of his neck and steady myself to tell him the part I kept secret, even from Augustus. This part is just for the two of us.

"I saw Mom and Dad up there," I tell Peter. His eye immediately starts to glisten anew. "They were so happy, Pete. They were together, and they were rejoicing, and there was no pain or suffering or illness. It was so beautiful, man."

We lean our heads against each other and cry, the tears dropping into the dirt. The invisible weight I felt lifted after my trip to the throne room—I know that same weight is lifting off his shoulders

now, too. He took Mom's death so much harder than I did, so I know it means everything to him to hear she and Dad are OK.

"Colin, come here," I say, waving for the old man to join us. He slides around beside us and places his hands on both our shoulders, tears on his cheeks. I look at him and share the other piece—the piece I saved just for him.

"I saw how my dad died," I tell him. "Malphas put all these doubts in my head about what happened. It caused me to lose trust in you, and I'm sorry for that. I had the chance to go back and see for myself, and I saw it. He did die that night you were there. He was there to meet Malphas, but Gregori killed him."

Colin recoils and places his hand over his heart. For a second, I worry that he's having a heart attack. He's simply processing the news, though. He shakes his head, and his shaggy black hair, streaked with gray, sways side-to-side as he does.

"That doesn't make any sense," he says. "Gregori was our ally in the fight against Malphas. Why would he kill your father, Silas? I don't get it."

"Oh, God," I groan. "I have a lot to catch you all up on, as well."

Before I can say another word—before I can let my family know that Gregori was working with Malphas the entire time, that he stirred up the angelic insurrection and tried to kill me—an ear-splitting noise rings out from high above us. It's a deep, sonorous sound so powerful it ripples the air and kicks up dust from the ground. It's like my insides are being turned to jelly as I try to discern what we're hearing. The tone shifts just enough to offer a clue as to what it is.

It's a gong. And judging by the force and where the sound seems to be coming from, I have to assume it's a heavenly gong. But why is it being rung?

I squint at the others, who are huddled before me with their hands over their ears. I mouth the words "it's a gong" at them and

they both nod, then close their eyes. I share the sentiment: it's fine to know what it is, but when is it going to stop?

That's when a voice cuts through the cacophony—a voice inside my mind.

Silas, can you hear me?

Augustus, is that you?

I know it's him. It's his voice, but I need to hear him say it. With Bron dead, I've been pushing away the possibility that Augustus and Lilith could die. I need them to be alive: for their own sake, for mine, and for Bron's heroic sacrifice.

If my great-great-grandfather is dead because I chose to come here...well, I don't think my heart would be able to take it. It's already dealing with enough guilt.

It's me. We did it, Silas. That smug bastard is dead.

How? I mean, I know you're good, Augustus, but I was so worried.

The next voice belongs to Lilith.

Well, he had some help. But your ancestor is a certified badass, kid.

Thank you, Lilith.

Now comes the million-dollar question.

The angels. Does that mean...they're falling?

They are—and they're coming your way. We can see them. Do you?

With the voices quiet, I notice that the gong has stopped. We're looking around the empty clearing, which is eerily quiet now that our ears aren't under assault. I'm about to respond that I don't see anything when I lift my eyes up and gasp.

Dotting the sky are thousands of streaks of light. They're like shooting stars, only slower, tracing a slight arc as they angle toward our position. I can't tell from here, but I can picture it: at the front of each streak, rather than a rock, it's an angel. Suffice it to say, when they land here, they're going to be royally pissed.

I turn to grab the others when they gasp and point over my shoulder. I wheel around and immediately spot what grabbed their

attention: among the cascade of streaking lights is a fiery red dot moving faster than all the others. We all trace its path down through the canopy of trees and feel the aftershock as it craters the ground a few hundred feet away. I turn back to Peter and Colin.

"How wide is the zone for catching the angels?" I ask them.

"Couple miles," Colin answers. "But judging by how many are falling, we need to haul ass out of here."

"We have to check out that red dot that crashed, right?" Peter asks, only half-joking. I was thinking the same thing. This is the dot I saw in my vision. I thought it might be an archangel originally, but they're all dead now. Could it be Michael's flaming sword? Perhaps Augustus sent it down here as a gift to help us fight the demons, or maybe to guard the angels' zone like it guarded the Garden of Eden.

I lead the way as we jog toward where it landed; as we go, I send a telepathic message back to Augustus that the angels are headed our way. We round a small hill and fight our way through some thick brush at the base of the crater. Before we make our way up to the lip, I send another message to Augustus.

A red dot crashed among the angels. Did you send us Michael's sword?

As we begin to climb the sloping wall of the crater and my curiosity crescendos, something odd happens. My neck prickles with heat...and I catch a whiff of something rotten. Like spoiled milk and week-old eggs left out in the sun.

No, I still have Michael's sword.

Augustus's reply sends a shiver down my spine. Not so much because of the words he said, but because of the dread I could hear in his voice. When we reach the lip of the crater and look down, I understand why Augustus responded the way he did...and why my demon senses have kicked into high gear.

Curled up in the pit ten feet beneath us is a demon with black craggy skin and rivers of lava crawling across his body like fiery snakes. But unlike his son, this demon is easily ten feet tall. As we

all stare down at his hulking form, our mouths agape, Augustus's voice makes me jump.

Oh my God, Silas. He got free. He was part angel at one point, so when Lightfall was activated, the cage must have been thrown open, and he was cast down. I didn't know. I swear to you, I didn't know. You have to get out of there, Silas. Run!

I grab the others and throw them down the side of the crater. We're running because I don't have to tell them whose body is lying in that hole. I don't have to describe the sheer terror I feel reaching its icy tendrils down my throat and threatening to strangle me— because I know they're feeling it too.

The sky's ablaze now as the falling angels draw nearer to our location. Any second, they'll begin raining down all around us and cratering the ground where we stand. We have to get out of here right now, so we run. We run, and we don't look back, even as the white light is replaced by a brilliant red glow coming from behind us. I don't stop even as the heat and the stench claw at my eyes and my throat.

Run, Silas. For the love of God, run!

There's no escaping, though. My powers are shot from the tornado I created earlier. I don't even have the strength to muster a wormhole and teleport us away. The cars aren't an option either. We'll be crushed by a falling angel (or several) before we get out of the clearing. We're trapped here. Trapped with fallen angels and something much worse. Something that wants to tear me limb from limb for what I did to his son, for what Augustus did to him all those years ago.

Asaroth wants me dead, and he's going to kill me if the angels don't do it first. But neither of them gets a chance because as we round the hill by Bron's body, he's not lying on the ground anymore. He's standing up, arms wide, sweeping us into an embrace that isn't a physical expression of his happiness that we're alive. It's the contact necessary for what comes next: as the first angels begin

WHAT COMES NEXT · 231

to land—*thoom thoom thoom*—all around us, a warm golden light pulls us away from the chaos.

As we soar backward, holding tight to Bron, a voice follows us into the void, one that only I can hear. A recognizable voice that is also terrifyingly unfamiliar.

I am coming for you, Silas Ford.

ACKNOWLEDGMENTS

I WROTE *THE DEVIL'S HALO* OVER THE COURSE OF three years. Once I found the start of the manuscript—which I wrote in ENG 203 at Western Kentucky University, taught by Sandra Wales—and realized how bad it was, I started working to rewrite it. If I remember correctly (doubtful at this point), that process started in 2011.

A few years later, in 2014, I published the book. Basking in the glow of that feeling all authors secretly relish, I can remember very clearly having this thought:

At least I know the next one won't take as long to write.

Well...about that. The book you're holding began shortly after I published its predecessor. On May 18, 2015, to be precise, with the opening line that didn't change in the (gulp) nearly *six* years it took me to finish *Fall of the Angels*.

I've changed so much as a writer since I created that Google Doc. I started working as a freelance editor for a company called Book in a Box (BIAB) in December 2015. In June 2016, I quit my

job to focus more on the writing assignments I was being offered by BIAB. I helped craft nine books for the company before being hired full-time in January 2019 by BIAB, which was now called Scribe.

It's been this journey with Scribe that both elongated my writing journey with *Fall of the Angels* and made me capable of finishing a second book, which I found to be more strenuous than writing the first book. In the pages that follow, I would like to thank some of the wonderful people from Scribe who made me into a better writer and, directly or indirectly, contributed to a book I'm proud bears my name.

First, I'd like to thank **Harlan "Hal" Clifford**. I knew of Hal early in my days as a freelancer with Scribe. He was like the final boss in a video game: if you talked with him, you were either a "boss" yourself...or you were about to be vanquished.

Later, once I became a Tribe member, Hal became my Whole Self guide, and I realized he wasn't quite the boogeyman I made him out to be. We talked once a month about what I wanted for my work, myself, and my relationships. For over a year, I talked to him about my desire to finish the book. As Scribe's Editor-in-Chief, Hal knew exactly what to say to encourage me and guide me toward the finish line. Hal, thank you for the continued support and push I needed to get this done.

Next, I'd like to thank **Rose Friel**, my publishing manager. Even though I work with Scribe and know exactly what goes into publishing a book, it's still a leap of faith (and a bit nerve-wracking) to hand over a manuscript that's like your baby. Rose was a faithful partner from the beginning and inspired confidence every step of the way. Rose, thank you for making this process smooth and painless for me.

I'd also like to thank **Erin Tyler** for her stellar work on my cover. I once heard Erin described as "one of the best cover designers in the world." I think that's selling her short, don't you? I think she is *the best* cover designer in the game right now. Erin, thank you for bringing your insane talents to my book. I'm forever grateful.

I'm also grateful for Scribe's leadership—namely **JeVon McCormick** and **Brittany Claudius**—for deciding to honor our company's mission by publishing the books of Tribe members free of charge. For those who don't know, that's a $12,000 service they offer to Tribe members who've worked with Scribe for at least eighteen months. Seriously, how many companies do you know that do this?

Scribe is special for many, many reasons, but this gracious gift is perhaps the best indication of why I'll be working with Scribe until I retire: they walk the walk. So, to JeVon and Brittany (and all our other leaders), thank you for this gift.

A lot of people have believed in me since I started working with Scribe, but none more so than **Zach Obront**. I once said I'd only leave Scribe if Zach left, and I wouldn't need to know where he was going or what he was doing. I'd just turn in my letter and help out however I could (unless it was hanging drywall or something like that—I would be useless there unless his company needed ad copy written).

While I was a freelancer, Zach brought me into a new offering where I learned to write short-form content under the tutelage of Caleb Kaiser. I wouldn't be doing what I'm doing now if it wasn't for what Zach and Caleb taught me during the brief time we were all together. About six months after I joined the Tribe, Zach became my direct support, and I've never had a better boss. Zach is somehow both utterly brilliant and incredibly supportive. How many bosses have you ever heard described that way? That's right: approximately zero. So, Zach, thank you for believing in me. You'll never know how much that belief means to me.

Finally, I have to thank **Tucker Max**. The most challenging part of my job was working with Tucker to craft stories, blog posts, and ad copy for Scribe. I don't mean that Tucker was challenging—if you know him from his *I Hope They Serve Beer in Hell* days, he's NOTHING like that person anymore. He's not only the smartest

person I've ever met (by far) but also possesses the rare ability to truly see people and understand what makes them tick. If you've been to a Guided Author workshop that he helps facilitate, you've seen this superpower firsthand.

So, when I say that working with Tucker was challenging, what I mean is that it forced me to raise my game. Tucker expected me to make that leap from Double-A to the Major Leagues when I got hired. The only problem? I wasn't quite capable of hitting metaphorical ninety-eight MPH fastballs yet. That said, I was terrified to let Tucker down. He'd gone to bat to get me hired, and I believed I owed it to him to justify that faith. That's why I was overcome with dread every time I sent him my work to review: I knew it would come back peppered with comments, and in my mind, each line he crossed out translated to an extra layer of disappointment in me.

Looking back now, I realize something: I wasn't scared of Tucker. I was scared of the writer he was turning me into, one edit at a time. Like a personal trainer, he was whipping me into shape with every "Make this sharp and interesting" comment he left for me in Google Docs. It's hard to put a number on it, but if I had to estimate, my writing improved 100 percent thanks to Tucker's coaching, feedback, and edits. That's not an exaggeration. I'm twice the writer I was in 2019, and Tucker is the main reason I can say that with confidence.

Tucker, thank you for seeing a better version of me when we started working together, and thanks for pushing me—hard—to become that person.

ABOUT THE AUTHOR

SINCE HE WAS FOUR YEARS OLD, JOSH RAYMER HAS been writing stories. Back then, it was construction paper and crayon drawings. Today, it's the first two novels in the Silas Ford series: *The Devil's Halo* and *Fall of the Angels*. Josh hopes the story of Silas's ongoing battle against the forces of darkness will be celebrated and shared by bookworms and reticent readers alike.

In addition to his fictional work, Josh also writes professionally for Scribe Media. His articles have appeared in *Forbes*, *Entrepreneur*, *Inc.*, and *Harvard Business Review*. When he's not writing, Josh enjoys traveling with his wife, Ali, and their son, Paxton. On Sundays, you can find him watching Colts football games with his family and friends. He has three dogs named Clark, Bruce, and Wally (named after Superman, Batman, and The Flash, respectively). You can follow him on Twitter @joshraymer and find his fantasy football takes on *The Big 3 IDP Podcast*.